The Brooklyn Follies

The Brooklyn Follies

Paul Auster

W F HOWES LTD

This large print edition published in 2006 by
W F Howes Ltd
Unit 4, Rearsby Business Park, Gaddesby Lane,
Rearsby, Leicester LE7 4YH

1 3 5 7 9 10 8 6 4 2

First published in the United Kingdom in 2005
by Faber and Faber Ltd

A CIP catalogue record for this book is available
from the British Library

ISBN 1 84632 783 0

Typeset by Palimpsest Book Production Limited,
Grangemouth, Stirlingshire
Printed and bound in Great Britain
by Antony Rowe Ltd, Chippenham, Wilts.

for my daughter
Sophie

OVERTURE

I was looking for a quiet place to die. Someone recommended Brooklyn, and so the next morning I traveled down there from Westchester to scope out the terrain. I hadn't been back in fifty-six years, and I remembered nothing. My parents had moved out of the city when I was three, but I instinctively found myself returning to the neighborhood where we had lived, crawling home like some wounded dog to the place of my birth. A local real estate agent ushered me around to six or seven brownstone flats, and by the end of the afternoon I had rented a two-bedroom garden apartment on First Street, just half a block away from Prospect Park. I had no idea who my neighbors were, and I didn't care. They all worked at nine-to-five jobs, none of them had any children, and therefore the building would be relatively silent. More than anything else, that was what I craved. A silent end to my sad and ridiculous life.

The house in Bronxville was already under contract, and once the closing took place at the end of the month, money wasn't going to be a problem. My ex-wife and I were planning to split the proceeds from the sale, and with four hundred thousand dollars in the bank, there would be more than enough to sustain me until I stopped breathing.

At first, I didn't know what to do with myself. I had spent thirty-one years commuting back and forth between the suburbs and the Manhattan offices of Mid-Atlantic Accident and Life, but now that I didn't have a job anymore, there were too many hours in the day. About a week after I moved into the apartment, my married daughter, Rachel, drove in from New Jersey to pay me a visit. She said that I needed to get involved in something, to invent a project for myself. Rachel is not a stupid person. She has a doctorate in biochemistry from the University of Chicago and works as a researcher for a large drug company outside Princeton, but much like her mother before her, it's a rare day when she speaks in anything but platitudes – all those exhausted phrases and hand-me-down ideas that cram the dump sites of contemporary wisdom.

I explained that I was probably going to be dead before the year was out, and I didn't give a flying fuck about projects. For a moment, it looked as if Rachel was about to cry, but she blinked back the tears and called me a cruel and selfish person instead. No wonder 'Mom' had finally divorced me, she added, no wonder she hadn't been able to take it anymore. Being married to a man like me must have been an unending torture, a living hell. *A living hell*. Alas, poor Rachel – she simply can't help herself. My only child has inhabited this earth for twenty-nine years, and not once has she come up with an original remark, with something absolutely and irreducibly her own.

Yes, I suppose there is something nasty about me at times. But not all the time – and not as a matter of principle. On my good days, I'm as sweet and friendly as any person I know. You can't sell life insurance as successfully as I did by alienating your customers, at least not for three long decades you can't. You have to be sympathetic. You have to be able to listen. You have to know how to charm people. I possess all those qualities and more. I won't deny that I've had my bad moments as well, but everyone knows what dangers lurk behind the closed doors of family life. It can be poison for all concerned, especially if you discover that you probably weren't cut out for marriage in the first place. I loved having sex with Edith, but after four or five years the passion seemed to run its course, and from then on I became less than a perfect husband. To hear Rachel tell it, I wasn't much in the parent department either. I wouldn't want to contradict her memories, but the truth is that I cared for them both in my own way, and if I sometimes found myself in the arms of other women, I never took any of those affairs seriously. The divorce wasn't my idea. In spite of everything, I was planning to stay with Edith until the end. She was the one who wanted out, and given the extent of my sins and transgressions over the years, I couldn't really

3

blame her. Thirty-three years of living under the same roof, and by the time we walked off in opposite directions, what we added up to was approximately nothing.

I had told Rachel my days were numbered, but that was no more than a hotheaded retort to her meddling advice, a blast of pure hyperbole. My lung cancer was in remission, and based on what the oncologist had told me after my most recent exam, there was cause for guarded optimism. That didn't mean I trusted him, however. The shock of the cancer had been so great, I still didn't believe in the possibility of surviving it. I had given myself up for dead, and once the tumor had been cut out of me and I'd gone through the debilitating ordeals of radiation treatment and chemo, once I'd suffered the long bouts of nausea and dizziness, the loss of hair, the loss of will, the loss of job, the loss of wife, it was difficult for me to imagine how to go on. Hence Brooklyn. Hence my unconscious return to the place where my story began. I was almost sixty years old, and I didn't know how much time I had left. Maybe another twenty years; maybe just a few more months. Whatever the medical prognosis of my condition, the crucial thing was to take nothing for granted. As long as I was alive, I had to figure out a way to start living again, but even if I didn't live, I had to do more than just sit around and wait for the end. As usual, my scientist daughter had been right, even if I'd been too stubborn to admit it. I had to keep myself busy. I had to get off my ass and do something.

It was early spring when I moved in, and for the first few weeks I filled my time by exploring the neighborhood, taking long walks in the park, and planting flowers in my back garden – a small, junk-filled patch of ground that had been neglected for years. I had my newly resurgent hair cut at the Park Slope Barbershop on Seventh Avenue, rented videos from a place called Movie Heaven, and stopped in often at Brightman's Attic, a cluttered, badly organized used-book store owned by a flamboyant homosexual named Harry Brightman (more about him later). Most mornings, I prepared breakfast for myself in the apartment, but since I disliked cooking and lacked all talent for it, I tended to eat lunch and dinner in restaurants – always alone, always with an open book in front of me, always chewing as slowly as possible in order to drag out the meal as long as I could. After sampling a number of options in the vicinity, I settled on the Cosmic Diner as my regular spot for lunch. The food there was mediocre at best, but one of the waitresses was an adorable Puerto Rican girl named Marina, and I rapidly developed a crush on her. She was half my age and already married, which meant that romance was out of the question, but she was so splendid to look at, so gentle in her dealings with me, so ready to laugh at my less than funny jokes, that I literally pined for her on her days off. From a strictly anthropological point of view, I discovered that Brooklynites are less reluctant to talk to strangers than any tribe I had previously encountered. They butt into one another's business at will (old women scolding young mothers for not dressing their children warmly enough, passersby snapping at dog walkers for yanking too hard on the leash); they argue like deranged four-year-olds over disputed parking spaces; they zip out dazzling one-liners as a matter of course. One Sunday morning, I went into a crowded deli with the absurd name of La Bagel Delight. I was intending to ask for a cinnamon-raisin bagel, but the word caught in my mouth and came out as *cinnamon-reagan*. Without missing a beat, the young guy behind the counter answered, 'Sorry, we don't have any of those. How about a pumpernixon instead?' Fast. So damned fast, I nearly wet my drawers.

After that inadvertent slip of the tongue, I finally hit upon an idea that Rachel would have approved of. It wasn't much of an idea, perhaps, but at least it was something, and if I stuck to it as rigorously and faithfully as I intended to, then I would have my project, the little hobbyhorse I'd been looking for to carry me away from the indolence of my soporific routine. Humble as the project was, I decided to give it a grandiose, somewhat pompous title – in order to delude myself into thinking that I was engaged in important work. I called it *The Book of Human Folly*, and in it I was planning to set down in the simplest, clearest language possible an account of every blunder, every pratfall, every embarrassment, every idiocy, every foible, and every inane act I had committed during my long and checkered career as a man. When I couldn't think of stories to tell about myself, I would write down things that had happened to people I knew, and when that source ran dry as well, I would take on historical events, recording the follies of my fellow human beings down through the ages, beginning with the vanished civilizations of the ancient world and pushing on to the first months of the twenty-first century. If nothing else, I thought it might be good for a few laughs. I had no desire to bare my soul or indulge in gloomy introspections. The tone would be light and farcical throughout, and my only purpose was to keep myself entertained while using up as many hours of the day as I could.

I called the project a book, but in fact it wasn't a book at all. Working with yellow legal pads, loose sheets of paper, the backs of envelopes and junk-mail form letters for credit cards and home-improvement loans, I was compiling what amounted to a collection of random jottings, a hodgepodge of unrelated anecdotes that I would throw into a cardboard box each time another story was finished. There was little method to my madness. Some of the pieces came to no more than a few lines, and a number of them, in particular the spoonerisms and malapropisms I was so fond of, were just a single phrase. *Chilled greaseburger* instead of *grilled cheeseburger*, for example, which came out of my mouth sometime during my junior year of high school, or the unintentionally profound, quasi-mystical utterance I delivered to Edith while we were engaged in one of our bitter marital spats: *I'll see it when I believe it.* Every time I sat down to write, I would begin by closing my eyes and letting my thoughts wander in any direction they chose. By forcing myself to relax in this way, I managed to dredge up considerable amounts of material from the distant past, things that until then I had assumed were lost forever. A moment from the sixth grade (to cite one such memory) when a boy in our class named Dudley Franklin let out a long, trumpet-shrill fart during a silent pause in the middle of a geography lesson. We all laughed, of course (nothing is funnier to a roomful of eleven-year-olds than a gust of broken wind), but what set the incident apart from the category of minor embarrassments and elevated it to classic status, an enduring masterpiece in the annals of shame and humiliation, was the fact that Dudley was innocent enough to commit the fatal blunder of offering an apology. 'Excuse me,' he said, looking down at his desk and blushing until his cheeks resembled a freshly painted fire truck. One must never own up to a fart in public. That is the unwritten law, the single most stringent protocol of American etiquette. Farts come from no one and nowhere; they are anonymous emanations that belong to the group as a whole, and even when every person in the room can point to the culprit, the only sane course of action is denial. The witless Dudley Franklin was too honest to do that, however, and he never lived it down. From that day on, he was known as Excuse-Me Franklin, and the name stuck with him until the end of high school.

The stories seemed to fall under several different rubrics, and after I had been at the project for approximately a month, I abandoned my one-box system in favor of a multi-box arrangement that allowed me to preserve my finished works in a more coherent fashion. A box for verbal flubs, another for physical mishaps, another for failed ideas, another for social gaffes, and so on. Little by little, I grew particularly interested in recording the slapstick moments of everyday life. Not just the countless stubbed toes and knocks on the head I've been subjected to over the years, not just the frequency with which my glasses have slipped out of my shirt pocket when I've bent down to tie my shoes (followed by the further indignity of stumbling forward and crushing the glasses underfoot), but the one-in-a-million howlers that have befallen me at various times since my earliest boyhood. Opening my mouth to yawn at a Labor Day picnic in 1952 and allowing a bee to fly in, which, in my sudden panic and disgust, I accidentally swallowed instead of spitting out; or, even more unlikely, preparing to enter a plane on a business trip just seven years ago with my boarding-pass stub wedged lightly between my thumb and middle finger, being jostled from behind, losing hold of the stub, and seeing it flutter out of my hand toward the slit between the ramp and the threshold of the plane – the narrowest of narrow gaps, no more than a sixteenth of an inch, if that much – and then, to my utter astonishment, watching it slide clear through that impossible space and land on the tarmac twenty feet below.

Those are just some examples. I wrote dozens of such stories in the first two months, but even though I did my best to keep the tone frivolous and light, I discovered that it wasn't always possible. Everyone is subject to black moods, and I confess that there were times when I succumbed to bouts of loneliness and dejection. I had spent the bulk of my working life in the business of death, and I had probably heard too many grim stories to stop myself from thinking about them when my spirits were low. All the people I had visited over the years, all the policies I had sold, all the dread and desperation I'd been made privy to while talking to my clients. Eventually, I added another box to my assemblage. I labeled it 'Cruel Destinies,' and the first story I put in there was about a man named Jonas Weinberg. I had sold him a million-dollar universal life policy in 1976, an extremely large sum for the time. I remember that he had just celebrated his sixtieth birthday, was a doctor of internal medicine affiliated with Columbia-Presbyterian Hospital, and spoke English with a faint German accent. Selling life insurance is not a passionless affair, and a good agent has to be able to hold his own in what can often turn into difficult, tortuous discussions with his clients. The prospect of death inevitably turns one's thoughts to serious matters, and even if a part of the job is only about money, it also concerns the gravest metaphysical questions. What is the point of life? How much longer will I live? How can I protect the people I love after I'm gone? Because of his profession, Dr Weinberg had a keen sense of the frailty of human existence, of how little it takes to remove our names from the book of the living. We met in his apartment on Central Park West, and once I had talked him through the pros and cons of the various policies available to him, he began to reminisce about his past. He had been born in Berlin in 1916, he told me, and after his father had been killed in the trenches of World War One, he had been raised by his actress mother, the only child of a fiercely independent and sometimes obstreperous woman who had never shown the slightest inclination to remarry. If I am not reading too much into his comments, I believe Dr Weinberg was hinting at the fact that his mother preferred women to men, and in the chaotic years of the Weimar Republic, she must have flaunted that preference quite openly. In contrast to the headstrong Frau Weinberg, the young Jonas was a quiet, bookish boy who

11

excelled at his studies and dreamed of becoming a scientist or a doctor. He was seventeen when Hitler took control of the government, and within months his mother was making preparations to get him out of Germany. Relatives of his father's lived in New York, and they agreed to take him in. He left in the spring of 1934, but his mother, who had already proved her alertness to the impending dangers for non-Aryans of the Third Reich, stubbornly rejected the opportunity to leave herself. Her family had been Germans for hundreds of years, she told her son, and she'd be damned if she allowed some two-bit tyrant to chase her into exile. Come hell or high water, she was determined to stick it out.

By some miracle, she did. Dr Weinberg offered few details (it's possible he never learned the full story himself), but his mother was apparently helped by a group of Gentile friends at various critical junctures, and by 1938 or 1939 she had managed to obtain a set of false identity papers. She radically altered her appearance – not hard for an actress who specialized in eccentric character roles – and under her new Christian name she wrangled herself a job as a book-keeper for a dry goods store in a small town outside Hamburg, disguised as a frumpy, bespectacled blonde. When the war ended in the spring of 1945, she hadn't seen her son in eleven years. Jonas Weinberg was in his late twenties by then, a full-fledged doctor completing his residency at Bellevue Hospital, and the moment he found out that his mother had survived the war, he began making arrangements for her to come visit him in America.

Everything was worked out to the smallest detail. The plane would be landing at such and such a time, would be parking at such and such a gate, and Jonas Weinberg would be there to meet his mother. Just as he was about to leave for the airport, however, he was summoned by the hospital to perform an emergency operation. What choice did he have? He was a doctor, and anxious as he was to see his mother again after so many years, his first duty was to his patients. A new plan was hastily put in motion. He telephoned the airline company and asked them to send a representative to speak to his mother when she arrived in New York, explaining that he had been called away at the last minute and that she should find a taxi to take her into Manhattan. A key would be left for her with the doorman at his building, and she should go upstairs and wait for him in the apartment. Frau Weinberg did as she was told and promptly found a cab. The driver sped off, and ten minutes into their journey toward the city, he lost control of the wheel and crashed head-on into another car. Both he and his passenger were severely injured.

By then, Dr Weinberg was already at the hospital, about to perform his operation. The surgery lasted a little over an hour, and when he had finished his work, the young doctor washed his hands, changed back into his clothes, and hurried out of the locker room, eager to return home for his belated reunion with his mother. Just as he stepped into the hall, he saw a new patient being wheeled into the operating room.

It was Jonas Weinberg's mother. According to what the doctor told me, she died without regaining consciousness.

AN UNEXPECTED ENCOUNTER

I have rattled on for a dozen pages, but until now my sole object has been to introduce myself to the reader and set the scene for the story I am about to tell. I am not the central character of that story. The distinction of bearing the title of Hero of this book belongs to my nephew, Tom Wood, the only son of my late sister, June. Little June-Bug, as we called her, was born when I was three, and it was her arrival that precipitated our parents' departure from a crowded Brooklyn apartment to a house in Garden City, Long Island. We were always fast friends, she and I, and when she married twenty-four years later (six months after our father's death), I was the one who walked her down the aisle and gave her away to her husband, a *New York Times* business reporter named Christopher Wood. They produced two children together (my nephew, Tom, and my niece, Aurora), but the marriage fell apart after fifteen years. A couple of years later, June remarried, and again I accompanied her to the altar. Her second husband was a wealthy stockbroker from New Jersey, Philip Zorn, whose baggage included two ex-wives and a nearly grown-up daughter, Pamela. Then, at the disgustingly early age of forty-nine, June suffered a massive cerebral hemorrhage while working in her garden one scorching afternoon in the middle of August and died before the sun rose again the next day. For her big brother, it was hands down the worst blow he had ever received, and not even his own cancer and near death several years later came close to duplicating the misery he felt then.

I lost contact with the family after the funeral, and until I ran into him in Harry Brightman's bookstore on May 23, 2000, I hadn't seen Tom in almost seven years. He had always been my favorite, and even as a small tyke he had impressed me as someone who stood out from the ordinary, a person destined to achieve great things in life. Not counting the day of June's burial, our last conversation had taken place at his mother's house in South Orange, New Jersey. Tom had just graduated with high honors from Cornell and was about to go off to the University of Michigan on a four-year fellowship to study American literature. Everything I had predicted for him was coming true, and I remember that family dinner as a warm occasion, with all of us lifting our glasses and toasting Tom's success. Back when I was his age, I had hoped to follow a path similar to the one my nephew had chosen. Like him, I had majored in English at college, with secret ambitions to go on studying literature or perhaps take a stab at journalism, but I hadn't had the courage to pursue either one. Life got in the way – two years in the army, work, marriage, family responsibilities, the need to earn more and more money, all the muck that bogs us down when we don't have the balls to stand up for ourselves – but I had never lost my interest in books. Reading was my escape and my comfort, my consolation, my stimulant of choice: reading for the pure pleasure of it, for the beautiful stillness that surrounds you when you hear an author's words reverberating in your head. Tom had always shared this love with me, and starting when he was five or six, I had made a point of sending him books several times a year – not just for his birthday or Christmas, but whenever I stumbled across something I thought he would like. I had introduced him to Poe when he was eleven, and because Poe was one of the writers he had dealt with in his senior thesis, it was only natural that he should want to tell me about his paper – and only natural that I should want to listen. The meal was over by then, and all the others had gone outside to sit in the backyard, but Tom and I remained in the dining room, drinking the last of the wine.

'To your health, Uncle Nat,' Tom said, raising his glass.

'To yours, Tom,' I answered. 'And to "Imaginary Edens: The Life of the Mind in Pre-Civil War America".'

'A pretentious title, I'm sorry to say. But I couldn't think of anything better.'

'Pretentious is good. It makes the professors sit up and take notice. You got an A plus, didn't you?'

Modest as always, Tom made a sweeping gesture with his hand, as if to discount the importance of the grade. I continued, 'Partly on Poe, you say. And partly on what else?'

'Thoreau.'

'Poe and Thoreau.'

'Edgar Allan Poe and Henry David Thoreau. An unfortunate rhyme, don't you think? All those *o*'s filling up the mouth. I keep thinking of someone shocked into a state of eternal surprise. Oh! Oh no! Oh Poe! Oh Thoreau!'

'A minor inconvenience, Tom. But woe to the man who reads Poe and forgets Thoreau. Not so?'

Tom smiled broadly, then raised his glass again. 'To your health, Uncle Nat.'

'And to yours, Dr Thumb,' I said. We each took another sip of the Bordeaux. As I lowered my glass to the table, I asked him to outline his argument for me.

'It's about nonexistent worlds,' my nephew said. 'A study of the inner refuge, a map of the place a man goes to when life in the real world is no longer possible.'

'The mind.'

'Exactly. First Poe, and an analysis of three of his most neglected works. "The Philosophy of Furniture," "Landor's Cottage," and "The Domain of Arnheim." Taken alone, each one is merely curious, eccentric. Put them together, and what

18

you have is a fully elaborated system of human longing.'

'I've never read those pieces. I don't think I've even heard of them.'

'What they give is a description of the ideal room, the ideal house, and the ideal landscape. After that, I jump to Thoreau and examine the room, the house, and the landscape as presented in *Walden*.'

'What we call a comparative study.'

'No one ever talks about Poe and Thoreau in the same breath. They stand at opposite ends of American thought. But that's the beauty of it. A drunk from the South – reactionary in his politics, aristocratic in his bearing, spectral in his imagination. And a teetotaler from the North – radical in his views, puritanical in his behavior, clear-sighted in his work. Poe was artifice and the gloom of midnight chambers. Thoreau was simplicity and the radiance of the outdoors. In spite of their differences, they were born just eight years apart, which made them almost exact contemporaries. And they both died young – at forty and forty-five. Together, they barely managed to live the life of a single old man, and neither one left behind any children. In all probability, Thoreau went to his grave a virgin. Poe married his teenage cousin, but whether that marriage was consummated before Virginia Clemm's death is still open to question. Call them parallels, call them coincidences, but these external facts are less important than the inner truth of each man's life. In their own wildly idiosyncratic ways, each took it upon himself to reinvent America. In his reviews and critical articles, Poe battled for a new kind of native literature, an American literature free of English and European influences. Thoreau's work represents an unending assault on the status quo, a battle to find a new way to live here. Both men believed in America, and both men believed that America had gone to hell, that it was being crushed to death by an ever-growing mountain of machines and money. How was a man to think in the midst of all that clamor? They both wanted out. Thoreau removed himself to the outskirts of Concord, pretending to exile himself in the woods – for no other reason than to prove that it could be done. As long as a man had the courage to reject what society told him to do, he could live life on his own terms. To what end? To be free. But free to what end? To read books, to write books, to think. To be free to write a book like *Walden*. Poe, on the other hand, withdrew into a dream of perfection. Take a look at 'The Philosophy of Furniture,' and you'll discover that his imaginary room was designed for exactly the same purpose. As a place to read, write, and think. It's a vault of contemplation, a noiseless sanctuary where the soul can at last find a measure of peace. Impossibly utopian? Yes. But also a sensible alternative to the conditions of the time. For the fact was, America had indeed gone to hell. The country was split in two, and we all know

20

what happened just a decade later. Four years of death and destruction. A human bloodbath generated by the very machines that were supposed to make us all happy and rich.'

The boy was so smart, so articulate, so well-read, that I felt honored to count myself as a member of his family. The Woods had been through their fair share of turmoil in recent years, but Tom seemed to have weathered the calamity of his parents' breakup – as well as the adolescent storms of his younger sister, who had rebelled against her mother's second marriage and run away from home at seventeen – with a sober, reflective, rather bemused attitude toward life, and I admired him for having kept his feet so firmly on the ground. He had little or no connection with his father, who had promptly moved to California after the divorce and taken a job with the *Los Angeles Times*, and much like his sister (though in far more muted form) felt no great fondness or respect for June's second husband. He and his mother were close, however, and they had lived through the drama of Aurora's disappearance as equal partners, suffering through the same despairs and hopes, the same grim expectations, the same never-ending anxieties. Rory had been one of the funniest, most fetching little girls I have ever known: a whirlwind of sass and bravura, a wise-acre, an inexhaustible engine of spontaneity and mischief. From the time she was two or three, Edith and I had always referred to her as the Laughing Girl, and she had grown up in the Wood household as the family entertainer, an ever more artful and rambunctious clown. Tom was just two years older than she was, but he had always looked out for her, and once their father left the picture, his mere presence had served as a stabilizing force in her life. But then he went off to college, and Rory went out of control – first escaping to New York, and then, after a brief reconciliation with her mother, vanishing into parts unknown. At the time of that celebratory dinner for Tom's graduation, she had already given birth to an out-of-wedlock child (a girl named Lucy), had returned home just long enough to dump the baby in my sister's lap, and had vanished again. When June died fourteen months later, Tom informed me at the funeral that Aurora had recently come back to reclaim the child – and had left again after two days. She didn't show up for her mother's burial service. Maybe she would have come, Tom said, but no one had known how or where to contact her.

In spite of these family messes, and in spite of losing his mother when he was only twenty-three, I never doubted that Tom would flourish in the world. He had too much going for him to fail, was too solid a character to be thrown off course by the unpredictable winds of sorrow and bad luck. At his mother's funeral, he had walked around in a dazed stupor, overwhelmed by grief. I probably should have talked to him more, but I was too stunned and shaken myself to offer him much of anything. A few hugs, a few shared tears, but that was the extent of it. Then he returned to Ann Arbor, and we fell out of touch. I mostly blame myself, but Tom was old enough to have taken the initiative, and he could have sent me a word whenever he'd chosen to. Or, if not me, then his first cousin, Rachel, who was also in the Midwest at the time, doing her postgraduate work in Chicago. They had known each other since infancy and had always gotten along well, but he made no move in her direction either. Every now and then, I felt a small twinge of guilt as the years passed, but I was going through a rough patch of my own (marriage problems, health problems, money problems), and I was too distracted to think about him very much. Whenever I did, I imagined him forging ahead with his studies, systematically advancing his career as he scaled the academic ladder. By the spring of 2000, I was certain he had landed a job at some prestigious place like Berkeley or Columbia – a young intellectual star already at work on his second or third book.

Imagine my surprise, then, when I walked into Brightman's Attic that Tuesday morning in May and saw my nephew sitting behind the front counter, doling out change to a customer. Luckily, I saw Tom before he saw me. God knows what regrettable words would have escaped my lips if I hadn't had those ten or twelve seconds to absorb the shock. I'm not only referring to the improbable fact that he was there, working as an underling in a secondhand bookstore, but also to his radically altered physical appearance. Tom had always been on the chunky side. He had been cursed with one of those big-boned peasant bodies constructed to bear the bulk of ample poundage – a genetic gift from his absent, semi-alcoholic father – but even so, the last time I'd seen him, he had been in relatively good shape. Burly, yes, but also muscular and strong, with an athletic bounce to his step. Now, seven years later, he had put on a good thirty or thirty-five pounds, and he looked dumpy and fat. A second chin had sprouted just below his jawline, and even his hands had acquired the pudge and thickness one normally associates with middle-aged plumbers. It was a sad sight to behold. The spark had been extinguished from my nephew's eyes, and everything about him suggested defeat.

After the customer finished paying for her book, I sidled up to the spot she had just vacated, put my hands on the counter, and leaned forward. Tom happened to be looking down at that moment, searching for a coin that had fallen to the floor. I cleared my throat and said, 'Hey there, Tom. Long time no see.'

My nephew looked up. At first, he seemed entirely befuddled, and I was afraid he hadn't recognized me. But an instant later he began to smile, and as the smile continued to spread across his face, I was heartened to see that it was the same Tom-smile of old. A touch of melancholy had been added to it,

24

perhaps, but not enough to have changed him as profoundly as I had feared.

'Uncle Nat!' he shouted. 'What the hell are you doing in Brooklyn?'

Before I could answer him, he rushed out from behind the counter and threw his arms around me. Much to my amazement, my eyes began to water up with tears.

FAREWELL TO THE COURT

Later that same day, I took him out to lunch at the Cosmic Diner. The glorious Marina served us our turkey club sandwiches and iced coffees, and I flirted with her a little more aggressively than usual, perhaps because I wanted to impress Tom, or perhaps simply because I was in such buoyant spirits. I hadn't realized how much I'd missed my old Dr Thumb, and now it turned out that we were neighbors – living, by pure happenstance, just two blocks from each other in the ancient kingdom of Brooklyn, New York.

He had been at Brightman's Attic for the past five months, he said, and the reason why I hadn't run into him earlier was because he always worked upstairs, writing the monthly catalogues for the rare-book-and-manuscript part of Harry's business, which was far more lucrative than the secondhand-book trade downstairs. Tom wasn't a clerk, and he never operated the cash register, but the regular clerk had gone off to a doctor's appointment that morning, and Harry had asked Tom to fill in for him until he returned to the store.

The job was nothing to brag about, Tom continued, but at least it was better than driving a taxi, which was what he'd been doing ever since he'd dropped out of graduate school and come back to New York.

'When was that?' I asked, doing my best to hide my disappointment.

'Two and a half years ago,' he said. 'I finished all my course work and passed my orals, but then I got stuck with the dissertation. I bit off more than I could chew, Uncle Nat.'

'Forget this *Uncle Nat* stuff, Tom. Just call me Nathan, the way everyone else does. Now that your mother's dead, I don't feel like an uncle anymore.'

'All right, Nathan. But you're still my uncle, whether you like it or not. Aunt Edith probably isn't my aunt anymore, I suppose, but even if she's been relegated to the category of ex-aunt, Rachel's still my cousin, and you're still my uncle.'

'Just call me Nathan, Tom.'

'I will, Uncle Nat, I promise. From now on, I'll always address you as Nathan. In return, I want you to call me Tom. No more Dr Thumb, all right? It makes me feel uncomfortable.'

'But I've always called you that. Even when you were a little boy.'

'And I've always called you Uncle Nat, haven't I?'

'Fair enough. I lay down my sword.'

'We've entered a new era, Nathan. The post-family, post-student, post-past age of Glass and Wood.'

'Post-past?'

'The *now*. And also the *later*. But no more dwelling on the *then*.'

'Water under the bridge, Tom.'

The ex-Dr Thumb closed his eyes, tilted back his head, and shot a forefinger into the air, as if trying to remember something he'd forgotten long ago. Then, in a somber, mock-theatrical voice, he recited the opening lines of Raleigh's 'Farewell to Court':

Like truthless dreams, so are my joys expired,
And past return are all my dandled days,
My love misled, and fancy quite retired:
Of all which past, the sorrow only stays.

PURGATORY

No one grows up thinking his destiny is to become a taxi driver, but in Tom's case the job had served as a particularly grueling form of penance, a way of mourning the collapse of his most cherished ambitions. It wasn't that he had ever wanted a great deal from life, but the little he had wanted turned out to have been beyond his grasp: to finish his doctorate, to find a place in some university English department, and then spend the next forty or fifty years teaching and writing about books. That was all he had ever aspired to, with a wife thrown into the bargain, maybe, and a kid or two to go along with her. It had never felt like too much to ask for, but after three years of struggling to write his dissertation, Tom finally understood that he didn't have it in him to finish. Or, if he did have it in him, he couldn't persuade himself to believe in the value of doing it anymore. So he left Ann Arbor and returned to New York, a twenty-eight-year-old has-been without a clue as to where he was headed or what turn his life was about to take.

At first, the taxi was no more than a temporary

solution, a stopgap measure to pay the rent while he looked for something else. He searched for several weeks, but all the teaching jobs in private schools were filled just then, and once he settled into the grind of his twelve-hour daily shifts, he found himself less and less motivated to hunt for other work. The temporary began to feel like something permanent, and although a part of Tom knew that he was letting himself go to hell, another part of him thought that perhaps this job would do him some good, that if he paid attention to what he was doing and why he was doing it, the cab would teach him lessons that couldn't be learned anywhere else.

It wasn't always clear to him what those lessons were, but as he prowled the avenues in his rattling yellow Dodge from five in the afternoon to five in the morning six days a week, there was no question that he learned them well. The disadvantages to the work were so obvious, so omnipresent, so crushing, that unless you found a way to ignore them, you were doomed to a life of bitterness and unending complaint. The long hours, the low pay, the physical dangers, the lack of exercise – those were the bedrock givens, and you could no more think of changing them than you could think of changing the weather. How many times had he heard his mother speak those words to him when he was a boy? 'You can't change the weather, Tom,' June would say, meaning that some things simply were what they were, and we had no choice but to accept them. Tom understood the principle, but that had never stopped him from cursing the snowstorms and cold winds that blew against his small, shivering body. Now the snow was falling again. His life had been turned into one long battle against the elements, and if there was ever a time to start grumbling about the weather, this was it. But Tom didn't grumble. And Tom didn't feel sorry for himself. He had found a method to atone for his stupidity, and if he could survive the experience without completely losing heart, then perhaps there was some hope for him after all. By sticking with the cab, he wasn't trying to make the best of a bad situation. He was looking for a way to make things happen, and until he understood what those things were, he wouldn't have the right to release himself from his bondage.

He lived in a studio apartment on the corner of Eighth Avenue and Third Street, a long-term sublet that had been passed on to him by the friend of a friend who had left New York and taken a job in another city – Pittsburgh or Plattsburgh, Tom could never remember which. It was a dingy one-closet cell with a metal shower in the bathroom, a pair of windows that looked out on a brick wall, and a pint-sized kitchenette that featured a bar refrigerator and a two-burner gas stove. One bookcase, one chair, one table, and one mattress on the floor. It was the smallest apartment he had ever lived in, but with the rent fixed at four hundred and twenty-seven dollars a month, Tom felt lucky to have it. For the first year after he moved in, he didn't spend much time there in any case. He tended to be out and about, looking up old friends from high school and college who had landed in New York, meeting new people through the old people, spending his money in bars, dating women when the opportunities arose, and generally trying to put together a life for himself – or something that resembled a life. More often than not, these attempts at sociability ended in painful silence. His old friends, who remembered him as a brilliant student and wickedly funny conversationalist, were appalled by what had happened to him. Tom had slipped from the ranks of the anointed, and his downfall seemed to shake their confidence in themselves, to open the door onto a new pessimism about their own prospects in life. It didn't help matters that Tom had gained weight, that his former plumpness now verged on an embarrassing rotundity, but even more disturbing was the fact that he didn't seem to have any plans, that he never spoke about how he was going to undo the damage he'd done to himself and get back on his feet. Whenever he mentioned his new job, he described it in odd, almost religious terms, speculating on such questions as spiritual strength and the importance of finding one's path through patience and humility, and this confused them and made them fidget in their chairs. Tom's intelligence had not been dulled by the job, but no one wanted to hear what he had to say anymore, least of all the women he talked to, who expected young men to be full of brave ideas and clever schemes about how they were going to conquer the world. Tom put them off with his doubts and soul-searchings, his obscure disquisitions on the nature of reality, his hesitant manner. It was bad enough that he drove a taxi for a living, but a philosophical taxi driver who dressed in army-navy clothes and carried a paunch around his middle was a bit too much to ask. He was a pleasant guy, of course, and no one actively disliked him, but he wasn't a legitimate candidate – not for marriage, not even for a crazy fling.

He began keeping more and more to himself. Another year went by, and so thorough was Tom's isolation by then that he wound up spending his thirtieth birthday alone. The truth was that he had forgotten all about it, and because no one called to congratulate him or wish him well, it wasn't until two o'clock the next morning that he finally remembered. He was somewhere out in Queens then, having just dropped off a pair of drunken businessmen at a strip club called the Garden of Earthly Delights, and to celebrate the beginning of the fourth decade of his existence, he drove over to the Metropolitan Diner on Northern Boulevard, sat down at the counter, and ordered himself a chocolate milk shake, two hamburgers, and a plate of French fries.

If not for Harry Brightman, there's no telling how long he would have remained in this purgatory. Harry's store was located on Seventh Avenue, just a few blocks from where Tom lived, and Tom had fallen into the habit of stopping in at Brightman's Attic as part of his daily routine. He rarely bought anything, but he liked to spend the odd hour or half hour before his shift began browsing among the used books on the ground floor. Thousands of items were crammed onto the shelves down there – everything from out-of-print dictionaries to forgotten bestsellers to leatherbound sets of Shakespeare – and Tom had always felt at home in that kind of paper mausoleum, flipping through piles of discarded books and breathing in the old dusty smells. On one of his early visits, he asked Harry a question about a certain Kafka biography, and the two of them had struck up a conversation. That was the first of many little chats, and while Harry wasn't always around when Tom came in (he spent most of his time upstairs), they talked often enough in the months that followed for Harry to have learned the name of Tom's hometown, to have been told the subject of Tom's aborted dissertation (*Clarel* – Melville's gargantuan and unreadable epic poem), and to have digested the fact that Tom had no interest in making love to men. In spite of this last disappointment, it didn't take Harry long to understand that Tom would make an ideal assistant for his rare-book-and-manuscript operation on the second floor. If he offered him the job once, he offered it a dozen times, but even though Tom continued to turn him down, Harry never gave up hope that one day he would say yes. He understood that Tom was in hibernation, wrestling blindly against a dark angel of despair, and that things would eventually change for him. That much was certain, even if Tom himself didn't know it yet. But once he did know it, all that taxi nonsense would immediately turn into yesterday's dirty laundry.

Tom enjoyed talking to Harry because Harry was such a droll and forthright person, a man of such needling patter and extravagant contradictions that you never knew what was going to come out of his mouth next. To look at him, you would have thought he was just another aging New York queen. All the surface rigmarole was calibrated to achieve that single effect – the dyed hair and eyebrows, the silk ascots and yachting club blazers, the sissified turns of speech – but once you got to know him a little. Harry turned out to be an astute and challenging fellow. There was something provocative about the way he kept coming at you, a darting, jabbing kind of intelligence that made you want to give good answers when he started reeling off those sly, overly personal questions of his. With Harry, it was never enough just to respond. There had to be some spark to what you said, some effervescent something that proved you were more than just another dullard plodding down the road of life. Since that was largely how Tom saw himself in those days, he had to work especially hard to keep up his end when talking to Harry. That work was what appealed to him most about their conversations. Tom liked having to think fast, and he found it invigorating to push his mind in unaccustomed directions for a change, to be forced to stay on his toes. Within three or four months of their first chat – at a time when they were barely even acquaintances, let alone friends or associates – Tom realized that of all the people he knew in New York, there wasn't a man or woman he talked to more openly than Harry Brightman.

And yet Tom continued to turn Harry down. For over six months he fended off the book dealer's proposals to come work for him, and in that time he invented so many different excuses, came up with so many different reasons why Harry should look for someone else, that his reluctance became a standing joke between them. In the beginning, Tom went out of his way to defend the virtues of his current profession, improvising elaborate theories about the ontological value of the cabbie's life. 'It gives you a direct path into the formlessness of being,' he would say, struggling not to smile as he mocked the jargon of his academic past, 'a unique entry point into the chaotic substructures of the universe. You drive around the city all night, and you never know where you're going next. A customer climbs into the backseat of your cab, tells you to take him to such and such a place, and that's where you go. Riverdale, Fort Greene, Murray Hill, Far Rockaway, the dark side of the moon. Every destination is arbitrary, every decision is governed by chance. You float, you weave, you get there as fast as you can, but you don't really have a say in the matter. You're a plaything of the gods, and you have no will of your own. The only reason you're there is to serve the whims of other people.'

'And what whims,' Harry would say, injecting a malicious glint into his eye, 'what naughty whims they must be. I'll bet you've caught a bundle of them in that rearview mirror of yours.'

'You name it. Harry, and I've seen it. Masturbation, fornication, intoxication in all its forms. Puke and semen, shit and piss, blood and tears. At one time or another, every human liquid has spilled onto the backseat of my cab.'

'And who wipes it up?'

'I do. It's part of the job.'

'Well, just remember, young man,' Harry would say, pressing the back of his hand against his forehead in a fake diva swoon, 'when you come to work for me, you'll discover that books don't bleed. And they certainly don't *defecate*.'

'There are good moments, too,' Tom would add, not wanting to let Harry have the last word. 'Indelible moments of grace, tiny exaltations, unexpected miracles. Gliding through Times Square at three-thirty in the morning, and all the traffic is gone, and suddenly you're alone in the center of the world, with neon raining down on you from every corner of the sky. Or pushing the speedometer up past seventy on the Belt Parkway just before dawn and smelling the ocean as it pours in on you through the open window. Or traveling across the

Brooklyn Bridge at the very moment a full moon rises into the arch, and that's all you can see, the bright yellow roundness of the moon, so big that it frightens you, and you forget that you live down here on earth and imagine you're flying, that the cab has wings and you're actually flying through space. No book can duplicate those things. I'm talking about real transcendence, Harry. Leaving your body behind you and entering the fullness and thickness of the world.'

'You don't have to drive a cab to do that, my boy. Any old car will do.'

'No, there's a difference. With an ordinary car, you lose the element of drudgery, and that's fundamental to the whole experience. The exhaustion, the boredom, the mind-numbing sameness of it all. Then, out of nowhere, you suddenly feel a little burst of freedom, a moment or two of genuine, unqualified bliss. But you have to pay for it. Without the drudgery, no bliss.'

Tom had no idea why he resisted Harry in this way. He didn't believe a tenth of the things he said to him, but each time the subject of changing jobs came up again, he would dig in his heels and start spinning his ludicrous counter-arguments and self-justifications. Tom knew he would be better off working for Harry, but the thought of becoming a book dealer's assistant was hardly a thrilling prospect, hardly what he had in mind when he dreamed of overhauling his life. It was too small a step, somehow, too puny a thing to settle for after having lost so much. So the courtship continued, and the more Tom came to despise his job, the more stubbornly he defended his own inertia; and the more inert he became, the more he despised himself. The jolt of turning thirty under such bleak circumstances had an effect on him, but not enough to force him into action, and even though his meal at the counter of the Metropolitan Diner had ended with a resolution to find another job no later than one month from that night, when a month had passed he was still working for the 3-D Cab Company. Tom had always wondered what the *D*'s stood for, and now he thought he knew. Darkness, Disintegration, and Death. He told Harry he would take his offer under consideration, and then he did nothing, just as he had always done. If not for the stuttering, juiced-up crackhead who jammed a gun into his throat at the corner of Fourth Street and Avenue B one frigid night in January, who knows how long the standoff would have continued? But Tom finally got the message, and when he went into Harry's shop the next morning and told him he had decided to accept the job, his days as a hack were suddenly over.

'I'm thirty years old,' he told his new boss, 'and forty pounds overweight. I haven't slept with a woman in over a year, and for the past twelve mornings I've dreamed about traffic jams in twelve different parts of the city. I could be wrong, but I think I'm ready for a change.'

A WALL FALLS

So Tom went to work for Harry Brightman, little realizing that Harry Brightman did not exist. The name was no more than a name, and the life that belonged to it had never been lived. That didn't prevent Harry from telling stories about his past, but since that past was an invention, nearly everything Tom thought he knew about Harry was false. Forget the childhood in San Francisco with the socialite mother and the doctor father. Forget Exeter and Brown. Forget the disinheritance and the flight to Greenwich Village in the summer of 1954. Forget the vagabond years in Europe. Harry was from Buffalo, New York, and he had never been a painter in Rome, had never managed a theater in London, and had never been an auction-house consultant in Paris. The only money in the family had come from the weekly paycheck his father brought home from his job as a mail sorter at the central post office, and when Harry left Buffalo at eighteen, it wasn't to go to college but to enlist in the navy. After his discharge four years later, he did manage to earn some undergraduate credits – at De Paul University in Chicago – but he felt too old for studying by then and quit after three semesters. Chicago was where he stayed, however, and the story of how he had come to New York nine years earlier (after losing his money in a London stock fraud) was no more than another work of fiction. Nevertheless, it was true that he had been in New York for nine years, and it was also true that he hadn't known the first thing about the book business when he arrived there. But his name hadn't been Harry Brightman then; it had been Harry Dunkel. And he hadn't come to New York by way of London. He had flown in from O'Hare Airport, and for the past two and a half years his mailing address had been the federal penitentiary in Joliet, Illinois.

That would account for Harry's reluctance to tell the truth. It's no small job having to start your life again at fifty-seven, and when a man's only assets are the brain in his head and the tongue in his mouth, he has to think carefully before he decides to open that mouth and speak. Harry wasn't ashamed of what he had done (he had been caught, that was all, and since when was bad luck considered a crime?), but he certainly had no intention of talking about it. He had worked too hard and too long to fashion the little world he lived in now, and he wasn't about to let anyone know how much he had suffered. Therefore, Tom was kept in the dark about Harry's career in Chicago, which included an ex-wife, a thirty-one-year-old daughter, and an art gallery on Michigan

Avenue that Harry had run for nineteen years. If Tom had known about the swindle and Harry's arrest, would he still have accepted the job Harry offered him? Possibly. But then again, perhaps not. Harry couldn't be certain, and for that reason he bit his tongue and never said a word.

Then, on a rain-soaked morning in early April, less than a month after I moved into the neighborhood, which was roughly three and a half months after Tom started working at Brightman's Attic, the great wall of secrecy came tumbling down.

It started with an unannounced visit from Harry's daughter. Tom happened to be downstairs when she walked into the store – dripping wet, with water streaming off her clothes and hair, a strange, disheveled creature with darting eyes and a foul, acrid smell hovering around her body. Tom recognized it as the smell of the permanently unwashed, the smell of the insane.

'I want to see my father,' she said, crossing her arms and clasping her elbows with trembling, nicotine-stained fingers.

Since Tom knew nothing about Harry's former life, he had no idea what she was talking about. 'You must be mistaken,' he said.

'No,' she shot back at him – suddenly agitated, bristling with anger. 'I'm Flora!'

'Well, Flora,' Tom said, 'I think you've come to the wrong place.'

'I can have you arrested, you know. What's your name?'

'Tom,' Tom said.

'Of course. Tom Wood. I know all about you. In the middle of life's journey, I lost my way in a dark wood. But you're too ignorant to know that. You're one of those little men who can't see the forest for the trees.'

'Listen,' Tom said, speaking to her in a soft, mollifying voice. 'You might know who I am, but there's nothing I can do to help you.'

'Don't get cheeky with me, mister. Just because you're made of wood, that doesn't mean you're good. *Comprendo*? I'm here to see my father, and I want to see him *right now*!'

'I don't think he's in,' Tom said, abruptly reversing his tactics.

'Like hell he isn't. The jailbird lives in the apartment upstairs. Do you think I'm stupid?'

Flora ran her fingers through her wet hair, spraying water onto a tower of newly acquired books that sat on a table near the front counter. Then, coughing deeply, she pulled out a pack of Marlboros from a pocket in her torn, loose-fitting dress. After she had lit up a cigarette, she tossed the burning match onto the floor. Tom hid his surprise and calmly snuffed it out with his foot. He didn't bother to tell her that smoking was forbidden in the shop.

'Who are we talking about?' he asked.

'Harry Dunkel. Who else?'

'Dunkel?'

'It means *dark*, in case you didn't know. My

father is a dark man, and he lives in a dark wood. He pretends he's a bright man now, but that's only a trick. He's still dark. He'll always be dark – right up to the day he dies.'

DISTURBING REVELATIONS

It took Harry seventy-two hours to persuade Flora to go back on her medication – and a full week to talk her into returning to her mother in Chicago. The day after her departure, he invited Tom to join him for dinner at Mike & Tony's Steak House on Fifth Avenue, and for the first time since his release from prison nine years earlier, he spilled the beans about his past – the whole brutal, asinine story of his misspent life, alternately laughing and weeping as he unburdened himself to his incredulous assistant.

He had started out in Chicago as a salesclerk in the perfume department at Marshall Field's. After two years, he had advanced to the somewhat more exalted position of assistant window dresser, and no doubt that was where he would have stayed if not for his unlikely union with Bette (pronounced *bet*) Dombrowski, the youngest daughter of multi-millionaire Karl Dombrowski, commonly referred to as the Diaper-Service King of the Midwest. The art gallery that Harry opened the following year was created entirely with Bette's money, but just because that money brought him hitherto unimaginable comforts and social status, it would be wrong to assume that he married her only because she was rich or that he walked into his new life under false pretenses. He was never anything less than frank with her on the subject of his sexual proclivities, but not even that could stop Bette from finding Harry to be the most desirable man she had ever known. She was already in her mid-thirties then, a homely, inexperienced woman who was rapidly heading toward permanent spinsterhood, and she knew that if she didn't assert herself with Harry, she was destined to live out the rest of her days in her father's house as an object of scorn, the clumsy maiden aunt of her brothers' and sisters' children, an exile stranded in the heart of her own family. Fortunately, she was less interested in sex than in companionship, and she dreamed of sharing her life with a man who would bestow on her some of the sparkle and self-confidence she lacked. If Harry wanted to indulge in an occasional dalliance or clandestine romp, she would have no objections. Just so long as they were married, she said, and just so long as he understood how much she loved him.

There had been women in Harry's life before. From the earliest years of his adolescence, his sexual history had been an indiscriminate catalogue of lusts and longings that fell on both sides of the fence. Harry was glad he had been built that way, glad that he was immune to the prejudice that would have forced him to spend his life spurning the charms of one half of humanity, but

46

until Bette proposed to him in 1967, it had never occurred to him that he might enter into a fixed domestic arrangement, let alone find himself transformed into a husband. Harry had loved many times in the past, but he had rarely been loved in return, and Bette's ardor astonished him. Not only was she offering herself to him without reservation, but in the same breath she was granting him total liberty.

There were, of course, certain drawbacks to contend with as well. Bette's family, for one thing, and the bullying interference from her blowhard father, who would periodically threaten to cut his daughter out of his will unless she divorced 'that obnoxious pansy.' And then, even more unsettling perhaps, there was the matter of Bette herself. Not the person or the soul of Bette, but her body, the outer manifestations of Bette, with her small squinting eyes and the off-putting black hairs that adorned her fleshy forearms. Harry had an instinctive, highly developed taste for the beautiful, and he had never fallen for anyone who was less than attractive. If anything made him hesitate about marrying her, it was this question of her looks. But Bette was so kind, and ever so intent on pleasing him, that Harry took the plunge, knowing that his first job as a married man would be to mold his wife into a facsimile of a woman who could – in the proper light and under the proper circumstances – arouse a flicker of desire in him. Some of the improvements were simple enough to achieve. Her glasses were replaced by contact lenses; her wardrobe was revamped; her arms and legs were subjected to painful depilatory treatments at regular intervals. But there were other factors that Harry couldn't control, efforts that his new bride would have to make entirely on her own. And Bette did make them. With all the discipline and self-abnegation of a holy sister of God, she managed to diet away close to one-fifth of her body weight in the first year of their marriage, dropping from a dowdy 155 to a slender 126. Harry was moved by the struggles of his strong-willed Galatea, and as Bette blossomed under the care and scrutiny of her husband's watchful gaze, their growing admiration for each other developed into a solid, lasting friendship. Flora's birth in 1969 was not the result of some prearranged one-night stand. Harry and Bette slept together often enough in the early years of their marriage to make a pregnancy almost inevitable, an a priori fait accompli. Who among Harry's friends would have predicted such a turnaround? He had married Bette because she had promised him his freedom, but once they settled in together, he discovered that he had little or no interest in exercising it.

The gallery opened its doors in February 1968. It was the fulfillment of a long-standing dream for the thirty-four-year-old Harry, and he did everything he could to make the operation a success. Chicago wasn't the center of the art world, but neither was it some Podunk backwater, and there was enough wealth floating around the city for a clever man to induce some of it to wind up in his pocket. After a period of deep reflection, he decided to call his gallery Dunkel Frères. Harry had no brothers, but he felt the name lent a certain Old World quality to the enterprise, hinting at a long family tradition in the business of buying and selling art. As he saw it, the marriage between the German proper noun and the French modifier would create an arresting, altogether agreeable confusion in the minds of his customers. Some would take the blending of languages to signify a background in Alsace. Others would think he was from a German-Jewish family that had emigrated to France. Still others wouldn't have the first idea what to make of him. No one would ever be certain of Harry's origins – and when a man can produce an air of mystery about himself, he always has the upper hand when dealing with the public.

He specialized in the work of young artists – paintings mostly, but also sculptures and installation pieces, along with a couple of Happenings, which were still in fashion in the late sixties. The gallery sponsored poetry readings and *soirées musicales*, and because Harry was interested in all forms of the beautiful, Dunkel Frères did not confine itself to a narrow aesthetic position. Pop and Op, minimalism and abstraction, pattern painting and photographs, video art and the New Expressionism – as the years went by, Harry and his phantom brother exhibited works that embodied every trend and inclination of the period. Most of the shows flopped. That was to be expected, but more dangerous to the future of the gallery were the defections of the half dozen or so real artists Harry discovered along the way. He would give a young kid his or her first break, promote the work with his customary flair and panache, build up a market for it, begin turning a comfortable profit, and then, after two or three shows, the artist would decamp to a gallery in New York. That was the problem with being based in Chicago, and Harry understood that for the genuinely talented ones, it was a move they had to make.

But Harry was a lucky man. In 1976, a thirty-two-year-old painter named Alec Smith walked into the gallery with a packet of slides. Harry was absent that day, but when the receptionist handed him the envelope the following afternoon, he removed a sleeve of transparencies and held it up against a window for a quick look – expecting nothing, prepared to be let down – and realized that he was looking at greatness. Smith's work had everything. Boldness, color, energy, and light. Figures swirled through fierce, slashing strokes of paint, vibrating with an incandescent roar of emotion, a human cry so deep, so true, so passionate, that it seemed to express both joy and despair at the same time. The canvases resembled nothing Harry had seen before, and so powerful was the effect they had on him that his hands began to shake. He sat down, examined all forty-seven pictures on a portable light table, and then immediately picked up the phone and called Smith to offer him a show.

Unlike the other young artists Harry had supported, Smith wanted nothing to do with New York. He had already spent six years there, and after being rejected by every gallery in town, he had returned to Chicago a bitter and angry man, seething with contempt for the art world and every blood-sucking, money-grubbing whore who was in it. Harry called him his 'surly genius,' but in spite of Smith's rude and sometimes combative nature, the roughneck was a thoroughbred at heart. He understood the meaning of loyalty, and once he was corralled into the Dunkel Frères stable, he had no intention of trying to break loose. Harry was the man who had rescued him from oblivion, and therefore Harry would remain his dealer for life.

Harry had found his first and only major artist, and for the next eight years Smith's work kept the gallery solvent. After the success of the 1976 show (all seventeen paintings and thirty-one drawings were gone by the end of the second week), Smith high-tailed it out of town with his wife and young son and bought a house in Oaxaca, Mexico. From then on, the artist refused to budge, and he never set foot in America again – not even to attend the annual exhibitions of his work in Chicago, much less the museum retrospectives that were mounted in various cities around the country as his reputation began to grow. If Harry wanted to see him, he had to fly down to Mexico – which he did on average twice a year – but mostly they stayed in touch by letter and the occasional phone call. None of that posed a problem for the director of Dunkel Frères. Smith's output was prodigious, and every other month new crates of canvases and drawings would arrive at the gallery in Chicago, to be sold for ever more delicious and elevated sums. It was an ideal setup, and no doubt it would have continued for many decades if Smith hadn't filled his body with tequila three nights before his fortieth birthday and jumped off the roof of his house. His wife insisted it was a prank that had gone wrong; his mistress claimed it was suicide. One way or the other, Alec Smith was dead, and the *S.S. Harry Dunkel* was about to sink.

Enter a young artist named Gordon Dryer. Harry had given him his first show just six months before the Smith catastrophe – not because he was impressed by his work (severe, overly rational abstractions that produced not one sale nor one positive review), but because Dryer himself was an irresistible presence, a thirty-year-old who looked no older than eighteen, with a delicate, feminine face, slim, marble-white hands, and a mouth that Harry wanted to kiss from the first moment he saw it. After sixteen years of conjugal life with Bette, Tom's future employer finally succumbed. Not just to some small, fly-by-night crush, but to a delirious, full-blown intoxication, an improbable, burning love. And the ambitious

Dryer, so desperate to show his work at Dunkel Fréres, allowed himself to be seduced by the squat, fifty-year-old Harry. Or perhaps it was the other way around, and Dryer was the one who did the seducing. However it happened, the deed took place when the gallery owner went to the artist's studio to look at his most recent canvases. The beautiful boyman was quick to divine Harry's intentions, and after twenty minutes of inconsequential chatter about the virtues of geometric minimalism, he casually dropped to his knees and unzipped the dealer's pants.

After the tepid response to Dryer's show, the unzippings multiplied, and before long Harry was stopping in at the painter's studio several times a week. Dryer fretted that Harry would eliminate him from the roster of his artists, and he had nothing but his body to offer as compensation. Harry was too smitten to understand that he was being used, but even if he had understood, it probably wouldn't have made a difference. Such is the madness of the human heart. He kept the affair a secret from Bette, and because the fifteen-year-old Flora was already beginning to manifest the first, incipient signs of her encroaching schizophrenia, he spent as much time at home with his family as his schedule allowed. The afternoons were for Gordon, but at night he slipped back into his role as dutiful husband and father. Then the announcement of Smith's death came crashing down on him, and Harry began to panic. There were still a number of works to be sold, but after six months or a year the stock would be exhausted. Then what? Dunkel Frères hardly broke even as it was, and Bette had already thrown too much money into the place for Harry to turn to her and ask for more help. With Smith suddenly gone, the gallery was bound to go under. If not today, then tomorrow, and if not tomorrow, then the day after that. For the truth was that Harry had failed to grasp the first thing about how to run a business. He had relied on the cantankerous Smith to support his extravagances and self-indulgent methods (the opulent parties and dinners for two hundred people, the private jets and chauffeur-driven cars, the moronic gambles on second- and third-rate talents, the monthly stipends to artists whose work didn't sell), but the goose had taken a swan dive in Mexico, and henceforth there would be no more golden eggs.

That was when Dryer came up with the plan to rescue Harry from his troubles. Sucking and fucking could go just so far, he realized, but if he could make himself truly indispensable, his career as an artist would be saved. In spite of the cold intellectualism of his work, Dryer had enormous natural gifts as a draftsman and colorist. He had suppressed them in the name of an idea, a notion of art that valued rigor and exactitude above all else. He hated Smith's gushing Romanticism, with its florid gestures and pseudo-heroic impulses, but that didn't mean he couldn't imitate the style if

54

he chose to. Why not continue to create Smith's work after the artist was dead? The final paintings and drawings of the young master who had been cut down in his prime. A public exhibition would be too risky, of course (Smith's widow would hear about it and eventually call their bluff), but Harry could sell the pieces from the back room of the gallery to Smith's most fervent collectors, and as long as Valerie Smith knew nothing about it, the scam would yield a pure, one hundred percent profit.

Harry resisted at first. He knew that Gordon had hit on a brilliant idea, but the idea scared him – not because he was against it, but because he didn't think the boy had the stuff to pull off the job. And anything less than perfect, dead-on clones of Smith's work would probably land him in jail. Dryer shrugged, pretending it had just been a passing thought, and then started talking about something else. Five days later, when Harry returned to the studio for another one of his afternoon visits, Dryer unveiled the first of his Alec Smith originals, and the astonished art dealer was forced to admit that he had underestimated the abilities of his young protégé. Dryer had reinvented himself as Smith's double, purging every shred of his own personality in order to slip into the mind and heart of a dead man. It was a remarkable turn of theater, a piece of psychological witchcraft that struck both terror and awe in poor Harry's brain. Not only had Dryer duplicated the look and feel of one of Smith's canvases, copying the harsh palette-knife strokes, the dense coloration, and the random, accidental drips, but he had taken Smith ever so slightly farther than Smith had ever gone himself. It was Smith's *next painting*, Harry realized, the one he would have started on the morning of January twelfth if he hadn't jumped off the roof of his house and died on the night of the eleventh.

Over the next six months, Dryer produced twenty-seven more canvases, along with several dozen ink drawings and charcoal sketches. Then, very slowly and methodically, tamping down his enthusiasm in an uncharacteristic display of tight-lipped control, Harry began fobbing off the bogus works to various collectors around the world. The game continued for more than a year, in which time twenty of the paintings were dispensed with, netting close to two million dollars. Because Harry was the front man – and therefore the one who stood to have his reputation destroyed – the forgers agreed on a seventy-thirty split. Fifteen years later, when Harry poured out his confession to Tom over dinner in Brooklyn, he described those months as the most exhilarating and grue-some period of his life. He was trapped in a state of constant fear, he said, and yet notwithstanding the horror, notwithstanding the conviction that he would ultimately be caught, he was happy, as happy as he had ever been. Each time he managed to sell another faux-Smith to a Japanese corporate executive or an Argentinian real estate developer, his pounding, overtaxed heart would jump through forty-seven hoops of joy.

In the spring of 1986, Valerie Smith sold her house in Oaxaca and moved back to the States with her three children. In spite of her tempestuous, often violent marriage to the philandering Smith, she had always been a staunch defender of his work, and she was familiar with every picture he had painted from his early twenties until his death in 1984. Following the initial show at Dunkel Frères, she and her husband had become friendly with a plastic surgeon named Andrew Levitt, a well-heeled collector who had bought two paintings from Harry in 1976 and had amassed a total of fourteen Smiths by the time Valerie went to dinner at his house in Highland Park ten years later. How could Harry have known that she would move back to Chicago? How could he have known that Levitt would invite her to his house – the same Levitt to whom he had sold a magnificent fake-Smith just three months earlier? Needless to say, the rich doctor proudly pointed to his new purchase on the living room wall, and needless to say, the perceptive widow instantly saw the work for what it was. She had never liked Harry, but she had always given him the benefit of the doubt for Alec's sake, knowing that the director of Dunkel Frères was the man most responsible for turning her husband's career around. But now her husband was dead, and Harry was up to no good, and the enraged Valerie Denton Smith was out to destroy him.

Harry denied everything. With seven of the sham works still locked in the storeroom of the gallery, however, it wasn't difficult for the police to mount a case against him. He continued to profess ignorance, but then Gordon skipped town, and in the aftermath of that betrayal, Harry lost all courage. In a moment of despair and self-pity, he finally broke down and told Bette the truth. Another mistake, another wrong move in a long line of stumbles and erroneous judgments. For the first time in all the years he had known her, she lashed out at him in anger – a tirade of invective that included such words as *sick, greedy, disgusting,* and *perverted.* Bette quickly apologized, but the damage had already been done, and even though she went out and hired one of the best lawyers in the city to defend him, Harry understood that his life was in ruins. The investigation dragged on for ten months, a slow gathering of evidence culled from such far-flung places as New York and Seattle, Amsterdam and Tokyo, London and Buenos Aires, and then the Cook County district attorney indicted Harry on thirty-nine counts of fraud. The press announced the news in bold front-page headlines. Harry was looking at a ten- to fifteen-year sentence if he lost his case in court. On the advice of his lawyer, he opted to plead guilty, and then, to reduce his sentence still further, implicated Gordon Dryer in the hoax, contending that the swindle had been his idea from the start and that he (Harry) had been coerced into acting as his accomplice when Dryer vowed to expose their affair. The reward for this co-operation was a maximum term of five years, with the guarantee of substantial time off for good behavior. Detectives followed Dryer's trail to New York and arrested him at a New Year's Eve party in a Christopher Street saloon, just minutes after 1988 began. He pleaded guilty as well, but with no names to give and no bargains to offer, Harry's ex-lover was sent away for seven years.

But worse was still to come. Just as Harry was preparing to go to prison, old man Dombrowski finally prevailed upon Bette to file for divorce. He employed the same intimidation tactics he had used in the past – threatening to cut her out of his will, threatening to stop her allowance – but this time he meant it. Bette was no longer in love with Harry, but neither had she been planning to desert him. In spite of the scandal, in spite of the disgrace he'd brought down on himself, it hadn't once crossed her mind to end their marriage. The problem was Flora. On the verge of nineteen now, she had already been in and out of two private mental hospitals, and her prospects for even a partial recovery were nil. Care at that level entailed staggering expenses, sums in excess of a hundred thousand dollars for each stay, and if Bette lost her father's monthly check, she would have no alternative but to send her daughter to a state institution the next time she broke down – an idea she simply refused to accept. Harry understood her dilemma, and because he had no solution to offer of his own, he reluctantly gave his blessing to the divorce, all the while swearing to kill her father the moment he was released from prison.

He had been turned into a pauper, a penniless convict without a single resource or plan, and once he had served his time in Joliet, he would be cast to the four winds like a fistful of confetti. Oddly enough, it was his much-despised father-in-law who stepped in and saved him – but at a price, at such a ruthless, exacting price that Harry never recovered from the shame and revulsion he felt when he accepted the old man's proposition. But he did it. He was too weak not to, too terrified about his future not to accept, but the moment he put his signature on the contract, he knew that he had signed away his soul and would be damned forever.

He had been in prison for almost two years at that point, and Dombrowski's terms couldn't have been simpler. Harry would move to another part of the country, and in exchange for a sufficient amount of money to set himself up in a new business, he would agree never to return to Chicago and never contact Bette or Flora again. Dombrowski considered Harry a moral degenerate, an example of some debased sub-species of organism that did not fully qualify as human, and he held him personally accountable for Flora's illness. She was crazy because Harry had impregnated Bette with his sickly, mutant sperm, and now that he had proven himself to be a fraud and a criminal as well, he would be condemned to a post-prison life of poverty and suffering unless he renounced all claims to his fatherhood. Harry renounced. He caved in to Dombrowski's ugly demands, and from that capitulation a new life became possible for him. He chose Brooklyn because it was New York and yet not New York, and the chances of running into any of his old art world colleagues were slim. There was a bookstore for sale on Seventh Avenue in Park Slope, and even though Harry knew nothing about the book business, the shop appealed to his taste for bric-a-brac and antiquarian clutter. Dombrowski bought the entire four-story building for him, and in June of 1991 Brightman's Attic was born.

Harry was crying by then, Tom said, and for the rest of the dinner he talked about Flora, remembering the last tormented day he'd spent with her before going off to prison. She was in the middle of another crack-up, spinning into the mania that would eventually land her in the hospital for the third time, but she was still lucid enough to recognize Harry as her father and talk to him in cogent sentences. Somewhere or other, she had come across a set of statistics that calculated how many people in the world were born and died each second on a given day. The numbers were stupendous, but Flora had always been good at math, and she quickly extrapolated the totals into groups of ten: ten births every forty-one seconds, ten deaths every fifty-eight seconds (or whatever the figures happened to be). This was the truth of the world, she told her father at breakfast that morning, and in order to get a grip on that truth, she had decided to spend the day sitting in the rocking chair in her room, shouting out the word *rejoice* every forty-one seconds and the word *grieve* every fifty-eight seconds to mark the passing of the ten departed souls and celebrate the arrival of the ten newly born.

Harry's heart had been broken many times, but now it was no more than a pile of ashes clogging up a hole in his chest. On the final day of his freedom, he spent twelve hours sitting on his daughter's bed watching her rock back and forth in the chair and alternately shout the words *rejoice* and *grieve* as she followed the arc of the second hand that moved steadily around the dial of the alarm clock on her bedside table. 'Rejoice!' she cried out. 'Rejoice for the ten who are born, who will be born, who have been born every forty-one seconds. Rejoice for them and do not stop. Rejoice unceasingly, for this much is certain, this much is true, and this much is beyond doubt: ten people live who did not live before. Rejoice!'

And then, gripping the arms of the chair tightly as she accelerated the pace of her rocking, she looked into her father's eyes and shouted, 'Grieve! Grieve for the ten who have vanished. Grieve for the ten whose lives are no more, who begin their journey into the vast unknown. Grieve endlessly for the dead. Grieve for the men and women who were good. Grieve for the men and women who were bad. Grieve for the old whose bodies failed them. Grieve for the young who died before their time. Grieve for a world that allows death to take us from the world. Grieve!'

ON RASCALS

Until I ran into Tom at Brightman's Attic, I don't think I had talked to Harry more than two or three times – and then only in passing, the shortest of short, perfunctory exchanges. After listening to Tom's tale of his boss's past, I found myself curious to learn more about this singular character, to meet the scoundrel face to face and observe him in action with my own eyes. Tom said he would be happy to introduce him to me, and so once our two-hour meal at the Cosmic Diner came to an end, I decided to accompany my nephew back to the store and fulfill my wish that very afternoon. I paid the check at the front register, then returned to our table and left a twenty-dollar tip for Marina. It was an absurdly excessive amount – nearly double the cost of the lunch itself – but I didn't care. My heart-throb beamed forth a resplendent smile of thanks, and the vision of her happiness put me in such excellent spirits that I instantly made up my mind to call Rachel that evening with the news that her long-lost cousin had been found. After her dreary, disputatious visit to my apartment in early April,

I was still on my daughter's shit list, but now that I had reconnected with Tom, and now that the smiling Marina Gonzalez had just blown me a kiss as I made my way out of the restaurant, I wanted everything to be right with the world again. I had already called Rachel once to apologize for having spoken so harshly to her, but she had hung up on me after thirty seconds. Now I would call again, and this time I wouldn't stop groveling until the air had finally been cleared between us.

The bookstore was five and a half blocks from the restaurant, and as Tom and I strolled along Seventh Avenue in the softness of the May afternoon, we continued to talk about Harry, the erstwhile Dunkel of Dunkel Frères, who had fled the dark wood of his former self to emerge as a bright sun in the firmament of duplicity.

'I've always had a soft spot for rascals,' I said. 'They might not make the most reliable friends, but think how drab life would be without them.'

'I'm not sure Harry's a rascal anymore,' Tom answered. 'He's too full of regret.'

'Once a rascal, always a rascal. People never change.'

'A matter of opinion. I say they can.'

'You never worked in the insurance business. The passion for deceit is universal, my boy, and once a man acquires a taste for it, he can never be cured. Easy money – there's no greater temptation than that. Think of all the wise guys with their staged car accidents and personal injury

65

scams, the merchants who burn down their own stores and warehouses, the people who fake their own deaths. I watched this stuff for thirty years, and I never got tired of it. The great spectacle of human crookedness. It keeps coming at you from all sides, and whether you like it or not, it's the most interesting show in town.'

Tom emitted a brief noise, an outrush of air that fell midway between a snicker and a guffaw. 'I love hearing you spout your bullshit, Nathan. I hadn't realized it until now, but I've missed it. I've missed it a lot.'

'You think I'm joking,' I said, 'but I'm giving it to you straight. The pearls of my wisdom. A few pointers after a lifetime of toiling in the trenches of experience. Con men and tricksters run the world. Rascals rule. And do you know why?'

'Tell me. Master. I'm all ears.'

'Because they're hungrier than we are. Because they know what they want. Because they believe in life more than we do.'

'Speak for yourself, Socrates. If I wasn't so hungry all the time, I wouldn't be carrying around this giant gut.'

'You love life, Tom, but you don't believe in it. And neither do I.'

'You're beginning to lose me.'

'Think of Jacob and Esau. Remember them?'

'Ah. Okay. Now you're making sense.'

'It's an awful story, isn't it?'

'Yes, truly awful. It gave me no end of trouble

when I was a kid. I was such a moral, upright little person back then. I never lied, never stole, never cheated, never said a cruel word to anyone. And there's Esau, a galumphing simpleton just like me. By all rights, Isaac's blessing should be his. But Jacob tricks him out of it – with his mother's help, no less.'

'Even worse. God seems to approve of the arrangement. The dishonest, double-crossing Jacob goes on to become the leader of the Jews, and Esau is left out in the cold, a forgotten man, a worthless nobody.'

'My mother always taught me to be good. 'God wants you to be good,' she'd say to me, and since I was still young enough to believe in God, I believed what she said. Then I came across that story in the Bible, and I didn't understand a thing. The bad guy wins, and God doesn't punish him. It didn't seem right. It still doesn't seem right.'

'Of course it does. Jacob had the spark of life in him, and Esau was a dumbbell. Good-hearted, yes, but a dumbbell. If you're going to choose one of them to lead your people, you'll want the fighter, the one with cunning and wit, the one with the energy to beat the odds and come out on top. You choose the strong and clever over the weak and kind.'

'That's pretty brutal stuff, Nathan. Take your argument one step further, and the next thing you'll be telling me is that Stalin should be revered as a great man.'

'Stalin was a thug, a psychotic murderer. I'm talking about the instinct for survival, Tom, the will to live. Give me a wily rascal over a pious sap any day of the week. He might not always play by the rules, but he's got spirit. And when you find a man with spirit, there's still some hope for the world.'

IN THE FLESH

When we were within a block of the store, it suddenly occurred to me that Flora's visit to Brooklyn meant that Harry was still in touch with his ex-wife and daughter – a clear violation of the contract he'd signed with Dombrowski. If so, why hadn't the old man swooped down on him and reclaimed the deed to the building on Seventh Avenue? According to my understanding of their bargain, that would have been grounds for Bette's father to have taken control of Brightman's Attic and for Harry to have been tossed out on his ear. Had I missed something, I asked Tom, or was there another wrinkle to the story he'd forgotten to tell me?

No, Tom hadn't left anything out. The contract was no longer valid for the simple reason that Dombrowski was dead.

'Did he die of natural causes,' I asked, 'or did Harry kill him?'

'Very funny,' Tom said.

'You're the one who brought it up, not me. Remember? You said Harry swore he was going to kill Dombrowski the day he got out of prison.'

'People say lots of things, but that doesn't mean they have any intention of doing them. Dombrowski kicked the bucket three years ago. He was ninety-one, and he died of a stroke.'

'According to Harry.'

Tom laughed at the remark, but at the same time I sensed that he was becoming a little annoyed by my jesting, sarcastic tone. 'Stop it, Nathan. Yes, according to Harry. Everything is according to Harry. You know that as well as I do.'

'Don't feel guilty, Tom. I'm not going to betray you.'

'Betray me? What are you talking about?'

'You're having second thoughts about letting me in on Harry's secrets. He told you his story in confidence, and now you've broken that confidence by telling the story to me. Don't worry, chum. I might act like an ass sometimes, but my lips are sealed. Got it? I don't know a goddamned thing about Harry Dunkel. The only person I'm going to shake hands with today is Harry Brightman.'

We found him in his office on the second floor, sitting behind a large mahogany desk and talking to someone on the phone. He was wearing a purple velour jacket, I remember, with a multi-colored silk handkerchief sprouting from the left front pocket. The hanky resembled some rare tropical flower, an efflorescence that immediately caught one's eye in the brownish, grayish environment of the book-lined room. Other sartorial particulars escape me now, but I wasn't interested in Harry's clothes so much as in examining his broad, jowly face, his exceedingly round, somewhat bulging blue eyes, and the curious configuration of his upper teeth – which fanned out in a way that suggested a jack-o'-lantern, with small gaps between them. He was a strange little pumpkinhead of a man, I decided, a popinjay with utterly hairless hands and fingers, and only his voice, a smooth and resonant baritone, undercut the overall foppishness of his manner.

As I listened to that voice talk into the phone, Harry waved a greeting to Tom, then lifted an index finger into the air, silently telling him that he'd be with us in a minute. The subject of the conversation eluded me, since Brightman did less talking than his invisible interlocutor, but I gathered that he was discussing the sale of a nineteenth-century first edition with a customer or fellow book dealer. The title of the work wasn't mentioned, however, and my thoughts soon began to wander. To keep myself occupied, I walked around the room inspecting the books on the shelves. By my rough count, there must have been seven or eight hundred volumes in that neatly organized space, with works ranging from the quite old (Dickens and Thackeray) to the relatively new (Faulkner and Gaddis). The older books were mostly leather-bound, whereas the contemporary ones all had transparent protective covers wrapped around their dust jackets. Compared to the jumble and chaos of the shop downstairs, the second floor was a paradise of tranquility and order, and the total value of the collection must have run well into the fat six figures. For a man who hadn't had a pot to piss in less than a decade earlier, the former Mr Dunkel had done rather nicely for himself, rather nicely indeed.

The telephone conversation ended, and when Tom explained who I was, Harry Brightman stood up from his chair and shook my hand. Perfectly friendly, flashing his jack-o'-lantern teeth with a welcoming smile, the very model of decorum and good manners.

'Ah,' he said, 'the famous Uncle Nat. Tom's spoken of you often.'

'I'm just Nathan now,' I said. 'We dropped the uncle business a few hours ago.'

'*Just Nathan,*' Harry replied, furrowing his brows in mock consternation, 'or *Nathan* pure and simple? I'm a little confused.'

'Nathan,' I said. 'Nathan Glass.'

Harry pressed a finger against his chin, striking the pose of a man lost in thought. 'How interesting. Tom Wood and Nathan Glass. Wood and Glass. If I changed my name to Steel, we could open an architecture firm and call ourselves Wood, Glass, and Steel. Ha ha. I like that. Wood, Glass, and Steel. *You want it, we'll build it.*'

'Or I could change my name to Dick,' I said, 'and people could call us Tom, Dick, and Harry.'

'One never uses the word *dick* in polite society,'

Harry said, pretending to be scandalized by my use of the term. 'One says *male organ*. In a pinch, the neutral term *penis* is acceptable. But *dick* won't do, Nathan. It's far too vulgar.'

I turned to Tom and said, 'It must be fun working for a man like this.'

'Never a dull moment,' Tom answered. 'He's the original barrel of monkeys.'

Harry grinned, then shot an affectionate glance at Tom. 'Yes, yes,' he said. 'The book business is so amusing, we get stomachaches from laughing so hard. And you, Nathan, what line of work are you in? No, I take that back. Tom's already told me. You're a life insurance salesman.'

'Ex-life insurance salesman,' I said. 'I took early retirement.'

'Another ex,' Harry said, sighing wistfully. 'By the time a man gets to be our age, Nathan, he's little more than a series of exes. *N'est-ce pas*? In my own case, I could probably reel off a dozen or more. Ex-husband. Ex-art dealer. Ex-navy man. Ex-window dresser. Ex-perfume salesman. Ex-millionaire. Ex-Buffalonian. Ex-Chicagoan. Ex-convict. Yes, yes, you heard me right. Ex-convict. I've had my spots of trouble along the way, as most men have. I'm not afraid to admit it. Tom knows all about my past, and what Tom knows, I want you to know, too. Tom's like family to me, and since you're related to Tom, you're in my family as well. You, the ex-Uncle Nat, now known as Nathan, pure and simple. I've paid my debt to society, and my conscience is clear.

X marks the spot, my friend. Now and forever, X marks the spot.'

I hadn't been prepared for Harry to come out with such a naked admission of guilt. Tom had warned me that his boss was a man filled with contradictions and surprises, but in the context of such a farcical and rambunctious conversation, I found it baffling that he suddenly should have seen fit to confide in a total stranger. Perhaps it had something to do with his earlier confession to Tom, I thought. He'd found the courage to let the cat out of the bag, so to speak, and now that he'd done it once, maybe it wasn't so difficult for him to do it a second time. I couldn't be certain, but for the moment it seemed to be the only hypothesis that made sense. I would have preferred to ponder the question a little longer, but circumstances didn't allow it. The conversation went charging ahead, full of the same silly remarks as before, the same ludicrous witticisms, the same blithering japery and pseudo-histrionic turns, and all in all I had to admit that I was favorably impressed by my pumpkin-headed rascal. He was somewhat exhausting to be with, perhaps, but he didn't disappoint. By the time I left the bookstore, I had already invited Tom and Harry to join me for dinner on Saturday night.

It was a little past four when I returned to my apartment. Rachel was still on my mind, but it was too early to call her (she didn't get home from work until six), and as I imagined myself picking up the phone and dialing her number, I realized that it was probably just as well. Relations had turned so bitter between us, I felt there was a good chance she would hang up on me again, and I dreaded the prospect of another rebuff from my daughter. Instead of calling, I decided to write her a letter. It was a safer approach, and if I kept my name and return address off the envelope, the odds were that she would open the letter and read it rather than tearing it up and throwing it in the garbage.

I thought it would be simple, but it took me six or seven shots before I felt I'd struck the right tone. Asking forgiveness from someone is a complicated affair, a delicate balancing act between stiff-necked pride and tearful remorse, and unless you can truly open up to the other person, every apology sounds hollow and false. As I worked on the successive drafts of the letter (growing more and more dejected in the process, blaming myself for everything that had gone wrong with my life, whipping my poor, rotten soul like some medieval penitent), I was reminded of a book Tom had sent me for my birthday eight or nine years back, in the golden age before June died and Tom was still the brilliant and promising Dr Thumb. It was a biography of Ludwig Wittgenstein, a philosopher I had heard of but never read – not an unusual circumstance, since most of my reading was confined to fiction, with nary the smallest dabble in other fields. I found it to be an absorbing, well-written book, but one story stood out from all the others, and it had stayed with me ever since. According to the author, Ray Monk, after Wittgenstein wrote his *Tractatus* as a soldier during World War One, he felt that he had solved all the problems of philosophy and was finished with the subject for good. He took a job as a school-master in a remote Austrian mountain village, but he proved unfit for the work. Severe, ill-tempered, even brutal, he scolded the children constantly and beat them when they failed to learn their lessons. Not just ritual spankings, but blows to the head and face, angry pummelings that wound up causing serious injuries to a number of children. Word got out about this outrageous conduct, and Wittgenstein was forced to resign his post. Years went by, at least twenty years if I'm not mistaken, and by then Wittgenstein was living in Cambridge, once again pursuing philosophy, by then a famous and respected man. For reasons I forget now, he went through a spiritual crisis and suffered a nervous breakdown. As he began to recover, he decided that the only way to restore his health was to march back into his past and humbly apologize to each person he had ever wronged or offended. He wanted to purge himself of the guilt that was festering inside him, to clear his conscience and make a fresh start. That road naturally led him back to the small mountain village in Austria. All his former pupils were adults now, men and women in their mid – and late twenties, and yet the memory of their violent schoolmaster had not dimmed with the years. One by one, Wittgenstein knocked on their doors and asked them to forgive him for his intolerable cruelty two decades earlier. With some of them, he literally fell to his knees and begged, imploring them to absolve him of the sins he had committed. One would think that a person confronted with such a sincere display of contrition would feel pity for the suffering pilgrim and relent, but of all of Wittgenstein's former pupils, not a single man or woman was willing to pardon him. The pain he had caused had gone too deep, and their hatred for him transcended all possibility of mercy.

In spite of everything, I felt reasonably certain that Rachel didn't hate me. She was pissed off at me, she resented me, she was frustrated with me, but I didn't think her animosity was strong enough to create a permanent rift between us. Still, I couldn't take any chances, and by the time I got around to composing the final draft of the letter, I was in a state of full and utter repentance. 'Forgive your stupid father for shooting his mouth off,' I began, 'and saying things he now mortally regrets. Of all the people in the world, you're the one who means the most to me. You're the heart of my heart, the blood of my blood, and it torments me to think that my idiotic remarks could have caused any bad blood between us. Without you, I am nothing. Without you, I am no one. My darling, beloved Rachel, please give your moronic old man a chance to redeem himself.'

I went on in that vein for several more paragraphs, ending the letter with the good news that her cousin Tom had magically popped up in Brooklyn and was looking forward to seeing her again and meeting Terrence (her English-born husband, who taught biology at Rutgers). Perhaps we could all have dinner together in the city one night. Sometime soon, I hoped. In the coming days or weeks – whenever she was free.

It had taken me over three hours to finish the job, and I felt exhausted, both physically and mentally drained. It wouldn't do to have the letter sitting around the apartment, however, so I immediately went out and mailed it, dropping it into one of the boxes in front of the post office on Seventh Avenue. It was dinnertime by then, but I didn't feel the least bit hungry. Instead, I walked on for several more blocks and went into Shea's, the local liquor store, and bought myself a fifth of Scotch and two bottles of red wine. I am not a heavy drinker, but there are moments in a man's life when alcohol is more nourishing than food. This happened to be one of them. Reconnecting with Tom had given a big boost to my morale, but now that I was alone again, it suddenly hit me what a pathetic, isolated person I had become – an aimless, disconnected lump of human flesh. I am not normally prone to bouts of self-pity, but for the next hour or so I pitied myself with all the abandon of a morose adolescent. Eventually, after two Scotches and half a bottle of wine, the gloom began to lift, and I sat down at my desk and added another chapter to *The Book of Human Folly*, a choice anecdote about the toilet bowl and the electric razor. It went back to the time when Rachel was in high school and still living at home, a chilly Thanksgiving Thursday, roughly three-thirty in the afternoon, with a dozen guests about to descend on the house at four. At no small expense, Edith and I had just remodeled the upstairs bathroom, and everything in it was spanking new: the tiles, the cupboards, the medicine cabinet, the sink, the bathtub and shower, the toilet, the whole works. I was in the bedroom, standing before the closet mirror and knotting my tie; Edith was down in the kitchen, basting the turkey and attending to last-minute details; and the sixteen – or seventeen-year-old Rachel, who had spent the morning and early afternoon writing up a physics lab report, was in the bathroom, scrambling to get ready before the guests arrived. She had just finished showering in the new shower, and now she was standing in front of the new toilet, her right foot perched on the rim of the bowl, shaving her leg with a battery-operated Schick razor. At some point, the machine slipped out of her hand and fell into the water. She reached in and tried to pull it out, but the razor had lodged itself tightly in the flush-hole of the toilet, and she couldn't get a purchase on it. That was when she opened the door and cried out, 'Daddy,' (she still called me *Daddy* then) 'I need some help.'

Daddy came. What tickled me most about our predicament was that the razor was still buzzing and vibrating in the water. It was a strangely insistent and irritating noise, a perverse aural accompaniment to what was already a bizarre, perhaps even unprecedented conundrum. Add in the noise, and it became both bizarre and hilarious. I laughed when I saw what had happened, and once Rachel understood that I wasn't laughing at her, she laughed along with me. If I had to choose one moment, one memory to hoard in my brain from all the moments I've spent with her over the past twenty-nine years, I believe that one would be it.

Rachel's hands were much smaller than mine. If she couldn't get the razor out, there was little hope that I could do any better, but I gave it a shot for form's sake. I removed my jacket, rolled up my sleeves, flung my tie over my left shoulder, and reached in. The buzzing instrument was locked in so firmly, I didn't have a chance.

A plumber's snake might have been useful, but we didn't have a plumber's snake, so I undid a wire hanger and stuck that in instead. Slender as the wire was, it was far too thick to help.

The doorbell rang then, I remember, and the first of Edith's many relatives arrived. Rachel was still in her terry-cloth robe, sitting on her knees as she watched my futile attempts to trick the razor out with the wire, but time was marching on, and I told her she should probably get dressed.

'I'm going to disconnect the toilet and turn it upside down,' I said. 'Maybe I can poke the little fellow out from the other end.' Rachel smiled, patted me on the shoulder as if she thought I'd gone mad, and stood up. As she was leaving the bathroom, I said, 'Tell your mother I'll be down in a few minutes. If she asks you what I'm doing, tell her it's none of her business. If she asks again, tell her I'm up here fighting for world peace.'

There was a toolbox in the linen closet next to the bedroom, and once I'd turned off the valve to the toilet, I took out a pair of pliers and detached the toilet from the floor. I don't know how much the thing weighed. I managed to lift it off the ground, but it was too heavy for me to feel confident that I could turn it over without dropping it, especially in such a cramped space. I had to get it out of the room, and because I was afraid of damaging the wood floor if I put it down in the hall, I decided to carry it downstairs and take it into the backyard.

With every step I took, the toilet seemed to become a few pounds heavier. By the time I reached the bottom of the stairs, I felt as if I were holding a small white elephant in my arms. Fortunately, one of Edith's brothers had just entered the house, and when he saw what I was doing, he came over and lent a hand.

'What's going on, Nathan?' he asked.

'I'm carrying a toilet,' I said. 'We're going to take it outside and put it in the backyard.'

All the guests had arrived by then, and everyone gawked at the weird spectacle of two men in ties and white shirts carrying a musical toilet through the rooms of a suburban house on Thanksgiving Day. The smell of turkey was everywhere. Edith was serving drinks. A Frank Sinatra song was playing in the background ('My Way,' if I remember correctly), and dear, overly self-conscious Rachel looked on with a mortified expression on her face, knowing that she was responsible for disrupting her mother's carefully planned party.

We got the elephant outside and turned it over on the brown autumn grass. I can't recall how many different tools I pulled out of the garage, but not one of them worked. Not the rake handle, not the screwdriver, not the awl and hammer – nothing. And still the razor buzzed on, singing its interminable one-note aria. A number of guests had joined us in the yard, but they were becoming hungry, cold, and bored, and one by one they all drifted back into the house. But not me, not the single-minded, see-it-to-the-end Nathan Glass. When I finally understood that all hope was lost, I took a sledgehammer to the toilet and smashed it to bits. The indomitable razor slid out onto the ground. I switched it off, put it in my pocket, and handed it to my blushing daughter when I returned to the house. For all I know, the damned thing is still working today.

After throwing the story into the box labeled 'Mishaps,' I polished off the other half of the bottle and then climbed into bed. Truth be told (how can I write this book if I don't tell the truth?), I put myself to sleep by masturbating. Doing my best to imagine what Marina Gonzalez looked like without any clothes on, I tried to trick myself into believing that she was just about to enter the room and slip under the covers with me, impatient to coil her smooth, warm flesh around mine.

THE SPERM BANK SURPRISE

As it happened, masturbation turned out to be one of the topics Tom and I discussed over lunch the following afternoon (in a Japanese restaurant this time, since it was Marina's day off at the diner). It started when I asked him if he had managed to re-establish contact with his sister. As far as I knew, the last time anyone in the family had seen her was before June's death, when she had come home to New Jersey to reclaim the infant Lucy. That was in 1992, a good eight years ago now, and from the fact that Tom hadn't mentioned her to me the day before, I assumed my niece had somehow dropped off the face of the earth, never to be heard from again.

Not so. In late 1993, less than a year after my sister's burial, Tom and a pair of his graduate student buddies came up with a scheme to earn some quick cash. There was an artificial-insemination clinic on the outskirts of Ann Arbor, and the three of them decided to offer their services as donors to the sperm bank. It was undertaken as a lark, Tom said, and not one of them stopped to consider the consequences of what they were doing: filling up vials of ejaculated semen in order to impregnate women they would never see or hold in their arms, who in turn would give birth to children – *their children* – whose names, lives, and destinies would remain forever unknown to them.

They were each led into a small, private room, and in order to get them into the spirit of the project, the clinic had thoughtfully provided the donors with a stack of dirty magazines – picture after picture of young naked women in alluring erotic poses. Given the nature of the male beast, such images rarely fail to induce stiff and pulsing erections. Always serious about his work, Tom diligently sat down on the bed and began flipping through the magazines. After a minute or two, his pants and underwear were down around his ankles, his right hand was gripping his cock, and as his left hand continued to turn the pages of the magazines, it was only a matter of time before the job would be finished. Then, in a publication he later identified as *Midnight Blue*, he saw his sister. There was no doubt that it was Aurora – one glance, and Tom knew who it was. Nor had she even bothered to disguise her name. The six-page spread of more than a dozen photos was entitled 'Rory the Magnificent,' and it featured her in various stages of undress and provocation: decked out in a transparent nightie in one picture, a garter belt and black stockings in another, knee-high patent-leather boots in another, but by the fourth page it was pure Rory from top to bottom, fondling her small breasts, touching her genitals, sticking out her ass, opening her legs so wide as to leave nothing to the imagination, and in every picture she was grinning, at times even laughing, her eyes all lit up in an exuberant rush of happiness and abandon, with no trace of reluctance or anxiety, looking as if she were having the time of her life.

'It nearly killed me,' Tom said. 'In two seconds, my dick went soft as a marshmallow. I pulled up my pants, buckled my belt, and got out of there as fast as I could. It knocked me flat, Nathan. My little sister, vamping in a skin magazine. And to find out about it in such a terrible way – out of the blue, sitting in that goddamn clinic at the very moment I'm trying to jerk off. It made me sick, sick to my stomach. Not just because I hated seeing Rory like that, but because I hadn't heard from her in two years, and those pictures seemed to confirm my worst nightmares about what had happened to her. She was only twenty-two, and already she'd fallen into the lowest, most degrading kind of work: selling her body for money. It was all so sad, it made me want to cry for a month.'

When you've lived as long as I have, you tend to think you've heard everything, that there's nothing left that can shock you anymore. You grow a little complacent about your so-called knowledge of the world, and then, every once in a while, something comes along that jolts you out of your smug cocoon of superiority, that reminds you all over again that you don't understand the first thing about life. My poor niece. The genetic lottery had been too kind to her, and she had come up with all the winning numbers. Unlike Tom, who had inherited his shape from the Woods, Aurora was a Glass through and through, and as a family we are universally thin, angular, and tall. She had developed into a carbon copy of her mother – a long-legged, dark-haired beauty, as lithe and supple as June herself. Natasha from *War and Peace*, as opposed to her brother's big-footed, awkward Pierre. It goes without saying that everyone wants to be beautiful, but beauty in a woman can sometimes be a curse, especially if you're a young woman like Aurora: a high school dropout with no husband and a three-year-old kid to support, with a wild and rebellious streak in you, willing to thumb your nose at the world and take on any risk that comes your way. If you're hard up for money, and if your looks are your prime selling point, why would you hesitate to strip off your clothes and reveal yourself to the camera? As long as you can handle the situation, giving in to an offer like that can mean the difference between eating and not eating, between living well and barely living at all.

'Maybe she only did it that one time,' I said, doing what little I could to comfort Tom. 'You know, she's having trouble paying the bills, and a photographer comes along and proposes the job to her. One day's work for a nice bundle of cash.'

Tom shook his head, and from the sullen expression on his face, I understood that my remark was no more than a futile exercise in wishful thinking. Tom didn't know all the facts, but he was certain that the story had neither begun nor ended with that photo session for *Midnight Blue*. Aurora had been a topless dancer in Queens (at the Garden of Earthly Delights, of all places, the very club where Tom had dropped off the drunken businessmen on the night of his thirtieth birthday), had appeared in more than a dozen porn films, and had posed for nudie magazines six or seven times. Her career in the sex business had lasted a solid eighteen months, and because she was well paid for her work, she probably would have kept at it a good deal longer if not for something that occurred just nine or ten weeks after Tom spotted her picture in *Midnight Blue*.

'Nothing bad, I hope,' I said to him.

'Worse than bad,' Tom replied, suddenly on the verge of tears. 'She was gang-raped on the set of a film. By the director, the cameraman, and half the crew.'

'Jesus Christ.'

'They really worked her over, Nathan. She was bleeding so much by the end, she had to check herself into a hospital.'

'I'd like to kill the fucks who did that to her.'

'Me too. Or at least put them in jail, but she

refused to press charges. All she wanted was to get away, to get the hell out of New York. That's when I heard from her. She wrote me a letter in care of the English department at the university, and when I realized what kind of spot she was in, I called her and said she should come out to Michigan with Lucy and live with me. She's a good person, Nathan. You know that. I know that. Everyone who's ever come near her knows that. There isn't a bad bone in her body. A bit out of control, maybe, a bit headstrong, but entirely innocent and trusting, the least cynical person in the world. Good for her that she wasn't ashamed of working in porn, I suppose. She thought it was fun. Fun! Can you imagine? She didn't understand that the business is filled with creeps, the vilest cruds in the universe.'

So Aurora and the three-year-old Lucy moved to the Midwest and settled into the top two floors of a rented house with Tom. Aurora had been making decent money before her departure, but most of it had gone into rent, clothes, and a full-time nanny for Lucy, which meant that her savings were nearly exhausted. Tom had his fellowship, but he was living on a restricted graduate-student budget, with a part-time job at the university library to help make ends meet. They talked about calling their father in California to ask for a loan, but in the end they decided against it. The same with their stepfather in New Jersey, Philip Zorn. Rory's belligerent teenage antics had ravaged the household for years, and they were reluctant to turn to a man who had grown to despise his stepdaughter during the great battles of those earlier days. Tom never said a word to his sister about it, but he knew that Zorn secretly blamed Aurora for their mother's death. She had put June through a prolonged siege of turmoil and despair, and the only recompense for all that suffering had been the unexpected gift of being able to raise her infant grand-daughter. Then that was snatched away from her as well, and Zorn felt it was the anguish of having to part with the child that had killed her. It was a sentimental reading of the story, perhaps, but who's to say he wasn't right? To be perfectly honest, on the day of the funeral the same thought had also occurred to me.

Instead of asking for handouts, Rory found herself a job waiting tables at the priciest French restaurant in town. She had no experience, but she charmed the owner with her smile, her long legs, and her pretty face, and because she was a clever girl, she caught on quickly and mastered the routine within days. It was a big comedown from her high-voltage life in New York, perhaps, but the last thing Aurora was looking for now was excitement. Chastened and bruised, still haunted by the vicious thing that had been done to her, she longed for nothing more than a dull and uneventful respite, a chance to recover her strength. Tom mentioned bad dreams, sudden outbursts of sobbing, long, moody silences. For all that, he also remembered the months she spent with him as a happy time, a time of great solidarity and mutual affection, and now that he had his sister back, there was the unrelenting pleasure of being able to assume the role of big brother again. He was her friend and protector, her guide and support, her rock.

As Aurora slowly regained the spunk and élan of her former self, she started talking about getting a high school equivalency diploma and applying to college. Tom encouraged her to go ahead with the plan, promising to help with the work if she found any of it too difficult. It's never too late, he kept telling her, it's never too late to start again, but in some sense it already was. Weeks passed, and as Rory continued to put off the decision, Tom understood that her heart wasn't in it. On her days off from the restaurant, she began turning up on open-mike nights at a local club, singing blues songs with three musicians she had met one evening while serving them dinner, and before long the quartet had decided to band together and form a group. They called themselves Brave New World, and once Tom saw them perform, he knew that Rory's fleeting impulse to go on with her education had been stopped dead in its tracks. His sister could sing. She'd always had a good voice, but now that she was older, and now that her lungs had been subjected to the tars and fumes of fifty thousand cigarettes, a new and compelling quality had been added to it – something deep and throaty and sensual, an aching, hard-knocks candor that made you sit up in your chair and listen. Tom was both happy and frightened for her. Within a month, she had taken up with the bass guitarist, and he knew it was only a matter of time before she and Lucy would be leaving with him and the two others for some larger city – Chicago or New York, Los Angeles or San Francisco, anywhere in America that wasn't Ann Arbor, Michigan. Deluded or not, Aurora saw herself as a star, and she would never find joy or fulfillment unless the eyes of the world were looking at her. Tom understood that now, and he made no more than a weak, pro forma attempt to talk her out of going. Skin movies yesterday; blues songs today; God knows what tomorrow. He prayed that the bass guitarist, whose name also happened to be Tom, wasn't as stupid as he looked.

When the inevitable moment arrived, Brave New World and their little mascot climbed into a used Plymouth van with eighty thousand miles on it and headed for Berkeley, California. Seven months went by before Tom heard from her again: a telephone call in the middle of the night, and her voice on the other end singing 'Happy Birthday' to him, as sweet and innocent as ever.

Then nothing. Aurora vanished as thoroughly and mysteriously as she had before turning up in Michigan, and for the life of him Tom couldn't understand why. Wasn't he her friend? Wasn't he someone she could count on no matter what kind of trouble she was in? He felt hurt, then angry, then miserable, and as the long months of silence stretched on for more than another year, his misery mutated into a deep and ever-growing despond, a conviction that something terrible had happened to her. In the fall of 1997, he finally gave up on his doctoral thesis. The night before he left Ann Arbor, he collected all his notes, all his diagrams and lists, all the countless rough drafts of his thirteen-part debacle, and one by one burned every page in an oil drum in the back-yard. As soon as the great Melvillean bonfire was extinguished, one of his housemates drove him to the bus depot, and an hour later he was on the road to New York. Three weeks after his arrival, he began his stint as a yellow cab man, and then, just six weeks after that, Aurora unexpectedly called. Neither frantic nor upset, Tom said, neither in desperate straits nor asking for money – she just wanted to see him.

They met for lunch the next day, and for the first twenty or thirty minutes he couldn't stop looking at her. She was twenty-six now and still lovely, as lovely as any woman on earth, but her entire presentation of self had changed. She still looked like Aurora, but it was a different Aurora who sat in front of him now, and Tom couldn't decide if he preferred the new version or the old. In the past, she had worn her lavish, tumbling hair long; there had been makeup, large jewelry, rings on every finger, and a flair for decking herself out in inventive, unorthodox clothes: green leather boots and Chinese slippers, motorcycle jackets and silk skirts, lacy gloves and outrageous scarves, a demi-punk, demi-glamorous style that seemed to express her youth and brave fuck-you spirit. Now, in comparison, she looked positively prim. Her hair had been cut in a short bob; she had no makeup on except for the tiniest slash of rouge on her lips; and her clothes were conventional to a fault: blue pleated skirt, white cashmere sweater, and a pair of nondescript brown high heels. No earrings, just one ring on the fourth finger of her right hand, and nothing around her neck. Tom hesitated to ask, but he wondered if the big eagle tattoo on her left shoulder was still there – or if, in some effort to purify herself, to expunge all traces of her former life, she had gone through the painful procedure of having the ornate, multi-colored bird removed.

There was no question that she was glad to see him, but at the same time he sensed how reluctant she was to talk about anything but the present. She offered no apologies for having been out of touch for so long, and when it came to her comings and goings since leaving Ann Arbor, she skimmed over the facts in just a few sentences. Brave New World broke up after less than a year; she sang with a couple of other groups in northern California; there were men, and then more men, and she began taking too many drugs. Eventually, she parked Lucy with two of her friends – a lesbian couple in their late forties who lived in Oakland – and checked herself into a rehab clinic, where she managed to get herself clean after six months. The entire saga was recounted in under two minutes, and because it had flown by him so quickly, Tom was too bewildered to press her for more details. Then she started talking about someone named David Minor, her group leader at the clinic, who had already turned himself around by the time she left detox and entered the program. He was single-handedly responsible for saving her, she said, and without him she never would have pulled through. More than that, he was the only man she had ever met who didn't think she was dumb, who didn't have sex on the brain twenty-four hours a day, who wasn't after her just for her body. Except Tom, of course, but sisters weren't allowed to marry their brothers, were they? It was against the law, and so she was going to marry David instead. They had already moved to Philadelphia and were staying with his mother while they both looked for work. Lucy was in a good school, and David was planning to adopt her after the wedding. That was why she had come to New York: to ask for Tom's blessing and find out if he would be willing to give her away at the ceremony. Yes, Tom said, of course he would, he would be honored. But what about their father, he asked, wasn't it his job to walk down the aisle with his daughter? Maybe so, Aurora said, but he didn't care about either one of them, did he? He was all wrapped up with his new wife and new kids, and besides, he was too cheap to spring for the airfare from L.A. to Philadelphia. No, she said, it had to be Tom. Tom and no one else.

He asked her to tell him something more about David Minor, but she spoke only in the vaguest generalities, which seemed to suggest that she didn't know as much about her future husband as she should have. David loved her, he respected her, he was kind to her, and so on, but there was nothing solid enough in those phrases for Tom to form a picture of who the man was. Then, her voice dropping almost to a whisper, Aurora added, 'He's very religious.'

'Religious? What sort of religion?' Tom asked, trying not to sound alarmed.

'Christianity. You know, Jesus and all that stuff.'

'What does that mean? Does he belong to a specific denomination, or are we talking about a born-again fundamentalist?'

'Born-again, I guess.'

'And what about you, Rory? Do you believe in all that?'

'I try to, but I don't think I'm very good at it. David says I need to be patient, that one day my eyes will open and I'll see the light.'

'But you're half Jewish. By Jewish law, you're all Jewish.'

'I know. Because of Mom.'

'And?'

'David says it doesn't matter. Jesus was Jewish, too, and he was the son of God.'

'David seems to say a lot of things. Is he the one who got you to cut your hair and change the way you dress?'

'He never forces me to do anything. I did it because I wanted to.'

'With David's encouragement.'

'Modesty befits a woman. David says it helps my self-esteem.'

'David says.'

'Please, Tommy, try to be nice. I know you don't approve, but I've finally found a chance for a little happiness, and I'm not going to let it slip through my fingers. If David wants me to dress this way, what difference does it make? I used to walk around looking like a slut. This is better for me. I feel safer, more pulled together. After all the screwed-up things I did, I'm lucky I'm still alive.'

Tom backed off and changed his tone, and they parted company that afternoon with fierce hugs and earnest kisses, swearing never to fall out of touch again. Tom was convinced that Aurora meant it this time, but as the date of the wedding approached, he still hadn't received an invitation from her – nor a letter, nor a telephone message, nor a word of any kind. When he called the number with the Philadelphia area code she had scribbled onto a paper napkin for him during lunch, a mechanical voice announced that the number was no longer in service. He then tried to track her down through local information, but of the three David Minors he spoke to, not one of them had heard of a woman named Aurora Wood. True to form, Tom blamed himself. His negative comments about Minor's religion had probably hurt Rory's feelings, and if she had gone ahead and told her fiancé about her atheist brother in New York, perhaps he had forbidden her to invite him to the wedding. From the little Tom had heard about Minor, he sounded like that kind of man: one of those over-bearing zealots who laid down the law to others, a sanctimonious prick.

'Any news from her since?' I asked.

'Nothing,' Tom said. 'It's been about three years since we had that lunch, and I have no idea where she is.'

'What about the telephone number she gave you? Do you think it was real?'

'Rory has her faults, but lying isn't one of them.'

'If they moved, then, you should have been able to contact her through the mother.'

'I tried, but nothing came of it.'

'Strange.'

'Not really. What if her name wasn't Minor? Husbands die, after all. People get divorced. Maybe she married again and was using her second husband's name.'

'I feel sorry for you, Tom.'

'Don't. It's not worth it. If Rory wanted to see me, she'd call. I'm pretty much resigned to it by now. I miss her, of course, but what the hell can I do about it?'

'And your father. When was the last time you saw him?'

'About two years ago. He had to come to New York for an article he was working on, and he invited me out to dinner.'

'And?'

'Well, you know what he's like. Not the easiest man in the world to talk to.'

'And what about the Zorns? Are you still in touch with them?'

'A little. Philip invites me out to New Jersey for Thanksgiving every year. I never liked him much when he was married to my mother, but I've gradually changed my mind about him. Her death really tore him apart, and when I understood how much he'd loved her, I couldn't bear a grudge anymore. So we have a mild, respectful sort of friendship now. The same with Pamela. She'd always struck me as a brainless snob, one of those people who cared too much about what college you went to and how much money you earned, but she seems to have improved over the years. She's thirty-five or thirty-six now and lives in Vermont with her lawyer husband and two kids. If you want to go to New Jersey with me this Thanksgiving, I'm sure they'd be happy to see you.'

'I'll have to think it over, Tom. For the time being, you and Rachel are about the only family I can stomach. One more ex-relative, and I'm liable to choke.'

'How is old cousin Rachel? I haven't even asked.'

'Ah, there's the rub, my boy. In herself, I believe she's fine. Good job, decent husband, comfortable apartment. But we had a little tiff a couple of months ago, and the fence is far from mended. In a word, there's a good chance she never wants to talk to me again.'

'I feel sorry for you, Nathan.'

'Don't. It's not worth it. I'd rather you let me feel sorry for you.'

THE QUEEN OF BROOKLYN

When Tom and I met again for lunch the following afternoon, we both understood that we were in the process of creating a small ritual. We didn't articulate it in so many words, but excepting the times when other plans or obligations arose, we would make it our business to get together as often as possible to share our midday meal. No matter that I was twice his age and had once been known as Uncle Nat. As Oscar Wilde once put it, after twenty-five everyone is the same age, and the truth was that our present circumstances were almost identical. We both lived alone, neither one of us was involved with a woman, and neither one of us had many friends (in my case none at all). What better way to break the monotony of solitude than to chow down with your confrère, your *semblable*, your long-lost Tomassino, and chew the fat as you shoveled in your grub?

Marina was on duty that day, looking terrific in a pair of tight-fitting jeans and an orange blouse. It was a delectable combination, since it gave me something to study and admire when she came toward us (the front view of her ample, poignant breasts) and also when she walked away (the back view of her rounded, somewhat bulky rear end). After my recent fantasy of our late-night tryst, I felt a little more reticent with her than I normally did, but there was still the matter of the outrageous gratuity I'd left for her the last time I'd been in, and she was all smiles with us when she took our orders, knowing (I think) that she had conquered my heart forever. I can't recall a word we said to each other, but I must have wound up with a rather dopey smile on my face, for once she walked off toward the kitchen, Tom remarked on how odd I looked and asked if anything was wrong. I assured him I was in top form, and then, in the next breath, I heard myself confessing to my mad, unrequited crush. 'I'd move heaven and earth for that girl,' I said, 'but it won't do me a bit of good. She's married, and one hundred percent Catholic to boot. But at least she gives me a chance to dream.'

I braced myself for Tom to burst out laughing at me, but he did nothing of the kind. With an utterly solemn expression on his face, he reached his arm across the table and patted me on the hand. 'I know just how you feel, Nathan,' he said. 'It's a terrible thing.'

Now it was Tom's turn to confess. Now I was hearing my nephew tell me that he, too, was in love with an unattainable woman.

He called her the B.P.M. The initials stood for

the Beautiful Perfect Mother, and not only had he never spoken a word to her, he didn't even know her name. She lived in a brownstone on a block midway between his apartment and Harry's bookstore, and every morning on his way to breakfast he would see her sitting on the front stoop of her building with her two young children, waiting for the yellow bus to arrive and take them to school. She was remarkably attractive, Tom said, with long black hair and luminous green eyes, but what stirred him most about her was the way she held and touched her children. He had never seen maternal love expressed so eloquently or simply, with more tenderness or outright joy. Most mornings, the B.P.M. would be sitting between the two children, an arm wrapped around each of their waists as they leaned into her for support, nuzzling and kissing them in turn, or else dandling them on her knees as she enclosed them in a double embrace, an enchanted circle of hugging, singing, and laughter. 'I walk by as slowly as I can,' Tom continued. 'A spectacle like that needs to be savored, and so I usually pretend I've dropped something on the ground, or pause to light a cigarette – anything to prolong the pleasure by just a few seconds. She's so beautiful, Nathan, and to see her with those kids, it almost makes me want to start believing in humanity again. I know it's ridiculous, but I probably think about her twenty times a day.'

I kept my feelings to myself, but I didn't like

the sound of it. Tom was just thirty years old, in the prime of his young manhood, and yet when it came to women and the pursuit of love, he had all but given up on himself. His last steady girlfriend had been a fellow graduate student named Linda Something-or-other, but they had broken up six months before he left Ann Arbor, and since then his luck had been so bad that he'd gradually withdrawn from circulation. Two days earlier, he'd told me that he hadn't been out on a date in over a year, which meant that his silent worship of the B.P.M. now constituted the full extent of his love life. I found that pathetic. The boy needed to gather up his courage and start making an effort again. If nothing else, he needed to get laid – and stop frittering away his nights dreaming about some beatific earth mother. I was in the same boat, of course, but at least I knew my dream girl's name, and whenever I repaired to the Cosmic Diner and sat down at my regular table, I could actually talk to her. That was enough for an old has-been like myself. I had already danced my dance and had my fun, and what happened to me was of little importance. If the opportunity came along to add another notch to my belt, I wouldn't have said no, but it was hardly a matter of life and death. For Tom, everything hinged on having the guts to barrel himself back into the thick of the game. Otherwise, he would go on languishing in the darkness of his private, two-by-four hell, and as the years went by he would slowly turn bitter, slowly turn into someone he wasn't meant to be.

'I'd like to see this creature for myself,' I said. 'You make her sound like an apparition from another world.'

'Anytime, Nathan. Just come to my apartment one morning at a quarter to eight, and we can walk down her block together. You won't be disappointed, I guarantee it.'

And so it was that we met early the next morning and walked down Tom's favorite street in Brooklyn. I assumed he was exaggerating when he started talking about the 'hypnotic power' of the Beautiful Perfect Mother, but it turned out that I was wrong. The woman was indeed perfect, indeed a sublime incarnation of the angelic and the beautiful, and to watch her sitting on the front steps of her house with her arms wrapped around those two small kids was enough to bring a flutter to an old curmudgeon's heart. Tom and I were standing on the other side of the street, tactfully positioned behind the trunk of a tall locust tree, and what moved me most about my nephew's beloved was the absolute freedom of her gestures, an unself-conscious abandon that allowed her to live fully in the moment, in an ever-present, ever-expanding now. I guessed her age to be around thirty, but her bearing was as light and unpretentious as a young girl's, and I found it refreshing that such a lovely figure of a woman would show herself in public dressed in a pair of white overalls and a checkered flannel shirt. It was a sign of confidence, I felt, an indifference to the opinions of others that only the steadiest, most grounded souls possess. I wasn't about to abandon my secret infatuation with Marina Gonzalez, but by every objective standard of feminine beauty, I knew she couldn't hold a candle to the B.P.M.

'I'll bet she's an artist,' I said to Tom.

'What makes you say that?' he replied.

'The overalls. Painters always like to wear overalls. Too bad Harry's gallery went out of business. We could have organized a show for her.'

'It could be that she's pregnant again. I've seen her with her husband a couple of times. A tall blond guy with big shoulders and a wispy beard. She's just as affectionate with him as she is with the kids.'

'Maybe she's both.'

'Both?'

'Both pregnant and an artist. A pregnant artist in her dual-purpose overalls. On the other hand, take note of her slender form. I cast my eyes toward the region of her belly, but I detect no bulge.'

'That's why she's wearing the overalls. They're loose enough to hide it.'

As Tom and I continued to speculate on the meaning of the overalls, the school bus pulled up in front of the house across the street, and the B.P.M. and her two little ones were momentarily blocked from view. I realized that I didn't have a moment to spare. In another few seconds, the bus would drive off down the block, and the B.P.M. would turn around and go back into her house. I had no intention of spying on the woman again (there are some things you just don't do), and if this was my only chance, then I had to act immediately. For the sake of my bashful, lovesick nephew's mental health, I felt obliged to destroy the spell he was living under, to demystify the object of his longing and turn her into what she really was: a happily married Brooklyn housewife with two kids and perhaps another on the way. Not some saintly, unapproachable goddess, but a flesh-and-blood woman who ate and shat and fucked – just like everyone else.

Given the circumstances, there was only one possible choice. I had to cross the street and talk to her. Not just a few words, but a full-fledged conversation that would go on long enough for me to wave Tom over and force him to join in. At the very least, I wanted him to shake her hand, to touch her, so he would finally get it through his thick skull that she was a tangible being and not some disembodied spirit who lived in the clouds of his imagination. So off I went – rashly, impulsively, without the first idea of what I was going to say to her. The bus was just beginning to move again when I got to the other side of the street, and there she was, standing on the curb directly in front of me, blowing a last kiss to her two darlings, who had already found their seats on the bus and were now part of a mob of three dozen howling tots. Putting on my most pleasant and reassuring salesman's face, I advanced toward her and said, 'Excuse me, but I wonder if I could ask you a question.'

'A question?' she answered, a bit taken aback, I think, or else merely startled that a man was now standing in front of her where just a moment before there had been a bus.

'I've just moved into the neighborhood,' I continued, 'and I'm looking for a decent art supply store. When I saw you standing here in your overalls, I thought maybe you were an artist yourself. Ergo, it popped into my head to ask.'

The B.P.M. smiled. I couldn't tell whether it was because she didn't believe me or because she was amused by the lameness of my question, but as I studied her face and saw the crinkles forming around her eyes and mouth, I understood that she was a tad older than I had thought at first. Perhaps thirty-four or thirty-five – not that it made the least bit of difference or detracted from her youthful luster in any way. She had spoken only two words to me so far – *A question?* – but in those three short syllables I had heard the resonant tonality of a born Brooklynite, that unmistakable accent so ridiculed in other parts of the country, but which I find to be the most welcoming, most human of all American voices. On the strength of that voice, the gears started rotating in my head, and by the time she spoke to me again, I had already sketched out the story of her life. Born here, I said to myself, and raised here as well, perhaps in the very house she was standing in front of now. Working-class parents, since the Brooklyn gentrification boom didn't begin until the mid-seventies, meaning that at the time of her birth (mid- to late sixties) the neighborhood had still been a shabby, rundown area inhabited by struggling immigrants and blue-collar families (the Brooklyn of my own child-hood), and the four-story brownstone that loomed behind her, which was now worth at least eight or nine hundred thousand dollars, had been bought for next to nothing. She attends the local schools, stays in the city for college, loves several men and breaks more than a few hearts, eventually marries, and when her parents die she inherits the house she lived in as a girl. If not precisely that, then something very close to it. The B.P.M. was too comfortable in her surroundings to have been a stranger, too settled in her own skin to have come from somewhere else. This was her place, and she reigned over the block as if it had been her realm from the first minute of her life.

'Do you always judge people by what they wear?' she asked.

'It wasn't a judgment,' I said, 'just a guess. Maybe a stupid guess, but if you're not a painter or a sculptor or an artist of some kind, then it's the first time I've ever guessed wrong about anyone. That's my specialty. I look at people and figure out who they are.'

She cracked another smile and laughed. Who is

this silly person, she must have been wondering, and why is he talking to me like this? I decided the moment had come to introduce myself. 'I'm Nathan, by the way,' I said. 'Nathan Glass.'

'Hello, Nathan. I'm Nancy Mazzucchelli. And I'm not an artist.'

'Oh?'

'I make jewelry.'

'That's cheating. Of course you're an artist.'

'Most people would call it a craft.'

'I suppose it depends on how good your work is. Do you sell the things you make?'

'Of course. I have my own business.'

'Is your store in the neighborhood?'

'I don't have a store. But a bunch of places on Seventh Avenue carry my stuff. I also sell things out of the house.'

'Ah, I see. Have you lived here long?'

'All my life. Born and bred on this very spot.'

'A Park Sloper through and through.'

'Yeah. Right down to the marrow in my bones.'

There it was: a full confession. Sherlock Holmes had done it again, and as I marveled at my devastating powers of deduction, I wished there had been two of me so I could have patted myself on the back. I know it sounds arrogant, but how often does one achieve a mental triumph of that magnitude? After listening to her speak just two words, I had nailed the whole bloody thing. If Watson had been there, he would have been shaking his head and muttering under his breath.

Meanwhile, Tom was still standing on the other side of the street, and I figured it was long past time to bring him into the conversation. As I turned around and gestured for him to come over, I informed the B.P.M. that he was my nephew and that he ran the rare-book-and-manuscript division of Brightman's Attic.

'I know Harry,' Nancy said. 'I even worked for him one summer before I was married. A hell of a guy.'

'Yeah, a hell of a guy. They don't make them like that anymore.'

I knew that Tom was peeved at me for dragging him into a situation he wanted no part of, but he nevertheless came over and joined us – blushing, his head down, looking like a dog who was about to be whipped. I suddenly regretted what I was doing to him, but it was too late to put a stop to it, too late to offer any apologies, and so I plunged ahead and introduced him to the Queen of Brooklyn, all the while swearing on my sister's grave that I would never, never butt into the affairs of anyone else again.

'Tom,' I said, 'this is Nancy Mazzucchelli. She and I were having a discussion about local art supply stores, but then we got sidetracked onto the subject of jewelry. Believe it or not, she's lived in this house all her life.'

Without daring to lift his eyes from the ground, Tom extended his right arm and shook Nancy's hand. 'It's a pleasure to meet you,' he said.

'Nathan tells me you work for Harry Brightman,' she replied, blissfully unaware of the momentous thing that had just happened. Tom had finally touched her, had finally heard her speak, and regardless of whether that would be enough to break the spell of his enchantment, contact had been made, which meant that Tom would henceforth have to confront her on new ground. She was no longer the B.P.M. She was Nancy Mazzucchelli, and pretty as she was to look at, she was just an ordinary girl who made jewelry for a living.

'Yes,' Tom said, 'I've been there for about six months. I like it.'

'Nancy used to work in the store herself,' I said. 'Before she was married.'

Instead of answering my comment, Tom looked at his watch and announced that he had to be going. Still understanding nothing, the object of his adoration calmly waved good-bye. 'Nice to meet you, Tom,' she said. 'See you around, I hope.'

'I hope so, too,' he answered, and then, much to my surprise, he turned to me and shook my hand. 'We're still on for lunch, right?'

'Absolutely,' I said, relieved to know that he wasn't as upset as I had imagined. 'Same time, same place.'

And off he went, shambling down the block with his heavy-footed gait, gradually shrinking into the distance.

Once he was out of earshot, Nancy said, 'He's very shy, isn't he?'

'Yes, very shy. But a good and noble person. One of the best people on earth.'

The B.P.M. smiled. 'Do you still want the name of an art store?'

'Yes, I do. But I'd also be interested in looking at your jewelry. My daughter's birthday is coming up, and I still haven't bought her a present. Maybe you can help pick something out for me.'

'Maybe. Why don't we go inside and have a look?'

ON THE STUPIDITY OF MEN

I wound up buying a necklace that cost something in the neighborhood of a hundred and sixty dollars (thirty dollars off the original price because I paid in cash). It was a fine and delicate piece of work, with bits of topaz, garnet, and cut glass strung along a thin gold chain, and I felt certain it would look attractive sitting around Rachel's slender neck. I had lied about her birthday – which was still three months down the road – but I figured it wouldn't hurt matters to send an additional peace offering as a follow-up to the letter I'd written on Tuesday. When all else fails, bombard them with tokens of your love.

Nancy's workshop was in a back room on the bottom floor of the house, and the windows looked out on the garden, which wasn't a garden so much as a tiny playground, with a swing set in one corner, a plastic slide in another, and a host of toys and rubber balls in between. As I sifted through the various rings, necklaces, and earrings she had for sale, we chatted in a comfortable sort of way about any number of topics. She was an easy person to talk to – very open, very generous, altogether warm and friendly – but, alas, not so terribly bright as it turned out, since it wasn't long before I learned that she was a devoted believer in astrology, the power of crystals, and all kinds of other New Age hokum. Oh, well. Nobody's perfect, as the old movie line goes – not even the Beautiful Perfect Mother. Too bad for Tom, I thought. He was going to be sorely disappointed if he ever managed to get into a serious conversation with her. But then again, perhaps that was all for the best.

I had figured out some of the essential facts of her life, but I was still curious to know if my other Holmesian theories were valid or not. I therefore continued to question her – not making a big point of it, but jumping in whenever the opportunity presented itself, trying to go about it as subtly as I could. The results were somewhat mixed. I had been right about the matter of her schooling (P.S. 321, Midwood High, Brooklyn College for two years before dropping out to test her luck as an actress, which hadn't come to anything) but wrong about inheriting the house from her deceased parents. Her father was dead, but her mother was very much above ground. She occupied the largest bedroom on the top floor, rode her bicycle through Prospect Park every Sunday, and at fifty-eight was still working as a secretary for a law firm in midtown Manhattan. So much for my infallible genius. So much for Glass's unerring eye.

Nancy had been married for seven years and referred to her husband as both Jim and Jimmy.

When I asked if he was Mazzucchelli or if she'd kept her maiden name, she laughed and said that he was pure Irish. Well, I answered, at least Italy and Ireland both began with the letter *I*. That got another laugh out of her, and then, still laughing, she told me that her mother's first name and her husband's last name were identical.

'Oh,' I said. 'And what name is that?'

'Joyce.'

'Joyce?' I paused for a moment in a kind of addled wonder. 'Are you telling me you're married to a man named James Joyce?'

'Uh-huh. Just like the writer.'

'Incredible.'

'The funny thing is, Jim's parents don't know the first thing about literature. They hadn't even heard of James Joyce. They named Jim after his mother's father, James Murphy.'

'Well, I hope your Jim isn't a writer. It wouldn't be much fun trying to publish work with that name branded on your head.'

'No, no, my Jim doesn't write. He's a Foley walker.'

'A what?'

'A Foley walker.'

'I have no idea what that is.'

'He makes sound effects for movies. It's part of postproduction. The mikes don't always pick up everything on the set. But say the director wants to have the sound of someone's feet crunching on a gravel driveway, you know? Or turning the page of a book, or opening a box of crackers – that's what Jimmy does. It's a cool job. Very exact, very interesting. They really work hard at getting things right.'

When Tom and I met for lunch at one o'clock, I duly reported every scrap of information I'd managed to glean from my talk with Nancy. He was in particularly jovial spirits, and more than once he thanked me for having taken the initiative that morning and coerced him into his face-to-face encounter with the B.P.M.

'I didn't know how you'd react,' I said. 'By the time I got to the other side of the street, I was pretty sure you'd be angry with me.'

'You took me by surprise, that's all. You did a good thing, Nathan, a brave and excellent thing.'

'I hope so.'

'I'd never seen her up close before. She's absolutely stunning, isn't she?'

'Yes, very pretty. The prettiest girl in the neighborhood.'

'And kind. That most of all. You can feel the kindness radiating from every pore of her body. She's not one of those stuck-up, standoffish beauties. She likes people.'

'Down to earth, as the saying goes.'

'Yes, that's it. Down to earth. I don't feel intimidated anymore. The next time I see her, I'll be able to say hello, to talk to her. Little by little, we might even become friends.'

'I hate to disillusion you, but after talking to her this morning, I don't think you two have much

117

in common. Yes, she's a lovely kid, but there ain't too much going on upstairs, Tom. Average intelligence at best. College dropout. No interest in books or politics. If you asked her who the secretary of state was, she wouldn't be able to tell you.'

'So what? I've probably read more books than any person in this restaurant, and what good has it done me? Intellectuals suck, Nathan. They're the most boring people in the world.'

'That could be. But the first thing she'll want to know about you is what your astrological sign is. And then you'll have to talk about horoscopes for the next twenty minutes.'

'I don't care.'

'Poor Tom. You're really stuck on her, aren't you?'

'I can't help it.'

'So what's the next step? Marriage, or just a plain old affair?'

'If I'm not mistaken, I believe she's married to someone else.'

'A minor detail. If you want him out of the picture, all you have to do is ask. I have good connections, son. But for you, I'd probably take care of the job myself. I can see the headlines now: EX-LIFE INSURANCE SALESMAN MURDERS JAMES JOYCE.'

'Ha ha.'

'I'll say one thing about your Nancy, though. She makes very nice jewelry.'

'Do you have the necklace with you?'

I reached into my inside breast pocket and pulled out the long, narrow box that contained my morning's purchase. Just as I was opening the lid, Marina arrived at the table with our sandwiches. Not wanting to exclude her from the unveiling, I slid the box in her direction so she could look as well. The necklace was mounted lengthwise on a bed of white cotton wool, and as she leaned over to examine it, she promptly announced her verdict. '*Ah, qué linda*,' she said, 'such a pretty thing.' Tom seconded her opinion with a silent nod, no doubt too moved to speak because he was thinking about his darling Nancy, whose celestial hands had wrought the small glimmering object that sat before him.

I lifted the necklace from the box and held it out toward Marina. 'Why don't you put it on?' I said. 'So we can see what it looks like.'

That was my original intention – simply to have her model it for us – but once she took the necklace in her hands and held it up against her light brown skin (that small area of exposed flesh just below the unfastened top button of her turquoise blouse), I suddenly changed my mind. I wanted to give it to her as a present. I could always buy another necklace for Rachel, but this one suited Marina so perfectly that it already seemed to belong to her. At the same time, if I gave the impression that I was coming on to her (which I was, of course, but with no hope), she might have felt that I was putting her in an awkward position and refused to accept it.

'No, no,' I said. 'Don't just hold it up. Put it on, so we can make sure it hangs right.' As she fumbled with the clasp in back, I hastily tried to think of something that would overcome her resistance. 'Someone told me it's your birthday today,' I said. 'Is that true, Marina, or was that guy just pulling my leg?'

'Not today,' she answered. 'Next week.'

'This week, next week, what difference does it make? It's coming soon, and that means you're already living inside the birthday aura. It's written all over your face.'

Marina finished putting on the necklace and smiled. 'Birthday aura? What's that?'

'I bought this necklace today for no particular reason. I wanted to give it to someone, but I didn't know who that person was. Now that I see how good it looks on you, I want you to have it. That's what the birthday aura is. It's a powerful force, and it makes people do all sorts of strange things. I didn't know it at the time, but I was buying the necklace for you.'

At first she seemed happy, and I thought there wasn't going to be a problem. From the way she looked at me with those vivid brown eyes of hers, there was no question that she wanted to keep it, that she was touched and flattered by the gesture, but then, once the initial surge of pleasure had passed, she began to think about it a little, and I saw doubt and confusion enter those same brown eyes. 'You're a terrific guy, Mr Glass,' she said, 'and I really appreciate it. But I can't take presents from you. It ain't right. You're a customer.'

'Don't worry about that. If I want to give something to my favorite waitress, who's going to stop me? I'm an old man, and old men are free to do what they want.'

'You don't know Roberto,' she said. 'He's a very jealous guy. He won't like me taking things from other men.'

'I'm not a man,' I said. 'I'm just a friend who wants to make you happy.'

At that point, Tom finally added his two cents to the discussion. 'I'm sure he doesn't mean any harm,' he said. 'You know what Nathan's like, Marina. He's a nutty person – always doing crazy, impulsive things.'

'He's crazy, all right,' she said. 'And also very nice. It's just that I don't want any trouble. You know how it is. One thing leads to another, and then boom.'

'Boom?' Tom said.

'Yeah, boom,' she replied. 'And don't ask me to explain what that means.'

'All right,' I said, suddenly understanding that her marriage was far less tranquil than I had supposed. 'I think I have a solution. Marina keeps the necklace, but she doesn't take it home. It stays here in the restaurant at all times. She wears it at work, and then she stores it in the cash register overnight. Tom and I can come in every day and admire the necklace, and Roberto will never know a thing.'

It was such a preposterous, underhanded proposal, such a devious, rawboned bit of chicanery that Tom and Marina both cracked up laughing.

'Wow,' Marina said. 'You're one hell of a sneaky old man, Nathan.'

'Not as old as all that,' I said.

'And what happens if I forget I'm wearing the necklace?' she asked. 'What happens if I go home one night and still have it on?'

'You'd never do that,' I said. 'You're too smart.'

And so I forced the birthday present on the young and guileless Marina Luisa Sanchez Gonzalez, and for my efforts I received a kiss on the cheek, a prolonged and tender kiss that I will remember to the end of my days. Such are the perks allotted to stupid men. And I am nothing if not a stupid, stupid man. I got my kiss and my beaming smile of thanks, but I also got more than I'd bargained for. Its name was Trouble, and when I reach the point in my story when I was introduced to Mr Trouble, I will give a full account of what happened. But it is only Friday afternoon now, and there are other, more pressing matters to attend to. The weekend is about to begin, and less than thirty hours after Tom and I left the Cosmic Diner, we were both sitting in another restaurant with Harry Brightman, eating dinner, drinking wine, and wrestling with the mysteries of the universe.

A NIGHT OF EATING AND DRINKING

Saturday evening. May 27, 2000. A French restaurant on Smith Street in Brooklyn. Three men are sitting at a round table in the rear left corner of the room: Harry Brightman (formerly known as Dunkel), Tom Wood, and Nathan Glass. They have just finished giving their orders to the waiter (three different appetizers, three different main courses, two bottles of wine – one red, one white) and have resumed drinking the aperitifs that were brought to the table not long after they entered the restaurant. Tom's glass is filled with bourbon (Wild Turkey), Harry is sipping a vodka martini, and as Nathan downs another mouthful of his neat, single-malt Scotch (twelve-year-old Macallan), he wonders if he isn't in the mood for a second drink before the meal is served. So much for the setting. Once the conversation begins, further stage directions will be kept to a minimum. It is the author's opinion that only the words spoken by the above-mentioned characters are of any importance to the narrative. For that reason, there will be no descriptions of the clothes they are wearing, no comments on the food they eat, no pauses when one

123

of them stands up to visit the men's room, no interruptions from the waiter, and not one word about the glass of red wine that Nathan spills on his pants.

TOM: I'm not talking about saving the world. At this point, I just want to save myself. And some of the people I care about. Like you, Nathan. And you, too, Harry.

HARRY: Why so glum, boy? You're about to eat the best dinner you've had in years, you're the youngest person sitting at this table, and as far as I know, you still haven't contracted a major disease. Look at Nathan over there. He's had lung cancer, and he never even smoked. And I've had two heart attacks. Do you see us grumbling? We're the happiest men in the world.

TOM: No you're not. You're just as miserable as I am.

NATHAN: Harry's right, Tom. It's not as bad as all that.

TOM: Yes it is. If anything, it's even worse.

HARRY: Please define 'it.' I don't even know what we're talking about anymore.

TOM: The world. The big black hole we call the world.

HARRY: Ah, the world. Well, of course. That goes without saying. The world stinks. Everyone knows that. But we do our best to avoid it, don't we?

TOM: No we don't. We're right in the thick of it, whether we like it or not. It's all around us, and every time I lift my head and take a good look at it, I'm filled with disgust. Sadness and disgust. You'd think World War Two would have settled things, at least for a couple of hundred years. But we're still hacking each other to pieces, aren't we? We still hate each other as much as we ever did.

NATHAN: So that's what we're talking about. Politics.

TOM: Among other things, yes. And economics. And greed. And the horrible place this country has turned into. The maniacs on the Christian Right. The twenty-year-old dot-com millionaires. The Golf Channel. The Fuck Channel. The Vomit Channel. Capitalism triumphant, with nothing to oppose it anymore. And all of us so smug, so pleased with ourselves, while half the world is starving to death and we don't lift a finger to help. I can't take it anymore, gentlemen. I want out.

HARRY: Out? And where are you going to go? Jupiter? Pluto? Some asteroid in the next galaxy? Poor Tom-All-Alone, like the Little Prince marooned on his rock in the middle of space.

TOM: You tell me where to go, Harry. I'm open to any and all suggestions.

NATHAN: A place to live life on your own terms. That's what we're talking about, isn't it? 'Imaginary Edens' revisited. But in order to do that, you have to be willing to reject society. That's what you told me. It was a long time ago, but I think you also used the word *courage*. Do you have the courage, Tom? Does any one of us have the courage to do that?

TOM: You still remember that old paper, huh?

NATHAN: It made a big impression on me.

TOM: I was just a wee undergraduate back then. I didn't know much, but I was probably smarter than I am now.

HARRY: We're referring to what?

NATHAN: The inner refuge, Harry. The place a man goes to when life in the real world is no longer possible.

HARRY: Oh. I used to have one of those. I thought everyone did.

TOM: Not necessarily. It takes a good imagination, and how many people have that?

HARRY (*closing his eyes; pressing his forefingers against his temples*): It's all coming back to me now. The Hotel Existence. I was just ten years old, but I can still remember the exact moment when the idea occurred to me, the exact moment when I found the name. It was a Sunday afternoon during the war. The radio was on, and I was sitting in the living room of our house in Buffalo with a copy of *Life* magazine, looking at pictures of the American troops in France. I had never been inside a hotel, but I had walked past enough of them on my trips downtown with my mother to know that they were special places, fortresses that protected you from the squalor and meanness of everyday life. I loved the men in the blue uniforms who stood in front of the Remington Arms. I loved the sheen of the brass fittings on the revolving doors at the Excelsior. I loved the immense chandelier that hung in the lobby of the Ritz. The sole purpose of a hotel was to make you happy and comfortable, and once you signed the register and went upstairs to your room, all you had to do was ask for something and it was yours. A hotel represented the promise of a better world, a place that was more than just a place, but an opportunity, a chance to live inside your dreams.

NATHAN: That explains the hotel part. Where did you find the word *existence*?

HARRY: I heard it on the radio that Sunday afternoon. I was only half listening to the program, but someone was talking about *human existence*, and I liked the way it sounded. *The laws of existence*, the voice said, and *the perils we must face in the course of our existence.* Existence was bigger than just life. It was everyone's life all together, and even if you lived in Buffalo, New York, and had never been more than ten miles from home, you were part of the puzzle, too. It didn't matter how small your life was. What happened to you was just as important as what happened to everyone else.

TOM: I still don't follow. You invent a place called the Hotel Existence, but where is it? What was it for?

HARRY: For? Nothing, really. It was a retreat, a world I could visit in my mind. That's what we're talking about, no? Escape.

NATHAN: And where did the ten-year-old Harry escape to?

HARRY: Ah. That's a complicated question. There were two Hotel Existences, you see. The first one, the one I made up that Sunday afternoon during the war, and then a second one, which didn't get going until I was in high school. Number one, I'm sorry to say, was pure corn and boyish sentimentality. But I was just a small fellow back then, and the war was everywhere, everyone talked about it all the time. I was too young to fight, but like most fat, dumb little boys, I dreamed of becoming a soldier. Ugh. Oh, ugh and double ugh. What empty dolts we mortals be. So I imagine this place called the Hotel Existence, and I immediately turn it into a refuge for lost children. I'm talking about European children, of course. Their fathers had been shot down in battle, their mothers were lying under the ruins of collapsed churches and buildings, and there they were, wandering through the rubble of bombed-out cities in the cold of winter, scavenging for food in forests, children alone, children in pairs, children in gangs of four and six and ten, rags tied around their feet instead of shoes, their gaunt faces splattered with mud. They lived in a world without grown-ups, and because I was such a fearless, altruistic soul, I anointed myself as their savior. That was my mission, my purpose in life, and every day for the rest of the war I would parachute into some demolished corner of Europe to rescue the lost and starving boys and girls. I would struggle down burning mountainsides, swim across exploding lakes, machine-gun my way into dank wine cellars, and each time I found another orphan, I would take the child by the hand and lead him to the Hotel Existence. It didn't matter what country I was in. Belgium or France, Poland or Italy, Holland or Denmark – the hotel was never far away, and I always managed to get the kid there before nightfall. Once I'd guided him through the formalities of registering at the front desk, I would turn around and leave. It wasn't my job to run the hotel – only to find the children and take them there. Anyway, heroes don't rest, do they? They aren't allowed to sleep in soft beds with down comforters and three pillows, and they don't have time to sit down in the hotel kitchen to eat a helping of lamb stew with all those succulent potatoes and carrots steaming in the bowl. They have to go back into the night and do their job. And my job was to save the children. Until the last bullet had been fired, until the last bomb had been dropped, I had to go on looking for them.

TOM: What happened after the war was over?

HARRY: I gave up my dreams of manly courage and noble self-sacrifice. The Hotel Existence shut down, and when it opened again a few years later, it was no longer sitting in a meadow somewhere in the Hungarian countryside, and it no longer looked like a baroque castle plucked from the boulevards of Baden-Baden. The new Hotel Existence was a much smaller and shabbier affair, and if you wanted to find it now, you had to go to one of those big cities where real life began only after dark. New York, maybe, or Havana, or some dingy side street in Paris. To enter the Hotel Existence was to think of words like *hobnob*, *chiaroscuro*, and *fate*. It was men and women eyeing you discreetly in the lobby. It was perfume and silk suits and warm skin, and everyone always walked around with a highball in one hand and a burning cigarette in the other. I'd seen it all in the movies, and I knew how it was supposed to look. The regulars downstairs in the piano bar sipping their dry martinis. The casino on the second floor with the roulette table and the muffled dice bouncing on the green felt, the baccarat dealer whispering in an oily foreign accent. The ballroom on the lower level with the plush leather booths and the singer in the spotlight with her smoky voice and shimmering silver dress. Those were the props that helped get things started, but no one came just for the drinks or the gambling or the songs, even if the singer that night was Rita Hayworth, flown in from Buenos Aires for one performance only by her current husband and manager, George Macready. You had to ease yourself into the flow, get a few shots into you before you could settle down to business. Not business, really, but the game, the infinitely pleasurable game of deciding which person you would go upstairs with later that night. The first move was always with the eyes – never anything but the eyes. You would let them wander around from this one to that one for a few minutes, calmly drinking your drink and smoking your cigarette, testing out the possibilities, searching for a glance that might be aimed in your direction, maybe even luring someone with a little smile or a flick of the shoulder to start looking at you. Men and women both, it didn't matter to me. I was still a virgin in those days, but I already knew enough about myself to know that I didn't care. Once,

Cary Grant sat down next to me in the piano bar and began rubbing my leg. Another time, the dead Jean Harlow came back from her grave and made passionate love to me in room four-twenty-seven. But there was also my French teacher, Mademoiselle Des Forêts, the slender Québecoise with the pretty legs and the bright red lipstick and the liquid brown eyes. Not to speak of Hank Miller, the varsity quarterback and hotshot ladies' man of the senior class. Hank probably would have punched me to death if he'd known what I was doing to him in my dreams, but the fact was that he didn't know. I was only a sophomore then, and I never would have had the courage to address such an august figure as Hank Miller during the day, but at night I could meet him in the bar at the Hotel Existence, and after a few drinks and some friendly small talk, I could take him upstairs to room three-oh-one and introduce him to the secrets of the world.

TOM: Adolescent jerk-off material.

HARRY: You could say that. But I prefer to think of it as the product of a rich inner life.

TOM: This is getting us nowhere.

HARRY: Where do you want us to go, dear Tom? We're sitting here waiting for the next course, drinking a splendid bottle of Sancerre, and entertaining ourselves with meaningless stories. There's nothing wrong with that. In most parts of the world, it would be considered the height of civilized behavior.

NATHAN: The kid's in the dumps, Harry. He needs to talk.

HARRY: I'm aware of that. I have eyes in my head, don't I? If Tom doesn't approve of my Hotel Existence, then maybe he should tell us something about his. Every man has one, you know. And just as no two men are alike, each man's Hotel Existence is different from all the others.

TOM: I'm sorry. I don't mean to be a bore. This was supposed to be a fun night, and I'm spoiling it for both of you.

NATHAN: Forget about it. Just answer Harry's question.

TOM: *(a long silence; then in a low voice, as if speaking to himself):* I want to live in a new way, that's all. If I can't change the world, then at least I can try to change myself. But I don't want to do it alone. I'm alone too much as it is, and whether it's my fault or not, Nathan is right. I'm in the dumps. Ever since we talked about Aurora the other day, I haven't stopped thinking about her. I miss her. I miss my mother. I miss everyone I've lost. I get so sad sometimes, I can't believe I don't just drop dead from the weight that's crushing down on me. What's my Hotel Existence, Harry? I don't know, but maybe it has something to do with living with others, with getting away from this rathole of a city and sharing a life with people I love and respect.

HARRY: A commune.

TOM: No, not a commune – a community. There's a difference.

HARRY: And where would this little utopia of yours be?

TOM: Somewhere out in the country, I suppose. A place with a lot of land and enough buildings to accommodate all the people who wanted to live there.

NATHAN: How many people are you talking about?

TOM: I don't know. It's not as if I've worked anything out yet. But both of you would be more than welcome.

HARRY: I'm flattered that I'm so high on your list. But if I move to the country, what happens to my business?

TOM: You'd move it with you. You make ninety

percent of your money through the mail as it is. What difference does it make what post office you use? Yes, Harry, of course I'd want you to be a part of it. And maybe Flora, too.

HARRY: My dear, demented Flora. But if you asked her, Bette would also have to be invited. She's ailing now, you know. Trapped in a wheelchair with Parkinson's, the poor woman. I can't say how she'd react, but in the end she might welcome the idea. And then there's Rufus.

NATHAN: Who's Rufus?

HARRY: The young man who works behind the counter at the bookstore. The tall, light-skinned Jamaican with the pink boa. A few years ago, I found him crying his heart out in front of a building in the West Village and brought him home. By now, I've more or less adopted him. The bookstore job helps pay his rent, but he's also one of the best drag queens in the city. He works on the weekends under the name of Tina Hott. A fabulous performer, Nathan. You should catch his act sometime.

NATHAN: Why would he want to leave the city?

HARRY: Because he loves me, for one thing. And because he's H.I.V. positive and scared out of his wits. A change of scenery might do him some good.

NATHAN: Fine. But where are we going to come up with the money to buy a country estate? I could chip in something, but it wouldn't be nearly enough.

TOM: If Bette wants to join us, maybe she'd be willing to open the coffers and help.

HARRY: Out of the question. A man has his pride, sir, and I'd rather croak ten times over before I asked that woman for another penny.

TOM: Well, if you sold your building in Brooklyn, that might raise enough to swing it.

HARRY: A mere drop in the bucket. If I'm going to spend my waning years in the boondocks, I want to do it in grand style. No bumpkin stuff for me, Tom. I turn myself into a country squire, or the deal is off.

TOM: A little here, then, and a little there. We'll think of some other people who might want to get involved, and if we pool our resources, maybe we can pull it off.

HARRY: Don't fret, boys. Uncle Harry will take care of everything. At least he hopes he will. If all goes according to plan, we can expect a large infusion of cash in the near future. Enough to tip the balance and make our dream come true. That's what we're talking about, isn't it? A dream, a wild dream of removing ourselves from the cares and sorrows of this miserable world and creating a world of our own. A long shot, yes, but who's to say it can't happen?

TOM: And where is this 'infusion of cash' going to come from?

HARRY: Let's just say I have a business venture in the works, and we'll put the matter aside until further notice. If my ship comes in, the new Hotel Existence is a sure thing. If it doesn't – well, at least I'll have gone down fighting the good fight. A man can't do any more than that, can he? I'm sixty-six years old, and after all the ups and downs of my . . . my somewhat dubious career, this is probably my last chance to walk off with some big-time money. And when I say big, I mean very big. Bigger than either one of you can imagine.

CIGARETTE BREAK

At the time, I didn't take any of this talk seriously. Tom was in low spirits – that was all – and Harry was simply trying to cheer him up, to put some wind in his sails and lift him out of the doldrums. I must say that I liked Harry for humoring Tom and playing along with his impractical fantasy, but the idea that Harry would actually leave Brooklyn and move to some remote country settlement struck me as pure nonsense. The man was made for the city. He was a creature of crowds and commerce, of good restaurants and expensive clothes, and even if he was only half gay, his closest friend turned out to be a black transvestite who went to work sporting a pair of rhinestone clip-on earrings and a pink feather boa. Put a man like Harry Brightman in some rustic backwater, and the neighboring peasants would run him out of town with pitchforks and knives.

On the other hand, I felt reasonably certain that Harry's business venture was on the level. The old reprobate had some new deal cooking, and I was burning with curiosity to find out what it was. Even if he didn't want to talk about it in front of

Tom, I hoped he would make an exception for me. My opportunity came just after we ordered dessert, when Tom excused himself and went into the bar area to smoke a cigarette (his newest tactic in the ongoing campaign to shed some pounds).

'Big money,' I remarked to Harry. 'Sounds interesting.'

'The chance of a lifetime,' he said.

'Any particular reason you don't want to talk about it?'

'I'm afraid of disappointing Tom, that's all. Some minor issues still have to be worked out, and until the business is settled, there's no point in getting overly excited.'

'I have some extra money lying around, you know. Quite a lot, in fact. If you need another investor to go in with you, I might be willing to help.'

'That's very generous of you, Nathan. Fortunately, I'm not looking for a partner. But that doesn't mean I wouldn't welcome your advice. I'm fairly confident my associates are on the up-and-up – but not one hundred percent confident. And doubt is a burdensome thing to live with, especially with so much at stake.'

'How about another dinner, then? Just the two of us. You can lay the whole thing out for me, and I'll tell you what I think.'

'Sometime next week?'

'Just pick a day, and I'll be there.'

ON THE STUPIDITY OF MEN (2)

At eleven o'clock the next morning, I stopped in at one of the local jewelry stores to buy a substitute necklace for Rachel. I didn't want to disturb the B.P.M. by ringing her bell on a Sunday morning, but I specifically asked the saleswoman to show me any and all pieces they carried that bore Nancy Mazzucchelli's mark. The woman smiled, said she was an old friend of Nancy's, and then promptly opened a glass cabinet from which she extracted eight or ten examples of her work, placing them on the counter for me one article at a time. As luck would have it, the last necklace turned out to be almost identical to the one that now slept at night in the cash register at the Cosmic Diner.

I was planning to head straight back to my apartment. A couple of anecdotes had occurred to me while walking to the store, and I was eager to return to my desk and add them to the ever-expanding *Book of Human Folly*. I hadn't bothered to count up the entries I'd written so far, but there must have been close to a hundred by then, and from the way they kept coming to me, surging up at all hours of the day and night (sometimes even in my dreams), I suspected there was more than enough material to go on with the project for years. Not twenty seconds after leaving the store, however, who should I run into but Nancy Mazzucchelli, the B.P.M. herself? I had been living in the neighborhood for two months, had taken long walks every morning and afternoon, had gone into countless shops and restaurants, had sat outdoors at the Circle Café watching hundreds of people stride down the avenue, but until that Sunday morning I had never once caught a glimpse of her in public. I don't mean to imply that she had escaped my notice. I look at everyone, and if I had seen this woman before (who was no less than the reigning monarch of Park Slope), I would have remembered her. Now, following our impromptu meeting in front of her house on Friday, the pattern abruptly changed. Like a word you add to your vocabulary late in life – and which you then start hearing everywhere you turn – Nancy Mazzucchelli was suddenly everywhere I turned. It began with that Sunday encounter, and from then on scarcely a day went by when I didn't run into her at the bank or the post office or on some street in the neighborhood. Eventually, I was introduced to her children (Devon and Sam); her mother Joyce; and her Foley-walker husband, Jim, the James Joyce who was not James Joyce. From total stranger, the B.P.M. rapidly became one of the fixtures of my life. Even if she is referred to only seldom in the future pages of this book, she is always there. Watch for her between the lines.

That first Sunday, nothing of any importance was said. Hi Nathan, hi Nancy, how are you, not bad, how's Tom, beautiful weather, nice seeing you, and so on. Small-town chat in the heart of the big city. If there is any detail significant enough to report, it would be the fact that she wasn't wearing her overalls. The day was unusually warm, and Nancy was dressed in a pair of blue jeans and a white cotton T-shirt. Because the shirt was tucked into the pants, I could see that her stomach was flat. That didn't mean she wasn't pregnant, of course, but even if she was in the early days of her first trimester, she hadn't been wearing the overalls on Friday to mask any bulge. I made a mental note to tell Tom about it the next time I saw him.

First thing Monday morning, I sent the necklace to Rachel, along with a short note (*Thinking of you – Love, Dad*), but by nine o'clock that evening I was beginning to worry. I had mailed my letter to her on Tuesday night. Assuming it had gone out early Wednesday morning, it should have reached her by Saturday – Monday at the latest. My daughter had never been much of a letter writer (she did most of her communicating by e-mail, which I didn't have), and therefore I was expecting her to contact me by phone. Saturday and Sunday had already come and gone without a word, which meant that Monday had to be the day she would call. Anytime after six, when she came home from work and read my letter. No matter how badly I had offended her, I found it inconceivable that Rachel wouldn't respond to what I had written. I sat in my apartment waiting for the phone to ring, but by nine o'clock nothing had happened. Even if she had decided to put off calling until after dinner, dinner would have been over by nine. A little desperate, a little afraid, more than a little embarrassed by how desperate and afraid I was, I finally summoned the courage to dial her number. No one there. The answering machine clicked on after four rings, but I hung up before the beep sounded.

Same result on Tuesday.

Same result on Wednesday.

Not knowing what else to do, I decided to call Edith and ask her what was going on. She and Rachel were in constant touch, and while I felt some trepidation about having to talk to my ex, there was no reason to suppose she wouldn't give me a straight answer. X marks the spot, as Harry had so eloquently put it. By now, the only contact I had with my former helpmeet was looking at her signature on the backs of my canceled alimony checks. She had filed for divorce in November 1998, and one month later, long before the decree came through, I was diagnosed with cancer. To her credit, Edith allowed me to stay on in the house for as long as necessary, which explained why we had been so slow to put it on the market.

After the sale, she'd used a portion of her money to buy a condo in Bronxville – which Rachel, with her usual flair for colorful language, had told me was 'very nice.' She'd also started taking adult education classes at Columbia, had traveled at least once to Europe, and, if the gossip mill was correct, was getting it on with an old lawyer friend of ours, Jay Sussman. His wife had died two years earlier, and since he'd always had the hots for Edith (husbands are good at detecting such things), it was only natural that he should make a move on her once I exited the scene. The merry widower and the gay divorcée. Well, good for both of them. Jay was pushing seventy, of course, but who was I to object to a tango dinner or two and some twilight nooky? To be perfectly frank, I wouldn't have minded a dose of that for myself.

'Hi there, Edith,' I said when she answered the phone. 'It's the ghost of Christmas past.'

'Nathan?' She sounded surprised to hear from me – and also a little disgusted.

'I'm sorry to bother you, but I need some information, and you're the only person who can give it to me.'

'This isn't one of your bad jokes, is it?'

'I wish.'

She sighed loudly into the receiver. 'I'm busy right now. Make it fast, okay?'

'Busy entertaining, I presume.'

'Presume whatever you like. I don't have to tell you a thing, do I?' She let out a strange, piercing laugh – a laugh that was so bitter, so triumphant, so full of smoldering, contradictory impulses, that I scarcely knew what to make of it. The laugh of a liberated ex-wife, perhaps. The last laugh.

'No, of course not. You're free to do what you want. All I'm asking for is some information.'

'About what?'

'Rachel. I've been trying to get in touch with her since Monday, but no one seems to be home. I just want to make sure that she and Terrence are all right.'

'You're such an idiot, Nathan. Don't you know anything?'

'Apparently not.'

'They went to England on May twentieth and won't be back until June fifteenth. The Rutgers semester ended. Rachel was invited to give a paper at a conference in London, and now they're spending some time with Terrence's parents in Cornwall.'

'She never told me.'

'Why should she tell you anything?'

'Because she's my daughter, that's why.'

'If you acted more like a father, maybe she would. That was a crummy thing you did to her, Nathan, blowing up at her like that. Who gives you the right? She was so hurt . . . so fucking hurt.'

'I called to apologize, but she hung up on me. Now I've written her a long letter. I'm trying to repair the damage, Edith. I really do love her, you know.'

'Then get down on your knees and beg for mercy. But don't expect any help from me. My days as a mediator are over.'

'I'm not asking for your help. But if she happens to call from England, you might want to mention that there's a letter waiting for her when she gets home. And a necklace, too.'

'Forget it, bub. I ain't saying a word. Not a single goddamn word. Got it?'

So much for the myth of tolerance and goodwill among divorced couples. By the time the conversation ended, I was half in the mood to hop on the next train to Bronxville and strangle Edith with my bare hands. The other half of me wanted to spit. But give the old girl her due. Her wrath had been so violent, so blistering in its denunciations and contempt, it actually helped me come to a decision. I would never call her again. Never again for the rest of my life. Under no circumstances, not ever again. The divorce had disentangled us in the eyes of the law, dissolving the marriage that had held us together for so many years, but even so, there was one thing we still had in common, and because we would go on being Rachel's parents for as long as we lived, I had assumed that connection would prevent us from sinking into a state of permanent animosity. But no longer. That telephone call was the end, and from now on Edith would be no more than a name to me – five tiny letters that signified a person who had ceased to exist.

The next day, Thursday, I ate lunch alone. Tom was in Manhattan with Harry that afternoon, negotiating with the widow of a recently dead novelist about the books in her husband's library. According to Tom, this novelist seemed to have known every important writer of the past fifty years, and his shelves were crammed with books that had been signed and dedicated to him by his illustrious friends. 'Association copies,' as these books were called in the business, and because they were much sought after by collectors, Tom said, they invariably fetched good prices. He also said that outings of this sort were the thing he liked best about working for Harry. Not only did they allow him to quit the confines of his second-floor office in Brooklyn, but they gave him a chance to watch his boss in action. 'He puts on quite a show,' he said. 'Never stops talking. Never stops bargaining. Flatter, denigrate, cajole – an endless feint and dodge. I don't believe in re-incarnation, but if I did, I'd swear he'd been a Moroccan rug merchant in another life.'

Wednesday was Marina's day off. Without Tom to keep me company, I was particularly looking forward to seeing her on Thursday, but when I walked into the Cosmic Diner at one o'clock, she wasn't there. I talked to Dimitrios, the owner of the restaurant, and he explained that she'd called in sick that morning and would probably be out for a few days. I felt deeply and absurdly dejected. After the tongue-lashing I'd been given by my ex-wife the night before, I wanted to reaffirm my faith in the female sex, and who better to help me than the gentle Marina Gonzalez? Before entering the restaurant, I had already imagined her wearing the necklace (which had been the case on Monday and Tuesday), and I knew that the mere sight of her would do me a world of good. With a heavy heart, therefore, I slid into an empty booth and placed my order with Dimitrios, who was filling in for my absent love. As usual, I was carrying a book in my jacket pocket (*Confessions of Zeno*, which I'd bought on Tom's recommendation), and given that I had no one to talk to that day, I opened Svevo's novel and began to read.

After two paragraphs, the man known as Mr Trouble came knocking at my door. This was the encounter I alluded to some fifteen or twenty pages ago, and now that the moment has arrived for me to talk about it, I cringe at the memory of what happened between us. This person, this thing I prefer to call Trouble, this nightmare being who emerged from the depths of nowhere, masqueraded himself as a thirty-year-old U.P.S. deliveryman with a muscular, well-toned body and an angry expression in his eyes. No, *anger* doesn't do justice to what I saw in that face. *Fury* would be closer to it, I think, or perhaps *rage*, or even *homicidal madness*. Whatever it was, when he stormed into the restaurant and asked Dimitrios in a loud, bellicose voice if Nathan was there, Nathan Glass, I knew Mr Trouble went by the code name of

Roberto Gonzalez. I also knew that the necklace was no longer in the cash register. Poor Marina had forgotten to take it off when she went home on Tuesday night. A small blunder, perhaps, but I couldn't help thinking of how she had employed the word *boom* when she tried to turn down my gift, and when I coupled that word with Dimitrios's announcement that she would be out 'for a few days,' I wondered how badly the son-of-a-bitch had beaten her.

Marina's husband parked himself on the bench directly opposite me and leaned across the table. 'Are you Nathan?' he asked. 'Nathan fucking Glass?'

'That's right,' I said. 'But my middle name isn't Fucking. It's Joseph.'

'Okay, smart-ass. Tell me why you did it.'

'Did what?'

He reached into his pocket and slammed the necklace down on the table. 'This.'

'It was a birthday present.'

'To my wife.'

'Yes. To your wife. What's wrong with that? Marina serves me lunch every day. She's a terrific girl, and I wanted to show my gratitude. I tip her when I pay my bill, don't I? Well, consider the necklace a big tip.'

'It ain't right, man. You don't fuck around with married women.'

'I'm not fucking around. I just gave her a present, that's all. I'm old enough to be her father.'

149

'You got a dick, don't you? You still got balls, don't you?'

'The last time I looked, they were still there.'

'I'm warning you, mister. You lay off Marina. She's my bitch, and I'll kill you if you ever come near her again.'

'Don't call her a bitch. She's a woman. And you're damn lucky to have her as a wife.'

'I'll call her whatever I want, asshole. And this,' he said, as he picked up the necklace and dangled it before my eyes, 'this piece of shit you can eat for breakfast tomorrow morning.' He grabbed hold of it with his two hands, and with one sharp jerk of the wrists snapped apart the gold chain. Some of the beads slid off and bounced on the Formica table; others landed in his palm, and as he stood up to take his leave, he threw them in my face. If not for my glasses, I might have caught one in the eye. 'Next time, I kill you!' he shouted, jabbing his finger at me like some deranged marionette. 'You lay off her, you bastard, or you're dead!'

By now, everyone in the restaurant was looking at us. It wasn't every day that you sat down to lunch and were treated to such an absorbing spectacle, but now that Mr Trouble had told me off, the action seemed to be coming to an end. Or so I thought. Gonzalez had already turned from me and was heading in the direction of the door, but the path between the booths and tables was narrow, and before he could make his exit, the towering, broad-bellied Dimitrios was standing in his way.

Thus began Act Two. Hemmed in, his brains still on fire, the overwrought Gonzalez started yelling at the top of his voice. 'You keep that scum-bag out of here!' he said (referring to me). 'You keep him out, or else Marina don't work for you no more! She quits!'

'Then she quits,' said the owner of the Cosmic Diner. 'This is my restaurant, and nobody tells me what to do in *my restaurant*. Without my customers, I don't have nothing. So get your ass out of here and tell Marina she's done. I don't want to see her no more. And you – you come in my place again, I call the cops.'

There was some pushing and shoving after that, but strong and muscular as Gonzalez was, Dimitrios was too big for him, and eventually, following another wave of threats and counter-threats, Marina's husband vanished from the premises. The fool had lost his wife her job. But worse than that – far worse than that – I realized I would probably never see her again.

Once calm had been restored to the diner, Dimitrios walked over to my table and sat down. He apologized for the disturbance and offered me lunch on the house, but when I tried to talk him out of firing Marina, he wouldn't budge. He had been a willing co-conspirator in our necklace-cash register ploy, but business was business, he said, and even though he liked Marina 'a hell of a lot,' he didn't want to take any chances with that crazy husband of hers. Then he said something that burned into me like the scald of a branding iron. 'Don't worry about it,' he said. 'It's not your fault.'

But it was my fault. I was to blame for the whole mess, and I despised myself for the wrong I'd done to the innocent Marina. Her first impulse had been to refuse the necklace. She understood what kind of man her husband was, but rather than listen to what she said to me, I had forced her to take it, and that stupid move, that stupid, stupid move, had led to nothing but trouble. God damn me, I said to myself. Cast my body into hell, and let me burn there for a thousand years.

That was the last time I had lunch at the Cosmic Diner. I continue to pass it every day on my walks down Seventh Avenue, but I still haven't found the courage to go back in.

MONKEY BUSINESS

That evening (Thursday) I met Harry for dinner at Mike & Tony's Steak House on the corner of Fifth Avenue and Carroll Street. This was the same restaurant where he had made his disturbing revelations to Tom a couple of months earlier, and I believe he chose it because he felt comfortable there. The front half of the establishment was a neighborhood bar where the smoking of cigarettes and cigars was actively encouraged, and sporting events could be watched on a large TV mounted on the wall near the entrance. Walk through that room, however, open the thickly paned double glass doors at the rear, and you found yourself in an altogether different environment. The restaurant at Mike & Tony's was a small, carpeted chamber with shelves of books lining one wall, a few black-and-white photographs hanging on another, and no more than eight or ten tables. In other words, a quiet, intimate beanery, blessed with the further advantage of tolerant acoustics that allowed one to be heard even while speaking in a hushed voice. To Harry's mind, the place must have felt as snug and private as a confessional box. At any rate, that's where he preferred to do his confessing – first to Tom, and now to me.

As far as Harry knew, my understanding of his pre-Brooklyn life was limited to just a few basic facts: born in Buffalo, ex-husband of Bette, father of Flora, time spent in prison. He wasn't aware that Tom had already supplied me with a host of particulars, but I wasn't about to let him know that. I therefore played dumb as Harry marched me through the familiar story of the Alec Smith bamboozle and his subsequent falling out with Gordon Dryer. At first I didn't understand why he was bothering to tell me these things. What connection did they have with his current business deal? I wondered, and then, ever more confused, I put the question directly to Harry. 'Just bear with me,' he said. 'In due time, all will come clear.'

I didn't say much through the early part of the meal. The uproar at the diner that afternoon had left me badly shaken, and as Harry rattled on with his story, my thoughts kept wandering off to Marina and her idiot husband and the whole chain of circumstances that had led me to buy that cursed bauble from the B.P.M. But Tom's boss was in good form that night, and with the aid of a predinner Scotch and the wine I drank to accompany my platter of Blue Point oysters, I gradually pulled out of my funk and started to focus on the business at hand. Harry's account of his Chicago crimes matched neatly with Tom's retelling of them, but with one notable and amusing difference. With

Tom, Harry had broken down and wept. He had been overcome by remorse, berating himself for having destroyed his marriage, his livelihood, his name. With me, on the other hand, he sounded thoroughly unrepentant, even boasting of the remarkable coup he'd managed to keep going for two solid years, and he looked back at his adventure in art forgery as one of the most glorious periods of his life. How to explain this radically altered tone? Had he been putting on an act for Tom to win his sympathy and understanding? Or, coming on the heels of Flora's disastrous visit to Brooklyn, had that first confession been a true cry from the heart? Perhaps. All men contain several men inside them, and most of us bounce from one self to another without ever knowing who we are. Up one day and down the next; morose and silent in the morning, laughing and cracking jokes at night. Harry had been low when he talked to Tom, but now that his business venture was in the works, he was flying high with me.

Our T-bones were brought to the table, we switched to a bottle of red, and then, at long last, the other shoe dropped. Harry had all but told me he was building up to a surprise, but even if he'd given me a hundred chances to guess what it was, I never would have predicted the startling piece of news that calmly fell from his lips.

'Gordon's back,' he said.

'Gordon,' I repeated, too stunned to say anything else. 'You mean Gordon Dryer?'

'Gordon Dryer. My old comrade in sin and frolic.'

'How in the world did he track you down?'

'You make it sound like a bad thing, Nathan. It's not. I'm very, very happy.'

'After what you did to him, I'd think he'd want to kill you.'

'That's what I thought at first, but it's all over now. The rancor, the bitterness. The poor fellow threw himself into my arms and asked me to forgive him. Can you imagine that? He wanted me to forgive *him*.'

'But you're the one who put him in jail.'

'Yes, but the scheme was Gordon's idea in the first place. Without him to get things rolling, neither one of us would have served any time. That's what he blames himself for. He's done a lot of soul-searching over the years, and he told me he'd gotten to the point where he couldn't live with himself if I thought he still bore me a grudge. Gordon's not a child anymore. He's forty-seven now, and he's grown up a lot since the old days in Chicago.'

'How many years did he spend in prison?'

'Three and a half. Then he moved to San Francisco and started painting again. Without much success, I'm sorry to report. He kept himself together by giving private drawing lessons, an odd temp job here and there, and then he fell for a man who lives in New York. That's why he's in the city now. He left San Francisco and moved in with him early last month.'

'Someone with money, I suppose.'

'I don't know all the details. But I think he earns enough to support them both.'

'Lucky Gordon.'

'Not so lucky. Not really, when you think of all he's been through. And besides, I'm the one he loves. He's very attached to his friend, but I'm the one he loves. And I love him back.'

'I don't mean to dig into your private life, but what about Rufus?'

'Rufus is my heart, but our relations are strictly platonic. In all the years I've known him, we haven't spent a single night together.'

'But Gordon is different.'

'Very different. He's not young anymore, but he's still a beautiful man. I can't tell you how kind he is to me. We don't get to see each other often, but you know what secret affairs are like. So many lies to be told, so many arrangements to be made. But whenever it happens, the old spark is still there. I'd thought I was finished with all that, over the hill, but Gordon's rejuvenated me. Bare skin, Nathan. It's the only thing worth living for.'

'One thing anyway, I'll grant you that.'

'If you can think of a better one, let me know.'

'I thought we came here to discuss business.'

'That's precisely what we're doing. Gordon's a part of it, you see. We're in it together.'

'Again?'

'It's a tremendous plan. So brilliant, I get goose bumps every time I think about it.'

'Why do I have this crazy feeling you're about to tell me you're involved in another fraud? Is the business legal or illegal?'

'Illegal, of course. Where's the fun if there's no risk?'

'You're incorrigible, Harry. After all that's happened to you, I'd think you'd want to toe the straight and narrow for the rest of your life.'

'I've tried. For nine long years I've tried, but it's no use. There's an imp inside me, and if I don't let him out to make some mischief now and then, the world just gets too damned dull. I hate feeling grumpy and bored. I'm an enthusiast, and the more dangerous my life becomes, the happier I am. Some people gamble at cards. Other people climb mountains or jump out of airplanes. I like tricking people. I like seeing how much I can get away with. Even as a kid, one of my dreams was to publish an encyclopedia in which all the information was false. Wrong dates for every historical event, wrong locations for every river, biographies of people who never existed. What kind of person imagines doing a thing like that? A crazy person, I suppose, but Christ, how that idea used to make me laugh. When I was in the navy, I was almost court-martialed for mislabeling a set of nautical maps. I did it on purpose. I don't know why, but the urge came over me, and I couldn't stop myself. I talked my commanding officer into believing it was an honest mistake, but it wasn't. That's who I am, Nathan. I'm generous,

I'm kind, I'm loyal, but I'm also a born prankster. A couple of months ago, Tom mentioned a theory someone had come up with about classical literature. It was all a hoax, he said. Aeschylus, Homer, Sophocles, Plato, the whole lot of them. Invented by some clever Italian poets during the Renaissance. Isn't that just the most wonderful thing you've ever heard? The great pillars of Western civilization, and every one of them a fake. Ha! How I would have loved to have taken part in that little gag.'

'So what is it this time? More forged paintings?'

'No, a forged manuscript. I'm in the book business now, remember?'

'Gordon's idea, no doubt.'

'Well, yes. He's extremely smart, you know, and he understands my weaknesses.'

'Are you sure you want to tell me about it? How do you know I can be trusted?'

'Because you're a man of honor and discretion.'

'How do you know that?'

'Because you're Tom's uncle. And he's a man of honor and discretion as well.'

'Then why not tell Tom?'

'Because Tom is too pure. He's too good, and he doesn't have a head for business. You've been around the block, Nathan, and I'm relying on your experience for some intelligent counsel.'

'My advice would be to drop the whole thing.'

'I can't do that. The venture is too far along for me to back out now. And besides, I don't want to.'

'All right. But when this thing blows up in your face, don't forget that I warned you.'

'*The Scarlet Letter.* You're familiar with the title, yes?'

'I read it in English class my junior year. Miss O'Flaherty, fourth period.'

'We all had to read it in high school, didn't we? An American classic. One of the most famous books ever written.'

'Are you telling me that you and Gordon are going to forge a manuscript of *The Scarlet Letter*? What about Hawthorne's original?'

'That's the beauty of it. Hawthorne's manuscript disappeared. Except for the title page – which is sitting in a vault at the Morgan Library as we speak. But no one knows what happened to the rest of the book. Some people think it was burned, either by Hawthorne himself or in a warehouse fire. Others say the printers simply threw the sheets in the garbage – or else used them to light their pipes. That's my favorite version. A ragtag crew of Boston print-shop workers lighting their corncobs with *The Scarlet Letter*. But whatever the real story is, there's enough uncertainty to the business to imagine that the manuscript was never lost. Just misplaced, so to speak. What if Hawthorne's publisher, James T. Fields, took it home with him and put it in a box somewhere with a pile of other papers? Eventually, the box is moved to the attic. Years later, the box is inherited by one of Fields's children, or else it's left in the house, and when the house is sold, the box becomes the property of the new owners. Do you see what I'm talking about? There are enough doubts and mysteries to lay the groundwork for a miraculous discovery. It happened with a stash of Melville letters and manuscripts just a few years ago in a house in upstate New York. If Melville papers can be found, why not Hawthorne?'

'Who's forging the manuscript? Gordon isn't qualified to do something like that, is he?'

'No. He's going to be the person who finds it, but the actual work is being done by a man named Ian Metropolis. Gordon heard about him from someone he met in prison, and apparently he's the best there is, an out-and-out genius. He's forged Lincoln, Poe, Washington Irving, Henry James, Gertrude Stein, and God knows who else, but in all the years he's been at it, he hasn't been caught once. No record, no suspicions hovering around him. A shadow-man lurking in the dark. It's a complex and demanding job, Nathan. First of all, there's the matter of finding the right paper – mid-nineteenth-century paper that will hold up to X-rays and ultraviolet exams. Then you have to study all of Hawthorne's extant manuscripts and learn how to imitate his handwriting – which was quite sloppy, by the way, almost illegible at times. But mastering the physical technique is only a small part of it. It's not as if you just sit down with a printed version of *The Scarlet Letter* and copy it out by hand. You have to know every one of

Hawthorne's private tics, the errors he made, his idiosyncratic use of hyphens, his inability to spell certain words correctly. *Ceiling* was always *cieling*; *steadfast* was always *stedfast*; *subtle* was always *subtile*. Whenever Hawthorne wrote *Oh*, the typesetters would change it to *O*. And so on and so on. It takes a lot of preparation and hard work. But well worth it, my friend. A complete manuscript will probably go for three to four million dollars. Gordon's offered me twenty-five percent for my services, which means that we're looking at something close to a million bucks. Not too shabby, is it?'

'And what are you supposed to do for your twenty-five percent?'

'Sell the manuscript. I'm the humble but respected purveyor of rare books, autographs, and literary curios. It lends legitimacy to the project.'

'Have you come up with a buyer yet?'

'That's the part that worries me. I suggested that we sell it directly to one of the libraries in town – the Berg Collection, the Morgan, Columbia University – or else put it up for auction at Sotheby's. But Gordon has his heart set on a private collector. He says it's safer to keep the business from going public, and I suppose I see his point. Still, it makes me wonder if he has real confidence in Metropolis's work.'

'What does Metropolis say?'

'I don't know. I've never met him.'

'You're involved in a four-million-dollar swindle with a man you've never met?'

'He doesn't allow anyone to see his face. Not even Gordon. All their contacts have been by phone.'

'I don't like the sound of this, Harry.'

'Yes, I know. A little too cloak-and-daggery for my taste as well. Nevertheless, things seem to be moving forward now. We've found our buyer, and two weeks ago we let him have a sample page. Believe it or not, he's taken it around to a number of experts, and they've all confirmed that it's genuine. I just got a check from him for ten thousand dollars. As a down payment, so we won't offer the manuscript to anyone else. We're supposed to conclude the sale after he comes back from Europe next Friday.'

'Who is he?'

'A stocks-and-bonds man named Myron Trumbell. I've looked him up. A Park Avenue blue-blood, positively rolling in money.'

'Where did Gordon find him?'

'He's a friend of his friend, the man he's living with now.'

'Whom you haven't met either.'

'No. Nor do I want to. Gordon and I are secret lovers. Why would I want to meet my rival?'

'I think you're walking into a trap, old man. They're setting you up.'

'Setting me up? What are you talking about?'

'How many pages of the manuscript have you seen?'

'Just the one. The page I handed over to Trumbell two weeks ago.'

'What if it's the only one, Harry? What if there is no Ian Metropolis? What if Gordon's new friend turns out to be none other than Myron Trumbell himself?'

'Impossible. Why would anyone go to such lengths . . .'

'Revenge. One bad turn deserves another. Tit for tat. All those wonderful qualities human beings are so renowned for. I'm afraid your Gordon isn't what you think he is.'

'That's too dark, Nathan. I refuse to believe it.'

'Have you deposited Trumbell's check?'

'I put it in the bank three days ago. As a matter of fact, I've already spent half of it on a pile of new clothes.'

'Send the money back.'

'I don't want to.'

'If you don't have enough in your account, you can borrow the rest from me to make up the difference.'

'Thank you, Nathan, but I don't need your charity.'

'They've got you by the balls, Harry, and you don't even know it.'

'Think what you like, but I'm not bowing out now. I'm marching ahead, come hail, sleet, or flood. If you're right about Gordon, then my life's finished anyway. So what difference does it make? And if you're wrong – which I know you are – then I'll invite you to another dinner and you can toast my success.'

A KNOCK ON THE DOOR

Saturdays and Sundays, Tom slept in. Harry's store was open on the weekends, but Tom didn't have to go to work, and since there was no school on those days, rising early would have been pointless. He wouldn't have found the B.P.M. on the front steps of her house waiting for the bus to pick up her children, and without that lure to pull him from the warm sheets of his bed, he didn't bother to set his alarm clock. Shades drawn, his body enveloped in the womblike dark of his tiny home, he would sleep until his eyes opened of their own accord – or, as often happened, a noise from somewhere in the building jolted him awake. On Sunday, June fourth (three days after my disastrous run-in with Roberto Gonzalez, which was also the day of my disconcerting talk with Harry Brightman), it was a noise that tore my nephew from the depths of slumber – in this case, the noise of a small hand knocking softly and tentatively on his door. It was a few minutes past nine, and once Tom managed to register the sound, once he roused himself from his bed and stumbled across the room to open the door, his life took a new and startling turn. To put it bluntly, everything changed for him, and it is only now, after much laborious preparation, after much raking and hoeing of the ground, that my chronicle of Tom's adventures begins to take flight.

It was Lucy. A silent, nine-and-a-half-year-old Lucy with short dark hair and her mother's round hazel eyes, a tall, preadolescent girl dressed in ragged red jeans, scuffed white Keds, and a Kansas City Royals T-shirt. No bag, no jacket or sweater slung over her arm, nothing but the clothes on her back. Tom hadn't seen her in six years, but he recognized her at once. Altogether different somehow, and yet exactly as she'd been – in spite of a full new set of adult teeth, in spite of the longer, thinner look to her face, in spite of the many inches she had grown. There she stood at the door, smiling up at her disheveled, sleep-worn uncle, studying him with the rapt, unblinking eyes he remembered so well from the old days in Michigan. Where was her mother? Where was her mother's husband? Why was she alone? How had she gotten there? Tom paused after each question, but not a single word came from Lucy's mouth. For a few moments, he wondered if she hadn't gone deaf, but then he asked her if she remembered who he was, and she nodded her head. Tom opened his arms, and she walked readily into his embrace, pressing her forehead against his chest and hugging him back as tightly as she could. 'You must be starving,' Tom said at last, and then he opened the door wide and let her into the dismal coffin he called his room.

He fixed her a bowl of Cheerios, poured her a glass of orange juice, and by the time he'd finished making a pot of coffee for himself, both the glass and the bowl were empty. He asked if she wanted something more, and when she nodded yes and smiled, he set about preparing a couple of pieces of French toast for her, which she doused in a puddle of maple syrup and scarfed down in a minute and a half. At first, Tom attributed her silence to exhaustion, to anxiety, to hunger, to any one of several possible causes, but the fact was that Lucy didn't look tired, appeared to be perfectly comfortable in her surroundings, and now that she had polished off the food, hunger had been scratched from the list as well. And yet she continued to say nothing in response to his questions. A few nods and shakes of the head, but no words, no sounds, no effort to use her tongue at all.

'Have you forgotten how to talk, Lucy?' Tom asked.

A shake of the head.

'What about the T-shirt. Does it mean you came here from Kansas City?'

No response.

'What do you want me to do with you? I can't send you back to your mother if you don't tell me where she lives.'

No response.

'Would you like me to give you a pencil and a pad of paper? If you don't want to talk, then maybe you could write down your answers for me.'

A shake of the head.

'Have you stopped talking forever?'

Another shake of the head.

'Good. I'm glad to hear it. And when are you allowed to start talking again?'

Lucy thought for a moment, then held two fingers up to Tom.

'Two. But two what? Two hours? Two days? Two months? Tell me, Lucy.'

No response.

'Is your mother all right?'

A nod.

'Is she still married to David Minor?'

Another nod.

'Why did you run away, then? Don't they treat you well?'

No response.

'How did you get to New York? By bus?'

A nod.

'Do you still have your ticket receipt?'

No response.

'Let's see what's in your pockets. Maybe we'll find some answers there.'

Lucy obliged by digging her hands into all four pockets of her jeans and yanking out the contents, but nothing of significance was found. A hundred and fifty-seven dollars in cash, three sticks of chewing gum, six quarters, two dimes, four pennies, and a piece of paper with Tom's name, address, and phone number written on it – but no bus ticket, no clue to tell him where her trip had begun.

'All right, Lucy,' Tom said. 'Now that you're here, what are you planning to do? Where are you going to live?'

Lucy pointed her finger at her uncle.

Tom let out a short, incredulous laugh. 'Take a good look at where you are,' he said. 'There's barely enough room for one person here. Where do you think you're going to sleep, little girl?'

A shrug, followed by a large, ever more beautiful smile – as if to say, *We'll figure it out*.

But there was no figuring it out, at least not in Tom's mind. He knew nothing about children, and even if he'd been living in a twelve-room mansion with a full staff of servants, he still wouldn't have had the faintest interest in becoming his niece's substitute parent. A normal child would have been challenging enough, but a child who refused to talk and stubbornly resisted giving out any information about herself was a simple impossibility. And yet what was he going to do? For the time being he was stuck with her, and unless he could force her to tell him where her mother was, there would be no getting rid of her. That didn't mean he wasn't fond of Lucy or felt indifferent to her welfare, but he knew she had come to the wrong person. Of all the people even remotely connected to her, he was the worst man for the job.

I had no interest in taking care of her either, but at least there was an extra room in my apartment, and when Tom called later that morning and told me about his predicament (panic in his voice, almost screeching into the phone), I said I would be willing to put her up until we found a solution to the problem. They arrived at my place on First Street just after eleven. Lucy smiled when Tom introduced her to her great-uncle Nat, and she seemed happy to receive the welcoming kiss I planted on the crown of her head, but I soon discovered that she was no more willing to talk to me than she was to him. I had been hoping to trick a few words out of her, but all I got were the same nods and shakes of the head that Tom had been subjected to earlier. Strange, unsettling little person. I was no expert in child psychology, but it seemed clear to me that there was nothing physically or mentally wrong with her. No retardation, no signs of autism, nothing organic to impede her interaction with others. She looked you straight in the eye, understood everything you said, and smiled as often and affectionately as any two children put together. What was it, then? Had she suffered some terrible trauma that had shut down her ability to talk? Or, for reasons that were still impenetrable, had she decided to take a vow of silence, pushing herself into voluntary mutism in order to test her will and courage – a kid's game that she would eventually grow tired of? Her face and arms were free of bruises, but at some point during the day I was determined to coax her into the bath to get a look at the rest of her body. Just to satisfy myself that no one had beaten or abused her.

I put her in front of the TV in the living room and switched on the set to a twenty-four-hour cartoon channel. Her eyes lit up with pleasure when she saw the animated figures prance across the screen – so much so that it occurred to me that she wasn't in the habit of watching television, which in turn led me to start thinking about David Minor and the harshness of his religious beliefs. Had Aurora's husband banned TV from the house? Were his convictions so strong that he wanted to shield his adopted daughter from the frenzied carnival of American pop culture – that godless free-for-all of glitz and garbage that poured out endlessly from every cathode tube in the land? Perhaps. We wouldn't know anything about Minor until Lucy told us where she lived, and for now she wasn't saying a word. Tom had guessed Kansas City because of the T-shirt, but she had refused to confirm or deny it, which meant that she didn't want us to know – for the simple reason that she was afraid we would send her back. She had run away from home, after all, and happy children did not run away from home. That much was certain, whether the home had a TV in it or not.

With Lucy parked on the floor of the living room, eating pistachio nuts and watching an episode of *Inspector Gadget*, Tom and I withdrew to the kitchen, where she wouldn't be able to overhear our conversation. We talked for a good thirty or forty minutes, but nothing came of it except ever-mounting confusion and worry. So many mysteries and imponderables to be dealt with, so little evidence on which to build a plausible case. Where had Lucy found the money for the trip? How had she known Tom's address? Had her mother helped her get away, or had she absconded on her own? And if Aurora had been involved, why hadn't she contacted Tom in advance or at least sent a note with Lucy? Perhaps there had been a note, we said, and Lucy had lost it. One way or another, what did the girl's departure tell us about Aurora's marriage? Was it the disaster we both feared, or had Tom's sister finally seen the light and embraced her husband's vision of the world? And yet, if harmony reigned in the household, what was their daughter doing in Brooklyn? Round and round it went, the two of us traveling in circles, talking, talking, talking, but unable to answer a single question.

'Time will tell,' I said at last, not wanting to prolong the agony. 'But first things first. We have to find a place for her to live. You can't keep her, and neither can I. So what do we do?'

'I'm not putting her in foster care, if that's what you mean,' Tom said.

'No, of course not. But there must be someone we know who'd be willing to take her in.

Temporarily, I mean. Until we manage to track down Aurora.'

'That's asking a lot, Nathan. It could go on for months. Maybe forever.'

'What about your stepsister?'

'You mean Pamela?'

'You said she's pretty well off. Big house in Vermont, two kids, lawyer husband. If you told her it's just for the summer, maybe she'd go along with it.'

'She detests Rory. All the Zorns do. Why would she want to put herself out for Rory's kid?'

'Compassion. Generosity. You said she's improved over the years, didn't you? Well, if I promise to cover Lucy's expenses, maybe she'd see it as a joint family venture. All of us pulling together for the common good.'

'You're a persuasive old coot, aren't you?'

'Just trying to get us out of a tight squeeze, Tom. Nothing more than that.'

'All right, I'll get in touch with Pamela. She'll turn me down, but I might as well give it a shot.'

'That's the spirit, son. Lay it on good and thick. A double grease job with syrup and molasses.'

He didn't want to make the call from my apartment, however. Not only because Lucy was there, he said, but because he would feel too self-conscious knowing I was around. Delicate, finicky Tom, the most sensitive soul in the world. No problem, I replied, but there wasn't any need for him to walk back to his place. Lucy and I would go out, and he could be alone when he talked to Pamela, with the added bonus of being able to charge the long-distance call to my bill. 'You saw what the kid is wearing,' I said. 'Those ratty jeans and worn-out sneakers. It just won't do, will it? You call Vermont, and I'll take her out to buy some new clothes.'

That settled the matter. After a hastily prepared lunch of tomato soup, scrambled eggs, and salami sandwiches, Lucy and I went on a shopping binge. Silent or not, she seemed to enjoy the expedition as much as any other young girl would have under similar circumstances: total freedom to choose whatever she wanted. At first we stuck mostly to the basics (socks, underwear, long pants, short pants, pajamas, a hooded sweatshirt, a nylon wind-breaker, nailclippers, toothbrush, hairbrush, and so on), but then followed the hundred-and-fifty-dollar pair of neon-blue sneakers, the all-wool Brooklyn Dodgers replica baseball cap, and, some-what to my surprise, a glistening duo of authentic, patent-leather Mary Janes, along with the red-and-white cotton dress we bought at the end – the old classic, with the round collar and the sash that tied in back. By the time we carried our haul to my apartment, it was well past three o'clock, and Tom was no longer there. A note was sitting on the kitchen table.

Dear Nathan
Pamela said yes. Don't ask me how I did it, but I had to work on her for over an

hour before she finally gave in. One of the most grueling, punishing conversations I've ever had. For now, it's only on a 'trial basis,' but the good news is that she wants us to get Lucy up there *tomorrow*. Something to do with Ted's schedule and some shindig at the local country club. I assume we can use your car, yes? I'll drive if you don't feel up to it. I'm off to the bookstore now to talk to Harry about taking some time off. I'll wait for you there. A presto.

Tom

It hadn't occurred to me that things would happen so fast. I felt relieved, of course, glad that our problem had been solved in such a quick and efficient way, but a part of me also felt disappointed, perhaps even a little bereft. I was beginning to like Lucy, and all during our shopping trip through the neighborhood, I had gradually warmed to the prospect of having her around for a while – days, I imagined, perhaps even weeks. It wasn't that I had changed my mind about the situation (she couldn't live in my apartment forever), but a short period would have been more than bearable for me. I had missed so many opportunities with Rachel when she was young, and now, suddenly, here was a little girl who needed looking after, who needed someone to buy clothes for her and put food in her stomach, who needed an adult with enough time on his hands to pay attention to her and try to draw her out of her baffling silence. I had no objections to assuming that role, but the show was apparently traveling from Brooklyn to New England, and I had been replaced by another actor. I tried to comfort myself with the thought that Lucy would be better off in the country with Pamela and her kids, but what did I know about Pamela? I hadn't seen her in years, and our few encounters in the past had left me cold.

Lucy wanted to wear her new dress and the Mary Janes to the bookstore, and I agreed on the condition that she take a bath first. I was an old hand at giving baths to children, I said, and to prove my point I pulled a photo album from the bookcase and showed her some pictures of Rachel – one of which, miraculously, showed my daughter sitting in a bubble bath at age six or seven. 'That's your cousin,' I said. 'Did you know that she and your mother were born just three months apart? They used to be great friends.' Lucy shook her head and flashed one of her biggest smiles of the day. She was beginning to trust her Uncle Nat, I felt, and a moment later we marched down the hall to the bathroom. As I filled the tub with water, Lucy compliantly stripped off her clothes and waded in. Except for a small, mostly hardened scab on her left knee, there wasn't a scratch on her. Clean, smooth back; clean, smooth legs; and no swelling or abrasions around her genitals. It was only a quick eyeball exam, but whatever the cause of her silence, I saw nothing to suggest that she had been roughed up or molested. To celebrate my discovery, I sang her the full version of 'Polly Wolly Doodle' as I washed and rinsed her hair.

Fifteen minutes after I pulled her out of the tub, the telephone rang. It was Tom, calling from the bookstore, wondering what had happened to us. He had finished talking to Harry (who had granted his request for a few days off) and was eager to get out of there.

'I'm sorry,' I said. 'Shopping took longer than expected, and then I decided Lucy could use a bath. Say good-bye to the little ragamuffin, Tom. Our girl looks like she's about to go to a birthday party at Windsor Castle.'

A short discussion followed about what to do for dinner. Since Tom wanted to get an early start in the morning, he thought it would be best if we planned something for around six o'clock. Besides, he added, Lucy's appetite was so big, she'd probably be ravenous by then anyway.

I turned to Lucy and asked her what she thought of pizza. When she replied by licking her lips and patting her stomach, I told Tom to meet us at Rocco's Trattoria – which served the best pizza in the neighborhood. 'Six o'clock,' I said. 'Meanwhile, Lucy and I will go to the video store and look for a movie we can all watch after dinner.'

The movie turned out to be *Modern Times*, which struck me as a weirdly inspired choice. Not only had Lucy never seen or heard of Chaplin (further evidence of the collapse of American education), but this was the film in which the tramp talks for the first time. The words might be gibberish, but sounds nevertheless came flying from his mouth, and I wondered if that moment wouldn't stir up something in Lucy, perhaps give her pause to reflect on the meaning of her intractable silence. In the best of all possible worlds, I thought maybe it would even snap her out of it for good.

Until the dinner at Rocco's, she had been on her best behavior. Everything I had asked of her she had done willingly and obediently, and not once had a frown creased her forehead. But Tom, in a rare burst of thoughtlessness, abruptly dropped the news of our impending trip to Vermont just minutes after we sat down at the table. There was no buildup, no propaganda extolling the wonders of Burlington, no argument about why she would be better off with Pamela than with her two uncles in Brooklyn. That was when I saw her frown for the first time, then cry for the first time, then sulk through the better part of the meal. Hungry as she must have been, she didn't touch her pizza when it was set down before her, and it was only my nonstop talking that delivered us from what might have escalated into a full-blown war of nerves. I began by doing the groundwork Tom had neglected to take care of: the hymns and panegyrics, the Chamber of Commerce tap dance, the lengthy encomium on Pamela's legendary kindness. When those speeches failed to produce the desired result, I switched tactics and promised her that Tom and I would stay around until she was comfortably settled in, and then, going even further, took the supreme risk of assuring her that the decision was entirely in her hands. If she didn't like it there, we would gather up her things and drive back to New York. But she had to give it a real chance, I said, no less than three or four days. Agreed? She nodded her head. And then, for the first time in half an hour, she smiled. I called for the waiter and asked him if it wouldn't be too much trouble to reheat her pizza in the kitchen. Ten minutes later, he carried it back to the table, and Lucy dug in.

The Chaplin experiment yielded only mixed results. Lucy laughed, emitting the first sounds we had heard from her all day (even her tears at dinner had rolled down her cheeks in silence), but several minutes before we came to the restaurant scene, the spot in the film where Charlie breaks into his memorable nonsense song, her eyes had already closed and she had drifted off to sleep. Who could blame her? She had arrived in New York only that morning, having traveled God knows how many hundreds of miles, which meant that for much if not all of the previous night she had been sitting on the bus. I carried her into the spare bedroom as Tom opened the already made-up sofa bed and pulled down the top sheet and blanket. No one sleeps more soundly than the young, especially the exhausted young. Even as I lowered her body onto the mattress and tucked her in, she didn't open her eyes once.

The next day began with a curious and troubling event. At seven o'clock, I walked in on the sleeping Lucy with a glass of orange juice, a plate of scrambled eggs, and two pieces of buttered toast. I put the food down on the floor and then reached out and gently shook her arm. 'Wake up, Lucy,' I said. 'It's time for breakfast.' After three or four seconds, she opened her eyes, and then, following a short spell of absolute bewilderment (*Where am I? Who is this strange man looking down at me?*), she remembered who I was and smiled. 'How did you sleep?' I asked.

'Real good, Uncle Nat,' she answered, pronouncing the words with what sounded like a southern accent. 'Like a big old stone at the bottom of a well.'

Bang. There it was. Lucy had talked. Without prompting or encouragement, without pausing to consider what she was about to do, she had calmly opened her mouth and talked. Was the reign of silence officially over, I wondered, or had she simply forgotten about it in the stupor of emerging wakefulness?

'I'm glad,' I said, not wanting to jinx things by mentioning what had just happened.

'Are we still going to stinky Vermont today?' she asked.

Each new word, each new sentence added to my cautious feeling of hope.

'In about an hour,' I said. 'Look, Lucy, juice and toast and eggs.'

As I bent down and lifted the food off the floor, she broke into another one of her big smiles. 'Breakfast in bed,' she announced. 'Just like Queen Nefertiti.'

I thought we were out of the woods by then, but what did I know – what did I know about anything? I had the glass of juice in my right hand, and just as she was reaching out to take it from me, the sky fell on top of her. I have rarely witnessed a face change expression more rapidly than hers did at that moment. In a single flash, the bright smile turned into a look of piercing, devastating horror. She clamped her hand over her mouth, and within seconds her eyes were brimming with tears.

'Don't worry, sweetheart,' I said. 'You haven't done anything wrong.'

But she had. According to her lights she had, and from the look on that tormented little face of hers, it was as if she had committed an unpardonable sin. In a sudden blast of anger at herself, she started banging the side of her head with the heel of her left hand, a wild pantomime display that seemed to express how stupid she thought she was. She did it three times, four times, five times, but just as I was about to grab her arm and make her stop, she thrust out her left hand and held up one finger, emphatically jabbing it toward my face. She was in a fury. Eyes burning with disgust and self-loathing, she began slapping her left hand with her right, as if rebuking the hand for having had the gall to hold up that one finger. Then the slapping stopped, and she thrust out her left hand again. This time she was holding up two fingers. As before, she jabbed the air with bitter emphasis. First one finger, then two fingers. What was she trying to tell me? I couldn't be sure, but I suspected it had something to do with time, with the number of days that were left before she would allow herself to speak again. She had been down to one day when she woke up that morning, but now that some words had accidentally slipped out of her, she had to punish herself by adding another day to her silence. One, therefore, had become two.

'Is that it?' I asked. 'Are you telling me you'll start talking again in two days?'

No response. I asked again, but Lucy wasn't about to divulge her secret. No nod of the head, no shake of the head, no nothing. I sat down beside her and started stroking her hair.

'Here, Lucy,' I said, handing her the glass of orange juice. 'Time to eat your breakfast.'

RIDING NORTH

The car was a relic from my old life. I had no use for the thing in New York, but I had been too lazy to bother selling it, and so it sat in a parking garage on Union Street between Sixth and Seventh Avenues, never once driven or looked at since my move to Brooklyn. A 1994 lime-green Oldsmobile Cutlass, a shockingly ugly piece of hardware. But the car did what it was supposed to do, and after two long months of idleness, the engine kicked over with the first turn of the key.

Tom was the pilot; I rode shotgun; Lucy sat in back. In spite of the promises I'd made to her the night before, she still wanted nothing to do with Pamela and Vermont, and she resented the fact that we were taking her there against her will. Logically speaking, she had a point. If the ultimate decision was in her hands, what was the purpose of driving over three hundred miles to get her there when the only result would be to drive another three hundred miles to bring her back? I had told her she had to give the Pamela experiment a legitimate chance. She had pretended to agree, but I knew her mind was already made up and nothing was going to change it. So she sat in the backseat of the car, looking sullen and withdrawn, a pouting, innocent victim of our cruel machinations. She fell asleep as we were passing the outskirts of Bridgeport on 1-95, but until then she did little else but stare out the window, no doubt thinking evil thoughts about her two wicked uncles. As later events would prove, I was wrong about that. Lucy was far more resourceful than I had imagined, and rather than sit there fuming with anger, she was planning and thinking, using her considerable intelligence to hatch a plot that would turn the tables on us and put her in control of her own destiny. It was a brilliant scheme, if I do say so myself, a true rascal's scheme, and one can only tip one's hat to ingenuity taken to such an exalted level. But more about that anon.

While Lucy cogitated and napped in the rear, Tom and I talked in the front. He hadn't been behind the wheel of a car since quitting his taxi job in January, and the mere fact that he was driving again seemed to work like a tonic on his system. I had been with him nearly every day for the past two weeks, and not once had I seen him lighter or happier than he was that morning in early June. After he'd negotiated us through the city traffic, we hit the first of several highways that would take us north, and it was out there on those open roads that he began to relax, to slough off the burden of his miseries and temporarily stop hating the world. A relaxed Tom was a talkative Tom. That was rule of thumb for the ex-Dr Thumb, and from approximately eight-thirty in the morning until well past noon, he showered me with a torrent of words – a veritable flood of stories, jokes, and lectures on matters both pertinent and arcane.

It started with a comment about *The Book of Human Folly*, my diminutive, half-assed work in progress. He wanted to know how it was coming along, and when I told him I was charging ahead with no end in sight, that each story I wrote seemed to give birth to another story and then another story and then another story, he clapped me on the shoulder with his right hand and pronounced this astonishing verdict: 'You're a writer, Nathan. You're becoming a real writer.'

'No, I'm not,' I said. 'I'm just a retired life insurance salesman who has nothing better to do with himself. It helps pass the time, that's all.'

'You're wrong, Nathan. After years of wandering in the desert, you've finally found your true calling. Now that you don't have to work for money anymore, you're doing the work you were meant to do all along.'

'Ridiculous. No one becomes a writer at sixty.'

The former graduate student and literary scholar cleared his throat and begged to differ with me. There were no rules when it came to writing, he said. Take a close look at the lives of poets and novelists, and what you wound up with was unalloyed chaos, an infinite jumble of exceptions. That was because writing was a disease, Tom continued, what you might call an infection or influenza of the spirit, and therefore it could strike anyone at any time. The young and the old, the strong and the weak, the drunk and the sober, the sane and the insane. Scan the roster of the giants and semi-giants, and you would discover writers who embraced every sexual proclivity, every political bent, and every human attribute – from the loftiest idealism to the most insidious corruption. They were criminals and lawyers, spies and doctors, soldiers and spinsters, travelers and shut-ins. If no one could be excluded, what prevented an almost sixty-year-old ex-life insurance agent from joining their ranks? What law declared that Nathan Glass had not been infected by the disease?

I shrugged.

'Joyce wrote three novels,' Tom said. 'Balzac wrote ninety. Does it make a difference to us now?'

'Not to me,' I said.

'Kafka wrote his first story in one night. Stendhal wrote *The Charterhouse of Parma* in forty-nine days. Melville wrote *Moby-Dick* in sixteen months. Flaubert spent five years on *Madame Bovary*. Musil worked for eighteen years on *The Man Without Qualities* and died before he could finish. Do we care about any of that now?'

The question didn't seem to call for a response.

'Milton was blind. Cervantes had one arm. Christopher Marlowe was stabbed to death in a bar-room brawl before he was thirty. Apparently, the knife went straight through his eye. What are we supposed to think of that?'

'I don't know, Tom. You tell me.'

'Nothing. A big fat nothing.'

'I tend to agree with you.'

'Thomas Wentworth Higginson 'corrected' Emily Dickinson's poems. A puffed-up ignoramus who called *Leaves of Grass* an immoral book dared to touch the work of the divine Emily. And poor Poe, who died crazy and drunk in a Baltimore gutter, had the misfortune to select Rufus Griswold as his literary executor. Little knowing that Griswold despised him, that this so-called friend and supporter would spend years trying to destroy his reputation.'

'Poor Poe.'

'Eddie had no luck. Not while he lived, and not even after he died. They buried him in a Baltimore cemetery in 1849, but it took twenty-six years before a stone was erected over his grave. A relative commissioned one immediately after his death, but the job ended in one of those black-humor fuck-ups that leave you wondering who's in charge of the world. Talk about human folly, Nathan. The marble yard happened to be situated directly below a section of elevated railroad tracks. Just as the carving of the stone was about to be finished, there was a derailment. The train toppled into the yard and crushed the stone, and because the relative didn't have enough money to order another one, Poe spent the next quarter century lying in an unmarked grave.'

'How do you know all this stuff, Tom?'

'Common knowledge.'

'Not to me it isn't.'

'You never went to graduate school. While you were out there making the world safe for democracy, I was sitting in a library carrel, cramming my head full of useless information.'

'Who finally paid for the stone?'

'A bunch of local teachers formed a committee to raise the funds. It took them ten years, if you can believe it. When the monument was finished, Poe's remains were exhumed, carted across town, and reburied in a Baltimore churchyard. On the morning of the unveiling, there was a special ceremony held at something called the Western Female High School. A terrific name, don't you think? *The Western Female High School*. Every important American poet was invited, but Whittier, Longfellow, and Oliver Wendell Holmes all found excuses not to come. Only Walt Whitman bothered to make the trip. Since his work is worth more than all the others' put together, I look at it as an act of sublime poetic justice. Interestingly enough, Stéphane Mallarmé was also there that morning. Not in the flesh – but his famous sonnet, 'Le Tombeau d'Edgar Poe,' was written for the occasion, and even if he didn't manage to finish it in time for the ceremony, he was nevertheless there in spirit. I love that, Nathan. Whitman and Mallarmé, the twin fathers of modern poetry, standing together in the Western Female High School to honor their mutual forebear, the disgraced and disreputable Edgar Allan Poe, the first true writer America gave to the world.'

Yes, Tom was in excellent form that day. Somewhat manic, I suppose, but there was no question that his rambling, erudite chatter helped cut the tedium of the drive. He would jog along in one direction for a while, come to a fork in the road, and then veer off sharply in another direction, never pausing to decide if left was better than right or vice versa. All roads led to Rome, so to speak, and since Rome was nothing less than all of literature (about which he seemed to know everything), it didn't matter which decision he made. From Poe, he suddenly bounced forward to Kafka. The link was the age of the two men at the time of their deaths: Poe at forty years and nine months, Kafka forty years and eleven months. It was the kind of obscure fact that only Tom would have remembered or cared about, but having spent half my life studying actuarial tables and thinking about the death rates of men in various professions, I found it rather interesting myself.

'Too young,' I said. 'If they'd been around today, there's a good chance that drugs and antibiotics would have saved them. Look at me. If I'd had my cancer thirty or forty years ago, I probably wouldn't be sitting in this car now.'

'Yes,' Tom said. 'Forty is too young. But think of how many writers didn't even make it that far.'

'Christopher Marlowe.'

'Dead at twenty-nine. Keats at twenty-five. Georg Büchner at twenty-three. Imagine. The greatest German playwright of the nineteenth century, dead at twenty-three. Lord Byron at thirty-six. Emily Brontë at thirty. Charlotte Brontë at thirty-nine. Shelley, just one month before he would have turned thirty. Sir Philip Sidney at thirty-one. Nathanael West at thirty-seven. Wilfred Owen at twenty-five. Georg Trakl at twenty-seven. Leopardi, Garcia Lorca, and Apollinaire all at thirty-eight. Pascal at thirty-nine. Flannery O'Connor at thirty-nine. Rimbaud at thirty-seven. The two Cranes, Stephen and Hart, at twenty-eight and thirty-two. And Heinrich von Kleist – Kafka's favorite writer – dead at thirty-four in a double suicide with his lover.'

'And Kafka is your favorite writer.'

'I think so. From the twentieth century, anyway.'

'Why didn't you do your dissertation on him?'

'Because I was stupid. And because I was supposed to be an Americanist.'

'He wrote *Amerika*, didn't he?'

'Ha ha. Good point. Why didn't I think of that?'

'I remember his description of the Statue of Liberty. Instead of a torch, the old girl is holding an upraised sword in her hand. An incredible image. It makes you laugh, but at the same time it scares the shit out of you. Like something from a bad dream.'

'So you've read Kafka.'

'Some. The novels and maybe a dozen stories. A long time ago now, back when I was your age.

But the thing about Kafka is that he stays with you. Once you've dipped into his work, you don't forget it.'

'Have you looked at the diaries and letters? Have you read any biographies?'

'You know me, Tom. I'm not a very serious person.'

'A pity. The more you learn about his life, the more interesting his work becomes. Kafka wasn't just a great writer, you see, he was a remarkable man as well. Did you ever hear the story about the doll?'

'Not that I can remember.'

'Ah. Then listen carefully. I offer it to you as the first piece of evidence in support of my case.'

'I'm not sure I follow.'

'It's very simple. The object is to prove that Kafka was indeed an extraordinary person. Why begin with this particular story? I don't know. But ever since Lucy turned up yesterday morning, I haven't been able to get it out of my head. There must be a connection somewhere. I still haven't figured out exactly how, but I think there's a message in it for us, some kind of warning about how we're supposed to act.'

'Too much preamble, Tom. Just get down to it and tell the story.'

'I'm blathering again, aren't I? All this sunshine, all these cars, all this rushing along at sixty and seventy miles an hour. My brain's exploding, Nathan. I feel pumped up, ready for anything.'

191

'Good. Now tell me the story.'

'All right. The story. The story of the doll . . . It's the last year of Kafka's life, and he's fallen in love with Dora Diamant, a young girl of nineteen or twenty who ran away from her Hasidic family in Poland and now lives in Berlin. She's half his age, but she's the one who gives him the courage to leave Prague – something he's been wanting to do for years – and she becomes the first and only woman he lives with. He gets to Berlin in the fall of 1923 and dies the following spring, but those last months are probably the happiest months of his life. In spite of his deteriorating health. In spite of the social conditions in Berlin: food shortages, political riots, the worst inflation in German history. In spite of the certain knowledge that he is not long for this world.

'Every afternoon, Kafka goes out for a walk in the park. More often than not, Dora goes with him. One day, they run into a little girl in tears, sobbing her heart out. Kafka asks her what's wrong, and she tells him that she's lost her doll. He immediately starts inventing a story to explain what happened. "Your doll has gone off on a trip," he says. "How do you know that?" the girl asks. "Because she's written me a letter," Kafka says. The girl seems suspicious. 'Do you have it on you?' she asks. 'No, I'm sorry,' he says, 'I left it at home by mistake, but I'll bring it with me tomorrow.' He's so convincing, the girl doesn't know what to think anymore. Can it be

192

possible that this mysterious man is telling the truth?

'Kafka goes straight home to write the letter. He sits down at his desk, and as Dora watches him write, she notices the same seriousness and tension he displays when composing his own work. He isn't about to cheat the little girl. This is a real literary labor, and he's determined to get it right. If he can come up with a beautiful and persuasive lie, it will supplant the girl's loss with a different reality – a false one, maybe, but something true and believable according to the laws of fiction.

'The next day, Kafka rushes back to the park with the letter. The little girl is waiting for him, and since she hasn't learned how to read yet, he reads the letter out loud to her. The doll is very sorry, but she's grown tired of living with the same people all the time. She needs to get out and see the world, to make new friends. It's not that she doesn't love the little girl, but she longs for a change of scenery, and therefore they must separate for a while. The doll then promises to write the girl every day and keep her abreast of her activities.

'That's where the story begins to break my heart. It's astonishing enough that Kafka took the trouble to write that first letter, but now he commits himself to the project of writing a new letter every day – for no other reason than to console the little girl, who happens to be a complete stranger to him, a child he ran into by accident one afternoon in a park. What kind of man does a thing like that? He kept it up for three weeks, Nathan. *Three weeks*. One of the most brilliant writers who ever lived sacrificing his time – his ever more precious and dwindling time – to composing imaginary letters from a lost doll. Dora says that he wrote every sentence with excruciating attention to detail, that the prose was precise, funny, and absorbing. In other words, it was Kafka's prose, and every day for three weeks he went to the park and read another letter to the girl. The doll grows up, goes to school, gets to know other people. She continues to assure the girl of her love, but she hints at certain complications in her life that make it impossible for her to return home. Little by little, Kafka is preparing the girl for the moment when the doll will vanish from her life forever. He struggles to come up with a satisfactory ending, worried that if he doesn't succeed, the magic spell will be broken. After testing out several possibilities, he finally decides to marry off the doll. He describes the young man she falls in love with, the engagement party, the wedding in the country, even the house where the doll and her husband now live. And then, in the last line, the doll bids farewell to her old and beloved friend.

'By that point, of course, the girl no longer misses the doll. Kafka has given her something else instead, and by the time those three weeks are up, the letters

194

have cured her of her unhappiness. She has the story, and when a person is lucky enough to live inside a story, to live inside an imaginary world, the pains of this world disappear. For as long as the story goes on, reality no longer exists.'

OUR GIRL, OR *COKE IS IT*

There are two ways to travel from New York City to Burlington, Vermont: the fast way and the slow way. For the first two-thirds of the trip, we chose the fast way, a trajectory that included such urban roads as Flatbush Avenue, the BQE, Grand Central Parkway, and Route 678. After we crossed the Whitestone Bridge into the Bronx, we continued north for several miles until we came to 1-95, which led us out of the city, through the eastern part of Westchester County, and on through lower Connecticut. At New Haven, we turned off onto 1-91. That was where we spent the bulk of the journey, traversing what remained of Connecticut and all of Massachusetts until we reached the southern border of Vermont. The quickest route to Burlington would have been to stay on 1-91 until White River Junction and then turn west onto 1-89, but once we found ourselves on the outskirts of Brattleboro, Tom declared that he was sick of superhighways and preferred switching over to smaller, emptier back-country roads. And so it was that we abandoned the fast way for the slow way. It would add another hour or two to the trip, he said, but at least we would have a chance to see something other than a procession of fast-moving, lifeless cars. Woods, for example, and wildflowers along the edge of the road, not to mention cows and horses, farms and meadows, village greens and an occasional human face. I had no objection to this change of plans. What did I care whether we made it to Pamela's house at three o'clock or five o'clock? Now that Lucy had opened her eyes again and was staring out the side window in back, I felt so guilty about what we were doing to her that I wanted to put off getting there as long as we could. I opened our Rand McNally road atlas and studied the map of Vermont. 'Get off at Exit Three,' I said to Tom. 'We're looking for Route Thirty, which squiggles up diagonally to the northwest. After about forty miles, we'll start bobbing and weaving until we get to Rutland, find Route Seven, and take that straight to Burlington.'

Why do I linger over these trivial details? Because the truth of the story lies in the details, and I have no choice but to tell the story exactly as it happened. If we hadn't made that decision to get off the highway at Brattleboro and follow our noses to Route 30, many of the events in this book never would have taken place. I am thinking especially of Tom when I say that. Both Lucy and I profited from the decision as well, but for Tom, the long-suffering hero of these Brooklyn Follies, it was probably the most important decision of his life.

At the time, he had no inkling of the consequences, no knowledge of the whirlwind he had set in motion. Like Kafka's doll, he thought he was simply looking for a change of scenery, but because he left one road and took another, Fortune unexpectedly reached out her arms to him and carried our boy into a different world.

The gas tank was nearly empty; our stomachs were nearly empty; our bladders were full. About fifteen or twenty miles northwest of Brattleboro, we stopped for lunch at a crummy roadside restaurant called Dot's. FOOD AND GAS, as the highway signs aptly put it, and that was the order in which we chose to fulfill our needs. Food and gas at Dot's, and then more gas at the Chevron station across the road. Here, too, our casual decision to do things one way and not another turned out to have a significant effect on the story. If we had filled up the gas tank first, Lucy never would have been able to pull off her electrifying stunt, and no doubt we would have continued all the way to Burlington as planned. But because the tank was still empty when we sat down to eat, the opportunity was suddenly there, and the little one didn't hesitate. It felt like a catastrophe at the time, but if our girl hadn't done what she did, our boy never would have fallen into the nurturing arms of Dame Fortune, and leaving or not leaving the highway would have been a moot point.

Even now, I can't quite comprehend how she did it. Certain contingencies worked in her favor, but even taking into account those stray bits of luck, there was something almost demonic about the daring and efficiency of her sabotage. Yes, the restaurant was set back from the road by about a hundred feet, which protected her from the eyes of passing motorists. Yes, all the parking places directly in front of the restaurant were full, which meant that we left our car off to the side, out of range of the two picture windows built into the façade of the sagging one-story building. And yes, there was the double bonus that Tom and I happened to sit down with our backs to those windows. But how in the world could she have thought quickly enough to translate the presence of an outdoor Coke machine (fortuitously positioned within ten feet of our parked car) into a weapon in her fight against the Burlington Solution? The three of us entered the restaurant together, and the first thing we did was head straight for the toilets. Then we sat down at a table and ordered our hamburgers and tuna salads and grilled cheese sandwiches. The moment the waitress was finished with us, Lucy made it known by pointing to her lap that she had more business to attend to in the bathroom. No problem, I said, and off she went, looking like any other American girl in her paisley shorts and hundred-and-fifty-dollar neon-blue sneakers. While she was gone, Tom and I talked about how pleasant it was to be out of the city, even sitting in a dark and mangy joint like Dot's, surrounded by truckers and farmers in yellow and red baseball caps emblazoned with logos from companies that manufactured work tools and heavy machinery. Tom was still going at full verbal tilt, and I got so caught up in what he was saying that I lost track of Lucy. Little did we know at the time (the facts didn't come out until later) that our girl had left the restaurant through a rear door and was frantically feeding coins and dollar bills into the Coke machine outside. She bought at least twenty cans of that gooey, sugar-laden concoction, and one by one she poured the entire contents of each can into the gas tank of my once healthy Oldsmobile Cutlass. How could she have known that sugar was a deadly poison to internal combustion engines? How could the brat have been so damn clever? Not only did she bring our journey to an abrupt and conclusive halt, but she managed to do it in record time. Five minutes would be my guess, seven at the most. However long it was, we were still waiting for our food when she returned to the table. She was suddenly full of smiles again, but how could I have guessed the cause of her happiness? If I had bothered to think about it at all, I would have assumed it was because she had taken a good shit.

When the meal was over and we climbed back into the car, the engine coughed forth one of the most peculiar noises in automotive history. I have sat here thinking about that noise for the past twenty minutes, but I still haven't found the correct words to describe it, the one unforget-table phrase that would do it justice. *Raucous chortling? Hiccupping pizzicati? A pandemonium of guffaws?* I'm probably not up to the task – or else language is too feeble an instrument to capture what I heard, which resembled something that might have come from the mouth of a choking goose or a drunken chimpanzee. Eventually, the guffaws modulated into a single, drawn-out note, a loud, tuba-like eructation that could have passed for a human burp. Not exactly the belch of a satisfied beer drinker, but a sound that recalled the slow, agonizing rumble of indiges-tion, a basso discharge of air seeping from the throat of a man afflicted with terminal heartburn. Tom cut the engine and tried again, but the second turn of the key produced no more than a faint groan. The third resulted in silence. The symphony had come to an end, and my poisoned Olds was in cardiac arrest.

'I think we're out of gas,' Tom said.

It was the only sensible conclusion to be drawn, but when I leaned to my left and looked at the fuel gauge, it showed that the tank was about one-eighth full. I pointed my finger at the red needle. 'Not according to this,' I said.

Tom shrugged. 'It must be broken. Lucky for us there's a gas station across the road.'

As Tom presented his flawed diagnosis of the car's condition, I turned around to glance at said gas station through the rear window – a tumbledown, two-pump garage that looked as if it hadn't had a paint job since 1954. In doing so, my eyes came into contact with Lucy's. She was sitting directly behind Tom, and because I had no idea that she was responsible for the mess we found ourselves in, I was somewhat puzzled by the serene, almost supernatural contentment I saw on her face. The engine had just poured out its cacophonous jungle medley, and under normal circumstances you would think those laughable sounds would have gotten a rise out of her: alarm, amusement, agitation, something. But Lucy had withdrawn deep into herself – floating weightlessly on a cloud of indifference, a pure spirit detached from her own body. I understand now that she was rejoicing over the success of her mission, giving silent thanks to the all-powerful one for helping her accomplish a miracle. Sitting with her in the car that afternoon, however, I was merely perplexed.

'Are you still with us, Lucy?' I asked.

She gave me a long, impassive stare, and then she nodded her head.

'Don't be upset,' I continued. 'We'll have the car running again in no time.'

Needless to say, I was wrong. It would be tempting to give a blow-by-blow account of the comedy that ensued, but I don't want to try the reader's patience by discussing matters that are not, strictly speaking, relevant to the story. In the case of the car, the upshot is all that counts. I will therefore dispense with the jerrican of high-octane gas that Tom lugged back from the garage across the road (since it didn't help) and omit any references to the tow truck that eventually hauled the Cutlass over to that same garage (what other choice did we have?). The only fact that bears mentioning is that neither one of the fellows who ran the garage (a father-and-son team known as Al Senior and Al Junior) could figure out what was wrong with the car. Junior and Senior were roughly the same ages as Tom and myself respectively, but whereas I was thin and Tom was stout, the bodies of the young Al and the old Al resembled ours in reverse: the son was lean, the father was fat.

After examining the engine for several minutes and finding nothing, Al Junior slammed the hood shut. 'I'm going to have to take this baby apart,' he said.

'It's that bad, huh?' I replied.

'I'm not saying it's bad. But it's not too good either. No sir, not too good at all.'

'How long will it take to fix it?'

'That depends. Maybe a day, maybe a week. First thing, I got to locate the problem. If it's something simple, no sweat. If it's not, we might have to order you some new parts from the dealer, and that could drag on for a while.'

It sounded like a fair and honest assessment, and given that I was thoroughly ignorant on the subject of cars, I didn't see what else I could do but offer him the job – no matter how long it took. Tom, who was no mechanic either, seconded that course of action. All well and good, perhaps, but now that we were stranded on a back road in rural Vermont, what were we going to do with ourselves while the two Als worked on resuscitating our ailing machine? One option was to rent a car and push on to Burlington, then spend the rest of the week with Pamela and pick up the Oldsmobile on our way back to New York. Or, more simply, rent rooms at a local inn and pretend that we were on vacation until the car was ready.

'I've had enough driving for today,' Tom said. 'I vote for staying put. At least until tomorrow.'

I was inclined to agree with him. As for Lucy – the wordless, ever-watchful Lucy – one can well imagine how little she protested our decision.

Al Senior recommended a couple of spots in Newfane, a village we had driven through about ten miles back. I went into the office and called both numbers, but it turned out that neither inn had any rooms available. When I reported what had happened, the big man looked miffed. 'Cruddy tourists,' he said. 'It's only the first week of June, and summer's already in full swing.'

For the next half minute or so, we all stood around with our hands in our pockets, watching father and son think. At long last, Al Junior broke the silence. 'What about Stanley, Dad?'

'Hmmm,' his father said. 'I don't know. What makes you think he's back in business?'

'I heard he's planning to open up this year,' the young man answered. 'That's what Mary Ellen told me. She bumped into Stanley at the post office last week.'

'Who's Stanley?' I asked.

'Stanley Chowder,' Al Senior said, lifting his arm and pointing west. 'He used to have an inn about three miles up that hill there.'

'Stanley Chowder,' I repeated. 'That's one hell of a funny name.'

'Yeah,' big Al said. 'But Stanley doesn't care. I think he kind of likes it.'

'I once knew a man named Elmer Doodlebaum,' I said, suddenly realizing that I enjoyed talking to the two Als. 'How'd you like to be saddled with that moniker all your life?'

Al Senior grinned. 'Not much, mister. Not much at all. But at least people would remember it. I've been Al Wilson since the day I was born, which is maybe half a step up from being called John Doe. There's nothing to sink your teeth into with a name like that. Al Wilson. There must be a thousand Al Wilsons in Vermont alone.'

'I think I'll give Stanley a try,' Al Junior said. 'You never can tell. If he isn't outside mowing that lawn of his, maybe he'll pick up . . .'

As the slender son went into the office to make the call, his plump father leaned back against my car, pulled a cigarette from his shirt pocket (which he put in his mouth but didn't light), and then told us the sad story of the Chowder Inn.

'That's what Stanley does now,' he said. 'He mows his lawn. From early in the morning until

205

late in the afternoon, he rides around on his red John Deere and mows his lawn. It starts when the snow melts in April, and it doesn't stop until the snow starts falling again in November. Every day, rain or shine, he's out there riding around his property, mowing the lawn for hours on end. When winter comes, he stays inside and watches television. And when he can't stand watching television anymore, he gets into his car and drives down to Atlantic City. He checks into one of the casino hotels and plays blackjack for ten straight days. Sometimes he wins, sometimes he loses, but Stanley doesn't care. He has enough money to live on, and if he squanders a few bucks every now and then, so what?

'I've known him a long time – more than thirty years now, I think. He used to be a C.P.A. down in Springfield, Mass. Back around sixty-eight or sixty-nine, he and his wife Peg bought that big white house up on the hill, and after that they'd come for the weekends, for summer vacations, for the Christmas holidays, whenever they could. Their big dream was to turn the place into an inn and live there full-time after Stanley retired. So four years ago, Stanley quits his job as a C.P.A., he and Peg sell their house in Springfield, and they move up here to open the Chowder Inn. I'll never forget how hard they worked that first spring, rushing to get things ready for the Memorial Day weekend. Everything goes as planned. They pretty up the place until it sparkles like a jewel. They hire a chef and two housemaids, and then, just when they're about to book their first reservations, Peg has a stroke and dies. Right there in the kitchen in the middle of the day. One minute she's alive, talking to Stanley and the chef, and the next minute she's crumpled up on the floor, breathing her last. It happened so quick, she died before the ambulance ever left the hospital.

'That's why Stanley mows his lawn. Some people think he's gone a little crazy, but whenever I talk to him, he's the same old Stanley I met thirty years ago, the same guy he's always been. He's grieving for his Peg, that's all. Some men take to drink. Some men look for a new wife. Stanley mows his lawn. There's no harm in that, is there?

'I haven't seen him in a while, but if Mary Ellen got the story right – and I've never known her not to – then that's good news. It means that Stanley's getting better, that he wants to start living again. Al Junior's been gone for a couple of minutes now. I could be wrong, but I'll bet Stanley picked up the phone, and they're working out the arrangements for getting you three up the hill. That would be something, wouldn't it? If Stanley's open for business, you'll be the first paying customers in the history of the Chowder Inn. My oh my. That would really be something, wouldn't it?'

DREAM DAYS AT THE HOTEL EXISTENCE

I want to talk about happiness and well being, about those rare, unexpected moments when the voice in your head goes silent and you feel at one with the world.

I want to talk about the early June weather, about harmony and blissful repose, about robins and yellow finches and bluebirds darting past the green leaves of trees.

I want to talk about the benefits of sleep, about the pleasures of food and alcohol, about what happens to your mind when you step into the light of the two o'clock sun and feel the warm embrace of air around your body.

I want to talk about Tom and Lucy, about Stanley Chowder and the four days we spent at the Chowder Inn, about the thoughts we thought and the dreams we dreamed on that hilltop in southern Vermont.

I want to remember the cerulean dusks, the languorous, rosy dawns, the bears yelping in the woods at night.

I want to remember it all. If all is too much to ask, then some of it. No, more than some of it.

Almost all. Almost all, with blanks reserved for the missing parts.

The taciturn yet convivial Stanley Chowder, practiced mower of lawns, astute poker player and Ping-Pong dervish, aficionado of old American movies, Korean War veteran, father of a thirty-two-year-old daughter with the unlikely name of Honey – a fourth-grade public school teacher who lives in Brattleboro. Stanley is sixty-seven but fit for his age, with a full head of hair and clear blue eyes. Five-eightish, stockily built, a firm grip when he shakes my hand.

He drives down the hill to pick us up. After greeting Al Junior and Al Senior, he introduces himself to us and then pitches in as we transfer our bags from the trunk of my car to the back of his Volvo station wagon. I notice that he moves quickly, almost rushing as he walks between the two vehicles. There is a nimble, nervous proficiency to his gestures. Stanley is no dawdler. Idleness breeds thought, and thoughts can be dangerous, as anyone who lives alone will readily understand. After listening to Al Senior's account of Peg's demise, I see Stanley as a lost and tormented figure. Accommodating, generous to a fault, but uncomfortable in his own skin, a shattered man struggling to pick up the pieces.

We say good-bye to the Wilsons and thank them for their help. Al Junior promises to give me daily progress reports on the state of my car.

A steep dirt road flanked by woods on both sides; bumpy terrain; an occasional low-hanging branch sweeps across the windshield as we climb toward the top of the hill. Stanley apologizes in advance for any problems we might encounter at the inn. He's been working alone for the past two weeks trying to get it into shape, but there's still much to be done. He was planning to open for the Fourth of July, but after Al Junior called and told him about our predicament, he 'wouldn't have felt right' about not putting us up for a few days. No staff has been hired yet, but he will make the beds and see to it that we're as comfortable as circumstances allow. He has already talked to his daughter in Brattleboro, and she has agreed to come to the inn every day and cook dinner for us. He assures us that she cooks well. Tom and I thank him for his kindness. Preoccupied with these multiple concerns, Stanley fails to notice that Lucy has yet to speak.

A three-story white house with sixteen rooms and a wraparound front porch. The sign at the edge of the driveway says *The Chowder Inn*, but a part of me already understands that we have come to the Hotel Existence. For the moment, I decide not to share this thought with Tom.

Before we are shown to our rooms, Tom calls Pamela from the ground-floor parlor to explain what happened to us. Stanley is upstairs making the beds. Lucy wanders off toward the sofa, and a moment later she is down on her knees petting Stanley's dog, an aging black Lab named Spot. Without wanting to, I think of Harry and the inane words that have been stuck in my head for the past two weeks: *X marks the spot.* The spot has now been turned into a four-legged animal, and as I watch the dog lick Lucy's face, I stand close to Tom on the off chance I'll be called upon to say a few words to Pamela. I'm not, but as I listen to Tom's end of the conversation, I'm surprised by his stepsister's irritable response to the news that our arrival in Burlington will be delayed. As if the trouble with the car were our fault. As if unforeseen events didn't occur all the time. But Pamela has just spent an hour and a half at the supermarket and is now in the kitchen 'working her head off' to get dinner ready for us before we show up. As a sign of hospitality and welcome, she's planned an elaborate, multicourse meal that includes everything from gazpacho to a home-baked pecan pie, and she's put out, nay furious, when she learns that all her efforts have been in vain. Tom offers a dozen apologies, but Pamela nevertheless continues to scold him. Is this the new and improved Pamela I've heard so much about? If she can't take a small disappointment in her stride, what kind of a stand-in mother will she be for Lucy? The last thing the girl needs is a neurotic bourgeois woman bearing down on her with impatient and impossible demands.

211

Even before Tom hangs up the phone, I decide that the Burlington Solution is dead. I cross Pamela's name off the list and appoint myself as Lucy's temporary guardian. Am I better qualified to take care of Lucy than Pamela is? No, in most ways probably not, but my gut tells me that I'm responsible for her – whether I like it or not.

Tom hangs up the phone and shakes his head. 'That's one pissed-off lady,' he says.

'Forget Pamela,' I answer.

'What do you mean?'

'I mean we're not going to Burlington.'

'Oh? Since when?'

'Since now. We'll stay here until the car is fixed, and then we'll all go back to Brooklyn together.'

'And what are you planning to do with Lucy?'

'She'll live with me in my apartment.'

'When we talked about it yesterday, you said you weren't interested.'

'I've changed my mind.'

'So we've driven all the way up here for nothing.'

'Not really. Look around you, Tom. We've landed in paradise. A couple of days of rest and relaxation, and we'll go home feeling like new men.'

Lucy is no more than ten feet from us as we exchange these words, and she hears every syllable we say. When I turn to look at her, she's blowing kisses to me with both hands – arms extended after each smack of her lips, like a triumphant leading lady on opening night. I'm happy to see her so

212

happy, but I'm also scared. Do I have any idea what I'm getting myself into?

Suddenly, I remember a line from a film I saw back in the late seventies. The title eludes me, both the story and characters have passed into oblivion, but the words are still ringing in my head, as if I heard them only yesterday. 'Children are a consolation for everything – except having children.'

As Stanley shows us to our rooms on the top floor, he explains that Peg, the late Mrs Chowder ('dead for four years now'), was responsible for choosing the furniture, the bed linens, the wall-paper, the Venetian blinds, the rugs, the lamps, the curtains, and every one of the many small objects that sit on top of the various tables, night-stands, and bureaus: the lace doilies, the ashtrays, the candlestick holders, the books. 'A woman of impeccable taste,' he says. To my mind, the décor is overly precious, a nostalgic attempt to re-create the atmosphere of a bygone New England that was in fact much grimmer and sparer than the soft, girlish rooms I am looking at now. But no matter. Everything is clean and comfortable, and there is one redeeming element that undercuts the otherwise pervasive tone of kitsch and fussi-ness: the pictures hanging on the walls. Contrary to what one might expect, there are no needle-point samplers, no badly executed watercolors of snowy Vermont landscapes, no Currier and Ives reproductions. The walls are covered with eight-by-ten black-and-white photographs of old Hollywood comedy stars. This is Stanley's single contribution to the look of the rooms, but it makes all the difference, injecting a dose of wit and levity into the staid surroundings. Of the three rooms he has prepared for us, one is devoted to the Marx Brothers, another to Buster Keaton, and the last to Laurel and Hardy. Tom and I give Lucy first choice, and she opts for Stan and Ollie at the end of the hall. Tom selects Buster, and I wind up between them with Groucho, Harpo, Chico, Zeppo, and Margaret Dumont.

First perusal of the grounds. Immediately after unpacking our bags, we go outside to visit Stanley's famous lawn. For several minutes, I am prey to a steady flow of shifting sensations. The feel of the soft, well-tended grass underfoot. The sound of a horsefly buzzing past my ear. The smell of the grass. The smells of the honeysuckle and lilac bushes. The bright red tulips planted around the edge of the house. The air begins to vibrate, and a moment later a small breeze is wafting over my face.

I drift along with my three companions and the dog, musing about absurd things, Stanley informs us that the property extends over a hundred acres, and I imagine how simple it would be to construct more buildings if the population of the Hotel Existence outgrows the capacity of the main house. I am dreaming Tom's dream and reveling in the possibilities. Sixty acres of woods. A pond. A neglected apple orchard, a collection of abandoned beehives, a shack in the woods for distilling maple syrup. And the grass of Stanley's lawn – the lovely, unending grass, stretching all around us and beyond.

It will never happen, I tell myself. Harry's scheme is bound to fail, and even if it doesn't, why should I presume Stanley would be willing to sell his house? On the other hand, what if Stanley stays with us and becomes a partner in the enterprise? Is he the sort of man who would grasp what Tom is hoping to achieve? I decide that I have to get to know him better, that I must spend as much time in his company as I can.

After twenty minutes or so, we circle back in the direction of the house. Stanley dashes into the garage to fetch some lawn chairs for us, and once we're installed, he excuses himself and disappears into the house. He has work to do, but the first paying guests in the history of the Chowder Inn are free to loaf in the sunlight as long as they want.

For a couple of minutes, I watch Lucy run across the lawn, throwing sticks to the dog. To my left, Tom is reading a play by Don DeLillo. I look up at the sky and study the passing clouds. A hawk wheels into view and then vanishes. When the hawk returns, I close my eyes. Within seconds, I am fast asleep.

At five o'clock, Honey Chowder makes her first appearance, pulling up in front of the house with a carload of groceries and two cases of wine. By now, Tom and I have left the lawn chairs and are sitting on the porch, talking about politics. We interrupt our denunciations of Bush II and the Republican Party, walk down the steps to the white Honda, and introduce ourselves to Stanley's daughter.

She's a large, freckle-faced woman with beefy upper arms and a bone-crunching handshake. She brims with confidence, with humor, with good will. A bit overbearing, perhaps, but what can you expect from a fourth-grade schoolteacher? Her voice is loud and somewhat hoarse, but I like it that she seems so ready to laugh, is unafraid of the bigness of her personality. She's a competent, can-do girl, I decide, and no doubt good fun in bed. Not pretty, but not not-pretty either. Radiant blue eyes, full lips, a thick mane of reddish-blonde hair. As we help her unload the grocery bags from the trunk of the car, I see her eyeing Tom with something more than detached curiosity. The lunkhead notices nothing, but I begin to wonder if this bossy, brainy young woman isn't the answer to my prayers. No more ethereal B.P.M.s, but an unmarried woman desperate to hook a man. A steamroller. A tornado. A hungry, fast-talking wench who could flatten our boy into submission.

For the second time that afternoon, I decide to keep my thoughts to myself and say nothing to Tom.

As Stanley promised, she cooks us an excellent dinner. Watercress soup, a pork loin roast, string beans with almonds, crème caramel for dessert, and generous pourings of wine. I feel a twinge of sympathy for Pamela and the aborted feast she was preparing for us, but I doubt the fare in Burlington could surpass what bedecks the table at the Chowder Inn.

The victorious Lucy, now liberated from her impending bondage, shows up at the table wearing her red-and-white checkered dress, her black patent-leather shoes, and her white anklets with the lacy fringes on top. I don't know if Stanley is impervious to the behavior of others or just overly discreet, but he still hasn't commented on Lucy's silence. Ten minutes into the meal, however, his blunt, sharp-eyed daughter begins asking questions.

'What's wrong with her?' she says. 'Doesn't she know how to talk?'

'Of course she does,' I reply. 'She just doesn't want to.'

'Doesn't want to?' Honey says. 'What does that mean?'

'It's a test,' I explain, blurting out the first lie that pops into my head. 'Lucy and I were talking the other day about hard things, and we decided that not talking is about the hardest thing a person can do. So we made a pact. Lucy agreed not to say a word for three days. If she can hold up her end of the bargain, I've promised to give her fifty dollars. Isn't that right, Lucy?'

Lucy nods.

'And how many days are left?' I continue.

Lucy holds up two fingers.

Ah, I say to myself, there we have it. The kid has finally fessed up. In two more days, the torture will come to an end.

Honey squints her eyes, at once dubious and alarmed. Children are her business, after all, and she senses that something is off. But I'm a stranger to her, and rather than press me about the queer and unhealthy game I've been playing with this little girl, she comes at the problem from another angle.

'Why isn't the child in school?' she asks. 'It's Monday, June fifth. Summer vacation doesn't begin for another three weeks.'

'Because . . .' I say, scrambling to concoct another fib, 'Lucy goes to a private school . . . and the academic year is shorter there than at public schools. She had her last class on Friday.'

Again, I'm convinced that Honey doesn't believe me. But short of crossing the line into an unacceptable rudeness, she can't very well go on interrogating me about matters that don't concern her. I like this chunky, forthright Chowder of a woman, and I also like her old man, who is sitting across the table from me, quietly chewing his food and sipping his wine, but I have no intention of letting them in on our family secrets. It's not that I'm ashamed of who we are – but my God, I tell myself, what a family it is. What a motley bunch of messed-up, floundering souls. What stunning examples of human imperfection. A father whose daughter wants nothing to do with him anymore. A brother who hasn't seen or heard from his sister in three years. And a little girl who's run away from home and refuses to speak. No, I'm not about to expose the Chowders to the truth of our fractured, good-for-nothing little clan. Not tonight I'm not. Not tonight, and no doubt not ever.

Tom must be thinking thoughts similar to mine, for he hastily jumps in and tries to steer the table talk in another direction. He begins by asking Honey about her work. How long has she been doing it, what motivated her to become a teacher in the first place, what does she think of the Brattleboro system, and so on. His questions are bland, stultifying in their banality, and as I look at his face while he talks to Honey, I can tell that he has no interest in her – not as a woman, not even as a person. But Honey is too tough to allow Tom's indifference to prevent her from giving bright and charming answers, and before long she is the one guiding the conversation, bombarding our boy with dozens of questions of her own. Her aggressiveness rocks Tom back on his heels for a few moments, but when he understands that his interlocutor is fully as clever as he is, he rises to the occasion and starts giving as good as he gets. Stanley and I scarcely say a word, but we are both amused by the verbal sparring match that has broken out before our eyes. Inevitably, the talk veers to politics and the upcoming elections in November. Tom rails against the right-wing takeover of

America. He cites the near destruction of Clinton, the anti-abortion movement, the gun lobby, the fascist propaganda of talk-radio shows, the cowardice of the press, the ban on the teaching of evolution in certain states. 'We're marching backward,' he says. 'Every day, we lose another piece of our country. If Bush is elected, there won't be anything left.' To my surprise, Honey is in total agreement with him. Peace reigns for approximately thirty seconds, and then she announces that she's planning to vote for Nader.

'Don't do that,' Tom says. 'A vote for Nader is a vote for Bush.'

'No, it's not,' Honey says. 'It's a vote for Nader. Besides, Gore will win Vermont. If I wasn't sure of that, I'd vote for him. This way I can make my little protest and still keep Bush out of office.'

'I don't know about Vermont,' Tom says, 'but I do know it's going to be a close election. If enough people think like you in the swing states, Bush will win.'

Honey struggles to suppress a smile. Tom is so damned earnest, she's itching to knock him from his high horse with some loopy, off-the-wall remark. I can see the joke coming, and I cross my fingers that it's a good one.

'Do you know what happened the last time a nation listened to a bush?' Honey asks.

No one says a word.

'Its people wandered in the desert for forty years.'

In spite of himself, Tom bursts out laughing.

The jousting contest has been brought to a sudden, decisive end, and Honey is the clear winner.

I don't want to get carried away, but I suspect that Tom has met his match. Whether anything comes of it is another story, to be told by time and the mysterious inclinations of the flesh. I tell myself to stay tuned for further developments.

Early the next morning, I call Al Junior at the gas station, but he still hasn't solved the riddle of the car. 'I'm working on it now,' he says. 'As soon as I have the answer, I'll be in touch.'

I marvel at how little this news affects me. If anything, I'm glad to be stuck on our hilltop for another day, glad not to have to think about returning to New York just yet.

I have a job to do that morning, but it's impossible to get Stanley to sit down long enough to engage him in a serious conversation. He cooks and serves us breakfast, but the moment he puts the plates in front of us, he rushes out of the kitchen and goes upstairs to make the beds. After that, he's busy with various projects around the house: screwing in lightbulbs, beating carpets, repairing broken window sashes. There's nothing to be done but look for an opportunity later in the day.

The morning air is cool and misty. We're wearing sweaters as we walk out onto the front porch and scan the wet, dew-drenched lawn. Eventually, the clouds will burn away and we'll be given another sparkling afternoon, but for now the shrubs and trees are barely visible.

Lucy has found a book in her room, and she carries it with her onto the porch. It's a small paperback, and since her hand is covering the title, I ask her to show me what it is. *Riders of the Purple Sage*, by Zane Grey. I ask her if it's any good, and she gives a vigorous nod of approval. Not just good, she seems to be telling me, but a masterpiece for all time. I find it a curious choice for a nine-year-old girl, but who am I to object? The kid likes to read, I say to myself, and I consider that a positive development, proof that our little runaway is no mental sluggard.

Tom plants himself in the chair next to mine as Lucy stretches out on the glider with her Western. He lights up an after-breakfast cigarette and says, 'Do you think Al Junior will ever fix the car?'

'Probably,' I answer. 'But I'm in no rush to get out of here. Are you?'

'No, not really. I'm beginning to like this place.'

'Do you remember our dinner with Harry last week?'

'When you spilled the red wine on your pants? How could I forget it?'

'I've been thinking about some of the things you said that night.'

'As I remember it, I said a lot of things. Most of them stupid things. Monumentally stupid things.'

'You were out of sorts. But you didn't say anything stupid.'

'You must have been too drunk to notice.'

'Drunk or not, there's one thing I have to know. Did you mean it about wanting to get out of the city – or was it just talk?'

'I meant it, but it was also just talk.'

'It can't be both. It has to be one or the other.'

'I meant it, but I also know it will never happen. Therefore, it was just talk.'

'And what about Harry's deal?'

'Just talk. You should know that about Harry by now. If anyone is "just talk," it's our old friend Harry Brightman.'

'I'm not going to disagree with you. But just for the sake of argument, imagine he was telling the truth. Imagine he's about to come into big money and would be willing to dump it into a country house. What would you say then?'

'I'd say, "Let's go ahead and do it."'

'Good. Now think carefully. If you could buy any place in the world, where would you want it to be?'

'I haven't thought that far ahead. Somewhere isolated, though. A place where other people wouldn't be right on top of us.'

'Somewhere like the Chowder Inn?'

'Yeah. Now that you mention it, this spot would work just fine.'

'Why don't we ask Stanley if he's willing to sell?'

'What for? We don't have enough money to buy.'

'You're forgetting Harry.'

'No, I'm not. Harry has his good points, but he's the last man I'd count on for something like this.'

'I admit it's a million-to-one shot, but just in case Harry's horse comes in, why not talk to Stanley? Just for the fun of it. If he says he's interested, at least we'll know what the Hotel Existence looks like.'

'Even if we never live here.'

'Exactly. Even if we never come back for the rest of our days.'

It turns out that Stanley had been thinking about selling the place for years. Only inertia and apathy have stopped him from 'taking the bull by the horns,' he says, but if the price is right, he'd chuck the whole thing in a minute. He can't stand living with Peg's ghost anymore. He can't stand the brutal winters. He can't stand the isolation. He's had it with Vermont, and all he dreams about is moving to the tropics, to some Caribbean island where the weather is warm every day of the year.

Then why work so hard at whipping the Chowder Inn into shape? I ask. No reason, he says. He has nothing better to do, and it helps ward off the boredom.

It's lunchtime. The four of us are sitting around the dining room table, eating cold cuts, fruit, and cheese. Now that the fog has lifted, sunlight blasts through the open windows, and every object in the room seems more defined, more vivid, more saturated with color. Our host is pouring out the sorrows of his life to us, but I feel remarkably happy just to be where I am, sitting in my own body, looking at the things on the table, breathing air in and out of my lungs, relishing the simple fact that I am alive. What a pity that life ends, I tell myself, what a pity that we aren't allowed to go on living forever.

Tom explains that we don't have the money to make an offer on the house now, but we might be in a position to do so in the coming weeks. Stanley says he doesn't know what the property is worth, but he can contact a local real estate agent and find out. The more we talk, the more enthusiastic he becomes. I don't know if he believes a word we say, but just being able to imagine a new life for himself seems to have turned him into a different man.

Why have I encouraged such nonsense? Everything hinges on the sale of a forged manuscript of *The Scarlet Letter*, and not only am I morally opposed to Harry's criminal scheme, I have no faith in it to begin with. More to the point: even if I did, I don't have any interest in moving to Vermont. I have only recently begun a new life of my own, and I'm perfectly content with the decision I made to settle in Brooklyn. After all those years in the suburbs, I find that the city agrees with me, and I've already grown attached to my neighborhood, with its shifting jumble of white and brown and black, its multi-layered chorus of foreign accents, its children and its trees, its striving middle-class families, its lesbian couples, its Korean grocery stores, its bearded Indian holy man in his white robes bowing to me whenever we cross paths on the street, its dwarfs and cripples, its aged pensioners inching along the sidewalk, its church bells and ten thousand dogs, its underground population of solitary, homeless scavengers, pushing their shopping carts down the avenues and digging for bottles in the trash.

If I don't want to leave all that, why have I pushed Tom into this pointless discussion about real estate with Stanley Chowder? To please Tom, I think. To show him that he can count on me to support his project, even though we both understand that the new Hotel Existence is built on a foundation of 'just talk.' I play along with Tom to prove that I'm on his side, and because Tom appreciates the gesture, he plays along with me. It's a mutual exercise in clear-eyed self-deception. Nothing will ever come of it, and therefore we can dream along together without having to worry about the consequences. Now that we've dragged Stanley into our little game, it almost begins to look real. But it isn't. It's still just hot air and hopeless fantasy, an idea as fake as Harry's Hawthorne manuscript – which probably doesn't even exist. But that doesn't mean the game isn't fun. You'd have to be dead not to enjoy talking about outlandish things, and what better place to do it than on a hilltop in the middle of a quiet New England nowhere?

After lunch, the rejuvenated Stanley challenges

me to a Ping-Pong match in the barn. I tell him I'm rusty, that I haven't played in years, but he won't take no for an answer. The exercise will do me good, he says, 'get the juices flowing again,' and so I reluctantly agree to play a game or two. Lucy accompanies us to the barn to witness the action, but Tom stays put, settling into a chair on the porch to smoke and read.

I quickly learn that Stanley doesn't play the kind of Ping-Pong I'm used to. The paddles and ball are the same, but in his hands it isn't a polite parlor activity so much as a full-blown, strenuous sport, a demonic, miniaturized form of tennis. He delivers his serves with a devastating, unhittable topspin, stands ten feet back from the table, and counters every shot I make as though I'm no more skilled than a four-year-old. He beats me three straight times – 21-0, 21-0, 21-0 – and once the massacre is over, there's nothing I can do but bow humbly to the victor and drag my exhausted body out of the barn.

Covered in sweat, I return to the house for a quick shower and a change of clothes. As I climb the steps of the front porch with Lucy, Tom tells me he called Brooklyn fifteen minutes ago. Harry is out on an errand, but Tom has left word with Rufus to have him call us back. 'To see if he's still interested,' Tom says. 'There's no point in getting Stanley's hopes up if Harry's changed his mind.'

I've been in the barn for less than half an hour,

but in that brief interlude I sense that Tom has been deep in thought. Something in his eyes tells me that our lunchtime talk with Stanley has altered his position concerning the new Hotel Existence. He's beginning to believe it can work. He's beginning to hope.

As it happens, the telephone rings the instant I step into the front hall. I pick up the receiver, and there's Brightman himself, chirping away on the other end of the line. I tell him about our car trouble, about the Chowder Inn, and about Stanley's eagerness to strike a bargain with us. 'This is the spot,' I continue. 'Tom's idea might have sounded a little strange when we were sitting in that restaurant in the city, but once you get up here the whole thing looks eminently reasonable. That's why he called. To find out if you're still in.'

'In?' Harry booms, sounding like some half-mad nineteenth-century actor. 'Of course I'm in. We shook hands on it, didn't we?'

'Not that I remember.'

'Well, maybe it wasn't an actual physical hand-shake. But we all agreed. I distinctly remember that.'

'A mental handshake.'

'That's it. A mental handshake. A true meeting of minds.'

'All contingent on the outcome of your little deal, of course.'

'Of course. That goes without saying.'

'So you're still planning to go ahead with it.'

'I know you're skeptical, but all the pieces are suddenly falling into place.'

'Oh?'

'Yes. And I'm happy to report an excellent bit of news. Don't think I didn't take your advice to heart, Nathan. I told Gordon I was having second thoughts, and if he didn't arrange a meeting for me with the elusive Mr Metropolis, I was backing out.'

'And?'

'I met him. Gordon brought him to the store, and I met him. A most interesting man. Barely said a word, but I knew that I was in the presence of a real pro.'

'Did he bring samples of his work?'

'A love letter from Charles Dickens to his mistress. A beautiful specimen.'

'I wish you luck, Harry. If not for your sake, then at least for Tom's.'

'You'll be proud of me, Nathan. After our talk the other night, I decided I needed to take some precautions. Just in case things go wrong. Not that they will – but when you've been around as many years as I have, you'd be a fool not to consider all the possibilities.'

'I don't think I follow.'

'You don't have to. Not now, in any case. If and when the time comes, you'll understand everything. It's probably the smartest move I've made in my life. A grand gesture, Nathan. The splurge of splurges. A vast swan dive into eternal greatness.'

I have no idea what he's talking about. Harry is in full bombastic flight, blustering forth his enigmatic pronouncements for the pure, self-indulgent pleasure of listening to his own voice, and I see no point in prolonging the conversation. Tom is standing next to me by then. Without bothering to say another word, I pass the phone to him and walk upstairs to take my shower.

The next morning, Lucy finally opens her mouth and speaks.

I am expecting answers and revelations, the unwrapping of manifold mysteries, a great beam of light shining into the darkness. I should have known better than to count on language as a more efficient form of communication than nods and shakes of the head. Lucy has resisted our attempts to pry something out of her for three solid days, and once she allows herself to talk, her words are scarcely more helpful to us than her silence was.

I begin by asking her where she lives.

'Carolina,' she says, drawling out the syllables with the same backwoods southern accent I had heard on Monday morning.

'North Carolina or South Carolina?'

'Carolina Carolina.'

'There's no such place, Lucy. You know that. You're a big girl. It's either North Carolina or South Carolina.'

'Don't be mad, Uncle Nat. Mama said not to tell.'

'Was it your mother's idea for you to go to Uncle Tom in Brooklyn?'

'Mama said go, and so I went.'

'Were you sad to leave her?'

'Real sad. I love my mama, but she knows what's right.'

'And what about your father? Does he know what's right?'

'Definitely. He's about the rightest man under the sun.'

'Why didn't you talk, Lucy? What made you keep quiet for so many days?'

'I did it for Mama. So she'd know I was thinking about her. That's how we do things back home. Daddy says silence purifies the spirit, that it prepares us to receive the word of God.'

'Do you love your father as much as your mother?'

'He's not my real father. I'm adopted. But I came out of Mama's womb. She carried me inside her for nine months, so she's the one I belong to.'

'Did she tell you why she wanted you to come north?'

'She said go, and so I went.'

'Don't you think Tom and I should talk to her? He's her brother, you know, and I'm her uncle. My sister was her mother.'

'I know. Grandma June. I used to live with her, but now she's dead.'

'If you give me your phone number, it will make things a lot simpler for all of us. I won't send you

231

back if you don't want to go. I just want to talk to your mother.'

'We don't have a phone.'

'What?'

'Daddy doesn't like phones. We used to have one, but then he gave it back to the store.'

'All right, then. What about your address? You must know that.'

'Yeah, I know it. But Mama said not to tell, and when Mama tells me something, that's what I do.'

This maddening, breakthrough conversation takes place at seven o'clock in the morning. Lucy has woken me up by knocking on my door, and she sits beside me on the bed as I rub my eyes open and begin my futile questioning. Next door, Tom is still asleep in the Buster Keaton room, but when he comes downstairs for breakfast an hour later, he is no more successful than I am in extracting information from her. Together, we go on grilling her for half the morning, but the kid is made of steel and won't budge. She won't even tell us what kind of work her father does ('He has a job') or if her mother still has the tattoo on her left shoulder ('I never see her without her clothes on'). The one fact she's willing to share with us is irrelevant to our purposes: her best friend is a girl named Audrey Fitzsimmons. Audrey wears glasses, we're told, but she's the best arm wrestler in the fourth grade. Not only does she beat all the girls, but she's stronger than all the boys as well.

Eventually, we give up in frustration, but not before Lucy reminds me that I promised to pay her fifty dollars the moment she started talking again.

'I never said that,' I tell her.

'Yes, you did,' she answers. 'The other night at dinner. When Honey asked you why I didn't speak.'

'I was trying to protect you. I didn't really mean it.'

'That makes you a liar, then. Daddy says liars are the lowest worms in the universe. Is that what you are, Uncle Nat? A nogood, lowly worm?'

Tom, who just a moment before was on the point of wringing her neck, suddenly bursts out laughing. 'You better cough up,' he says. 'You don't want her to lose respect for you, do you, Nathan?'

'Yeah,' Lucy chimes in. 'You want me to love you, don't you, Uncle Nat?'

Reluctantly, I take out my wallet and hand over the fifty dollars.

'You're some operator, Lucy,' I mumble.

'I know I am,' she says, tucking the bills into her pocket and gracing me with one of her gigantic smiles. 'Mama told me always to stick up for myself. A bargain's a bargain, right? If I let you welsh on the deal, you wouldn't like me anymore. You'd think I was a softy.'

'What makes you think I like you?' I ask.

'Because I'm so cute,' she says. 'And because you changed your mind about Pamela.'

It's all very funny, perhaps, but once she runs

off to play with the dog, I turn to Tom and ask, 'How the hell are we going to get her to talk?'

'She's talking,' he says. 'She's just not saying the right words.'

'Maybe I should threaten her.'

'That's not your style, Nathan.'

'I don't know. What if I tell her I've changed my mind again? If she doesn't answer our questions, we'll drive her up to Pamela and dump her there. No ifs, ands, or buts.'

'Fat chance.'

'I'm worried about Rory, Tom. If the kid doesn't open up, we'll never know what's going on.'

'I'm worried, too. For the past three years, the only thing I've done is worry. But frightening Lucy isn't going to help anyone. She's already been through enough.'

At eleven o'clock that same morning, Al Junior calls from the garage down the hill and tells me the problem has been solved. Sugar in the gas tank and fuel lines, he says. This pronouncement is so mystifying to me, I scarcely know what he's talking about.

'Sugar,' he repeats. 'It looks like someone poured about fifty cans of Coke into the tank. You want to mess up a person's car, there's no faster or simpler way to do it.'

'Good God,' I say. 'Are you telling me someone did it on purpose?'

'That's what I'm saying. Coke cans don't have

legs, do they? They don't have hands and fingers to flick themselves open with. The only explanation is that someone got it into his head to do a number on your car.'

'It had to have happened while we were eating lunch. The car was working fine until we parked in front of the restaurant. The question is: why would anyone do a shitty thing like that?'

'A hundred reasons, Mr Glass. Some rowdy kids, maybe. You know, a bunch of bored teenagers out to play a prank. That kind of vandalism goes on around here all the time. Or else it was someone who doesn't like people from New York. He sees the license plates on your car and decides to teach you a lesson.'

'That's ridiculous.'

'You'd be surprised. There's a lot of resentment against out-of-staters in this part of Vermont. The New York and Boston folks most of all, but I've even seen some morons pick fights with people from New Hampshire. It happened just the other day at Rick's Bar on Route Thirty. A guy walks in from Keene, New Hampshire, which is about one inch from the Vermont border, and some drunken local – I won't mention any names – smashes a chair over his head. 'Vermont for Vermonters!' he's yelling. 'Get your New Hampshire ass out of here!' It turned into a real slugfest. From what they tell me, it probably would have gone on all night if the cops hadn't broken it up.'

'You make it sound like we're living in Yugoslavia.'

'Yeah, I know what you mean. Every idiot's got his turf to defend, and damn the poor stranger who doesn't belong to your tribe.'

Al Junior rattles on for another minute or two, lamenting the state of the world in a doleful, disbelieving voice, and I imagine him shaking his head as the words come out of his mouth. Eventually, we resume talking about my sabotaged green sedan, and I'm told that he's about to get started on flushing the engine and fuel lines clean. I'm going to have to spring for new spark plugs, a new distributor cap, and sundry other replacement parts, but all I care about is getting the old jalopy up and running again. Al Junior predicts a clean bill of health by the end of the day. If he and his father have time, they'll drive up the hill in two cars and deliver the Cutlass to me that evening. If not, I should expect them the following morning. I don't bother to ask him what the repairs will cost. My mind is temporarily stuck in Yugoslavia, and I'm thinking about the horrors of Sarajevo and Kosovo, about the thousands of slaughtered innocents who died for no other reason than that they were supposedly different from the people who killed them.

Dark thoughts dog me until lunchtime, and I walk around the property alone, leaving Tom and Lucy to their own devices. It is the only grim patch during my stay at the Chowder Inn, but nothing has gone right this morning, and suddenly I feel the world pressing down on me from all sides. Lucy's deft, tight-lipped evasions; the growing anxiety about her mother; the malicious attack on my car; the unstoppable brooding about massacres in distant places – all of these things pour into my head and remind me there is no escape from the wretchedness that stalks the earth. Not even on the remotest hilltop in southern Vermont. Not even behind the locked doors and bolted porticoes of the make-believe sanctuary known as the Hotel Existence.

I cast about for a counter-argument, for an idea that will put the scales in balance, and eventually I start thinking about Tom and Honey. Nothing is certain at this point, but at dinner the previous night I sensed a considerable softening in his attitude toward her. Honey has been begging her father to move for years, and when Stanley told her about our potential interest in buying the house, she raised her glass and offered us a toast of thanks. Then she turned to Tom and asked him why on earth would he want to trade his life in the city for a dirt road in Vermont? Instead of mocking her with a facetious answer, he gave a full and measured explanation, reiterating many of the points he had made at our dinner with Harry on Smith Street in Brooklyn, but somehow he was more eloquent than he had been that night – more urgent, more persuasive as he delved into his despair over the future of America. It was Tom at his scintillating best, and as I watched Honey looking at him across the table, I saw little tears gathering in the corners of her eyes, and I knew, knew beyond any shadow of a doubt, that Stanley's buxom, big-hearted daughter was smitten with my nephew.

But what about Tom? I could see that he had begun to take notice of her, to talk to her in a less guarded and aggressive way, but what did that mean? It could have been a sign of growing interest, and it also could have been simple good manners.

One small moment from the end of the evening. Whether it answers the question or not, I submit it as a final piece of evidence.

By the time we finished dessert, Lucy was already upstairs in bed, and the four adults were all a bit drunk. Stanley proposed a friendly game of poker, and as he shuffled the cards and talked about his new life in the tropics (sitting under a palm tree with a rum punch in one hand and a Montecristo in the other, watching the surf roll in and out on the white shore at sunset), he quietly proceeded to beat our pants off, winning three out of every four hands we played. After the drubbing he'd given me at Ping-Pong that afternoon, how could I have expected any less? It seemed there was nothing the man didn't excel at, and both Tom and Honey laughed at their ineptitude, making wilder and wilder bets as Stanley continued to outsmart us all. It was a complicitous sort of laughter, I felt, and I made a conscious effort not to join in, studying the two youngsters from behind the shield of my cards. Then, as the game was breaking up, Tom said something that took me by surprise. 'Don't go back to Brattleboro,' he said to Honey. 'It's after midnight, and you've had too much to drink.'

Simple good manners – or a devious ploy to woo her into bed?

'I can drive that road with my eyes shut,' Honey answered. 'Don't worry about me, kiddo.'

She went on to explain that she had to get up especially early the next morning (something to do with a teacher-parent conference), but I could see that Tom's solicitude had touched her, or at least I imagined it had. Then she kissed everyone good-bye. First her father, next a light peck on the jaw for me, and last of all Tom. Not only did he get his kiss on the lips, but he was the recipient of a hug as well – a big hug, which went on several seconds longer than the situation seemed to call for.

'Night, all,' Honey said, waving to us as she walked to the front door. 'See you fellows tomorrow.'

She shows up the next day at four, bearing five lobsters, three bottles of champagne, and two different desserts. Another feast is prepared for us by our extravagantly gifted chef, and now that Lucy is willing to join in on the conversation, the fourth-grade teacher and the fourth-grade student talk shop for a good part of the meal, batting back and forth the titles of their favorite books. Al Junior and Al Senior have yet to show up with my car, but I announce that the Olds has been fixed and should be in our hands by tomorrow. With so much high-spirited talk flying around the table, I neglect to mention the cause of the breakdown, since I don't want to spoil the mood by bringing up such an unpleasant subject. Tom knows all about it by now, but he too is reluctant to report on the nasty trick that was played on us. Honey and Lucy are singing nonsense songs as they crack open their lobsters, and why interrupt their fun with a disheartening account of class resentments and provincial animosities?

When I take Lucy upstairs to bed, I realize that I'm too worn out to sit up late for a second night in a row, belting back glass after glass of wine with the others. The Chowders can both hold their alcohol, and with his great bulk and prodigious appetites, Tom can match them drink for drink, but I'm a skinny ex-cancer patient with a small capacity, and I dread waking up the next morning with a hangover.

I park myself on the edge of Lucy's bed and read to her from the Zane Grey novel until she closes her eyes and falls asleep. As I walk to my own room next door, I can hear laughter seeping up from the dining room below. I catch Stanley say something about being 'tuckered out,' and then Honey adds something about 'the Charlie Chaplin room' and 'maybe it's not such a bad idea.' It's difficult to know what they're talking about, but one possibility could be this: Stanley is about to go to bed, and Honey has drunk too much to drive home and plans to spend the night at the inn. If I'm not mistaken, the Charlie Chaplin room is the one immediately next to Tom's.

I crawl into my own bed and begin reading Italo Svevo's *As a Man Grows Older*. It's my second Svevo novel in less than two weeks, but *The Confessions of Zeno* made such a strong impression on me, I've decided to read everything by the author I can put my hands on. The original title in Italian is *Senilità*, and I find it a perfect book for an aging fart like me. An older man and his young mistress. The sorrows of love. Dashed hopes. After every paragraph or two, I pause for a moment and think about Marina Gonzalez, aching at the thought that I will never see her again. I'm tempted to masturbate, but I resist the urge because the rusty bedsprings are bound to give me away. Nevertheless, I slip my hand under the covers from time to time and briefly touch my cock. Just to make sure it's still there, to verify that my ancient friend is still with me.

Half an hour later, I hear footsteps tramping up the stairs. Two pairs of legs, two whispering voices: Tom and Honey. They walk down the hall in the direction of my door, then stop. I strain to catch a few words of their conversation, but they're talking too low for me to make anything out. Eventually, I hear Tom say 'good-night,' and a moment later the door of the Charlie Chaplin room opens and shuts. Three seconds after that, the same thing happens to the door of the Buster Keaton room.

The wall between me and Tom is thin – the flimsiest of Sheetrock partitions – and every sound he makes is audible to me. I hear him take off his shoes and unbuckle his belt, I hear him brush his teeth at the sink, I hear him sigh, I hear him hum, I hear him crawl under the covers of his creaking bed. I'm about to close my book and turn out the light, but no sooner do I reach for the lamp than I hear a faint knock on Tom's door. Honey's voice says, 'Are you asleep?' Tom says no, and when Honey asks if she can come in, our boy says yes, and by saying yes the hidden purpose of our turn off the interstate highway onto Route 30 is about to be fulfilled.

The sounds are so clear to me, I have no trouble following every detail of the action that unfolds on the other side of the wall.

'Don't get any ideas,' Honey says. 'It's not that I do this sort of thing every day.'

'I know,' Tom answers.

'It's just that it's been a long time.'

'For me, too. A very long time.'

I hear her slip into bed with him, and I hear everything that happens after that. Sex is such a strange and sloppy business, why bother to recount every slurp and moan that ensued? Tom and Honey deserve their privacy, and for that reason I will end my report of the night's activities here. If some readers object, I ask them to close their eyes and use their imaginations.

The next morning, Honey is long gone before the rest of the house rolls out of bed. It's another splendid day, perhaps the most beautiful day of the spring, but it turns out to be a day of surprises as well, and in the end those jolts will overwhelm the perfection of the landscape and the weather, pushing them to the back of my mind. If I remember that day at all, it's only as an unassembled jigsaw puzzle, a mass of isolated impressions. A patch of blue sky here; a silver birch there, reflecting the light of the sun off its bark. Clouds that look like human faces, like the maps of countries, like ten-legged dream animals. The sudden glimpse of a garter snake wending its way through the grass. The four-note lament of an unseen mockingbird. The thousand leaves of an aspen tree fluttering like wounded moths as the wind slides through the branches. One by one, each element is there, but the whole is lacking, the parts don't cohere, and I can do no more than search for the remnants of a day that doesn't fully exist.

It begins with the arrival of Al Junior and Al Senior at nine o'clock. Tom is still upstairs in the Buster Keaton room, comatose after his all-night romp with Honey. Lucy and I have been up since eight, and we're just leaving the house to go for a walk when the Wilsons show up in their two-vehicle convoy: a red Mustang convertible and my lime-green Cutlass. I let go of Lucy's hand to shake hands with those stalwart gentlemen. They tell me my car is as good as new, Al Senior presents me with a bill for their services, and I write them a check on the spot. Then, just when I think the transaction is over, Al Junior drops the first bomb of the day.

'The kicker is, Mr Glass,' he says, patting the roof of my car, 'it's a good thing that dope messed with your gas tank.'

'What do you mean?' I say, not knowing how to interpret this peculiar statement.

'After we talked yesterday morning, I thought I'd have the job finished in a couple of hours. That's why I said we'd be able to deliver the car to you last night. Remember?'

'Yes, I remember. But you also said it might not happen until today.'

'Yeah, I did say that, but the reason I gave you then isn't the reason why we couldn't get here till now.'

'No? What happened in the meantime?'

'I took your Olds out for a spin. Just to make sure everything was back to normal. It wasn't.'

'Oh?'

'I pushed the car up to sixty-five, seventy, and then I tried to slow down. Mighty hard to do when the brakes are shot. Lucky I didn't get myself killed.'

244

'The brakes . . .'

'Yeah, the brakes. I got the car back to the garage and had a look. The lining was worn thin, Mr Glass, just about to go.'

'What are you saying?'

'I'm saying that if you hadn't had that other problem with the gas tank, you never would have found out about this problem with the brakes. If you'd gone on driving much longer, you would have run into some pretty bad trouble. Accident trouble. Death trouble. All kinds of trouble.'

'So the shithead who poured Coke into the gas tank actually saved our lives.'

'That's what it looks like. Pretty weird, huh?'

After the Wilsons drive off in their red convertible, Lucy begins tugging on my sleeve.

'It wasn't no S-head that did it, Uncle Nat,' she says.

'S-head?' I answer. 'What are you talking about?'

'You said a naughty word. I'm not allowed to talk like that.'

'Oh, I see. *S*. Short for you-know-what.'

'Yeah. The S-word.'

'You're right, Lucy. I shouldn't use that kind of language when you're around.'

'You shouldn't use it, period. Whether I'm around or not.'

'You're probably right. But I was angry, and when a person's angry, he can't always control what he says. A bad man tried to wreck our car. For no reason. Just to be cruel, to hurt us. I'm sorry I used that word, but you can't really blame me for being upset.'

'It wasn't a bad man. It was a bad girl.'

'A girl? How do you know that? Did you see it happen?'

For a brief moment, she relapses into her old silence, nodding her head in answer to my question. Already, tears have begun to well up in her eyes.

'Why didn't you tell me?' I ask. 'If you saw it happen, you should have told me, Lucy. We could have caught the girl and put her in jail. And if the men at the garage had known what the problem was, they could have fixed the car right away.'

'I was scared,' she says, bowing her head, afraid to look me in the eye. The tears are spilling out of her in earnest now, and I see them land on the dry dirt below – salty ephemera, shining globules that momentarily darken and then vanish into the dust.

'Scared? Why should you be scared?'

Instead of responding to my question, she grabs hold of me with her right arm and digs her face into my ribs. I begin stroking her hair, and as I feel her body shudder against mine, I suddenly understand what she's been trying to tell me. I register a moment of genuine shock, then feel a wave of anger pass through me, but once the wave passes, it is gone. Anger gives way to pity, and I realize that if I begin scolding her now, I might lose her trust forever.

'Why did you do it?' I ask.

'I'm sorry,' she says, tightening her grip on me and blubbering into my shirt. 'I'm real, real sorry. I just kind of went crazy, Uncle Nat, and before I knew what I was doing, it was already done. Mama told me about Pamela. She's a mean person, and I didn't want to go there.'

'I don't know if she's mean or not, but it all turned out for the best, didn't it? You did a wrong thing, Lucy. A very wrong thing, and I never want you to behave like that again. But this time – this one time – the wrong thing turned out to be the right thing, too.'

'How can a wrong thing be a right thing? That's like saying a dog's a cat, or a mouse is an elephant.'

'Don't you remember what Al Junior told us about the brakes?'

'Yeah, I remember. I saved your life, didn't I?'

'Not to speak of your own life. And Tom's life, too.'

At long last, she disengages herself from my shirt, wipes the tears from her eyes, and gives me an intense, thoughtful look. 'Don't tell Uncle Tom I did it, okay?'

'Why not?'

'He won't like me anymore.'

'Of course he will.'

'No, he won't. And I want him to like me.'

'I still like you, don't I?'

'You're different.'

'In what way?'

'I don't know. You don't take things as hard as Uncle Tom. You're not as serious.'

'That's because I'm older.'

'Just don't tell him, okay? Swear to me you won't tell him.'

'All right, Lucy. I swear.'

She smiles then, and for the first time since she turned up on Sunday morning, I catch a glimpse of her mother as a young girl. Aurora. The absent Aurora, lost somewhere in the mythical land of Carolina Carolina, a shadow-woman beyond the reach of the living. If she is anywhere now, it is only in her daughter's face, in the little girl's loyalty to her, in Lucy's unbroken promise not to tell us where she is.

Tom rises at last. I find it difficult to read his state of mind, which seems to oscillate between somber contentment and a fidgety, awkward self-consciousness. At lunch he says not a word about the previous night's events, and I refrain from asking any questions, curious though I am to learn his side of the story. Has he fallen for the ebullient Miss C., I wonder, or does he plan to brush her off as a one-night fling? Is it all sex and nothing but sex, or are feelings involved in the equation as well? After we finish our lunch, Lucy trots off with Stanley to ride on the tractor and help him mow the lawn. Tom retires to the porch for his post-prandial smoke, and I settle into the chair next to his.

'How did you sleep last night, Nathan?' he asks.

'Pretty well,' I answer. 'Considering the thinness of the walls, it could have been a lot worse.'

'I was afraid of that.'

'It's not your fault. You didn't build the house.'

'I kept telling her to keep it down, but you know how it is. A person gets carried away, and there's nothing you can do about it.'

'Not to worry. To tell the truth, I was glad. I felt happy for you.'

'Me too. For one night, I was glad.'

'You'll have other nights, old man. That was only the beginning.'

'Who knows? She left early this morning, and it's not as if we did much talking while she was here. I have no idea what she wants.'

'More to the point – what do you want?'

'It's too early to tell. Everything happened so fast, I haven't had time to think about it.'

'Not that you've asked me, but in my opinion you two are a good match.'

'Yeah. Two fatsos colliding in the night. I'm surprised the bed didn't collapse.'

'Honey isn't fat. She's what they call "statuesque." '

'She's not my type, Nathan. Too tough. Too confident. Too many opinions. I've never been attracted to women like that.'

'That's why she'd be good for you. She'd keep you on your toes.'

Tom shakes his head and sighs. 'It would never work. She'd wear me out in less than a month.'

'So you're ready to give up after one night.'

'There's nothing wrong with that. One good night, and that's the end of it.'

'And what happens if she crawls into your bed again? Are you going to kick her out?'

Tom puts a match to a second cigarette, then pauses for a long moment. 'I don't know,' he says at last. 'We'll see.'

Unfortunately, neither Tom nor anyone else gets a chance to see.

A last surprise is waiting for us, and this one proves to be so large, so stinging, so colossal in its ramifications, that we have no choice but to hit the road that very afternoon. Our holiday at the Chowder Inn comes to a sudden and bewildering end.

Good-bye hilltop. Good-bye lawn. Good-bye Honey.

Good-bye to the dream of the Hotel Existence.

Tom utters the words 'We'll see' at approximately one o'clock. After Lucy's tractor ride with Stanley, I take her to the pond for a swim. When we return to the house forty minutes later, Tom delivers the news. Harry is dead. Rufus has just called from Brooklyn, weeping into the phone, barely able to get a word out of his mouth, to tell us that Harry has died, that Harry is gone. According to Tom, Rufus was too choked up to say any more. We understand nothing. Beyond the fact that we must leave Vermont at once, we understand nothing.

I pay Stanley what we owe him. As I sign the check with a trembling hand, I tell him that our partner is dead and that we're no longer in a position to buy the house. Stanley shrugs. 'I knew it wasn't serious,' he says. 'But that doesn't mean I didn't enjoy talking about it.'

Tom hands him a piece of paper with his address and telephone number on it. 'Please give this to Honey,' he says. 'And tell her I'm sorry.'

We pack our bags. We climb into the car. We go.

DOUBLE-CROSS

I considered it a homicide. It didn't matter that no one laid a hand on him, that no one shot him or stabbed him in the chest, that no one ran him down with a car. Even if words were his killers' only weapons, the violence they subjected him to was no less physical than a blow to the head with a hammer. Harry was not a young man. He had suffered two coronaries in the past three years, his blood pressure was high, his arteries were in a state of imminent collapse. How much torture could a body in that condition withstand? Not much, in my opinion. Not much at all.

There was only one witness to the outrage, but even though Rufus heard every word they said, he understood only the smallest part of it. That was because Harry hadn't bothered to tell him about the scheme he was hatching with Gordon Dryer, and when Dryer walked into the store early that afternoon with Myron Trumbell, Rufus took them for a pair of fellow dealers. He led them upstairs to Harry's office, and because Harry seemed exceptionally tense and excited when he opened the door, not at all himself, pumping the hands of his visitors like some windup doll, Rufus began to grow alarmed. Rather than return to his post at the cash register downstairs, he decided to stay where he was and listen in on the conversation by pressing his ear against the door.

They toyed with Harry for a few minutes before they circled in with their daggers, softening him up for the kill. Friendly greetings all around, casual remarks about the weather, unctuous compliments about Harry's taste in office furniture, admiring references to the neat array of first editions stacked along the shelves. For all the pleasant banter, Harry must have been confused. Metropolis hadn't finished his work on the manuscript, and without a completed forgery to hand over to Trumbell, he didn't understand why Gordon had chosen to drop by now.

'It's always a pleasure to see you,' he said, 'but I don't want Mr Trumbell to be disappointed. The manuscript is locked away in a vault at the Citibank on Fifty-Third Street in Manhattan. If you'd called in advance, I would have had it for you today. But unless I'm wrong, we weren't supposed to get together until next Monday afternoon.'

'In a bank vault?' Gordon said. 'So that's where you stashed away my discovery. I didn't know.'

'I thought I'd told you,' Harry continued, improvising as he went along, still unable to comprehend what Gordon was doing there with Trumbell four days before their scheduled meeting.

'I'm having second thoughts,' Trumbell said.

'Yes,' Gordon added, jumping in before Harry had a chance to reply. 'You see, Mr Brightman, a sale like this can't be taken lightly. Not when there's so much money involved.'

'I'm aware of that,' Harry said. 'That's why we had the first page examined by those experts. Not just one man, but two.'

'Not two,' Trumbell said. 'Three.'

'Three?'

'Three,' Gordon said. 'You can never be too careful, can you? Myron also took it to a curator at the Morgan Library. One of the top men in the field. He gave his verdict this morning, and he's convinced it's a forgery.'

'Well,' Harry stammered, 'two out of three isn't bad. Why trust this man's opinion over the two others?'

'He was very persuasive,' Trumbell said. 'If I'm going to buy this manuscript, there can't be any doubt. No doubt whatsoever.'

'I see,' Harry said, struggling to elude the trap they had set for him, but no doubt already beginning to lose heart, already demoralized beyond all imagining. 'I just want you to know that I've acted in good faith, Mr Trumbell. Gordon found the manuscript in his grandmother's attic and brought it to me. We had it checked out and were told it was genuine. You became interested in buying it. If you've changed your mind, I can only say I'm sorry. We can cancel the deal right now.'

'You're forgetting the ten thousand dollars you took from Myron,' Gordon said.

'No, I'm not,' Harry answered. 'I'll give him back the money, and then we're quits.'

'I don't think it's going to be that simple, Mr Brightman,' Trumbell said. 'Or should I call you Mr *Dunkel?* Gordon's told me quite a bit about you, Harry. Chicago. Alec Smith. Twenty-odd forged paintings. Prison. A new identity. You're a champion liar, Harry, and with a record like yours, I'd just as soon you kept those ten thousand dollars. That way I'll be able to press charges. You were planning to rip me off, weren't you? I don't like it when people try to take my money. It irritates me.'

'Who is this man, Gordon?' Harry said, his voice suddenly shaking, out of control.

'Myron Trumbell,' Gordon answered. 'My benefactor. My friend. The man I love.'

'So this is the one,' Harry said. 'There never was that other person.'

'Just the one,' Gordon replied. 'Always just the one.'

'Nathan was right,' Harry moaned. 'Nathan was right all along. Goddamn it, why didn't I listen to him?'

'Who's Nathan?' Gordon asked.

'A man I know,' Harry said. 'It doesn't matter. Someone I know. A fortune-teller.'

'You never could take good advice, could you, Harry?' Gordon said. 'Too fucking greedy. Too fucking full of yourself.'

255

That was when Harry began to crack. The cruelty in Gordon's voice was too much for him, and he was no longer able to pretend that he was talking business, discussing the ins and the outs of a deal that had gone wrong. This was love that had gone wrong, deception on a scale he had never encountered before, and the pain of it destroyed any power he might have had to resist the onslaught.

'Why, Gordon?' he said. 'Why are you doing this to me?'

'Because I hate you,' his ex-lover said. 'Haven't you figured that out by now?'

'No, Gordon. You love me. You've always loved me.'

'Everything about you disgusts me, Harry. Your bad breath. Your varicose veins. Your dyed hair. Your awful jokes. Your fat belly. Your knobby knees. Your puny cock. Everything. Every part of you makes me sick.'

'Then why come back after all these years? Couldn't you have left well enough alone?'

'After what you did to me? Are you insane? You destroyed my life, Harry. Now it's my turn to destroy yours.'

'You ran out on me, Gordon. You betrayed me.'

'Think again, Harry. Who turned me over to the cops? Who cut a deal for himself by pointing his finger at me?'

'And so now you turn me over to the cops. Two wrongs don't make a right, Gordon. At least you're alive. At least you're young enough to have something to look forward to. You put me back in jail, and I'm finished. I'm a dead man.'

'We don't want you to die, Harry,' Trumbell said, suddenly re-entering the conversation. 'We want to make a bargain with you.'

'A bargain? What kind of bargain?'

'We're not out for blood. We're only looking for justice. Gordon suffered because of you, and now we feel he deserves some compensation. Fair is fair, after all. If you co-operate with us, we won't say a word to the law.'

'But you're rich. Gordon has all the money he needs.'

'Certain members of my family are rich. Unfortunately, I'm not one of them.'

'I don't have any cash. I can scrape up the ten thousand I owe you, but that's about it.'

'You might be short on cash, but you have other assets we'd be willing to settle for.'

'Other assets? What are you talking about?'

'Look around you. What do you see?'

'No. You can't do that. You've got to be kidding.'

'I see books, Harry, don't you? I see hundreds of books. And not just any books, but first editions, even signed first editions. Not to speak of what's sitting in the drawers and cabinets below. Manuscripts. Letters. Autographs. Give us the contents of this room, and we'll consider the account square.'

'I'll be ruined. I'll be wiped out.'

'Consider the alternatives, Mr Dunkel-Brightman.

Which would you prefer: arrest on charges of fraud, or a quiet, peaceful life as the owner of a used-book store? Think about it carefully. Gordon and I will come back tomorrow with a large van and a team of moving men. It won't take more than a couple of hours, and then you'll be rid of us forever. If you try to stop us, I'll simply pick up the phone and call the police. You decide, Harry. Life or death. An empty room – or a second trip to prison. If you don't give us the books tomorrow, you're going to lose them anyway. You understand that, don't you? Be smart, Harry. Don't fight it. If you give up without a struggle, you'll be doing everyone a favor – especially yourself. Expect us between eleven and noon. I wish I could be more precise, but it's so hard to predict the traffic these days. *A demain,* Harry. Ta ta.'

The door opened then, and as Dryer and Trumbell pushed their way past him, Rufus looked into the office and saw Harry sitting at his desk with his head in his hands, sobbing like a young boy. If only Harry had stayed there for a few minutes and taken the time to reflect on what had just happened, he would have understood that Dryer and Trumbell had no case against him, that threatening to turn him in to the police was no more than an artless, heavy-handed bluff. How could they have proved that Harry knowingly tried to sell a forged manuscript without also implicating themselves? By confessing to their knowledge of the forgery, they would have been obliged to deliver the forger to the police, and what were the chances that Ian Metropolis would have admitted he was involved in the hoax? Assuming there was such a person as Ian Metropolis, of course, which struck me as less than likely. Ditto with the three so-called experts who had supposedly examined his work. My hunch was that Dryer and Trumbell had manufactured the Hawthorne page themselves, and with a gullible man like Harry as their victim, how hard would it have been to persuade him that he was looking at the penmanship of a master forger? Harry had told me he'd met Metropolis while we were in Vermont, but how could he be certain that man was who he claimed to be? The Dickens letter was of no importance. Whether genuine or fake, the letter had no bearing on the story. From start to finish, the plot to crush Harry had been a two-man operation, with a brief appearance by a third person posing as someone else. Two not-so-clever crooks and their anonymous crony. Bastards all.

But Harry wasn't thinking clearly that day. How could he think when his mind had been turned into an open wound, a suppurating mass of scrambled brain matter, exploded neurons, and short-circuited electrical impulses? Where was reason when the adored one of your life has just insulted you with a litany of monstrous denunciations, ripping apart your hapless self with the hatchet blows of his contempt? Where was mental equilibrium when that same man and his new cohort have declared their intention to rob you of everything you own and you feel powerless to stop them? Could anyone criticize Harry for lacking the wherewithal to take the long view? Could anyone fault him for being in a state of pure, animal panic?

When Rufus entered the office, Harry stood up from his desk and began to howl. He was beyond words then, incapable of forming a single coherent sentence, and the sounds that rushed out of his throat were so ghastly, Rufus said, so agonizing in their torment, that he began to shake with fear. Dryer and Trumbell were still on their way down the stairs to the ground floor, and without bothering to acknowledge Rufus's presence, Harry bolted out from behind his desk and began chasing after them. Rufus followed – but slowly, cautiously, nearly immobilized with dread. By the time he got to the bottom of the stairs, Dryer and Trumbell had already left the shop, and Harry was yanking open the front door – still howling, still in pursuit. A yellow cab was parked at the curb with its engine and meter running, and the two men climbed into the backseat before Harry could catch up with them. He shook his fist at the departing taxi, paused for a moment to scream two words – *Murderers! Murderers!* – and then, totally out of his mind, began charging down Seventh Avenue as fast as his legs could take him, bumping into pedestrians, staggering, falling down, picking himself up, but not stopping until he reached the next corner and the cab vanished from sight. Rufus watched it all from a distance, following the blurred form of Harry's body as tears streamed down his face.

At the moment Harry stopped at the corner, Nancy Mazzucchelli rounded that same corner and approached her former boss, stunned to see him in such a gruesome state. His cheeks were bright red, he was gasping for breath, the elbow of his jacket was torn, and his eternally well-groomed hair was flopping around on all sides of his scalp.

'Harry,' she said. 'What's wrong?'

'They've killed me, Nancy,' Harry replied, clutching his chest and continuing to gasp for air. 'They stuck a knife in my heart and killed me.'

Nancy put her arms around him and gently patted his back. 'Don't worry,' she said. 'Everything is going to be all right.'

But it wasn't all right; it wasn't the least bit all right. Just after Nancy spoke those words, Harry let out a long, faint groan, and then she felt his body go limp against hers. She tried to hold him up, but he was too heavy for her, and little by little they both sank to the ground. And so it was that Harry Brightman, once known as Harry Dunkel, father of Flora and ex-husband of Bette, died on a Brooklyn sidewalk one sultry afternoon in the year 2000, cradled in the arms of the B.P.M.

COUNTERATTACK

T om drove fast, and we made it back to Park Slope in less than five hours, pulling up in front of the store just as the sun was beginning to go down. Rufus and Nancy were waiting for us in Harry's upstairs apartment, huddled together in the darkened bedroom. It felt right to me that she should be present, but until Rufus began telling us what had happened earlier that day, I didn't understand why she was there. With so many pressing matters to attend to, it never even occurred to me to ask.

Neither one of them had met Lucy before, so introductions became the first point of business. Then Tom took our girl into the living room and planted her in front of the TV. Normally, that would have been my job, but I believe Tom was so startled to encounter the B.P.M. in such an unlikely setting that he had to withdraw for a moment to catch his breath. His queen had miraculously surfaced again, and no doubt his heart was racing, pounding madly in his lovesick chest.

Rufus was a good deal calmer than he had been on the phone that afternoon. The shock had begun to wear off a bit, and he was able to get through the story without too many interruptions. He and Nancy were sitting on the bed, and every time he broke down and cried, she would put her arms around him and hold on firmly until the tears had passed. She was somewhat weepy herself, but kindness was her specialty, and she understood that of all the people in the apartment that night, Rufus was the most desperate, the one most in need of comforting. As he went on talking to us in his slow, lilting Jamaican voice, my mind kept conjuring up images of Harry's corpse, which was laid out in a freezer at Methodist Hospital, just a few blocks from where we sat.

I hadn't known Harry well, but I had been fond of him in a peculiar sort of way (part fascination, part awe, part disbelief), and if he had died under any other circumstances, I doubt that I would have been as affected as I was. More than shock, more than sadness, I was filled with anger over the grotesque thing that had been done to him. It didn't help matters that I had predicted Dryer's double cross, that my instincts had told me the Hawthorne scam was no more than a ruse, an elaborate hoax within a hoax, and that revenge had been the single motive from the start. What good is knowledge if you don't use it to stop your friends from being destroyed? I had tried to warn Harry, but I hadn't been emphatic enough – I hadn't put in sufficient time and effort to make him understand why he should have backed out of the deal. And now he was dead – murdered in cold blood, and murdered in such a way that his killers would never be charged for their crime.

After Rufus had finished talking, my immediate impulse was to partake in some vengeance of my own. Tom had only the fuzziest idea of what the dispute with Dryer and Trumbell had been about (he knew it was connected to Harry's deal in some way, but that was all), and Rufus and Nancy were in the dark about everything. Unlike Tom, they had never even heard of Gordon Dryer, and neither one of them was aware of Harry's less than sterling past. I didn't take the trouble to fill them in on the details. There wouldn't have been any point. The only point was to get on the phone as quickly as possible – and make sure that no van turned up at the store the next morning. Dryer and his boyfriend might have killed Harry, but I wasn't going to let them rob him as well.

I asked Tom for the key to the downstairs office, and since he was in a state of extreme discombobulation at that moment (mourning the unexpected death of his boss, trembling with joy and terror at his sudden proximity to the B.P.M., doing what he could to console the all but inconsolable Rufus), he absentmindedly reached into his pocket and gave it to me. It was only when I was walking out the door that he came to his senses long enough to ask me what I was doing. 'Nothing,' I said vaguely. 'I just need to check on something. I'll be right back.'

I installed myself at Harry's desk and opened the top center drawer, thinking it might be a logical place for him to have put Dryer's telephone number. I was prepared to call information and track down Trumbell if necessary, but I was hoping to save a little time by looking in the drawer first. For once in my life, I got lucky. Affixed to a business-size envelope at the very top of the drawer was a square green Post-it with two words scribbled on it in ink – *Gordon's cell* – followed by a ten-digit number that began with a 917 area code. When I removed the Post-it from the envelope and stuck it on the desk beside the phone, I saw that the envelope had writing on it as well: *To Be Opened In The Event Of My Death.*

There were twelve typed pages folded up inside, a Last Will and Testament prepared by the Court Street law firm of Flynn, Bernstein, and Vallero, duly signed, witnessed, and executed on June 5, 2000, just one day before I had talked to Harry on the phone at the Chowder Inn. I scanned the contents of the document, and within three minutes I understood what he'd meant by his *grand gesture*, his *splurge of splurges*, his *vast swan dive into eternal greatness*. He had been referring to the will I now held in my hands, which was indeed something great, something altogether surprising and great, and which proved that he had listened to my warnings far more closely than I had imagined. Even as he'd refused to follow my advice, he had hedged his bets by embracing the possibility that Gordon was about to turn on him, and if such a betrayal were to come to pass, he felt that his life would be over – if not literally, then at least in the sense that the inner destruction would be more than he could bear. He had said as much to me at our dinner on June first: *If you're right about Gordon, then my life's finished anyway.* To think about Gordon as a duplicitous avenger was also to think about his own death. The first thought led naturally to the second, and in the end the two thoughts were one and the same. Hence the will. It was an overly dramatic step, perhaps, a near-hysterical response to the distress roiling inside him, but who could fault him for wanting to take (in his words) *some precautions*? In light of what had happened earlier that day, it turned out to be an act of supreme wisdom.

The two beneficiaries named in the will were Tom Wood and Rufus Sprague. They were to inherit the building on Seventh Avenue along with the business known as Brightman's Attic, including all goods and moneys that appertained to said business. Other, smaller bequests were mentioned as well – various books, paintings, and articles of jewelry to be given to people whose names were unfamiliar to me – but the bulk of Harry's estate was going to Tom and Rufus, with all income from Brightman's Attic to be divided equally between them. Considering that there was no mortgage on the building, and considering the value of the books and manuscripts in the room where I was currently sitting, the inheritance would amount to a small fortune, more money than either one of them had ever dreamed of. At the last possible moment, Harry had pulled off his grand gesture, his splurge of splurges. He had taken care of his boys.

I realized then how badly I had underestimated him. The man might have grown up into an imp and a scoundrel, but a part of him had remained the ten-year-old child who had fantasized about rescuing orphans from the bombed-out cities of Europe. For all his wisecracking irreverence, for all his peccadilloes and falsehoods, he had never stopped believing in the principles of the Hotel Existence. Good old Harry Brightman. Funny old Harry Brightman. If there had been a bottle of something on the desk, I would have poured myself a glass and raised a toast to his memory. Instead, I picked up the phone and dialed Gordon's number. In the long run, that probably amounted to the same thing.

He didn't answer, but a message came on after four rings and I heard his voice for the first time – an unusually calm and guarded voice, I felt, with little affect or inflection. Fortunately, he gave a second number where he could be reached (I assumed Trumbell's), which spared me the bother of having to look it up myself. I dialed again, fully expecting no one to be in, imagining that Dryer and Trumbell were out somewhere whooping it up, celebrating their triumph in Brooklyn that afternoon. Just as I was beginning to wonder if I should leave a message on the machine, the phone stopped ringing and I heard Dryer's voice for the second time in thirty seconds. To play it safe, I asked if I could talk to Gordon Dryer, even though I knew for certain that he was the man on the other end of the line.

'Speaking,' he said. 'Who is this?'

'Nathan,' I replied. 'We've never met, but I believe you've heard of me. Harry Brightman's friend. The fortune-teller.'

'I don't know what you're talking about.'

'Of course you do. When you and your friend visited Harry today, someone was standing on the other side of the door, listening in on your conversation. At one point, Harry mentioned my name. 'I should have listened to Nathan,' he said, and you asked him, 'Who's Nathan?' That's when Harry told you I was a fortune-teller. Remember now? We're not talking about the distant past, Mr Dryer. You heard those words just a few hours ago.'

'Who are you?'

'I'm the messenger of bad tidings. I'm the man who issues threats and warnings, who tells people what to do.'

'Oh? And what am I supposed to do?'

'I like your sarcasm, Gordon. I hear that coldness in your voice, and it confirms my feelings about who you are. Thank you. Thank you for making my job so simple.'

'All I have to do is hang up the phone, and that's the end of the conversation.'

'But you're not going to hang up, are you? You're scared shitless, and you'll do anything to find out what I know. Am I right or wrong?'

'You don't know a damn thing.'

'Guess again, Gordon. Let me try out some names on you, and we'll see what I know and don't know.'

'Names?'

'Dunkel Frères. Alec Smith. Nathaniel Hawthorne. Ian Metropolis. Myron Trumbell. How's that? Do you want me to go on?'

'All right, so you know who I am. Big deal.'

'Yes, big deal. Because I know what I know, I'm in a position to get what I want from you.'

'Ah. So that's it. You want money. You want us to cut you in on the deal.'

'Wrong again, Gordon. I'm not interested in money. There's just one thing you have to do for me. A very easy thing. It won't take but a minute of your time.'

'One thing?'

'Call up the moving company you hired for tomorrow and cancel the order. Tell them you've changed your mind and won't be needing the van.'

'Why would I do that?'

'Because your scam has done gone backfired on you, Gordon. The whole thing blew up in your face about five minutes after you left Harry's store.'

'What do you mean?'

'Harry's dead.'

'What?'

'Harry's dead. He went running after you along Seventh Avenue as you were driving away in the cab. The strain was too much for him. His heart gave out, and he died there on the street.'

'I don't believe you.'

'Believe it, buster. Harry's dead, and you killed him. Poor, stupid Harry. All he ever did was love you, and you pay him back by luring him into some crummy extortion scheme. Nice work, kid. You must be very proud of yourself.'

'It's not true. Harry's alive.'

'Call the morgue at Methodist Hospital in Brooklyn, then. You don't have to take my word for it. Just ask the guys in the white coats.'

'I will. That's exactly what I'll do.'

'Good. In the meantime, don't forget to call the movers. Harry's books stay in Harry's store. If you show up at Brightman's Attic tomorrow, I'll break your neck. And then I'll turn you over to the cops. Do you understand me, Gordon? I'm letting you off easy. I know all about the forged manuscript page, the ten-thousand-dollar check, everything. It's just that I don't want to see Harry's name get dragged into it. The man's dead, and I'll be damned if I do anything to hurt his reputation now. But that's only if you act like a good boy. You do what I tell you to do, or else I switch to Plan B and go after you with everything I've got. Do you hear me? I'll have you busted and thrown into jail. I'll fuck you up so bad, you won't want to live anymore.'

ADIEU

Rufus wanted no part of the building or the store. He wanted no part of Brooklyn, no part of New York City, no part of America. The only America he believed in was the one that had Harry Brightman in it, and now that Harry had left the country, Rufus felt it was time for him to be going home.

'I'll live with my granny in Kingston,' he said. 'She's my friend, the only friend I have in the world.'

Such was his startling reaction to the news of Harry's will. As for Tom, he just sat there in silence, not knowing what to think.

I returned to the upstairs apartment a little past ten. Nancy had already gone home to be with her children; Lucy had fallen asleep in front of the television and had since been transferred to Harry's bed, where she was stretched out on top of the covers with her clothes on and her mouth open, gurgling softly in the warm New York night; Tom and Rufus were in the living room, sitting in chairs and smoking. Tom looked pensive as he dragged on his Camel Filter. Rufus, who

271

was puffing on what appeared to be a joint, looked a little crazed.

High or not, he talked with great clarity after I read Harry's will to them. His mind was made up, and no matter what Tom said to him, he wouldn't budge from his position. The only thing he wanted was to talk about Harry, which he proceeded to do at great length, giving a long-winded, emotional account of their first meeting – Rufus in tears, having just been thrown out of the apartment he shared with his friend Tyrone, and Harry stepping out of the darkness, putting his arm around his shoulder, and asking if there was anything he could do to help – and then moving on to the thousand selfless acts Harry had bestowed on him over the past three years, in particular the offer of a job, but also paying for the costumes and jewelry he used in his Tina Hott performances, not to speak of Harry's unflagging generosity with the doctors' bills and his willingness to spring for the expensive medicines that were keeping Rufus alive. Was there ever a man as good as Harry Brightman? he asked. Not that he knew of, he said, answering his own question, and then, for the umpteenth time that night, he broke down and wept.

'You don't have any choice,' Tom said, finally emerging from his dazed silence. 'Whether you stay here or not, the money belongs to both of us. We're partners, and there's no way I'm going to steal your share. Half and half, Rufus. We split everything right down the middle.'

'Just send me the money for my meds,' Rufus whispered. 'I don't want anything else.'

'We'll sell the building and the store,' Tom said. 'We'll get rid of everything and share the profits.'

'No, Tommy,' Rufus said. 'You keep it. You're so smart, man, you'll make yourself rich if you hold on. This place isn't for me. I don't know nothing about books. I'm just a freak, man, a little colored freak who doesn't belong here. A girl in a boy's body. A dying boy who wants to go home.'

'You're not going to die,' Tom said. 'Your health is good.'

'We all die, baby,' Rufus said, lighting up another joint. 'Don't take it so hard. I'm cool with it, man. My granny will take good care of me. Just remember to call every once in a while, okay? Promise me that, Tommy. If you forget my birthday, I don't think I'll ever forgive you.'

As I listened to this exchange between the two young men, I began to feel somewhat choked up myself. It wasn't like me to succumb to strong displays of sentiment, but I was still reeling from my talk with Dryer, which had taken a lot more out of me than I had expected it would. I had assumed the role of tough guy for the confrontation, and I had borne down on him with a viciousness that made me sound like some gravel-voiced hood from an old B-movie. It wasn't that Dryer didn't deserve the full treatment, but until the words came out of my mouth, I hadn't known I was capable of such coarseness, of such brutality. Now, just minutes after that talk had ended, I was in the upstairs apartment again, listening to Rufus Sprague turn down the very things Dryer had wanted to steal from Harry. The contrast was too stark, too overwhelming not to feel moved by the differences between the two men. And yet Harry had loved them both, had stuck by each one of them with the same helpless ardor, the same unquestioning devotion. How was such a thing possible? I asked myself. How could a person so thoroughly misjudge one man and at the same time so accurately penetrate the true character of another? Rufus was just twenty-six or twenty-seven years old. Physically, he resembled an exotic creature from some alien planet, and with his small, perfect head, his honey-colored face, and his slender, elongated limbs, he was the very embodiment of the weakling, the pushover, the pansy. But there was something fierce in him as well, an unusual sort of idealism that rejected the vanities and desires that make the rest of us so vulnerable to the temptations of the world. For his sake, I hoped he would change his mind about the inheritance. I hoped he would start thinking like the rest of us and accept the property that had been left to him, but as I listened to Tom argue with him for the next two hours, I realized it was never going to happen.

The following day was given over to practical chores. Phone calls to Harry's friends (handled by Rufus), calls to Bette in Chicago and fellow book dealers in New York (handled by Tom), and calls to various funeral parlors around Brooklyn (handled by me). In his will, Harry had left instructions that his body should be cremated, but he hadn't stipulated how or where the ashes should be disposed of. After a lengthy discussion, it was decided that we would scatter them in a wooded area of Prospect Park. By New York City law, you aren't supposed to dump the ashes of dead people in public places, but we figured that if we secluded ourselves in some remote, rarely traveled spot, no one would notice us. The bill for burning Harry's body and securing the remains in a metal box tallied up to just over fifteen hundred dollars. With no one else in a position to contribute, I covered the entire cost myself.

On the afternoon of the ceremony – Sunday, June eleventh – I left Lucy with a babysitter and walked to the park with Tom, who carried the box of ashes in a green shopping bag with the Brightman's Attic logo on it. The weather had been vile since the start of the weekend, a sweltering, oppressive, ninety-six-degree onslaught of humidity and pounding light, and Sunday was the worst day of all, one of those barely breathable moments when New York is turned into an equatorial jungle outpost, the hottest, foulest place on earth. Simply to move was to feel your body awash in sweat.

The weather was probably responsible for the sparse turnout. Harry's Manhattan friends had opted to stay at home in their air-conditioned apartments, and our number was therefore reduced to a smattering of neighborhood loyalists. Among them were three or four Seventh Avenue shopkeepers, the owner of Harry's regular lunch spot, and the woman who had cut and dyed his hair. Nancy Mazzucchelli was present, of course, as was her husband, the ersatz James Joyce, better known as Jim or Jimmy. It was the first time I had met him, and I'm sorry to report that I was not favorably impressed. He was as tall and handsome as Tom had advertised, but he kept grumbling about the heat and the gnats swarming in the woods, and I took those complaints as a sign of childishness and inappropriate self-regard, particularly when he had come to pay his last respects to a man who would no longer have the pleasure of complaining about anything.

But no matter. There was only one thing that counted that day, and it wasn't connected to Nancy's husband or the weather. It was all about Rufus, who turned up twenty minutes after the rest of the party had assembled, striding into the gnat-filled copse just as we were about to begin the ceremony without him. By then, the prevailing opinion was that he had chickened out, that the prospect of seeing Harry reduced to an urnful of ashes had been too much for him, and he hadn't been up to the ordeal. Nevertheless, we gave him the benefit of the doubt, standing around in the turgid, suffocating air for all those minutes as we mopped our faces and checked the time on our wristwatches, hoping we had been wrong. When he finally appeared, it took a few moments before anyone recognized him. It wasn't Rufus Sprague who had joined us – it was Tina Hott, and the transformation was so radical, so mesmerizing, that I actually heard someone behind me gasp.

He was one of the most beautiful women I had ever seen. Decked out in full widow's regalia, with a tight black dress, three-inch black heels, and a black pillbox hat with a delicate black veil, he had turned himself into an incarnation of absolute femininity, an idea of the feminine that surpassed anything that existed in the realm of natural womanhood. The auburn wig looked like real hair; the breasts looked like real breasts; the makeup had been applied with skill and precision; and Tina's legs were so long and lovely to look at, it was impossible to believe that they were attached to a man.

But there was more to the effect she created than mere surface trappings, more than just clothes or wigs or makeup. The inner light of the feminine was there as well, and Tina's dignified, sorrowful bearing was a perfect representation of grieving widowhood, a performance by an actress of immense talent. All through the ceremony, she didn't say a word, standing among us in total silence as people delivered short speeches about Harry and Tom then opened the box and spread the ashes out on the ground. It seemed as if our business had been concluded, but before we turned to go, a chubby black boy of about twelve emerged from the fringes of the small forest and approached the group. There was a portable CD player in his outstretched arms, and he carried it as if he were bearing a crown on a velvet pillow. The boy, who was later identified as Rufus's cousin, placed the boom box at Tina's feet and pushed a button. Suddenly, Tina opened her mouth, and as the first bars of orchestral music came pouring through the speakers, she began lip-synching the words of the song that followed. After a moment or two, I recognized the voice of Lena Horne, singing the old song from *Show Boat*, 'Can't Help Lovin' Dat Man.' This was how Tina Hott performed in her Saturday night cabaret appearances: not as a singer, but as a faux-singer, mouthing the words of show tunes and jazz standards as sung by legendary female vocalists. It was magnificent and absurd. It was funny and heartbreaking. It was moving and comical. It was everything it was and everything it wasn't. And there was Tina, gesturing with her arms as she pretended to belt out the words of the song. Her face was all tenderness and love. Her eyes were wet with tears, and we all stood there transfixed, not knowing whether to cry with her or to laugh. As far as I'm concerned, it was one of the strangest, most transcendent moments of my life.

> Fish gotta swim, birds gotta fly
> I gotta love one man 'til I die . . .

That evening, Rufus boarded a plane and flew home to Jamaica. To the best of my knowledge, he has not been back since.

FURTHER DEVELOPMENTS

Tom was confused. So much had happened in such a short period of time, he felt unprepared to deal with the wealth of possibilities that had opened before him. Did he want to take over Harry's business and spend the rest of his days trafficking in rare and used books from a Park Slope storefront? Or, as he had proposed on the night of Harry's death, should he simply sell the whole operation and split the proceeds with Rufus? The fact that Rufus didn't want the money was of little importance. The building was a valuable piece of property, and if Rufus persisted in turning down his half of the sale, Tom would see to it that his grandmother accepted for him. Selling would generate a large sum of cash, no less than several hundred thousand dollars for each of them, and with his share Tom would be able to reinvent himself from the bottom up, to take off in any direction he wanted. But what did he want? That was the fundamental question, and for the time being it was the one question that had no answer. Was Tom still interested in pursuing the idea of the Hotel Existence?

Or would he prefer to return to his original post-Michigan plan and look for a job as a high school English teacher? And, if so, where? Did he want to stay in New York, or was he ready to pack it in and move to the country? We discussed these matters a hundred times in the days that followed, but other than giving up his tiny apartment and temporarily installing himself in Harry's place above the store, Tom continued to waffle, to brood, to sulk. Fortunately, he was under no immediate pressure to make a decision. Harry's will was about to commence its laborious journey through probate, and it would be months before the deed to the building was turned over to the beneficiaries. As for Harry's other assets – his meager bank account, a few stocks and bonds – those were frozen as well. Tom was sitting on a mountain of gold, but until the lawyers at Flynn, Bernstein, and Vallaro wrapped up the affairs of Harry's estate, he would actually be worse off than he had been before. He had lost his weekly salary, and unless he kept Brightman's Attic running at full tilt, he would scarcely have any income at all. I offered to lend him money, but he refused to consider it. Nor was he terribly keen on my suggestion that he shut down the business for the summer and go on a long vacation with Lucy and me. He owed it to Harry to keep the Attic alive, he said. It was a moral debt, and he felt honor-bound to stick it out to the end. Fine, I said. But how are you going to run the store on your own?

Rufus is gone, which means you don't have a sales-clerk. And you can't afford to hire a new one, can you? Where's his salary going to come from?

For the first time in all the years I had known him, Tom lost his temper. 'Fuck it, Nathan,' he said. 'Who the hell cares? I'll figure something out. Just mind your own business, okay?'

But Tom's business was also my business, and it pained me to see him in such a difficult spot. That's when I volunteered my services to the cause – for the nominal salary of one dollar a month. I would take over for Rufus, I said, and for as long as neces-sary I would suspend my retirement to carry out the taxing responsibilities of salesclerk on the ground floor of Brightman's Attic. If Tom wanted me to, I would even be happy to call him Boss.

And so it was that a new era of our lives began. I enrolled Lucy in a summer arts camp at the Berkeley Carroll School on Lincoln Place, and every morning after walking her the seven and a half blocks between apartment and camp, I would stroll back down the avenue and take my place behind the counter of the store. My work on *The Book of Human Follies* suffered from this altered routine, but I kept my hand in as best I could, scribbling during the late-night hours after Lucy had gone to bed, stealing fifteen minutes here or twenty minutes there whenever business in the store was slow. Much to my regret, the daily lunches with Tom were discon-tinued. There simply wasn't enough time to indulge in long, sit-down meals anymore, so we turned ourselves into brown baggers instead, eating our sandwiches and drinking our iced coffees in the stuffy confines of the Attic, polishing off the food in a matter of minutes. At four o'clock, Tom would relieve me of my duties behind the counter so I could fetch Lucy at camp. I would bring her back to the shop, and until we closed up at six, she would entertain herself by reading one of the four thousand two hundred books that lined the shelves on the ground floor.

Lucy remained a puzzle to me. In many respects, she was a model child, and the better we got to know each other, the more I liked her, the more I enjoyed having her around. Forgetting the question of her mother for a moment, there were a thousand positive things to be said about our girl. A complete stranger to big-city life, she adapted quickly to her new surroundings and began to feel at home in the neighborhood almost at once. Wherever Carolina Carolina might have been, the only language spoken there was English. Now, as we took our walks up and down Seventh Avenue, passing the dry cleaner, the grocery store, the bakery, the beauty parlor, the news-stand, the coffee shop, she was assaulted by a plethora of different tongues. She heard Spanish and Korean, Russian and Chinese, Arabic and Greek, Japanese, German, and French, but rather than feel intimidated or perplexed, she exulted in this variety of human sound. 'I want to talk like that,' she said to me one morning as we walked by the open door of some establishment or other and saw a dumpy little woman screaming at an old man. '*Mira! Mira! Mira!*' Lucy said, aping the woman's voice with uncanny exactitude. '*Hombre! Gato! Sucio!*' A minute later, she was doing a similar rendition of a man calling out to someone across the street in Arabic – words I wouldn't have been able to pronounce if my life had depended on it. The kid had an ear, and eyes to see with, and a mind to think with, and a heart to feel with. She had no trouble making friends at the camp, and by the end of the first week she had already been invited over by three different girls for so-called play dates. She didn't recoil from my good-night kisses and hugs; she wasn't picky about her food; she rarely made a fuss about anything. In spite of her frequently atrocious grammar (which I decided not to correct) and in spite of her fixation with watching TV cartoons (I put my foot down and limited her to one hour a day), I never once regretted having taken her in.

Still, there was the unsettling fact of her refusal to talk about her mother. Aurora was the unseen presence who dominated our little household, and no matter how many questions I asked, no matter how often I tried to trick Lucy into divulging some scrap of pertinent information, I continued to get nowhere. I suppose there was something admirable about such willpower in one so young, but I found it infuriating, and the longer the stand off went on, the more frustrated I became.

'You miss your mother, Lucy, don't you?' I asked her one night.

284

'I miss her something terrible,' she said. 'I miss her so bad, my heart aches.'

'You want to see her again, don't you?'

'More than anything. Every night I pray to God she'll come back to me.'

'She will. All you have to do is tell me where we can find her.'

'I'm not supposed to, Uncle Nat. I keep telling you the same thing, but it's like you don't hear what I'm saying.'

'I hear you. It's just that I don't want you to be sad anymore.'

'I can't talk about it. I made a promise, and if I break my promise, I'll burn in hell. Hell is forever, and I'm still a little girl. I'm not ready to burn forever.'

'There is no hell, Lucy. And you're not going to burn, not for one minute. Everyone loves your mother, and all we want to do is help her.'

'No, sir. That ain't the way it is. Please, Uncle Nat. Don't ask me any more questions about Mama. She's all right, and one day she'll come back to me. That's what I know, and that's the only thing I can tell you. If you keep it up, I'll just go back to the way I was when I first came here. I'll clamp my lips shut and won't say a word to you. And where would that get us? We have such a nice time when we talk together. As long as you're not asking me about Mama, it's about the best fun I have. Talking to you, I mean. You're such a jolly old soul, Uncle Nat. We don't want to spoil a good thing, do we?'

Outwardly, she appeared to be the happiest, most contented of children, but it disturbed me to think of the torments she must have been living through in order to hold on to her secret. It was too much to ask a nine-and-a-half-year-old person to walk around with such a heavy responsibility. Damage was being done to her, and I couldn't figure out a way to stop it. I talked to Tom about sending her to a psychiatrist, but he thought it would only be a waste of time and money. If Lucy wouldn't talk to us, then she certainly wouldn't talk to a stranger. 'We have to be patient,' he said. 'Sooner or later, it will become too much for her, and then everything will come pouring out. But she won't say a word until she's good and ready.' I took Tom's advice and temporarily bagged the idea of a doctor, but that didn't mean I thought much of his opinion. The kid was never going to be ready. She was so tough, so stubborn, so damned unbreakable, I was convinced she could hold out forever.

I started working for Tom on the fourteenth, three days after Harry's ashes were scattered in Prospect Park and Rufus went home to his Jamaican granny. The day after that, my daughter returned from England. I had been thinking about the fifteenth ever since my disastrous conversation with the now unmentionable one who had mothered my child, but in the maelstrom of events that followed our abrupt departure from the Chowder Inn, I had been too preoccupied to keep track of dates. It was indeed the fifteenth of June, but I was too out of it by then to know that. After closing up the store at six, Tom, Lucy, and I had an early dinner at the Second Street Café, and then Lucy and I returned to my apartment, where we were planning to spend the evening battling each other at a game of Monopoly or Clue. That was when I heard Rachel's message on the answering machine. Her plane had landed at one; she had walked into her house at three; she had read my letter at five. From the tone of her voice when she spoke the word *letter*, I understood that all was forgiven. 'Thank you, Dad,' she said. 'You have no idea how important it is to me. So much bad stuff has been happening lately, it's exactly what I needed to hear. If I can count on you now, I think I'll be able to get through anything.'

The next night, Tom babysat for Lucy, and I had dinner with Rachel in midtown Manhattan, not far from my old office at Mid-Atlantic Accident and Life. How rapidly the world shifts around us; how rapidly one problem is replaced by another, with scarcely a moment to bask in our victories. For close to a month, I had been fretting over the note I'd sent to my angry, alienated daughter, praying that my abject words of apology would cut through years of resentment and give me a second chance with her. By some miracle, the letter had accomplished everything I had hoped it would. We were back on solid ground together, and with all the acrimonies of the past now forgotten, the dinner that night should have been a joyous reunion, a time for jokes and laughter and whimsical recollections. But no sooner had I re-established myself as Rachel's father than I was called upon to help her through the worst predicament of her adult life. My girl was going through 'bad stuff.' She was in crisis, and who else could she turn to but her old man – incompetent fool though he might have been?

I booked a table for us at La Grenouille, the same exorbitantly priced, fussily decorated old New York-style French restaurant where (name deleted) and I had taken her to celebrate her eighteenth birthday. She showed up wearing the necklace I had sent her, the twin to the one that had caused so much grief at the Cosmic Diner, and glad as I was to see how well it suited her, how attractive it looked against the darkness of her eyes and hair, I couldn't help thinking about the other necklace at the same time, which provoked several pangs of remorse as I relived the disaster I had brought down on Marina Gonzalez. So many young women in their late twenties and early thirties, I said to myself, so many young female lives swirling around me. Marina. Honey Chowder. Nancy Mazzucchelli. Aurora. Rachel. Of all the women in that group, my daughter struck me as the most balanced and successful, the most solid, the one least likely to be swamped with difficulties, and yet there she was sitting across the table from me with tears in her eyes, telling me that her marriage was falling apart.

288

'I don't understand,' I said. 'The last time I saw you, everything was going well. Terrence was terrific. You were terrific. You'd just had your second anniversary, and you told me they'd been the happiest two years of your life. When was that? Late March? Early April? Marriages don't crumble that fast. Not when people are in love.'

'I'm still in love,' Rachel answered. 'It's Terrence I'm worried about.'

'The guy chased you halfway around the world to talk you into marrying him. Remember? He was the one who went after you. At first, you weren't even sure if you liked him.'

'That was a long time ago. This is now.'

'The last time we talked about now, you said you were thinking about having babies. You said Terrence was dying to become a father. Not a father in the abstract – but the father of your child. That's what men say when they're in love with the woman they live with.'

'I know. That's what I thought, too. But then we went to England.'

'America, England. What's the difference? You're still the same people wherever you are.'

'Maybe so. But Georgina isn't in America. She's in England.'

'Ah. So that's where we're going. Why didn't you come right out and say it?'

'It's hard. Just mentioning her name turns my stomach.'

'If it's any comfort, I find it a ridiculous name.

Georgina. It makes me think of some giggly Victorian girl with golden ringlets and fat red jowls.'

'She's a mousy little brunette with greasy hair and bad skin.'

'Doesn't sound like much competition to me.'

'She and Terrence went to university together. She was his first big love. Then she fell for someone else and broke up with him. That's when he came to America. He was so depressed, Dad. He told me he thought of committing suicide.'

'And now the someone else is out of the picture.'

'I'm not sure. All I know is that when we were in London, the three of us had dinner together, and Terrence couldn't take his eyes off her. It was like I wasn't even there. After that, he wouldn't stop talking about her. Georgina is so smart. Georgina is so funny. Georgina is such a good person. Two days later, he had lunch with her alone. Then we went to Cornwall to visit his parents, but after three or four days he took the train back to London to talk to his publisher about the book he's been writing. Or so he said. I think he went back to be with stupid Georgina Watson, the love of his life. It was so awful. He just left me out there in the country with his right-wing, anti-Semitic parents, and all I could do was pretend I was enjoying every minute of it. He slept with her. I know he did. He slept with her, and now he doesn't love me anymore.'

'Did you ask him?'

'You bet I did. The minute he came back to his

parents' house. We had a terrible fight. The worst fight since I've known him.'

'And what did he say?'

'He denied it. He said I was jealous and making up stories.'

'That's a good sign, Rachel.'

'Good? What do you mean good? He was lying to me, and now I'm never going to be able to trust him again.'

'Assume the worst. Assume that he slept with her and then came back and lied to you. It's still a good sign.'

'How can you keep saying that?'

'Because it means he doesn't want to lose you. He doesn't want the marriage to end.'

'What kind of marriage is that? When you can't trust the man you're married to, it's like not being married at all.'

'Look, dumpling, far be it from me to offer you advice. When it comes to marriage, I'm the least qualified person in the world to tell anyone what to do. You lived in the same house with me for the first eighteen years of your life, and I don't have to remind you what a botch of it I made with your mother. There were moments when I felt so sick of her, I actually wished she would die. I would imagine car crashes, train wrecks, falls down enormous flights of stairs. This is a terrible confession to make, and I don't want you to think I'm proud of myself – but it's important that you understand what a bad marriage is. Your mother and I had a bad marriage. We loved each other for a while, and then it all went bad. But still, we stuck it out for a long time, and bad as we were together, we managed to make you. You're the happy ending to the whole tragic story, and because you are who you are, I don't have a single regret about anything. Do you understand me, Rachel? I don't know Terrence well enough to have an opinion about him. But I do know that you don't have a bad marriage. People slip up. They do dumb things. But Georgina is on the other side of the ocean now, and unless you've linked yourself up with an incurable skirt chaser, I suspect this little episode is over and done with. Stick it out for a while and see what happens. Don't do anything rash. He told you he was innocent, and who's to say he wasn't telling the truth? Old loves are hard to get out of your system. Maybe Terrence had his head turned for a couple of moments, but now he's back in America with you, and if you love him as much as you say you do, there's a good chance everything will work out. As long as he doesn't turn into the kind of shit husband your father was, there's hope. Lots of hope. Hope for a happy future together. Hope for babies. Hope for cats and dogs. Hope for trees and flowers. Hope for America. Hope for England. Hope for the world.'

I had no idea what I was saying. The words tumbled out of me in a mad rush, an unstoppable deluge of nonsense and over-cooked emotions, and when I came to the end of my ridiculous speech, I saw that Rachel was smiling, smiling for the first time since she had walked into the restaurant. Perhaps that was all I could hope to accomplish. To let her know that I was with her, that I believed in her, and that the situation probably wasn't as dark as she thought it was. If nothing else, the smile told me that she was beginning to calm down, and as I kept on talking, I slowly steered her away from the subject at hand, knowing that the best medicine would be to make her forget Terrence for a while, to stop her from dwelling on the problem that had been obsessing her for weeks. Chapter by chapter, I filled her in on all the things that had happened to me since we'd last been together. Essentially, it was a truncated version of everything I've set down in this book so far. No, not quite everything – since I edited out the story of Marina and the other necklace (too sad, too humiliating), said nothing about my ugly telephone conversation with the unmentionable one, and spared her the painful details of the *Scarlet Letter* hoax. But nearly all the other elements were accounted for: *The Book of Human Folly*, cousin Tom, Harry Brightman, little Lucy, the trip to Vermont, Tom's fling with Honey Chowder, the contents of Harry's will, Tina Hott mouthing the words of 'Can't Help Lovin' Dat Man.' Rachel listened closely, doing her best to absorb so much startling information as she swallowed her food and drank her wine. As for me, the more I talked, the more I enjoyed myself. I had slipped into the role of ancient mariner, and I could have gone on spinning my tales until the end of the night. Rachel was especially eager to meet Lucy, and so we arranged for her to visit my apartment the following Sunday – with or without her husband, as she preferred. She was also looking forward to seeing Tom, she said, and then she asked the sixty-four-thousand-dollar question, 'What about Honey? Do you think anything is going to happen?'

'I doubt it,' I said. 'Tom left his number with her father and asked him to give it to her, but she hasn't called. And as far as I know, Tom hasn't called her. If I were a betting man, I'd say we've seen the last of Honey. Too bad, but the case appears to be closed.'

As usual, I was wrong. Exactly two weeks after my dinner with Rachel, on the last Friday of the month, Honey Chowder came striding into the bookstore wearing a white summer dress and a large straw hat with a floppy brim. It was five o'clock in the afternoon. Tom was sitting behind the front counter, reading an old softcover edition of *The Federalist Papers*. I had already picked up Lucy at camp, and she and I were in the back of the store, rearranging books in the History section. Not a single customer had been in for the past two hours, and the only sound to be heard was the muffled whir of an electric fan.

Lucy's face brightened when she saw Honey walk in. She was about to go running toward her, but I put my hand on her arm and whispered,

'Not yet, Lucy. Give them a chance to talk first.' Honey, whose eyes were fixed on Tom, hadn't noticed we were there. Like two secret agents, our girl and yours truly hid behind one of the bookcases and observed the following exchange.

'Hey there, Tom,' Honey said, plopping her purse down on the counter. Then she removed her hat and shook out her long, opulent hair. 'How's life?'

Tom glanced up from his book and said, 'Good Lord, Honey. What are you doing here?'

'We'll get to that later. First, I want to know how you are.'

'Not bad. Busy, a bit stressed out, but not bad. A lot has happened since I last saw you. My boss died, and it seems that I've inherited this store. I'm still trying to figure out what to do with it.'

'I'm not talking about business. I'm talking about you. The inner workings of your heart.'

'My heart? It's still beating. Seventy-two times a minute.'

'Which means you're still alone, doesn't it? If you'd fallen in love with someone, it would beat much faster than that.'

'Love? What are you talking about?'

'You haven't met anyone in the past month, have you?'

'No. Of course not. I've been much too busy.'

'Do you remember Vermont?'

'How could I forget it?'

'And the last night you were there. Do you remember that?'

'Yes. I remember that night.'

'And?'

'And what?'

'What do you see when you look at me, Tom?'

'I don't know, Honey. I see you. Honey Chowder. A woman with an impossible name. An impossible woman with an impossible name.'

'Do you know what I see when I look at you, Tom?'

'I'm not sure I want to know.'

'I see a great man, that's what I see. I see the finest person I've ever met.'

'Oh?'

'Yes, *oh*. And because that's what I see when I look at you, I've chucked everything and come down to Brooklyn to be part of your life.'

'Chucked everything?'

'That's right. The school year ended two days ago, and I gave them notice. I'm free as a bird.'

'But Honey, I'm not in love with you. I hardly even know you.'

'You will.'

'Will what?'

'First, you'll get to know me. And then you'll start to love me.'

'Just like that.'

'Yes. Just like that.' She paused for a moment and smiled. 'How's Lucy, by the way?'

'Lucy's fine. She's living with Nathan on First Street.'

'Poor Nathan. He's not up to all that work. The

girl needs a mother. From now on, she'll live with us.'

'You're awfully damn sure of yourself, aren't you?'

'I have to be, Tom. If I wasn't sure of myself, I wouldn't be here. I wouldn't have all my bags waiting outside in the car. I wouldn't know that you were the man of my life.'

At that point, I figured they had said enough to each other, and I let Lucy come out of hiding. She rushed across the room, heading straight for Honey.

'There you are, my little munchkin,' the ex-schoolteacher said, wrapping our girl in her arms and lifting her off the ground. When she finally put her down again, she asked, 'Did you hear what Tom and I were saying?'

Lucy nodded.

'And what do you think?'

'I think it's a nice plan,' Lucy said. 'If I live with you and Uncle Tom, I won't have to eat in restaurants anymore. You'll stuff me with all that tasty food you cook. And Uncle Nat can eat with us whenever he likes. And when you and Uncle Tom go out on the town, he can be my babysitter.'

Honey grinned. 'And you're going to be a good girl, aren't you? The best girl in the world.'

'No, ma'am,' Lucy said, looking back at her with the deadest of deadpan faces. 'I'm gonna be bad. I'm gonna be the baddest, meanest, cussingest little girl in the whole of God's creation.'

HAWTHORN STREET OR HAWTHORNE STREET?

Months passed. By the middle of October, the lawyers had finished their work on Harry's estate, and Tom and Rufus had become the legitimate owners of Brightman's Attic and the building it was housed in. Tom and Honey were already married by then, and Lucy, silent as ever on the subject of her mother's whereabouts, was enrolled as a fifth grader at the local public school, P.S. 321. Rachel was still with Terrence. One week after the Wood-Chowder wedding, she called to tell me that she was two months pregnant.

I continued to work in the bookstore, but after Honey's dramatic appearance at the end of June, we began sharing the job, which meant that I had to be there only half the time. On my days off I continued jotting down anecdotes for *The Book of Human Folly*, and just as Lucy had suggested, I filled in as babysitter whenever Tom and Honey went out at night. In their first months together, that proved to be a common occurrence. Honey had felt starved in the provinces, and now that she had landed in New York, she wanted to take advantage of everything the city had to offer: plays, movies, concerts, dance performances, poetry readings, moonlight jaunts on the Staten Island ferry. It did me good to see how the slothful, bovine Tom flourished under the energetic influence of his newfound wife. Within days of Honey's arrival, he ceased dithering about what to do with the inheritance and decided to put the building on the market. With their half of the money from the sale, they would have more than enough to buy a two- or three-bedroom apartment in the neighborhood, along with something left over to carry them until they found regular jobs – most likely as teachers in a private school for the next academic year. Months passed, and by mid-October Tom had lost close to twenty pounds, which brought him halfway back to resembling the young Dr Thumb of yore. Home cooking obviously agreed with him, and in spite of his predictions to the contrary, Honey didn't wear him out or beat him down or crush his spirit. Day by day, she slowly turned him into the man he was always destined to become.

With so many positive developments in the love department, the reader might be lulled into thinking that universal happiness reigned over our little patch of Brooklyn. Alas, not all marriages are destined to survive. Everyone knows that, but who among us would have guessed that the least happy person in the neighborhood during those months was Tom's former flame, the Beautiful Perfect Mother? It was true that her husband had made a bad impression on me in the woods of Prospect Park, but not in a hundred years would I have supposed he was dumb enough to take a wife like his for granted. The Nancy Mazzucchellis of this world are few and far between, and if a man should be lucky enough to win a Mazzucchelli heart, his job from that point on is to do everything in his power not to lose it. But men (as I have amply demonstrated in earlier chapters of this book) are stupid creatures, and pretty boy James Joyce turned out to be stupider than most. Because Nancy's mother and I struck up a friendship that summer (more about that later), I was a frequent dinner guest of the family, and it was within the precincts of their house on Carroll Street that I learned about Jimmy's past transgressions and saw his marriage to Nancy burst asunder. The tomfoolery had started even before there was such a person as the B.P.M. – a good six years back, when Nancy was pregnant with her first child, Devon. When she learned about her husband's affair with a Tribeca barmaid, she temporarily threw him out of the house, but once the baby was born, she didn't have the strength to resist his tearful promises that it would never happen again. But words count for little in such matters, and who knows how many secret liaisons followed? By Joyce's estimate, there were no less than seven or eight, counting one-night stands and quick fucks in the back stairwell at work. Nancy, ever generous and forgiving, tended to discount the rumors. But then Jim fell for fellow Foley walker Martha Ives, and that was that. He said he was in love, and on August 11, 2000, two months after I first saw him at Harry's funeral service, he packed up his bags and left.

Twelve days later, my oncologist told me that my lungs were still clean.

A scant four days after that, Rachel, in cahoots with Tom and Honey, hatched a devilish plot to trick me into thinking I was about to attend a ball game at Shea Stadium – when in fact it was a surprise party for my sixtieth birthday. The plan was for me to pick up Tom at his apartment, but the moment I walked through the door, a dozen people mobbed me with hugs, kisses, and slaps on the back, not to mention an outburst of wild shouting and singing. I was so unprepared for this assault of good will, I nearly threw up from the shock it gave to my system. The festivities lasted well into the night, and at one point I was prevailed upon to stand up and deliver a speech. The champagne had long since gone to my head, and I think I rambled for some time, spouting gibberish and incoherent jokes as my half-potted audience struggled to follow what I was saying. About the only thing that comes back to me from that screwy discourse is a brief aside on the linguistic acumen of Casey Stengel. If memory serves me right, I think I even ended my talk with a quotation from the master himself. 'They didn't call him the Old Professor for nothing,' I said. 'Not only was he the first manager of our beloved Mets, but, even more essential to the general good of mankind, he was the author of numerous sentences that have reshaped our understanding of the English language. Before I sit down, allow me to leave you with this priceless, unforgettable pearl, which sums up my own experience more accurately than any statement I've come across in the sixty years I've dwelled inside this flesh: "There comes a time in every man's life, and I've had plenty of them."'

The Subway Series came and went; the weather turned cool; Gore was running against Bush. To my mind, the outcome was never in doubt. Even with Nader gumming up the works, it seemed impossible that the Democrats could be defeated, and wherever I went in the neighborhood, almost everyone I talked to was of the same opinion. Only Tom, the most pessimistic of men when it came to American politics, looked worried. He believed it was too close to call, and if Bush turned out to be the winner, he said, we could forget all that claptrap about 'compassionate conservatism.' The man wasn't a conservative. He was an ideologue of the extreme right, and the instant he was sworn into office, the government would be controlled by lunatics.

Just one week before the election, Aurora finally surfaced – only to vanish again within thirty seconds. Contact came in the form of a telephone call to Tom, but no one was in the apartment that morning, and therefore we had nothing to go on but a truncated message left on the answering machine. I don't know how many times I listened to that message with Tom and Honey, but we rewound the tape often enough for me to have memorized every sentence of it. Each time I heard her voice, she sounded a little more despairing, a little more on edge, a little more afraid. She spoke softly, barely rising above a whisper from start to finish, but her words were so deadly, they carried all the impact of a scream.

Tom. It's me, Rory. I'm calling from a pay phone and I don't have much time. I know you've probably had it with me, but I've been missing Lucy so much, I just wanted to find out how she is. Don't think it was fun, Tommy. I thought and thought, but you were the only person I could count on. She couldn't stay here anymore. It's all going to pieces. It's bad news. I've been trying to get out myself, but it's too hard, I'm never alone . . . Write me a letter, okay? I don't have a phone, but you can reach me at eighty-seven Hawthorn Street in . . . Shit. Gotta go. Sorry. Gotta go.

The receiver slammed down on the hook, and the long-awaited call came to a sudden, inconclusive end. Our darkest anxieties had assumed the weight of fact, and still we had no idea where she was. Tom had been through similar moments with his sister in the past, and though he felt every bit as worried about her as I did, his alarm was tempered by exhaustion, by irritation, by years of disappointment and regret. 'She's the most irresponsible person I've ever known,' he said. 'Lucy's finally beginning to settle in with us, and now, after how many goddamn months, she calls to say she's missing her. What kind of mother is that? She wants me to write to her, and then she doesn't even tell us what town she lives in. It isn't fair, Nathan. Honey and I are doing all we can to help, and the last thing we need is more confusion, more drama. Enough is enough.'

'It might not be fair,' I said, 'but Rory's in some kind of trouble, and we have to find her. There's no other choice. Spare me your judgments until later, all right?'

The entire world changed for me after that. The 2000 election disaster was just a few days down the road, but even as Tom and Honey sat horrified in front of their television set for the next five weeks, watching the Republican Party call in their thugs to challenge the Florida returns and then manipulate the Supreme Court into staging a legal coup on their behalf, even as these offenses were committed against the American people and my nephew and his wife marched in demonstrations, sent letters to their congressman, and signed countless protests and petitions, I was preoccupied with only one thing: to hunt down Rory and bring her back to New York.

Eighty-seven Hawthorn Street. Or maybe it was Hawthorne Street, named after a man instead of a shrub – perhaps even Nathaniel Hawthorne, the long-dead novelist who had inadvertently caused the death of our sad, luckless friend. A bitter conjunction, signifying little or nothing, but spooky for all that, as if the same word appearing in two different contexts established a subterranean link between Harry and Aurora: the one gone forever, the other just beyond reach, both denizens of the invisible. Apart from that single clue, everything was blind guesswork, but because Lucy spoke with a southern accent, and because she had placed her mother in the nonexistent land of Carolina Carolina, I decided to begin my search in the real Carolinas, North and South. The pity was that Aurora and her husband didn't have a phone. If they had been listed in the book, it would have been possible to call information for every town and city in both states and find them by asking for the number of David Minor at 87 Hawthorn(e) Street. A laborious task, but one that was bound to yield a positive result. Since that option wasn't available to me, I had no choice but to proceed in reverse. One Sunday, I took the train down to Princeton Junction and spent twelve hours sitting in front of a computer screen with my pregnant daughter and her meek, chastened husband. Terrence might have lacked charm, but he was a technological superhero, and by the time I returned home the next morning, I had a printout that listed every Hawthorn Street and Hawthorne Street in both Carolinas. To my stupefaction, there were several hundred of them. Too many. In order to visit every number 87 on the list, I would have been on the road for six months.

That was when I turned to Henry Peoples, my old associate at Mid-Atlantic Accident and Life. He had been one of the company's top investigators, and over the years we had worked on a number of cases together, the most spectacular one being the so-called Dubinsky Affair, which had turned Henry into something of a minor legend in the field. Arthur Dubinsky had faked his death at fifty-one by killing a homeless man from the streets of New York and substituting that body for his own in a fiery car crash off a cliff in the Rockies. Maureen, his twenty-eight-year-old third wife, collected on the one-point-six-million-dollar policy, and then, just one month later, sold her Manhattan co-op and vanished from sight. Henry, who had been suspicious of Dubinsky from the start, had continued keeping tabs on Maureen, and when she suddenly upped and left New York, he filed a report with his department chief, who granted him permission to go after her. It took nine months of arduous legwork before he found Mrs Dubinsky – living with her perfectly intact husband on the island of Saint Lucia. We managed to recover eighty-five percent of the policy; Arthur Dubinsky wound up in prison for murder; and Henry and I were rewarded with large bonuses.

I worked with Peoples for more than twenty years, but I'm not going to pretend I ever liked him. He was an odd, unpleasant man who adhered to a strict vegetarian diet and demonstrated all the warmth and personality of an extinguished lamppost. Rumpled polyester suits (mostly brown), thick horn-rim glasses, perpetual dandruff, and an unnerving revulsion against small talk of any kind. You could show up at the office with your arm in a sling or a patch over your eye, and Henry wouldn't say a word. He would stare at you for a while, absorb the details of your injury, and then, without asking how you'd hurt yourself or whether you were in pain, calmly put his report on your desk.

Still, he had a knack for wriggling into holes and scaring up missing people, and now that he was retired, I wondered if he wouldn't be willing to take on the job for me. Fortunately, he hadn't moved from his old apartment in Queens, which he shared with his widowed sister and four cats. When I dialed his number, he picked up on the second ring.

'Just name a price,' I said. 'I'll pay anything you ask.'

'I don't want your money, Nathan,' he answered. 'Just cover my expenses, and it's a deal.'

'It could take months. I'd hate to see you lose so much time and get nothing out of it.'

'That's all right. It's not as if I have anything better to do with myself these days. I'll climb back into the saddle, and I'll get to live the glory years all over again.'

'The glory years?'

'Sure. All those good times we had together, Nathan. Dubinsky. Williamson. O'Hara. Lupino. You remember those cases, don't you?'

'Of course I remember them. I didn't know you were such a sentimentalist, Henry.'

'I'm not. Or at least I didn't think I was. But you can count on me. For old times' sake.'

'I'm assuming North Carolina or South Carolina. But I could be wrong.'

'Don't worry. As long as Minor used to have a phone, I'll be able to find him. It's in the bag.'

Six weeks later, Henry called me in the middle of the night and muttered four syllables into my ear: 'Winston-Salem.'

The next morning I was on a plane, flying south into the heart of tobacco country.

THE LAUGHING GIRL

Eighty-seven Hawthorne Street was a shabby two-story house on a half-rural, half-suburban road about three miles from the center of town. I lost my way several times before I found it, and when I parked my rented Ford Escort in the dirt driveway, I noticed that all the blinds on the front windows had been drawn. It was a gloomy, overcast Sunday in mid-December. The logical assumption was that no one was at home – or else that Rory and her husband lived in that house as if it were a cave, guarding themselves against the glare of natural light, fending off the impingements of the outside world, the sole members of a society of two. There was no doorbell, so I knocked. When nothing happened, I knocked again. Ever since Rory had left her message on Tom's machine, we had been expecting her to call back. But no more had been heard from her, and now that I was standing in front of what appeared to be an empty house, I was beginning to suspect that she no longer lived there. All sorts of gruesome thoughts jumped around in my head as I knocked for the third time. What if she had tried to run away, I asked myself, and Minor had caught up with her? What if he had taken her to another city, another state, and we had lost track of her forever? What if he had struck her down and accidentally killed her? What if the end had already come, and I was too late to help her, too late to carry her back to the world she belonged to?

The door opened, and there was Minor in the flesh, a tall, good-looking man of about forty, with dark, neatly combed hair and gentle blue eyes. I had built him up into such a monster over the past months, I was shocked to discover how unthreatening he looked, how *normal*. If there was anything strange about him, it was the fact that he was wearing a long-sleeved white shirt and a blue necktie knotted tightly at the collar. What kind of man walked around the house in a white shirt and tie? I wondered. It took a moment for me to come up with the answer. A man who had been to church, I said to myself. A man who observed the Sabbath and took his religion seriously.

'Yes?' he asked. 'What can I do for you?'

'I'm Rory's uncle,' I said. 'Nathan Glass. I happened to be in the neighborhood and thought I'd drop by to see her.'

'Oh? Is she expecting you?'

'Not that I'm aware of. As I understand it, you don't have a telephone.'

'That's correct. We don't believe in them. They

encourage too much chatter and idle talk. We prefer to save our words for more essential things.'

'Very interesting . . . Mr . . . Mr . . .'

'Minor. David Minor. I'm Aurora's husband.'

'That's what I thought. But I didn't want to presume.'

'Come in, Mr Glass. Unfortunately, Aurora isn't feeling well today. She's upstairs taking a nap, but you're more than welcome to come in. We're very open-minded in this neck of the woods. Even when others don't share our faith, we make every effort to treat them with dignity and respect. It's one of God's holy commandments.'

I smiled but said nothing. He had a pleasant enough manner, but already he was talking like a fanatic, and the last thing I needed was to tangle with him over theological issues. Give him his God and his church, I said to myself. The only reason I was there was to confirm whether Rory was in danger or not – and if she was, to get her out of that house as quickly as I could.

Based on the condition of the exterior (peeling paint, disintegrating shutters, weeds sprouting from the concrete steps), I was prepared to find some squalid assortment of broken, mismatched furniture cluttering the rooms within, but the place turned out to be more than presentable. Rory had inherited June's talent for doing much with little, and she had fashioned the living room into an austere but attractive environment, decorated with potted plants, handmade gingham curtains, and a large poster advertising a Giacometti museum show on the opposite wall. Minor gestured for me to take a seat on the couch, and I sat. He settled into a chair on the other side of the glass coffee table, and for the next few moments neither one of us said a word. I was tempted to plunge in at full tilt – demanding to go upstairs and talk to Aurora, grilling him with questions about Lucy, forcing him to explain why his wife was too scared to call her own brother – but I realized that this approach would probably backfire on me, and so I tiptoed into the conversation as delicately as I could.

'North Carolina,' I began. 'The last we heard, you were living with your mother in Philadelphia. What brought you down here?'

'Several things,' Minor said. 'My sister and her husband live in the area, and they found a good job for me. That job led to an even better job, and now I'm assistant manager at the True Value Hardware Store over at the Camelback Mall. It might not sound like much to you, but it's honest work, and I make a decent living. When I think about what I was like seven or eight years ago, it's a miracle I've come this far. I was a sinner, Mr Glass. I was a drug addict and a fornicator, a liar and a petty criminal, a betrayer of everyone who loved me. Then I found peace in the Lord, and my life was saved. I know it's hard for a Jewish person like yourself to understand us, but we're not just another sect of Bible-thumping,

312

fire-and-brimstone Christians. We don't believe in the apocalypse and the Day of Judgment; we don't believe in the Rapture or the End of Time. We prepare ourselves for life in heaven by living good lives on earth.'

'When you say *we*, who are you talking about?'

'Our church. The Temple of the Holy Word. We're a small group. Our congregation has just sixty members, but the Reverend Bob is an inspired leader, and he's taught us many things. "In the beginning was the Word, and the Word was with God, and the Word was God." '

'The Gospel according to Saint John. Chapter one, verse one.'

'So you're familiar with the Book.'

'To some extent. For a Jew who doesn't believe in God, more than most.'

'Are you telling me you're an atheist?'

'All Jews are atheists. Except for the ones who aren't, of course. But I don't have much to do with them.'

'You're not making fun of me, are you, Mr Glass?'

'No, Mr Minor, I'm not making fun of you. I wouldn't dream of it.'

'Because if you're making fun of me, I'll have to ask you to leave.'

'I'm interested in the Reverend Bob. I want to know what makes his church different from the others.'

'He understands what it means to sacrifice. If

the Word is God, then the words of men mean nothing. They're no more significant than the grunts of animals or the cries of birds. To breathe God into us and absorb His Word, the reverend instructs us to refrain from indulging in the vanity of human speech. That's the sacrifice. One day out of seven, every member of the congregation must maintain a full and unbroken silence for twenty-four straight hours.'

'That must be very difficult.'

'It is at first. But then you begin to adjust, and your days of silence become the most beautiful and fulfilling moments of the week. You can actually feel the presence of God within you.'

'And what happens when someone breaks the silence?'

'He has to begin all over again the next day.'

'And if your child is sick, and you have to call the doctor on your day of silence, what happens then?'

'Married couples are never silent on the same day. You get your spouse to make the call.'

'But how can you call if you don't have a phone?'

'You go to the nearest pay phone.'

'And what about children? Do they have days of silence as well?'

'No, children are exempt. They don't enter the fold until the age of fourteen.'

'Your Reverend Bob has it all figured out, doesn't he?'

'He's a brilliant man, and his teachings make life

better and simpler for us. We're a happy flock, Mr Glass. Every day, I get down on my knees and thank Jesus for sending us to North Carolina. If we hadn't come here, we never would have known the joys of belonging to the Temple of the Holy Word.'

As Minor talked, I had the impression that he would have been satisfied to go on extolling the virtues of the Reverend Bob for another six or ten hours, but I found it curious to see how carefully he avoided mentioning the names of his wife and adopted daughter. I hadn't traveled all the way down from New York to shoot the breeze about True Value Hardware and crack-pot temples of God. Now that we had spent some time together and he was beginning to feel a bit less nervous in my company, I figured the moment had come to change the subject.

'I'm surprised you haven't asked me about Lucy,' I said.

'Lucy?' he replied, looking genuinely taken aback. 'Do you know her?'

'Of course I know her. She's living with Aurora's brother and his new wife. I see her almost every day.'

'I thought you were out of touch with the family. Aurora said you lived in the suburbs somewhere, and no one had seen you in years.'

'That changed about six months ago. I'm back in touch. I'm in touch all the time.'

Minor gave me a short, wistful grin. 'How's the little one doing?'

'Do you care?'

'Of course I care.'

'Then why did you send her away?'

'It wasn't my decision. Aurora didn't want her anymore, and there was nothing I could do to stop her.'

'I don't believe you.'

'You don't know Aurora, Mr Glass. She's not all there in the head. I do everything I can to help and support her, but she shows no gratitude. I pulled her out of the depths of hell and saved her life, but she still won't give in. She still won't believe.'

'Is there any law that says she has to believe what you believe?'

'She's my wife. A wife should follow her husband. It's her duty to follow her husband in all things.'

It was difficult to know where we were headed now. The conversation was branching off in several directions at once, and my instincts were beginning to fail me. Minor's calm, soft-spoken question about Lucy seemed to demonstrate a sincere regard for her well being, and unless he was a ferociously gifted liar, a man who wouldn't hesitate to distort the truth whenever it served his purpose, I found myself in the awkward position of feeling a little sorry for him. At least for a few moments I did, and that sudden, unexpected rush of sympathy caught me with my guard down, turning what was supposed to be a naked clash of wills into something far more complex, far more human. But then he had started bad-mouthing Rory, blaming her for abandoning her own daughter, accusing her of mental instability, and then, even worse, had come out with that idiotic, reactionary pronouncement about marriage. Still, certain facts were nevertheless undeniable. He had rescued her from drugs and fallen in love with her, and based on Rory's past history, who was to say she wasn't prone to fits of irrational behavior, that she wasn't an impossible person to live with, that she wasn't partially out of her mind? On the other hand, perhaps the entire conflict could be boiled down to a single irresolvable point: Minor believed in the teachings of the Reverend Bob, and Rory didn't. And because she refused to believe, he had gradually come to hate her.

From where I was sitting on the couch, I had a clear view of the staircase that led to the second floor. As I pondered what to say next, I looked past Minor's left shoulder in that direction, momentarily distracted by something I'd seen out of the corner of my eye – a small, dark object that appeared for less than a second, then vanished before I could identify what it was. Minor began talking again, reiterating his ideas on what constituted a good and proper marriage, but he no longer had my full attention. I was looking at the stairs, belatedly understanding that the thing I had seen was probably the tip of a shoe – no doubt Aurora's shoe – and if that was the case, I hoped she'd been standing there for some time, eavesdropping on us since the start of my visit. Minor was so wrapped up in what he was saying, he still hadn't noticed that I wasn't looking directly at him. Fuck it, I said to myself. Enough cat and mouse. Enough beating around the bush. It's time to pull up the curtain on the second act.

'Come on down, Rory,' I said. 'It's your old Uncle Nat, and I'm not going to leave this house until I've talked with you.'

I jumped from the couch and skirted past Minor to the foot of the stairs, moving quickly on the off chance that he would try to stop me from going to her.

'She's asleep,' I heard him say behind me, just as I caught my first glimpse of Aurora's legs at the top of the stairs. 'She's been fighting the flu since Thursday and has a high fever. Come back in the middle of the week. You can talk to her then.'

'No, David,' my niece called out as she descended the stairs. 'I'm all right.'

She was wearing a pair of black jeans and an old gray sweat-shirt, and it was true that she looked under the weather, not at all in good form. Pale and thin, with dark circles under her eyes, she had to clutch the banister as she slowly made her way toward me, but in spite of the effects of flu and fever, she was smiling, smiling the great, luminous smile of the little Laughing Girl she had been so many years before.

318

'Uncle Nat,' she said, opening her arms to me. 'My knight in shining armor.' She threw herself against my body and hugged me with all her strength. 'How's my baby?' she whispered. 'Is my little girl all right?'

'She's fine,' I said. 'She can't wait to see you again, but she's doing fine.'

Minor was standing next to us by then, looking none too pleased by this display of family affection. 'Sweetheart,' he said. 'You really should go back upstairs and lie down. You were a hundred and one just half an hour ago, and it isn't good to walk around with a fever like that.'

'This is my Uncle Nat,' Rory said, still holding on to me for dear life. 'My mother's only brother. I haven't seen him in a long, long time.'

'I know that,' Minor said. 'But he can come back in a couple of days – as soon as you're feeling better.'

'You know what's best, don't you, David?' Rory said. 'You always know what's best. Silly me to come downstairs without your approval.'

'Don't go if you don't want to,' I said to her. 'You're not going to die if you stay here for a few more minutes.'

'Oh yes, I will,' she said, making no effort to hide her sarcasm. 'David thinks I'll die if I don't do everything he says. Isn't that right, David?'

'Calm down, Aurora,' her husband said. 'Not in front of your uncle.'

'Why not?' she answered. 'Why the goddamn fucking not?'

'Watch your tongue,' Minor reprimanded her. 'We don't talk like that in this house.'

'Oh, we don't, do we?' she said. 'Then maybe it's time for me to leave this goddamn fucking house. Maybe it's time for the vermin to clear out so you can be left alone with your pure thoughts and your pure tongue and your silent fucking God. This is it, Mr Holy. The goddamn moment of truth. My lucky day has finally come, and now Uncle Nat is going to get me out of here. Isn't that right, Uncle Nat? We're going to drive away in your car, and before the sun comes up tomorrow morning, I'll be with my Lucy again.'

'Just say the word,' I answered, 'and I'll take you wherever you want to go.'

'I'm saying it, Uncle Nat. I'm saying it now.'

Minor was so flabbergasted, he didn't know what to do. I was expecting him to make a lunge for her, to do everything he could to stop us from walking out of there, but the confrontation had erupted so quickly, so fiercely, that he didn't even say a word. I put my arm around Aurora, and before her husband knew what had hit him, we were already in my car, backing out of the driveway and leaving Hawthorne Street behind us for good.

FLYING NORTH

urora was in no condition to travel, but when I suggested that we check into a hotel somewhere and wait for her fever to come down, she shook her head and insisted that we get on the next plane to New York.

'David's smart,' she said. 'If we hang around here for just a few hours, he's bound to find us. Just pump me full of Advil or something, and I'll be okay.'

So I bought her the Advil, wrapped her in my overcoat, turned up the heat in the car, and drove straight to the airport. I had landed in Greensboro that morning, but since Minor would surely go looking for us there, Rory thought our best bet was to leave by way of Raleigh-Durham. It was a hundred-mile drive, and she slept for the full two hours we were on the road. After four Advils and the long nap, she woke up feeling better. Still wan, still a bit drained, but the fever had apparently broken, and after another dose of pills and two glasses of orange juice at the airport, she was strong enough to talk – which was precisely what we did for the next several hours: from the moment we took our seats at the departure gate to the moment we stepped out of a yellow cab in front of my house in Brooklyn that night.

'It's all my fault,' she said. 'I saw it coming a long time ago, but I was too weak to stand up for myself, too nervous to fight back. That's what happens when you think the other person is better than you are. You stop thinking for yourself, and pretty soon you don't own your own life anymore. You don't even realize it, Uncle Nat, but you're fucked. You're absolutely fucked . . .

'The first mistake was turning my back on Tom. After I got out of rehab, David and I left California and came east with Lucy. We lived with his mother in Philadelphia for six months, and things were good, about as good as any time I can remember. I was crazy in love with him. No man had ever been so nice to me, and I walked around with this incredible feeling that I was protected, that this smart, decent person actually knew who I was. We were both survivors. The two of us had been through so much, and there we were after all our ups and downs, standing on our feet together, about to get married . . .

'One day, I went to New York to see Tom, and I have to admit I found it a little depressing. He'd put on all this weight, he'd quit school and was driving a cab, and he was kind of testy with me, at least in the beginning. Not that I blamed him. I'd been out of touch for so long, why shouldn't he have resented me for it? There was no excuse.

I'd been running around California all that time, slowly going to the dogs, and I just couldn't bring myself to pick up the phone and call. I tried to explain, but it didn't do much good. But Tom was still my big brother, and now that I was getting married, I wanted him to walk me down the aisle and give me away – just like what you did with Mom when she got married. He said he'd be glad to do it, and all of a sudden it was like old times again, and I really started feeling happy. I had my brother back. I was marrying David, and Lucy, my amazing little Lucy, was living with her mother again – her dumb kid mother who was finally beginning to grow up. What else could I ask for? I had everything I wanted, Uncle Nat. Everything . . .

'Then I took the bus back to Philadelphia, and when I told David about inviting Tom to the wedding, he said it was impossible, out of the question. He'd been thinking about it the whole time I was in New York, and he'd decided that my brother was a bad influence on me. If I wanted to go ahead with the marriage, I would have to cut all ties to my past. Not just friends, but everyone in my family too. What are you talking about? I asked him. I love my brother. He's the best person in the world. But David didn't want to discuss it. We were starting a new life together, he said, and unless I made a clean break with everything that had corrupted me in the past, I would eventually slip back into my old ways. I had to choose. It was all or nothing, he said. An act of faith or an act of rebellion. Life with God or life without God. Marriage or no marriage. Husband or brother. David or Tom. A hopeful future or a miserable return to the past . . .

'I should have put my foot down. I should have told him I wasn't swallowing that horseshit, and if he thought he could marry me without inviting Tom to the wedding, there wasn't going to be any wedding – period. But I didn't do that. I didn't fight back, and when I let him have his way like that, it was already the beginning of the end. You can't give up power over yourself, not even when you believe in the other person, not even when you think the other person knows what's best. That's what did me in. It was more than just being scared of losing David. The really scary thing was that I thought he was probably right. I loved Tommy, but what had I ever done for him except cause a lot of trouble and heartache? Maybe it would be better if I cut the tie and left him alone. Maybe he would be better off if he never saw me again . . .

'No, David never hit me. He never hit Lucy, and he never hit me. He's not a violent person. His game is talk. Talk, talk, talk. And then more talk. He wears you down with his arguments, and because his voice is so kind and reasonable, because he expresses himself so well, he sort of sucks you into his brain – almost as if he's hypnotizing you. That's what saved me at the rehab clinic in Berkeley. The way he kept on talking to me, looking into my eyes with that caring expression on his face and that soft, steady voice of his. It's hard to resist him, Uncle Nat. He gets inside your head, and after a while you start to think he can never be wrong about anything . . .

'I know Tom was worried. He was afraid I was going to turn into one of those born-again holy rollers, but I'm not cut out for that kind of stuff. David kept working on me, but I only pretended to go along. If he wants to believe in that crap – fine, I don't care. It makes him happy, and I'm never going to be against anything that makes a person happy. I heard him talking to you in the house before, and what he said was true. He isn't into all that fundamentalist ranting and raving. He believes in Jesus and the afterlife, but compared to some of the things other people believe in, it isn't too heavy. His problem is that he thinks he can be a saint. He wants to be perfect . . .

'So yeah, I went to church with him every Sunday. I didn't have much choice, did I? But it wasn't all bad, at least not when we were in Philadelphia. I sang in the choir there, and you know how much I love to sing. Those hymns are some of the sappiest tunes ever written, but at least I got a chance to exercise my lungs once a week, and as long as David didn't push too hard on shoving Jesus down my throat, I wasn't what you'd call an unhappy camper. I sometimes think that if we hadn't left Philadelphia, everything would have worked out. But we both had trouble finding decent jobs. I had a part-time gig as a waitress in some sleazoid diner, and the best David could do after months of looking was night watchman in an office building on Market Street. We went to our N.A. meetings; we kept ourselves sober; Lucy liked her school; David's mom was a little nuts but basically all right – but we just couldn't earn enough money in that town. Then an opening turned up in North Carolina, and David jumped at the chance. True Value Hardware. Things got better after that, and then, about a year and a half ago, David met the Reverend Bob, and all of a sudden they got a whole lot worse . . .

'David was only seven when his father died. I'm not saying it's his fault, but I think he's been looking for a substitute father ever since. An authority figure. Someone strong enough to take him under his wing and guide him through life. That's probably why he joined the marines after high school instead of going to college. You know, take your orders from Big Daddy America, and Big Daddy will take care of you. Big Daddy took care of him all right. Shipped him out to Desert Storm and did a major number on his head. Fucked him up bad. David goes downhill for a bunch of years and ends up on horse. You already know that. I heard him tell you about it today, but the interesting thing to me is how he finally kicked it. Not with that A.A. line about trusting

326

in a higher power – but with real religion. He goes all the way to the top and gets the biggest father of them all. Mr God. Mr goddamn God, the ruler of the universe. But still, maybe that isn't enough. You can talk to your God and hope he listens to you, but unless your brain is tuned to the twenty-four-hour Schizophrenia Network, he isn't going to talk back. Pray all you want, but you won't hear a peep from Dad. You can study his words in the Bible, but the Bible is just a book, and books don't talk, do they? But the Reverend Bob talks, and once you start listening to him, you know you've found your man. He's the father you've been looking for, an actual flesh-and-blood human father, and every time he opens his mouth, you're convinced he's getting it straight from the big boss himself. God talks through this guy, and whenever he tells you to do something, you'd better do it or else . . .

'He's fifty-something years old, I guess. Tall and skinny, with a long nose and a fat cow of a wife named Darlene. I don't know when he started the Temple of the Holy Word, but it isn't a normal church like the one we went to in Philadelphia. The reverend calls himself a Christian, but he never says what kind, and I'm not even sure he gives a rat's ass about religion. It's all about controlling other people, about getting them to do weird, self-destructive things and make them believe they're serving the will of God. I think he's a fraud, a scam artist from the word go, but he has his followers in the palm of his hand, and they love him, they all love him, and David more than anyone else. What gets them so excited is the way he keeps coming up with new ideas, keeps changing his message. One Sunday it's about the evils of materialism and how we should shun worldly possessions and live in sacred poverty like the son of our dear Lord. The next Sunday it's about hard work and how we should earn as much money as we can. I told David I thought he was nuts and didn't want to expose Lucy to any more of that drivel. But David was a true convert by then, and he wouldn't listen to me. Two or three months later, the Reverend Bob suddenly decides that singing should be banned from the Sunday services. It's an offense against the ears of God, he says, and from now on we should worship him in silence. As far as I was concerned, that was the last straw. I told David that Lucy and I were quitting the church. He could keep on going as long as he liked, but we were never setting foot inside that place again. It was the first time I'd spoken up for myself since we were married – and it didn't do me an ounce of good. He pretended to be sympathetic, but the rules were that all families of the congregation had to attend services together every Sunday. If I dropped out, he would be excommunicated. Well, I said, just tell them that Lucy and I are sick, that we have a fatal disease and can't get out of bed. David gave me one of his sad, patronizing smiles. Prevarication is a sin, he said. If we don't speak the truth at all times, our souls will be barred at the gates of heaven and cast down into the jaws of hell . . .

'So we kept on going every week, and about a month after that the Reverend Bob came up with his next big idea. Secular culture was destroying America, he said, and the only way we could undo the damage was to reject everything it offered us. That was when he started issuing his so-called Sunday Edicts. First, everyone had to get rid of their television sets. Then it was radios. Then it was books – every book in the house except the Bible. Then it was telephones. Then it was computers. Then it was CDs, tapes, and records. Can you imagine? No more music, Uncle Nat, no more novels, no more poems. Then we had to cancel our magazine subscriptions. Then it was newspapers. Then we weren't allowed to go to the movies anymore. The idiot was on a rampage, but the more sacrifices he demanded of the congregation, the more they seemed to like it. As far as I know, not one family left . . .

'Finally, there weren't any more things to get rid of. The reverend stopped his attacks on the culture and media business and started hammering away at what he called 'the gut issues.' Every time we talked, we drowned out the voice of God. Every time we listened to the words of men, we neglected the words of God. From now on, he said, every member of the church above the age of fourteen would spend one day a week in total silence. In that way, we would be able to restore our connection with God, to hear him speaking within our souls. After all the other stunts he'd pulled on us, this seemed like a pretty mild demand . . .

'David works from Monday to Friday, so he chose Saturday as his day of silence. Mine was Thursday, but since no one was around until Lucy came home from school, I could do whatever I damn pleased. I sang songs, I talked to myself, I shouted curses at the almighty Reverend Bob. But once Lucy and David walked through the door, I had to put on an act. I served them dinner in silence, I tucked Lucy into bed in silence, I kissed David goodnight in silence. No big deal. Then, after about a month of this routine, Lucy got it into her head to follow my example. She was just nine years old. Not even the Reverend Bob was asking children to join in, but my little girl loved me so much, she wanted to do everything I did. For three Saturdays in a row, she didn't say a word. No matter how much I begged her not to do it, she refused to stop. She's such a smart kid, Uncle Nat, but you know how stubborn she can be. You've had the same treatment yourself, and once she makes up her mind, it's like trying to push over a building to get her to back down. Incredibly enough, David took my side, but I think a part of him was so proud of her for acting like an adult, he wasn't very forceful or convincing. Anyway, it had nothing to do with him. It was about me. About me and her. I told David that I had to talk to the Reverend Bob. If he would release me from my Thursday silences, it would take the burden off Lucy, and then she'd start acting like herself again . . .

'David wanted to come to the meeting with me, but I said no, I had to see the reverend alone. To make sure he wouldn't butt in, I set up the appointment for a Saturday, the day when David wasn't allowed to talk. Just drive me to the house, I said, and wait outside in the car. It shouldn't take too long . . .

'The Reverend Bob was sitting at the desk in his study, putting the final touches on the sermon he was supposed to deliver the next morning. Sit down, my child, he said, and tell me what the problem is. I explained about Lucy and why I thought he would be doing us a great service if he released me from my Thursday silences. Hmmm, he said. Hmmm. I have to think it over. I'll give you my decision by the end of next week. He was looking straight at me, and every time he spoke, his bushy eyebrows did this funny little twitching thing. Thank you, I said. I believe you're a wise man, and I know you'll see it in your heart to bend the rules in order to help a young child. I wasn't going to tell him what I really thought. Like it or not, I was a member of his fucking congregation, and I had to play along as if I meant what I was saying. I figured our business was over then, but when I stood up to go, he stretched out his right arm and waved me back into my seat. I've been watching you, woman, he said, and I want you to know that you get high marks on all fronts. You and Brother Minor are among the pillars of our community, and I'm certain I can depend on you to follow me in all matters, both sacred and profane. Profane? I said. What do you mean by *profane*? As you probably know, the reverend said, my wife Darlene was unable to bear children. Now that I've reached a certain age, I've begun to think about my legacy, and I find it tragic to contemplate leaving this earth without having produced an heir. You could always adopt, I said. No, he said, that's not good enough. I have to make a child out of my own flesh, a descendant of my own blood to carry on with the work I've started here. I've been watching you, woman, and of all the souls in my flock, you're the only one worthy to carry my seed. What are you talking about? I said. I'm married to someone else. I love my husband. Yes, I know that, he said, but for the sake of the Temple of the Holy Word, I'm asking you to divorce him and marry me. But you have a wife, I said. No one's allowed to have two wives, Reverend Bob, not even you. No, of course not, he said. Needless to say, I'll file for divorce as well. Let me think it over, I said. Everything's happening so fast, I don't know what to say. My head's spinning, my hands are shaking, and I'm completely confused. Don't worry, my child, the reverend said. Take all the time you need. But just so you understand the sorts of pleasures that await you, there's something

I want you to see. The reverend stood up from his chair, came around to the front of the desk, and unzipped his fly. He was standing right in front of me, and that unzipped fly wasn't two feet from my face. Look at this, he said, and then he pulled out his cock and showed it to me. To be honest, it was a fairly huge cock – much bigger than what you'd expect to find hanging between the legs of a scrawny guy like that. I've seen a lot of naked men in my time, and for sheer length and girth, I'd have to put the reverend's unit up there in the top ten percent. A porn-sized cock, if you know what I mean, but not the least bit attractive to my eyes. It was stiff and purplish red, but the hard-on made it all veiny, and at full extension it also curved to the left. A big cock, but also a disgusting one, and the man it belonged to disgusted me even more. I suppose I could have jumped up and run out of the house, but somewhere way off in the back of my mind I knew this asshole was offering me a priceless opportunity, and in exchange for a few repulsive moments, I could free us all from the morons of that church . . .

'This is the holy bone, the reverend said, holding the erection in his hand and wagging it in my face. God gave me this glorious gift, and the jism that spurts from it can engender the lives of angels. Take it in your hand, Sister Aurora, and feel the fire coursing through its veins. Put it in your mouth and taste the flesh our good Lord saw fit to endow me with . . .

'I did what he wanted, Uncle Nat. I closed my eyes and shoved that big veiny corncob into my mouth, and little by little I sucked him off. It was nasty. My poor nose rubbing up against his smelly crotch, my poor stomach churning around inside me, but I knew what I was doing, and I was glad. Just as he was about to come, I took him out of my mouth and finished the job with my hand, making sure his precious jism squirted all over my blouse. That was my evidence, the one thing I needed to bring the son-of-a-bitch down. Remember Monica and Bill? Remember the dress? Well, now I had my blouse, and it was as good as a weapon, as good as a loaded gun . . .

'When I got into the car, I was crying. I don't know if they were real tears or fake tears, but I was crying. I told David to start up the engine and head for home. He looked upset, but since he wasn't allowed to talk until the next morning, he couldn't ask me any questions. That was when I realized the thing could go in either one of two ways. I was about to tell him that the Reverend Bob had raped me. If David talked then, it would mean that he cared more about me than the goddamn Temple of the Holy Word. We could hand the blouse over to the cops, have it tested for DNA, and the reverend would be cooked in a vat of burning oil. But what if David didn't talk? It would mean that I was nothing to him, that he was sticking with old Bob the Father to the bitter end. There wasn't going to be much time to act. If David let me down, I would have to stop thinking about myself. Lucy was the one who had to be saved, and the only way to do that was to get her out of North Carolina. Not tomorrow or next week, but now, this minute, on the first bus leaving for New York . . .

'After we had gone about a hundred yards, I told him. The bastard raped me, I said. Look at my blouse, David. That's the Reverend Bob's semen. He pinned me down and wouldn't let go. He forced himself on me, and I wasn't strong enough to push him off. David pulled the car over to the side of the road and stopped. For a little while, I thought he was with me, and I felt bad that I'd doubted him, ashamed that I hadn't been willing to trust him. He reached out his hand and touched my face, and he had that sweet, soulful look in his eyes, the same beautiful, tender look that made me fall for him back in California. This is the man I married, I said to myself, and he still loves me. But I was wrong. He might have felt sorry for me, but he wasn't about to interrupt his silence and disobey the Reverend Bob's holy command. Talk to me, I said. Please, David, open your mouth and talk to me. He shook his head. He shook his head, and I started to cry again, and this time it was for real . . .

'We got back on the road, and after a minute or two I managed to pull myself together enough to tell him that we were sending Lucy up north to my brother Tom in Brooklyn. If he didn't do exactly what I told him to do, I would take the blouse to the police, press charges against the Reverend Bob, and our marriage would be over. You still want to be married to me, don't you? I asked. David nodded. All right, I said, then this is the deal. First, we pick up Lucy at the house. Then we drive to the A.T.M. at City Federal and withdraw two hundred dollars in cash. Then we go to the bus depot and you buy her a one-way ticket to New York with your MasterCard. Then we give her the money, put her on the bus, and kiss her good-bye. That's what you're going to do for me. What I'm going to do for you is this: the moment the bus leaves the terminal, I'll give you the blouse with your hero's cum stains on it, and you can destroy the evidence to save his ass. I'll also promise to stay with you, but only on one condition: that I never have to go near that church again. If you try to drag me back there, I'm gone from your life, gone from your life forever . . .

'I don't want to talk about saying good-bye to Lucy. It hurts too much to think about it. I said good-bye to her when I went into rehab, but this was different. This felt like the end of the world, and all I could do was hug her, and try not to crack up, and remind her to tell everyone that I was doing okay. I'm sorry she lost the letter I wrote Tom. I explained a lot in that letter, and it must have seemed awfully peculiar when she showed up empty-handed like that. I also tried to call Tom from the terminal, but everything was so rushed, and since I didn't have enough coins on me, I had to call collect. He wasn't home, but at least I knew he was still at his old address. I might have been acting crazy that day, but not crazy enough to send Lucy to New York without knowing exactly where Tom lived . . .

'I don't understand this Carolina Carolina business. I never told her not to say where I was. Why would I do that? I was sending her to Tom – and it never occurred to me that she wouldn't tell him about Winston-Salem. The poor kid. What I said to her was: Just let him know that I'm okay, that I'm doing fine. I should have known better. Lucy takes things so literally, she probably thought that when I used the word *just*, I meant that was the only thing I wanted her to say. She's always been like that. When she was three, I sent her to day care for a couple of hours every morning. After a few weeks, the teacher called me and said that she was worried about Lucy. When it was time for the children to have their milk, Lucy would always hang back until all the other kids had taken a carton before she'd take one for herself. The teacher didn't understand. Go get your milk, she'd say to Lucy, but Lucy would always wait around until there was just one carton left. It took a while for me to figure it out. Lucy didn't know which carton was supposed to be *her milk*. She thought all the other kids knew which ones were theirs, and if she waited until there was only one carton in the box, that one had to be hers. Do you see what I'm talking about, Uncle Nat? She's a little weird – but intelligent weird, if you know what I mean. Not like anyone else. If I hadn't used the word *just*, you would have known where I was all along . . .

'Why didn't I call again? Because I couldn't. No, not because we didn't have a phone in the house – because I was trapped. I'd promised David that I wouldn't leave him, but he didn't trust me anymore. The minute we got home from the bus terminal, he took me upstairs to Lucy's room and locked me in. Yes, Uncle Nat, he locked me in and kept me there for the rest of the day and all that night. When he started talking again the next morning, he told me that I had to be punished for lying about the Reverend Bob. Lying? I said. What the hell did that mean? There hadn't been any rape, he said. The only reason I'd insisted on going into the house alone was because I'd been planning to seduce him – and the poor man hadn't been able to resist my charms. Thank you, David, I said. Thank you for believing in me and understanding what a good wife I've been to you . . .

'Later that day, he boarded up the windows in the room. I mean, what's the use of a jail if the prisoner can crawl out the window, right? Then, very kindly, my dear husband carried up all the things we had put downstairs in the cellar after the Reverend Bob's Sunday Edicts. The television set, the radio, the CD player, the books. Isn't that against the rules? I asked. Yes, David said, but I talked to the reverend after services this morning, and he's given me a special dispensation. I want to make things as comfortable as possible for you, Aurora. Gee, I said, why are you so nice to me? Because I love you, David said. You did a wicked thing yesterday, but that doesn't mean I don't love you. To show the purity of that love, he came back a minute later with a big stew pot so I wouldn't have to piss and shit on the floor. By the way, he said, you'll be happy to learn that you've been excommunicated from the Temple. You're out, but I'm still in. I'm crushed, I said. I think this is the saddest day of my life . . .

'I don't know what was wrong with me, but the whole thing felt like a joke, and I couldn't take it seriously. I figured it would go on for just a few days, and then I'd split. Promise or no promise, I wasn't going to hang around there a minute longer than I had to . . .

'But the days became weeks, and then the weeks became months. David understood what I was thinking, and he wasn't about to let me go. He'd let me out of the room when he came home from work, but what chance did I have to get away? He was always watching me. If I tried to run for the door, how far could I have gone? About two steps, maybe. He's bigger and stronger than I am, and all he had to do was run after me and drag me back. The keys to the car were in his pocket, his money was in his pocket, and the only money I had was a bunch of change I'd found in one of Lucy's bureau drawers. I kept waiting and hoping, but I only managed to slip out of the house once. That was when I tried to call Tom. You remember that, don't you? By some miracle, David dozed off in the living room after dinner. There's a pay phone about a mile and a half down the road, and I ran down that road as fast as I could. If only I'd had the balls to put my hand in David's pocket and steal the car key. But I couldn't risk waking him up, so I went down that road on foot. David must have opened his eyes about ten minutes after I left, and needless to say, he went down that road in the car. What a fiasco. I didn't even have time to finish the damn message . . .

'Now you know why I look so pale, so worn out. I was locked up in that room for six months, Uncle Nat. Locked up like an animal in my own house for half a year. I watched television, I read books, I listened to music, but mostly what I did was think about how to kill myself. If I didn't go ahead with it, it's because I promised Lucy that I was going to come back for her one day, that one day we would live together again. But Christ, it wasn't easy, it wasn't easy at all. If you hadn't come for me this afternoon, I don't know how much longer I could have taken it. I probably would have died in that house. It's that simple, Uncle Nat. I would have died in that house, and then my husband and the good Reverend Bob would have carried me out in the middle of the night and dumped my body in an unmarked grave.'

A NEW LIFE

Because of my friendship with Joyce Mazzucchelli, who owned the house on Carroll Street that she shared with her B.P.M. daughter and two grandchildren, I was able to find new digs for Aurora and Lucy. There was an empty room on the third floor of the brownstone. In former times, it had served as a multipurpose workshop-studio for Jimmy Joyce, but now that Nancy's Foley walker ex-husband was gone, why couldn't they live there? I asked. Rory had no money and no job, but I would be willing to pay the rent until she got back on her feet, and now that Lucy was old enough to lend an occasional hand with Nancy's kids, it might work out to everyone's advantage.

'Forget about the rent, Nathan,' Joyce said. 'Nancy needs an assistant for her jewelry business, and if Aurora doesn't mind helping out with the cleaning and cooking, she can have the room for free.'

Good old Joyce. We had been monkeying around together for almost six months by then, and even though we lived in separate places, it was the rare week when we didn't spend at least two or three nights in the same bed – hers or mine, depending on what the mood and circumstances dictated. She was a couple of years younger than I was, which made her something of an old broad, but at fifty-eight, fifty-nine, she still had enough moves to keep things interesting.

Sex among aging people can have its embarrassments and comical longueurs, but there is also a tenderness to it that often eludes the young. Your breasts might sag, your cock might droop, but your skin is still your skin, and when someone you care about reaches out and touches you, or holds you in her arms, or kisses you on the mouth, you can still melt in the same way you did when you thought you would live forever. Joyce and I hadn't reached the December of our lives, but there was no question that May was well behind us. What we were together was an afternoon in mid- to late October, one of those bright fall days with a vivid blue sky above, a gusty nip in the air, and a million leaves still clinging to the branches – most of them brown, but with enough golds and reds and yellows left to make you want to stay outdoors as long as you can.

No, she wasn't the beauty her daughter was, and based on the early photographs I'd seen of her, she never had been. Joyce attributed Nancy's physical appearance to her late husband, Tony, a building contractor who had died of a heart attack in 1993. 'He was the handsomest man I ever met,'

342

she once told me. 'The spitting image of Victor Mature.' With her strong Brooklyn accent, the actor's name emerged from her mouth sounding something like *Victa Machuah*, as if the letter r had atrophied to such a degree that it had been expunged from the English alphabet. I loved that earthy, proletarian voice. It made me feel on safe ground with her, and as much as any of the other qualities she possessed, it told you that this was a woman without pretension, a woman who believed in who and what she was. She was the mother of the Beautiful Perfect Mother, after all, and how could she have raised a girl like Nancy if she hadn't known what she was about?

On the surface, we had almost nothing in common. Our backgrounds were entirely different (city Catholic, suburban Jew), and our interests diverged on nearly every point. Joyce had no patience for books and was a strict nonreader, whereas I shunned all physical exertion, striving for immobility as the ne plus ultra of the good life. For Joyce, exercise was more than just a duty, it was a pleasure, and her preferred weekend activity was getting up at six o'clock on Sunday morning and riding her bike through Prospect Park. She still worked, and I was retired. She was an optimist, and I was a cynic. She had been happily married, and my marriage – but enough about that. She paid little or no attention to the news, and I read the paper carefully every day. Back when we were children, she had rooted for the Dodgers, and I had rooted for the Giants. She was a fish and pasta person, and I was a meat and potatoes man. And yet – and what can be more mysterious about human life than this *yet?* – we got along like gangbusters. I had felt an immediate attraction the morning we were introduced (out on Seventh Avenue with Nancy), but it wasn't until we had our first long talk at Harry's funeral that I understood there might be a spark between us. In a fit of shyness, I had put off calling her, but then one day the following week she invited me to the house for dinner, and so the flirtation began.

Did I love her? Yes, I probably loved her. To the extent that I was capable of loving anyone, Joyce was the woman for me, the only candidate on my list. And even if it wasn't the full-blown, one hundred percent passion that supposedly defines the word *love*, it was something that fell just short of it – but so close to the mark as to render the distinction meaningless. She made me laugh a lot, which medical experts claim is good for one's mental and physical health. She tolerated my foibles and inconsistencies, endured my black funks, stayed calm during my blistering rants against the G.O.P., the C.I.A., and Rudolph Giuliani. She tickled me with her rabid devotion to the Mets. She astonished me with her encyclopedic knowledge of old Hollywood films and her talent for identifying every minor and forgotten actor who flitted across the screen.

(Look, Nathan, there's Franklin Pangborn . . . there's Una Merkel . . . there's C. Aubrey Smith). I admired her for having the courage to let me read to her from *The Book of Human Folly,* and then, in her good-natured ignorance, how she treated my piddling stories as literature of the first rank. Yes, I loved her to the full extent allowed by law (the law of my nature), but was I prepared to settle down and spend the rest of my life with her? Did I want to see her every day of the week? Was I mad enough about her to pop the big question? I wasn't sure. After the long disaster with Name Deleted, I was understandably hesitant to consider another stab at matrimony. But Joyce was a woman, and since the vast preponderance of women seem to prefer couplehood to singledom, I figured I owed it to her to prove that I meant business. In one of the darkest moments of that fall – two days after Rachel suffered a miscarriage, four days after Bush was illegally handed the election, and twelve days before Henry Peoples managed to zero in on the missing Aurora – I broke down and did it. To my immense surprise, the marriage proposal was greeted with hoots of raucous laughter. 'Oh, Nathan,' Joyce said, 'don't be such a nitwit. We're doing just fine the way we are. Why rock the boat and start making trouble for ourselves? Marriage is for young people, for kids who want to have babies. We've already done that. We're free. We can screw around like a pair of teenagers, and we're never going to get pregnant.

Just whistle, pal, and my big Italian ass is yours, okay? You get my ass, and I get your nice Yiddish you-know-what. You're my first Jew, Nathan, and now that you've parked yourself on my doorstep, I'm not about to give you up. I'm yours, baby. But forget about this marriage stuff. I don't want to be a wife anymore, and the fact is, my sweet, funny man, you'd make a terrible husband . . .'

In spite of these tough words, she started crying a moment later – suddenly overwrought, losing control of her emotions for the first time since I'd known her. I assumed that she was thinking about her dead Tony, remembering the man she had said yes to when she was hardly older than a girl, the husband she had lost when he was only fifty-nine, the love of her life. That might have been the case, but what she said to me was something entirely different. 'Don't think I don't appreciate it, Nathan. You're the best thing that's happened to me in a long time, and now this, now you give me this. I'm never going to forget it, angel. An old bag like me getting proposed to. I don't mean to blubber, but boy, boy oh boy, knowing you care that much hits me right where I live.'

I was relieved to know that I had touched her enough to produce those tears. It meant that there was something solid between us, a connection that wasn't going to be broken any time soon. But I also have to admit that I felt relieved that Joyce had turned me down. I had made my big gesture, but in all honesty I had been of two minds about it, and she knew me well enough to understand that yes, I would have made a terrible husband, and neither one of us had any business getting married. And so, to paraphrase the words of the immortal Dr Pangloss, everything turned out for the best – and for the first time in my life, I got to have my cake and eat it too.

Joyce dried her tears, and two weeks later Aurora and Lucy were living in her house. It was a sensible arrangement for all concerned, but even if logic demanded that mother and daughter should be reunited, one mustn't forget how difficult it was for Tom and Honey to let go of their young charge. They had been taking care of Lucy for months by then, and over the course of time the three-some had solidified into a close little family. I had felt a similar pang when I relinquished her to them back in the summer, and she had lived with me for only a few weeks. When I thought of the five and a half months they had spent with her, I couldn't help sympathizing with them – no matter how happy we all were that Aurora had landed safely in Brooklyn. 'She has to live with her mother,' I said to Tom, trying to be philosophical about it. 'But a part of Lucy still belongs to us, to each one of us. She's our girl, too, and nothing will ever change that.'

Hard as it was for them to lose her, their brief foray into parenthood had convinced Tom and Honey that they wanted children of their own. For the moment, they were preoccupied by a multitude of practical concerns – negotiating the sale of Harry's building, looking for a new apartment, applying for teaching jobs around the city – but once those chores were dispensed with, Honey threw away her diaphragm, and the two of them got down to the nightly business of attempting to start a family. In March of 2001, they moved into a co-op on Third Street between Sixth and Seventh Avenues: an airy, light-filled place on the fourth floor with a sizable living room in front, a modest kitchen and dining room in the center, and a narrow hallway that led to three small bedrooms in the back (one of which Tom converted into a study). By the time they set up house in that apartment, Brightman's Attic was no more. As one of the conditions for completing the sale of the building, the buyer had insisted that the books be removed from the premises, which had compelled Tom to spend a frantic period at the start of the year liquidating the entire stock of Harry's old business. Paperbacks were sold for five and ten cents, hardcovers were listed at three for a dollar, and the volumes that didn't sell by February first were shipped off to hospitals, charity organizations, and merchant seamen libraries. I helped out with these lugubrious tasks, and while the rare books and first editions on the second floor brought in a considerable amount of money (even at the rock-bottom prices Tom was willing to accept in order to transfer the whole collection to a single dealer in Great Barrington, Massachusetts), it was no fun taking part in the demolition of Harry's empire – especially when I learned what the new owner was planning to do with the space after it was empty. Books were giving way to women's shoes and handbags, and the top three floors were being converted into expensive co-op apartments. Real estate is the official religion of New York, and its god wears a gray pin-striped suit and goes by the name of Cash, Mr More-and-More Cash. If there was any consolation for me in this grim turn of events, it was the knowledge that Tom and Rufus would never be hard up again. For the two hundredth time since his death, my thoughts turned to Harry – and his vast swan dive into eternal greatness.

On a Thursday evening in early June, Honey announced that she was pregnant. Tom put his arm around her, then leaned across the dinner table and asked me if I would be the godfather. 'You're our only choice,' he said. 'For services rendered, Nathan, above and beyond the call of duty. For outstanding courage in the heat of battle. For risking life and limb to rescue your wounded comrade under intense fire. For prodding that same comrade to stand on his feet again and enter into this conjugal union. In recognition of these heroic acts, and for the benefit of our future offspring, you deserve to wear a title more fitting to your role than that of great-uncle. Therefore, I dub thee godfather – if thou wilt accept our humble supplication to assume the mantle of that burden. What shall it be, good sir? We await thine answer with pounding hearts.' The answer was yes. A yes followed by a long string of mumbled words, none of which I can remember now. Then I raised my glass to them, and unaccountably my eyes filled with tears.

Three days later, Rachel and Terrence drove in from New Jersey for Sunday brunch at my apartment. Joyce helped me prepare the spread, and as the four of us sat in the back garden eating our bagels and lox, I noticed that my daughter looked lovelier and happier than at any time in recent months. Her miscarriage in the fall had been a brutal disappointment, and she had been on shaky ground ever since – covering up her sadness by working too hard at her job, cooking elaborate gourmet meals for Terrence to prove that she was a worthy spouse in spite of her failure to bear a child, exhausting herself at every turn. But that day in the garden, the old luster was shining in her eyes again, and though she was normally reserved in company, she more than held her own in the four-way conversation, talking as much and as often as the rest of us. At one point, Terrence excused himself to go to the bathroom inside, and a moment later Joyce dashed off to the kitchen to fetch a new pot of coffee. Rachel and I were alone. I kissed her on the cheek and told her how beautiful she looked, and she responded to the compliment by returning the kiss and then leaning her head against my shoulder. 'I'm pregnant again,' she said. 'I took the test this morning, and the results were positive. There's a baby growing inside me, Dad, and this time it's going to live. I promise. I'm going to make you a grandfather, even if I have to stay in bed for the next seven months.'

For the second time in less than seventy-two hours, my eyes unexpectedly filled with tears.

Pregnant women were sprouting up all around me, and I was turning into something of a woman myself: a person who wept at the mere mention of babies, a lachrymose saphead who needed to walk around with a box of emergency tissues so as not to embarrass myself in public. Perhaps the house on Carroll Street was partly to blame for these lapses of manly decorum. I spent a good deal of time there, and now that Nancy's husband had been replaced by Aurora and Lucy, the household had become an entirely feminine universe. Its only male member was Sam, Nancy's three-year-old son, but as he could barely talk, his influence over its operations was severely limited. Otherwise, it was all girls, three generations of girls, with Joyce at the top, Nancy and Aurora in the middle, and the ten-year-old Lucy and the five-year-old Devon at the bottom. The interior of the brownstone was a living museum of female artifacts, with galleries devoted to the display of bras and panties, blow-dryers and tampons, makeup jars and lipstick tubes, dolls and jump ropes, nighties and bobby pins, curling irons and facial creams and endless, endless pairs of shoes. To go there was like visiting a foreign country, but since I adored every person who lived in that house, it was the single place on earth I preferred above all others.

In the months that followed Aurora's escape from North Carolina, a number of curious things happened chez Joyce. Because the door was always open to me, I was in a position to observe these dramas at close hand, and I watched in a state of perpetual wonder and surprise. With Lucy, for example, all bets were suddenly off. During her time with Tom and Honey, I had been apprehensive, expecting trouble to break out at any minute. Not only had she threatened to become 'the baddest, meanest, cussingest little girl in the whole of God's creation,' but it seemed inevitable to me that her mother's continued absence would eventually wear her down, turning her into a mopish, angry, disgruntled kid. But no. She had thrived in that apartment above Harry's old store, and her adjustment to her new surroundings had continued at a remarkable pace. By the time I brought Rory back to Brooklyn with me, Lucy's southern accent was gone, she had shot up at least four or five inches, and she was one of the best students in her class. Yes, she had often cried for her mother at night, but now that her mother had returned, one would assume our girl would have felt her prayers had been answered. No again. There was an early rush of happiness immediately following the reunion, but after a while resentments and hostilities began to surface, and by the end of their first month together, our smart, energetic, wise-cracking child had turned herself into a royal pain in the ass. Doors slammed; polite requests were greeted with sour derision; belligerent shouts resounded from the third floor; grumps devolved into sulks, sulks devolved into storms, storms devolved into tears; the words *no, stupid, shut up,* and *mind your own business* became an integral part of the daily discourse. With everyone else, Lucy's conduct was unchanged. Only her mother was subjected to these assaults, and as time went on, they became more and more relentless.

Demoralizing as this behavior was on the fragile Aurora, I began to see it as a necessary purge, a sign that Lucy was actively fighting for her life. The question of love wasn't at issue. Lucy loved her mother, but that same beloved mother had also thrown her onto a bus one hectic, crazy after-noon and shipped her off to New York, and for the next six months the girl had been abandoned. How can a little person absorb such a perplexing turn of events without feeling at least partially to blame? Why would the mother get rid of the child unless the child was bad, a creature unworthy of the mother's love? Through no fault of her own, the mother had slashed a wound across her daughter's soul, and how can the wound ever heal if the daughter doesn't cry out at the top of her lungs and announce to the world: I'm in pain; I can't stand it anymore; help me? The household would have been a more tranquil place if Lucy had kept quiet, but bottling up that scream would have caused her no end of trouble in the long run. She had to let it out. There was no other way to stop the bleeding.

I made an effort to see Aurora as often as I could, especially in those first difficult months when she was still struggling to find her bearings. The North Carolina horrors had marked her for life, and we both knew she would never fully recover from them, that no matter how well she managed to cope in the future, the past would always be with her. I offered to pay for regular sessions with a therapist if she thought they would help, but she said no, she'd rather just talk to me. Me. The bitter, solitary man who had crept home to Brooklyn less than a year earlier, the burnout who had convinced himself there was nothing left to live for – knuckle-headed me, Nathan the Unwise, who could think of nothing better to do than quietly wait to drop dead, now transformed into a confidant and counselor, a lover of randy widows, and a knight-errant who rescued damsels in distress. Aurora chose to talk to me because I was the one who had gone down to North Carolina and saved her, and even if we had been out of contact for many years prior to that after-noon, I was nevertheless her uncle, her mother's only brother, and she knew that she could trust me. So we got together for lunch several times a week and talked, just the two of us, sitting at a back table in the New Purity Diner on Seventh Avenue, and little by little we became friends, in the same way her brother and I had become friends, and now that both of June's children were back in my life, it was as if my baby sister had come alive in me again, and because she was the ghost who continued to haunt me, her children had now become my children.

The one thing Aurora had never shared with her mother, her brother, or anyone else in the family was the name of Lucy's father. She had guarded that secret for so many years by then, it seemed futile to broach the question anymore, but at one of our lunches in early April, without any prompting from me, the answer accidentally slipped out.

It all began when I asked her if she still had her tattoo. Rory put down her fork, broke into a big smile, and said, 'How do you know about that?'

'Tom told me. A big eagle on your shoulder, right? We wondered if you'd had it taken off, but Lucy wouldn't tell us.'

'It's still there. As big and pretty as ever.'

'And David was all right with that?'

'Not really. He saw it as a symbol of my fucked-up past and wanted me to get rid of it. I was willing to go along with him, but it turned out to be too expensive. When he realized we couldn't afford it, David did a one-hundred-and-eighty-degree about-face. That gives you a good idea of how he thinks, of why I could never win an argument against him. Maybe it's a good thing, he said. We'll leave the tattoo where it is, and every time we look at it, we'll remember how far you've come from the dark days of your youth. That's typical David for you: *the dark days of my youth.* He said it would be an amulet that I wore on my own skin, and it would protect me from further harm and suffering. An amulet. I had no idea what that was, so I looked it up in the dictionary. A charm for warding off evil spirits. Okay, I can buy that. It didn't do much for me when I was with David, but maybe it will help now.'

'I'm glad you still have it. I don't know why I'm glad, but I am.'

'Me too. I'm kind of attached to that stupid thing. I had it done in the East Village eleven years ago. To celebrate getting pregnant with Lucy. The same morning the nurse at the clinic told me I'd tested positive, I rushed out and got my tattoo.'

'A strange way to celebrate, no?'

'I'm a strange girl, Uncle Nat. And that was probably the strangest time of my life. I was renting some rathole apartment off Avenue C with two guys, Billy and Greg. Billy played the guitar, Greg played the fiddle, and I sang. We weren't too bad, really, considering how young we were. Most of the time, we'd perform out in Washington Square Park. Or else in the Times Square subway station. I loved the echoes in those underground halls, belting out my songs as people dropped their coins and dollars into Greg's fiddle case. Sometimes I sang stoned, and Billy would call me his floozy, woozy, boozy girl. Sometimes I sang sober, and Greg would call me the Queen of Planet X. Jesus Christ. Those were good times, Uncle Nat. When we couldn't earn enough playing our music, I'd go into stores and shoplift. They called me Fearless Fosdick. Rumbling down the aisles of a supermarket, stuffing steaks and chickens under my coat. Nothing was serious back then. One week I was in love with Greg. The next week I was in love with Billy. I slept with both of them, and then I wound up pregnant. I never knew which one was the father, and since neither one of them *wanted* to be the father, I kicked them both out.'

'So that's why you never told June. You didn't know.'

'Shit. I can't believe how dumb I am. Shit, shit, shit. I swore to myself I'd never tell anyone, and now I've gone ahead and done it.'

'It doesn't matter, Rory. Greg and Billy are just names to me. Don't say another word if you don't want to.'

'Greg died of an overdose about two years after Lucy was born. And Billy just kind of vanished. I don't know what happened to him. Somebody once told me that he went back home, finished college, and teaches music in some high school out in the Midwest. But who knows if it's the same Billy Finch? It could be someone else.'

Even after she arrived in Brooklyn, it was far from certain that Aurora had seen the last of David Minor. My name and address were in the telephone book, and it wouldn't have been difficult for him to track her down through me. I cringed at the thought of another confrontation with that self-righteous turd, but I kept my fears to myself and said nothing to Rory. Minor was such a painful subject for her, she could barely bring herself to talk about him, and I didn't want to stir up any new anxieties that would add to the problems she already had to contend with. As the months went by, I began to feel more hopeful, but it wasn't until late June that I was finally able to stop worrying and put the matter to rest. A thick white envelope appeared in my mailbox one morning, and because I carelessly failed to notice that the letter had not been addressed to Nathan Glass but to Aurora Wood in care of Nathan Glass, I opened it before I realized my mistake. The brief, handwritten cover note read as follows:

> *Dear One,*
>   *It's better this way.*
>   *Good luck – and may God ever be merciful to you.*
>
>   *David*

The note was attached to a seven-page document, which turned out to be a divorce decree from Saint Clair County in the State of Alabama, dissolving the marriage between David Wilcox Minor and Aurora Wood Minor on the grounds of desertion.

That day at lunch, I apologized to Rory for having opened her mail, and then I handed her the letter.

'What is it?' she asked.

'A note from your ex,' I said. 'Along with a bunch of official papers.'

'My ex? What does that mean?'

'Open it up and find out.'

As I watched her read the note and scan the document, I was struck by how little her expression changed. I had thought she would smile, perhaps even let out a laugh or two, but her face registered almost nothing. A slight flicker of some buried, enigmatic feeling, but it was impossible to know what the feeling was.

'Well,' she said at last. 'I guess that's that.'

'You're free, Rory. If you wanted to, you could marry someone else tomorrow.'

'I'm never going to let another man touch me for the rest of my life.'

'That's what you say now. Eventually, someone new will come along, and you'll start thinking about marriage again.'

'No, I mean it, Nathan. That part of my life is over and done with. When David locked me in that room, I said to myself: This is it, no more falling for men. Not a single good thing ever came of it. And nothing ever will.'

'You're forgetting Lucy.'

'Okay, one thing. But I already have my kid, and I don't need another.'

'Is everything all right? You sound awfully down on yourself.'

'I'm fine. I've never felt better.'

'You've been here for six months now. You live in Joyce's house, you work for Nancy, you take care of your girl, but maybe it's time to think about the next step. You know, start making plans.'

'What kind of plans?'

'It's not for me to say. Whatever you want.'

'But I like things the way they are.'

'What about singing? Aren't you tempted to get back into it?'

'Sometimes. But I don't want a career anymore. I wouldn't mind doing some weekend stuff around the neighborhood, but no more traveling, no more big ambitions. It's not worth it.'

'Are you happy making jewelry? Is it enough to satisfy you?'

'More than enough. I get to be with Nancy every day, and what can be better than that? There's no one like her in the whole world. I love her to pieces.'

'We all love her.'

'No, you don't understand. I mean, I *really* love her. And she loves me back.'

'Of course she does. Nancy is one of the most affectionate people I've ever known.'

'You still don't get it. What I'm trying to say is that we're *in love*. Nancy and I are lovers.'

'. . .'

'You should see your face, Uncle Nat. You look like you've swallowed a typewriter.'

'I'm sorry. It's just that I didn't know. I could see that you two hit it off. I could see that you liked each other, but . . . but I hadn't realized that it had gone that far. How long has it been going on?'

'Since March. It started about three months after I moved in.'

'Why didn't you tell me before?'

'I was afraid you'd tell Joyce. And Nancy doesn't want her to know. She thinks her mother will flip out.'

'So why tell me now?'

'Because I decided that you can keep a secret. You're not going to let me down, are you?'

'No, I'm not going to let you down. If you don't want Joyce to know, I won't tell her.'

'And you're not disappointed in me?'

'Of course not. If you and Nancy are happy, more power to you.'

'We have so much in common, you see. It's like we're sisters, and our minds are on the same wavelength. We always know what the other one is thinking and feeling. The men I've been with, it was always about words – talking, explaining, arguing, yacking all the time. With us, I just have to look at her, and she's inside my skin. I've never had that with anyone before. Nancy calls it a magic bond – but I just call it love, pure and simple. The real deal.'

'JUST LIKE TONY'

I kept my promise and didn't say anything to Joyce, but holding on to the secret had as much to do with protecting myself as it did with helping out the girls. If and when Joyce discovered the truth, I had no idea how she would react. I suspected that it wouldn't be calmly, and if that turned out to be so, then one possible result of her ire would be to look for someone to blame. And who better to cast in the role of fall guy than Aurora's uncle, the bungling moocher who had wrangled his unbalanced, corrupting niece into the heart of the Mazzucchelli household, whereupon she had connived to turn the innocent Nancy into a flaming, passionate lesbian? I imagined that Joyce would kick Rory and Lucy out of the house, and in the family mayhem that followed, I would be put in the position of having to defend my sister's daughter, which would so alienate Joyce from me that I would be booted out as well. We had been together for a year by then, and God knows that was the last thing I wanted to happen.

On a warm, quiet Sunday just after the end of

summer vacation, she joined me at my apartment for an evening of movie watching and Thai food. After we had phoned in our order to the restaurant, she turned to me and said, 'You won't believe what they've been up to.'

'Who are we talking about?' I asked.

'Nancy and Aurora.'

'I don't know. Making and selling jewelry. Looking after their kids. The usual grind.'

'They're sleeping together, Nathan. They're having an affair.'

'How do you know?'

'I caught them. I stayed here Thursday night, remember? I got up early the next morning, and instead of going straight to work, I went back home to change my dress. The plumber was supposed to come that afternoon, and I went upstairs to remind Nancy about the appointment. I opened the door of her bedroom, and there they were, the two of them lying naked on top of the covers, fast asleep in each other's arms.'

'Did they wake up?'

'No. I closed the door as softly as I could, and then I tiptoed down the stairs. What am I going to do? I'm so devastated, I feel like slitting my wrists. Poor Tony. For the first time since he left me, I'm glad he's dead. I'm glad he isn't around to see this . . . this *awful thing*. It would have broken his heart. His own daughter sleeping with another woman. It makes me want to throw up every time I think about it.'

'There's not a lot you can do, Joyce. Nancy is a grown woman, and she can sleep with any person she wants. The same with Aurora. They've both been through rough times. They've both had marriages break up on them, and they're both probably a little sick of men. It doesn't mean they're gay, and it doesn't mean it will last forever. If they can find some comfort in each other for the time being, where's the harm?'

'The harm is that it's disgusting and unnatural. I don't see how you can be so cool about it, Nathan, I really don't. It's like you don't even care.'

'People feel what they feel. Who am I to tell them they're wrong?'

'You sound like a gay rights activist. Pretty soon, you'll be telling me you've had affairs with men.'

'I'd rather cut off my right arm than go to bed with a man.'

'Then why defend Nancy and Aurora?'

'Because they're not me, for one thing. And because they're women.'

'What's that supposed to mean?'

'I'm not sure. I'm so attracted to women myself, I guess I can understand why a woman would be attracted to another woman.'

'You're a pig, Nathan. It turns you on, doesn't it?'

'I didn't say that.'

'Is that what you do when you're alone? Sit around here at night watching lesbo porn movies?'

'Hmmm. I never thought of that. It might be more fun than typing up my stupid book.'

'Don't make jokes. Here I am on the brink of a nervous breakdown, and you're cracking jokes.'

'Because it's none of our business, that's why.'

'Nancy's my daughter . . .'

'And Rory's my niece. So what? They don't belong to us. We just have them on loan.'

'What am I going to do, Nathan?'

'You can pretend you don't know anything about it and leave them in peace. Or else you can give them your blessing. You don't have to like it, but those are your only two choices.'

'I could throw them out of the house, couldn't I?'

'Yes, I suppose you could. And you'd wind up regretting it every day for the rest of your life. Don't go there, Joyce. Try to roll with the punches. Keep your chin up. Don't take any wooden nickels. Vote Democrat in every election. Ride your bike in the park. Dream about my perfect, golden body. Take your vitamins. Drink eight glasses of water a day. Pull for the Mets. Watch a lot of movies. Don't work too hard at your job. Take a trip to Paris with me. Come to the hospital when Rachel has her baby and hold my grandchild in your arms. Brush your teeth after every meal. Don't cross the street on a red light. Defend the little guy. Stick up for yourself. Remember how beautiful you are. Remember how much I love you. Drink one Scotch on the rocks every day. Breathe deeply. Keep your eyes open. Stay away from fatty foods. Sleep the sleep of the just. Remember how much I love you.'

Her reaction to the news was more or less as I had predicted, but at least she hadn't held me accountable for Rory's actions, which was all I was concerned about just then. I was sorry she had opened that door, sorry the facts had been revealed to her in such a shocking, indelible way, but eventually she would have to come to terms with the situation, whether she liked it or not. The meal came, and for the next little while we stopped talking about Nancy and Aurora and concentrated on our food. I remember feeling exceptionally hungry that night, and I bolted down my appetizers and spicy shrimp with basil in just a few minutes. Then we turned on the TV and started watching a film called *The Outriders*, a Western from 1950 starring Joel McCrea. At one point, the cowboys were sitting around a campfire chewing the fat, and the old geezer of the bunch (played by James Whitmore, I believe) delivered a line that got a loud guffaw from me. 'I kind of relish getting old,' he said. 'It takes the bother out of living.' I kissed Joyce on the cheek and whispered, 'That fathead doesn't know what he's talking about,' and for the first time that night, my still-rattled, unhappy darling laughed as well.

Ten minutes after Joyce emitted that laugh, my own life was coming to an end. We were sitting on the sofa watching the film, and suddenly I felt a pain in my chest. At first, I took it for heartburn, indigestion brought on by the food I had eaten, but the pain continued to grow, spreading across my upper body as if my insides had caught fire, as if I had swallowed a gallon of hot molten lead, and before long my left arm had gone numb and my jaw was tingling with the pinpricks of a thousand invisible needles. I had read enough about heart attacks to know that these were the classic symptoms, and since the pain kept building, kept climbing to ever more unbearable stages of intensity, I figured my moment had come. I tried to stand up, but after two steps I fell down and began writhing around on the floor. I was clutching my chest with both hands, I was struggling for breath, and Joyce was holding me in her arms, looking down at my face and telling me to hang in there. Somewhere in the distance, I heard her say, 'Oh, my God. Oh, my God, it's just like Tony,' and then she wasn't there anymore, and I heard her shouting at someone, telling him to send an ambulance to First Street. Remarkably enough, I wasn't scared. The attack had carried me into another zone, and questions of life and death were of no importance in that place. You merely accepted. You merely took what you were given, and if death was what I had been given that night, I was prepared to accept it. As the paramedics lifted me into the ambulance, I noticed that Joyce was there again, standing next to me with tears pouring down her face. If I remember correctly, I think I managed to smile at her. 'Don't die on me, baby,' she said. 'Please, Nathan, don't die on me.' Then the doors closed, and a moment later I was gone.

INSPIRATION

I didn't die. As it turned out, I didn't even have a heart attack. An inflamed esophagus was the cause of my agony, but no one knew that at the time, and for the rest of the night and the bulk of the following day, I was convinced my life was over.

The ambulance took me to Methodist Hospital at Sixth Street and Seventh Avenue, and because all the beds on the upper floors were full just then, they put me in one of the small cubicles reserved for cardiac patients in the Emergency Room downstairs. A thin green curtain divided me from the main desk (when the nurses remembered to close it), and except for an early visit to the X-ray Unit down the hall, I did nothing but lie on a narrow bed the whole time I was there. My body was hooked up to a heart monitor, and with an IV needle planted in my arm and plastic oxygen tubes stuck into my nostrils, I had no choice but to remain on my back. Blood was drawn from me every four hours. If a coronary had taken place, small bits of damaged tissue would have broken loose from the heart and filtered into the bloodstream, and eventually those bits would begin showing up in the tests. A nurse explained that it would be twenty-four hours before they knew for certain. In the meantime, I had to lie there and wait it out, alone with my fear and morbid imagination as my blood gradually told the story of what had or hadn't happened to me.

Paramedics kept wheeling in new patients, and one by one they passed before me with their epileptic seizures and intestinal blockages, their knife wounds and heroin overdoses, their fractured arms and bloody heads. Voices called out, telephones rang, food carts clattered along the floor. These things were happening no more than a body's length from the tips of my feet, and yet for all the effect they had on me, they might have been happening in another world. I don't think I've ever been more numb to my surroundings than I was that night, more locked into myself, more absent. Nothing felt real to me except my own body, and as I lay there wallowing in my brokenness, I became fixated on trying to visualize the circuits of veins and arteries that crisscrossed below my chest, the dense inner network of glop and blood. I was in there with myself, rooting around with a kind of scrambled desperation, but I was also far away, floating above the bed, above the ceiling, above the roof of the hospital. I know it doesn't make any sense, but lying in that boxed-in enclosure with the beeping machines and the wires clamped to my skin was the closest I have come to being nowhere, to being inside myself and outside myself at the same time.

That's what happens to you when you land in a hospital. They take off your clothes, put you in one of those humiliating gowns, and suddenly you stop being yourself. You become the person who inhabits your body, and what you are now is the sum total of that body's failures. To be diminished in such a way is to lose all right to privacy. When the doctors and nurses come in and ask you questions, you have to answer them. They want to keep you alive, and only a person who didn't want to live would give them false answers. If you happen to be in a small cubicle, and just three feet to your right another person is being questioned by a doctor or a nurse, you can't help overhearing what that person says. It's not that you necessarily want to know the answers, but you find yourself in a position that makes it impossible not to know them. That was how I was introduced to Omar Hassim-Ali, a fifty-three-year-old Egyptian-born car-service driver with a wife, four children, and six grandchildren. He entered the cubicle a little past one in the morning after experiencing chest pains while chauffeuring a fare across the Brooklyn Bridge. Within a matter of minutes, I had learned that he took pills for his high blood pressure, that he still smoked a pack a day but was trying to cut down, that he suffered from hemorrhoids and occasional bouts of dizziness, and that he had been living in America since 1980.

After the doctor left, Omar Hassim-Ali and I talked for close to an hour. It didn't matter that we were strangers. When a man thinks he's about to die, he talks to anyone who will listen.

I slept very little that night – a couple of catnaps of ten or fifteen minutes each – but an hour or so after dawn, I drifted off in earnest. At eight o'clock, a nurse came in to take my temperature, and when I looked over to my right, I saw that my room-mate's bed was empty. I asked her what had happened to Mr Hassim-Ali, but she couldn't give me an answer. Her shift had just come on duty, she said, and she didn't know anything about it.

Every four hours, the blood tests came back negative. There were morning visits from Joyce, from Tom and Honey, and from Aurora and Nancy – but no one was allowed to stay for more than a few minutes. In the early afternoon, Rachel showed up as well. They all began by asking the same question – *How was I feeling?* – and I gave them all the same answer: Fine, fine, fine, don't worry about me. The pain had vanished by then, and I was starting to feel more confident about my chances of getting out of there in one piece. I said, I didn't live through cancer in order to die from some dumb-ass coronary infarction. It was an absurd statement, but as the day wore on and the blood tests continued to come in negative, I clung to it as logical proof that the gods had decided to spare me, that the attack of the previous night had been no more than a demonstration of

371

their power to control my fate. Yes, I could die at any moment – and yes, I had been certain that I was about to die as I lay in Joyce's arms on the living room floor. If there was anything to be learned from this brush with mortality, it was that my life, in the narrowest sense of the term, was no longer my own. I had only to remember the pain that had ripped through me during the terrible siege of fire to understand that every breath that filled my lungs was a gift from those capricious gods, that from now on every tick of my heart would be granted to me through an arbitrary act of grace.

By ten-thirty, the empty bed was occupied by Rodney Grant, a thirty-nine-year-old roofer who had passed out while climbing a flight of stairs earlier that morning. His co-workers had called for an ambulance, and there he was in his skimpy hospital gown, a burly, large-muscled black man with the face of a young boy, looking positively frightened out of his wits. After his interview with the doctor, he turned to me and said that he was dying for a smoke. Did I think he would get into trouble if he went to the men's room and lit up a cigarette? You won't know until you try, I said, and off he went, unhooking himself from the heart monitor and wheeling his IV line down the hall. When he returned a few minutes later, he smiled at me and said, 'Mission accomplished.' At two o'clock, a nurse opened the curtain and informed him that he was being transferred to the Cardiac

Unit upstairs. Never having fainted before, never having been diagnosed with anything more worrisome than chicken pox and a mild case of hay fever, the young man was confused. 'It looks pretty serious, Mr Grant,' the nurse said. 'I know you're feeling better now, but the doctor needs to run some tests.'

I wished him luck when he left, and then I was alone in the cubicle again. I thought about Omar Hassim-Ali, trying to remember the names of his various children, and wondered if he hadn't been transferred to the upstairs unit as well. It was a reasonable supposition, but as I looked over at the empty cot to my right, I couldn't help imagining that he was dead. I didn't have a single scrap of evidence to confirm that hypothesis, but now that Rodney Grant had been escorted to his uncertain future, the bare bed seemed to be haunted by some mysterious force of erasure, blotting out the men who had lain on it and ushering them into a realm of darkness and oblivion. The empty bed signified death, whether that death was real or imagined, and as I pondered the implications of this idea, another idea gradually took hold of me, which overwhelmed all thoughts about everything else. By the time I saw where I was going, I understood that I had come up with the single most important idea I had ever had, an idea big enough to keep me occupied every hour of every day for the rest of my life.

I was no one. Rodney Grant was no one. Omar

Hassim-Ali was no one. Javier Rodriguez – the seventy-eight-year-old retired carpenter who took over the bed at four o'clock – was no one. Eventually, we would all die, and when our bodies were carried off and buried in the ground, only our friends and families would know we were gone. Our deaths wouldn't be announced on radio or television. There wouldn't be any obituaries in the *New York Times*. No books would be written about us. That is an honor reserved for the powerful and famous, for the exceptionally talented, but who bothers to publish biographies of the ordinary, the unsung, the workaday people we pass on the street and barely take the trouble to notice?

Most lives vanish. A person dies, and little by little all traces of that life disappear. An inventor survives in his inventions, an architect survives in his buildings, but most people leave behind no monuments or lasting achievements: a shelf of photograph albums, a fifth-grade report card, a bowling trophy, an ashtray filched from a Florida hotel room on the final morning of some dimly remembered vacation. A few objects, a few documents, and a smattering of impressions made on other people. Those people invariably tell stories about the dead person, but more often than not dates are scrambled, facts are left out, and the truth becomes increasingly distorted, and when those people die in their turn, most of the stories vanish with them.

My idea was this: to form a company that would

publish books about the forgotten ones, to rescue the stories and facts and documents before they disappeared – and shape them into a continuous narrative, the narrative of a life.

The biographies would be commissioned by friends and relatives of the subject, and the books would be printed in small, private editions – anywhere from fifty to three or four hundred copies. I imagined writing the books myself, but if demand ever became too heavy, I could always hire others to help with the work: struggling poets and novelists, ex-journalists, unemployed academics, perhaps even Tom. The cost of writing and publishing such books would be steep, but I didn't want my biographies to be an indulgence affordable only by the rich. For families of lesser means, I envisioned a new type of insurance policy whereby a certain negligible sum would be set aside each month or quarter to defray the expenses of the book. Not home insurance or life insurance – but biography insurance.

Was I crazy to dream that I could make something of this farfetched project? I didn't think so. What young woman wouldn't want to read the definitive biography of her father – even if that father had been no more than a factory worker or the assistant manager of a rural bank? What mother wouldn't want to read the life story of her policeman son who was shot down in the line of duty at age thirty-four? In every case, it would have to be a question of love. A wife or a husband, a son or a daughter, a parent, a brother or a sister – only the strongest attachments. They would come to me six months or a year after the subject had died. They would have absorbed the death by then, but they still wouldn't be over it, and now that everyday life had started for them again, they would understand that they would never be over it. They would want to bring their loved one back to life, and I would do everything humanly possible to grant their wish. I would resurrect that person in words, and once the pages had been printed and the story had been bound between covers, they would have something to hold on to for the rest of their lives. Not only that, but something that would outlive them, that would outlive us all.

One should never underestimate the power of books.

X MARKS THE SPOT

The results of the final blood test came in just after midnight. It was too late to discharge me from the hospital, so I stayed on until morning, feverishly planning the structure of my new company as I watched the exhausted Javier Rodriguez doze in the opposite bed. I thought of various names that would capture the spirit of the work that lay before me, and in the end I hit upon the neutral but descriptive *Bios Unlimited*. About an hour after that, I decided that my first move would be to contact Bette Dombrowski in Chicago and ask her if she would be interested in commissioning me to write a biography of her ex-husband. It seemed appropriate that the first book in the collection should be about Harry.

Then they let me go. I stepped out into the cool morning air, and I felt so glad to be alive, I wanted to scream. Overhead, the sky was the bluest of pure deep blues. If I walked quickly enough, I would be able to get to Carroll Street before Joyce left for work. We would sit down in the kitchen and have a cup of coffee together, watching the kids run around like chipmunks as their mothers

377

got them ready for school. Then I would walk Joyce to the subway, put my arms around her, and kiss her good-bye.

It was eight o'clock when I stepped out onto the street, eight o'clock on the morning of September 11, 2001 – just forty-six minutes before the first plane crashed into the North Tower of the World Trade Center. Just two hours after that, the smoke of three thousand incinerated bodies would drift over toward Brooklyn and come pouring down on us in a white cloud of ashes and death.

But for now it was still eight o'clock, and as I walked along the avenue under that brilliant blue sky, I was happy, my friends, as happy as any man who had ever lived.